HEISTING THE BEARD

HEISTING THE BEARD

J.C. PEREZ

MALEVOLENT BOOKS
Santa Monica, California

FIRST EDITION

Library of Congress Cataloging-in-Publication-Data is available on file.

ISBN: 978-1-936573-01-1

Malevolent Books, in association with Global ReLeaf, will plant two trees for each tree used in the manufacturing of this book. Global ReLeaf is an international campaign by American Forests, the nation's oldest nonprofit conservation organization and a world leader in planting trees for environmental restoration.

10 9 8 7 6 5 4 3 2 1

First and foremost, without the Love
and understanding of my family I am a lost soul.

I would first like to thank Martha Sickles, Craig
Kayser, and Jim Strader for their support and trust.

I dedicate this book to my loving wife, Francine
Marie Fossat, who's non ending love and belief in me
made this possible. You will always be remembered.

HEISTING THE BEARD

PROLOGUE

I sat up and looked around. Mierda, mira lo que viene!. I heard the sound of the other jeep coming and I was out in the open. I got up and started to run toward David and Anibal, but it was too late. The jeep came around the corner of the warehouse and the headlights caught me in mid stride. The guards opened fire and I could hear bullets whizzing by my head. Anibal was right, these fuckers don't question, they kill.

From out of the darkness I could hear the familiar zip zip zip sound of Anibal and David's silenced guns returning fire on the jeep that was now chasing me. They jammed on their brakes when they realized they were taking return fire and I heard the tires bring the jeep to a screeching halt, then gears grinding and tires screeching again. I turned to look and they were in reverse and in a hurry.

A dark shape came at me out of the darkness. I jumped to the side and fell down. I pointed my Uzi up at the shape as it came to a stop next to me and in that moment I wondered what the hell had gotten me to this point where I was about to die on my native Cuban soil.

CHAPTER 1

It was hot as hell out on the water. Not much of a breeze was blowing. It was only July and we still had the dog days of August ahead. No problem though. This salvage job wasn't going to take long and I would be spending most of it on the water.

Jobs like this only came along a few times a year and I was lucky to land this one.

Old Man Jamieson's son Bobby had taken his father's new 24-foot Mako out a couple of days earlier and left it underwater, just east of Alligator Reef. It was rough going that day; a little storm came through and Bobby made the most of it, jumping waves. Evidently he got hung up in-between waves and was swamped by an oncoming one. Now his father's boat rested under twenty feet of water.

Personally, I thought the Mako was overpowered with twin 250 Mercs. On a calm day at top speed, she'd "china walk," and that was unstable. Bobby did not have to do much to rock this boat.

Old Man Jamieson was really pissed off; he had just bought the boat and it wasn't insured yet. He offered to pay me a grand to have a look at it, so I went out. The water was clear but I dove down anyway to assess things.

I was down on the sandy bottom in seconds and swimming to the Mako dead ahead. Suddenly I caught the movement of something big, above me and to the right. I hadn't scoped the water before diving in, and now I was down here and something was stalking me. I turned from side to side and looked up and down, feeling my pulse quicken at the thought of being caught off guard by a fifteen-foot eating machine. A moment later the panic was over when I discovered the source of the movement. It was just a large grouper bumbling along.

The area around Alligator Reef has a strong current and is fertile feeding ground as a result. There's everything here, from five-foot barracudas to permit, yellowtails, and baitfish galore. All this activity attracts sharks. I was deathly scared of sharks and had a healthy respect for their territory.

I had never been very cautious around sea creatures in the past. Until one fateful day off the coast of Sandy Cay in the Bahamas I would dive in anywhere at anytime.

That was back in the day, when I ran on the wrong side. We had just finished a job and the weather was rough and one of our boats was broadsided by a big wave that seemed to have come out of nowhere. It capsized her and she went to the bottom in about twenty to thirty feet of water, just like Jamieson's boat, not deep. The difference was that our boat had some very valuable cargo on it which we had to retrieve, or else face the consequences of a very angry *padrino*. We quickly anchored off and prepared to dive to assess the situation. We would bring up the cargo, and then decide if we had time to bring up the boat.

Stress ran high, and we were anxious to do this salvage and get out of the area. This little treasure trove could bring you just as much comfort economically as it could mental and physical discomfort if we were caught. Millions of dollars were involved, but if we got caught we'd be doing ten to twenty.

Lusito "Fat Boy" Sanchez and I didn't hesitate—we dove right in. Fat Boy kept bitching about the timing of the wave, not because of our predicament, but because it was going to make him late getting back to Miami. This motherfucker didn't have a penny to his name when he arrived in Key West in 1980 in the Mariel Boatlift, and now he was fat and happy, a millionaire a few times over and he wasn't worried about the D.E.A., the Coast Guard, the Bahamian Defense Force, or even the thought of doing ten years or more. No, he was worried about getting back to his comfortable Miami and all the luxuries he could now afford.

Obnoxious as Fat Boy was, he was an excellent diver. He hadn't always been fat. He once dove with the Cuban national team and he knew what he was doing. As for me, I'd spent a lot of years in and around the water and I could handle myself out there in the wild better than most.

I didn't pay attention to his bullshit, but the noise he made was stressing me out. Without thinking, I dove in with him and began to swim the twenty-five yards or so to our sunken treasure.

What we should have done was take five minutes to check the area for sharks. That means a 360-degree look around, then getting out the binoculars and making the same sweep at a distance. You're looking for a fin or two, and ruling out sharks takes time, because they're not always at the surface. I sure as hell knew the routine now, but back then I had a different attitude thanks to all the bullshit nature shows that told you sharks weren't man-eaters and that they were safe to swim with.

Fat Boy Sanchez and I were on the bottom assessing our cargo when I noticed a school of about eight or so blacktip sharks, all around ten feet long. Once again, my wonderful television education from the gurus of the deep told me everything was okay. Don't worry, they mind their own business. So I paid attention to the job at hand; but then I glanced back because I realized something was not quite right about the sharks. They looked agitated, darting quickly from left to right, with their backs arched and their pectoral fins pointing almost straight down. I recognized this posture, once again from my television education, and knew it as anger or preparation for a feeding frenzy.

Because we were in shallows and there was a plentitude of baitfish and other fish, I thought they were onto a school nearby. I still wasn't overly worried. The gurus, in their infinite wisdom, never let me know that there was a chance that I could be the special of the day. No, no, blacktips weren't man-eaters, the experts told me.

As I continued my overview of the sunken boat while keeping an eye on the sharks a hard bump on the shoulder and side spun me around. I thought it was Fat Boy, but he was nowhere in sight. A blacktip swam away from me, still in his menacing posture. The bump he gave me was forceful, but not as painful as his brushing against me. Although sharkskin looks smooth, it's actually very rough, and it was as if I had been filed by a heavy-duty rasp. I started to bleed, not badly, but enough to tint the surrounding water with my blood.

Fuck the gurus. My survival instinct kicked in. I swam as hard as I could toward the surface boat. I didn't go more than a few feet when I realized I was swimming right into a pack of blacktips. I turned and swam back down, blood still oozing from my side and arm. I felt like a bait fish that had been flushed from his hiding hole. As I swam back down, my imagination ran wild. I could feel massive sharks biting me, and then my mind raced ahead to the gruesome conclusion: one thrashing Kiki being eaten alive by a man-eating shark. Just like in the nature shows.

Luckily the guys on the surface saw the sharks. They made a big commotion on the far side of the boat and lured the sharks that way, opening a route to the boat.

I swam as fast as I could. As I neared the surface I felt a jolt and I was yanked back down a few feet. I was running out of air and I began to panic, kicking my legs as hard as I could. My fears had come true—I had been attacked. I looked down at a cloud of red, and through it my foot gushed a stream of blood.

Below I could see one of the menacing sharks circling, chomping on my diving fin.

That shark wanted the real thing. It spit out the fin and circled back to have another go at me. I'm a fast swimmer, but I would have taken Olympic gold that day. I was like an underwater Tasmanian devil. I ripped through the twenty yards of water left between me and the surface boat, knowing that if I didn't make it now I was surely going to be a statistic. Considering the job I was on, I wasn't going to show up on the stats report. This one would go down as missing in action and nobody knows shit.

I raced to the top, watching the man-eater out of the corner of my eye. He was ten yards behind me when I got to the transom of the boat. I swam in between the two outboard engines and reached up to pull myself out of the water as much as possible. The boys on the boat were there waiting, and pulled me on deck just as that twelve-foot monster surfaced. The blacktip slammed into an engine, rocking the entire boat. Unsteady on my injured leg, I fell over on deck. I sat there for a moment, stunned, then checked out the leg. Blood gushed from deep gashes on my left heel and calf.

I looked up for help. There was Fat Boy Sanchez, sitting there with a towel in his hand and a shit-eating grin on his face while my blood painted the deck red.

He looked over at me and said, "Don't you know blacktips are very aggressive, *amigo?*"

I just stared at him while one of the boys brought me the first-aid kit. This would require a tourniquet.

"Fuck this," Fat Boy yelled, "we'll come back tomorrow and pull everything up." Then he turned in his seat, hit the throttles and pointed us to Bimini. "*Vamonos de aqui ante que nos coman*," he said, "Let's get out of here before they eat us." I was glad to see that there was something in life that would make Fat Boy compromise his luxurious Miami lifestyle. Sharks were serious business. I just needed a lesson in how serious.

The episode seemed to transpire over several hours, but actually took place in about two minutes. It was something I would never ever forget. It was pure, blood-curdling terror, and the agony of it all came rushing back to me when I approached Old Man Jamieson's sunken boat and saw the grouper. I had only been under water about thirty seconds. I quickly checked out Jamieson's boat, then surfaced and climbed up on my boat, the *Lean Back*. I looked at my arm, fully exposed goose bumps standing up the length of it. I started up my boat and headed it back to Islamorada. I glanced back once or twice at the spot where I had been anchored. A *brrrr* came out of my mouth and I shook like a shivering dog, thinking of what could have been the outcome of my carelessness. Damn, I thought, I hate sharks.

I looked into the glaring sun and turquoise waters that lay ahead and brought my thoughts back to the present and the task at hand, bringing up Jamieson's boat from the bottom.

The hull was undamaged, which was rare in these cases. Miraculously, the transom was also undamaged, but the bolts holding the engines onto the transom were sheared right off. The engines were lying on the bottom next to the boat, attached only by the cables. It was definitely salvageable.

Old Man Jamieson wanted it back, so we agreed on half the cost of the boat: Twenty grand. Jony from Hawk Marine and I would do this in one day. It was a sweet little job.

Most people without insurance on their boats would have to eat the loss. The cost of bringing the boat up was like throwing good money after bad. All they would get for it was a damaged boat and perhaps—depending on their tax bracket and the nature of their business or businesses—a write-off. Old Man Jamieson didn't care though, he had plenty of money. His father had bought up a lot of prime oceanfront real estate back in the 1940s and had sold most of it in the early eighties. He made millions, died in his prime and left it all to his only son, who made more millions. Jamieson still sat on some prime lots, and he lived in a big house on Ocean Lane in Islamorada.

He spent all his time on the water, fishing. The man was always on the water. He had a beautiful 19-foot Hewes that he took into the back country of Florida Bay, that big lagoon with all its little uninhabited keys stretching way up to the Everglades. He was an avid fly fisherman and split his fishing time between back country "skinny water" and deep sea. For the big blue water, he had a beautiful Ribovich.

His son Bobby wasn't a bad kid; just a real island boy, kind of like Sandy from the old TV show *Flipper*. He was never in any real trouble, but he came from money and his screw ups usually cost more than most people's.

Bobby's dad set him up with a little bait and tackle shop on the old Keys highway, down by the Cheeca Lodge golf course, and he did quite well. A lot of the charter captains from Bud and Mary's in Islamorada used him, and he had a good reputation as a fisherman, when he wasn't busting up expensive toys.

Other than his predilection for smoking weed, Bobby wasn't a problem. The kid didn't even drink, and weed didn't make him a bad guy in my book, or anybody else's book down here. The island was full of free spirits.

This time he just bit off a little more wave than he could chew, and Daddy had to foot the bill. Bobby wasn't spoiled though; I was sure Old Man Jamieson would find a way to make him work it off.

Jony attached the hoist and began to pull her up. It was mid-afternoon and I had returned to the sunken boat with some help.

"Do you have it all secured?" I asked him as he broke the surface.

He gave me a thumbs-up sign.

"Did you remember to cut the cables to the engines?"

Jony handed me the industrial-sized bolt cutters, and I took that as a "yes."

I grabbed them and put them on the deck of the *Lean Back*.

Jony pushed his dive mask on top of his head and took the respirator from his mouth.

"Does Jamieson want those engines?" I asked.

"No, he said I could have them if I wanted."

"Good. I'll come back tomorrow, bring them up, and take them back to the marina. Jorge will dry them out and have them running in no time. We can get $2,500 a piece for them."

"I'm going back down to pull the cord on the air bags I put in the cuddy cabin. When you see me coming up, start pulling her with the *Lean Back*."

I watched as Jony swam down to the Mako. After a half a minute, I saw a burst of escaped air bubble up and Jony began to ascend. I went to the throttles of the *Lean Back* and eased her forward. I was hoping things didn't start breaking up and ripping off of the boat. Jony and I had pulled up a few boats from shallow water before and I knew he had a way of tying them off that distributed the tension evenly, but I was always antsy about it.

The little 24-foot Mako began to rise and move forward as the *Lean Back* pulled her toward the surface. She was still partially submerged but she was floating and looked to be in good shape. I throttled back and released the tension on the tow ropes, then swung around and pulled up next to her. I put two bumpers between her and the *Lean Back* and tied them off. Jony had already swum over and climbed on board the now one-third-submerged Mako.

"She looks great considering. Did the kid get hurt at all?" Jony asked.

"Not a damn scratch," I said. "And he's so damn lucky, he managed to stuff it just 50 yards from another boat. They picked him up right away and brought him into port. He barely got wet. He hitchhiked home and about an hour later he was back at the bait and tackle shop calling his dad to break the bad news."

"Figures," said Jony.

I handed Jony a bilge pump. While I hooked it up to the battery of the *Lean Back*, he popped the hatch by the transom of the Mako and put the pump in the bottom of the boat. It wasn't long before we had the Mako fully up to her water line and were towing her back to Jamieson's dock on Ocean Lane.

We pulled the *Lean Back* up and around and swung the little Mako into place at the dock while Old Man Jamieson and Bobby looked on. Jony tossed them a line and they tied off the salvaged boat. I pulled back around and tied off to the dock, then talked to Old Man Jamieson for a few minutes. He thanked me and gave me a big, fat check for 20 grand. I pocketed it with a smile.

This kind of money would get me through to my next job and I could afford to do what I liked best for a while: fish and lounge around. Jony was already on board the *Lean Back* so I untied her and we headed home. Home for me was two slips at Bud and Mary's Marina on Islamorada, where I kept the *Lean Back* and my live-aboard sailboat, the *Quest*.

Islamorada was a beautiful place to live, for me and about five thousand other people. Quaint and quiet, with the requisite tourists of course, but it was not Key West. The tourism consisted mainly of families, so things stayed pretty quiet. Except where I lived. Bud and Mary's always had some pretty interesting characters. Some lived there, some worked there, and some were just passing though. The beer flowed freely and there were plenty of old salts with great stories to tell. The stories weren't just fishing stories; they were stories about smugglers, Cuban *balseros*, hurricanes, ocean tragedies, and even pirates. You name it, you could hear a tale about it at Bud and Mary's.

Islamorada was the self-proclaimed fishing capital of the world; the big boys went there to fish. Bud and Mary's Marina had been around since the forties, and it is loaded with nostalgia. I liked it there. It was home, at least until something else came along.

I pulled the *Lean Back* into her slip. Jony jumped off and ran down the dock to his truck in the parking lot; he wanted to be home before dark. He lived in Miami and it would take him about an hour and a half to get there.

I yelled to him, "Hey, Jony, I'll get the check cashed and call you to give you your piece."

"*Sin problema hermano.* I trust you," he shouted back as he started his truck and backed out.

After he left, I tied the boat off and cleaned her up a little. Then I stepped up onto the dock and walked the ten feet over to the next slip and the *Quest*, my 45 foot Hardin ketch.

Most of my neighbors were boat captains and they were all great folks. I never had to worry about my equipment, and they watched out for me.

I climbed up on the aft deck and was headed to the galley door when I heard someone call me. It was Jimmy Chase, a back country guide in his late twenties who was always at Bud and Mary's. "Hey, Kiki, there were two guys here about an hour ago looking at the *Quest*. I asked if I could help them but they just walked to the parking lot, got in their car and drove north."

"Thanks Jimmy," I said.

I was pretty tired from the day's salvage job so I didn't give it much thought. I walked into a steamy hot galley, put my things on the table, and opened up the windows. Leaving the boat to air out, I headed back topside, and then down the dock to Bud and Mary's deli. I got myself a sandwich and, back on the *Quest*, I washed it down with a half bottle of Bacardi before falling asleep on the couch.

CHAPTER 2

"What the hell are you saying? Am I hearing you right?" I asked the smiling fat man sitting across the table from me.

That morning I had woken up with sweat dripping down my face. I was sprawled out on the couch in the galley of the *Quest*. The sun shining through the window was blazing down on me. It was 8:00 am and the South Florida sun was already in full force.

Yeah, the *Quest* was hot and steamy. She had all the modern conveniences and was a great traveling sailboat, but there was no AC. Summertime was a bitch here and it took some getting used to. That's why I spent most of my time out on the water.

As I got up, groggy from the heat, I heard footsteps coming down the dock. I walked up the steps from the galley to the rear deck and saw two goons coming toward the *Quest*. It was easy to see that they weren't locals.

"Mr. Morales would like to see you, Mr. Logan," said the bigger one.

Banco "El Mono" Morales was a Cuban-American, born in Miami. He was called "the Fat Man" for obvious reasons, but he was also tall, about 6'2". He had a kind face and was balding on top, hair already half gone. Always smiling, happy by nature, he had an unassuming look that disarmed you. It was wise not to underestimate him though; he was a very, very intelligent man. He was also extremely gracious and very, very rich. He always wore black pants, expensive, custom-made Cuban guayabera shirts, a Rolex watch, and Italian shoes.

Officially, Banco's record was clean. His reputation however, was somewhat cloudy. Banco always had a faint air of mystery about him. He had connections from Budapest to Bangkok, from Hong Kong to Little Italy. Some say he'd been involved in the drug game. I had never seen anything . . . but then, I wasn't looking.

Banco was a patron of the arts, with a specific love for pre-Columbian artifacts and salvaged treasure from old Spanish galleons, specifically those lost in the Caribbean, an area whose waters he knew well. He donated to charity and was well known in Miami's social circles. Yet, for the most part, the elite Banco dreamed of being accepted by shunned him. Oh, they took his money for their little charities and shook his hand while taking his check, but that was about all the air they gave him. Fucking hypocrites. It was always about the goddamn money, wasn't it?

Banco played the game though, and he played it well. He always kept his cool; he never succumbed to envy and he never had anything bad to say about anyone. He was heavily connected worldwide and he knew that they knew it. Every once in a while one of Miami's Cuban elite would need something only Banco could handle. That's when he made them pay through the nose for his services. He provided service with a smile and made them think they were getting away cheap.

The important thing was: Banco was no joke. When he sent goons to tell you he wanted to talk to you, you paid attention, partly out of fear, but mainly to find out what he might have up his sleeve. I had worked with Banco on different jobs and they always paid well. The man never cheated you; his word was good.

It was late afternoon, and having responded to his summons, I was sitting at one of Banco's favorite hangouts, the Mutiny Club in Coconut Grove, enjoying his hospitality, eating shrimp, drinking imported beer, looking out at the gorgeous view, and listening to the most outrageous thing I had ever heard.

"Repeat that, Banco, I'm not sure I heard you right."

"Listen up, I'm only going to say this one more time, *mi amigito*, then you're either in or you're out. It's that simple, Enrique, you got it?" Banco said with a smirk. His calling me by my first name instead of my nickname told me he was serious.

"I got it, I got it. Now say it again."

"I know where there is a cache of Spanish treasure from the old *flotas*, and I am going after it.

"Castro pillaged it from different wrecks throughout the Caribbean—Jamaica, the Caymans, Haiti, the Dominican Republic, the Bahamas; you name it, and he pillaged it. It went on for years, until he was able to get some heavyweights from other countries involved. Then he stopped the small-scale robberies and began to concentrate on Cuban waters only. My sources tell me he had accumulated quite a nice little stash by then. My sources also told me where it is."

Banco leaned back, took a bite of a large shrimp from his plate, followed it with a big gulp of his *mojito*, smiled, and said, "What do you think, Kiki? Are you in or out?"

"What you're talking about is not a salvage job, it's a heist. You want me to hit "the Beard" himself; that's suicidal. You called me here, and I was thinking you needed some salvage work done, or maybe to pick up some of those little statues with the big noses you like so much, those pre-Columbians. You know, the ones from Central and South America, the real valuable ones that are probably already on an Interpol list. Instead, you ask me if I'm in or out to pull a heist on Cuba, on the Beard."

"Yeah, that's right. Fuck the Beard. You know how I feel about him, same as you do: I hate him," Banco snapped. "Anyway, it's not about the Beard, it's about greenbacks."

Banco was right; the Cuban in me hated what Castro and his revolution had done to Cuba. I had no qualms about stealing from a thief. Banco also knew my sense of adventure and my appreciation for greenbacks would have me listening.

I reached over and picked up a big coconut shrimp off Banco's plate and looked at him. I'd hear him out, if only to hear what crazy scheme he had in mind. "All right, I'm in. At least until I see what's up. So far, this sounds awful fucking crazy to me."

"Fair enough, I'll get hold of you in a few days and show you what I've got."

Banco stood up, wiped his mouth with a napkin, and said, "Enjoy your food. Have another drink; it's all taken care of. I'll talk to you soon." He turned, and walked out of the Mutiny Club and onto Bayshore Drive.

I finished my grouper sandwich, along with the rest of Banco's coconut shrimp, and washed it all down with another beer. I couldn't believe what Banco was up to, but he had me halfway hooked.

I sat there for a few minutes, enjoying the beautiful hostesses in the Mutiny. They were some of the most gorgeous women in Miami. Wearing mid-length, summery dresses and wide-brim island hats, every one of them looked like a model.

The Mutiny Club, located prominently on Bayshore Drive in Coconut Grove, had to keep up its reputation for understated elegance, and it did.

Everybody who was anybody came to the Mutiny. Politicians, business people, movie moguls, top cops, smugglers, actors, and musicians—you could catch some big time people here on any day of the week. Everybody knew who everybody was; there was no hostility, only fun and drinking in the laidback tropical atmosphere of Coconut Grove. Almost everybody dresses up when they come here, so I was a little out of place in my shorts, sandals, and summer shirt.

I got up, thanked my beautiful tanned hostess, and made my way to the door. Outside, the valet was waiting and I handed him my ticket. He brought my car around. It was a beautiful red Ferrari 308 GTS that I had gotten as a payment on a job I did down in Key West. It wasn't a Testarosa, but she ran and looked great. I got in the car, gave the valet a five and headed back to Islamorada, thinking about what Banco's plan might be.

When I got back to the *Quest*, there was a note on the galley door. It said: "Came by to see you, but you were out. Call you tomorrow. Nadine." I walked down into the galley. The *Quest* was a mess and needed a lady's touch. The half-empty bottle of Bacardi sat on the table next to an ashtray with a roach in it, and not the insect kind. I pulled the curtains closed in a feeble attempt to keep tomorrow's inevitable blasting sun and heat out as long as possible. Then I flopped down on the couch and fell asleep watching the evening news.

The phone rang. I could barely hear it in my half-asleep state. I wasn't sure if it was a dream or real. A Roadrunner cartoon was blaring on the TV, and the beep beep was confusing. I forced myself awake and wiped the sweat that was beginning to roll down my face as yet another steamy day heated up.

"Hello."

"Kiki, it's me, Nadine. Are you awake yet?"

"Hmm," was all I could muster.

"I'll be over in an hour or so," I heard her say before she hung up.

It was definitely too hot to go back to bed so I made some Cuban coffee, went up on deck, and sat down to enjoy my java. A light breeze made the heat somewhat bearable, but the sights, sounds and smells of the Keys made it all worth it. The gin-clear water made it seem like the *Quest* sat on a sheet of glass and I could look into another world down below. The water teemed with life, and I could see that the hot morning sun had awakened more than me. Fish darted about, looking for a meal, and tiny crabs crawled along looking for shelter before the snook and redfish turned them into a morning snack.

"*Salut, mon amour.* May I come aboard?"

I had been watching the leggy blonde as she approached the *Quest.*

"Come on up. You're just in time for coffee."

I reached over and gave her a hand up onto the deck. She gave me a kiss on each cheek, the typical French greeting. Her name was Nadine Delon. She was above average height with an above average body, lovely blond hair, and the most stunning blue eyes I had ever seen.

We had been going out for about a year now and somehow I hadn't scared her off yet. The relationship had been rocky at times, with its share of mild disagreements and heated arguments, but we both seemed to find something comforting and real in each other. Add in the great sex, and it was clear why neither of us would give up on the other.

Nadine had her hair in a loose braid. Little wisps of hair had escaped the braid, accentuating her beautiful face. She had a perpetual smile that gave her an innocent look. It had fooled me a few times, right before I got cut to the bone.

Nadine had a rough childhood. Her parents divorced when she was young. Her mother re-married and Nadine didn't see eye to eye with her stepfather. She was pretty much taking care of herself by the time she was fourteen, and at sixteen she hopped a boat in the port town of Le Havre in Normandy, France and sailed to Martinique.

At nineteen, she caught a ride on a boat heading to Miami, before it went on to Brazil. Unfortunately, they ran into a storm in the Devil's Triangle and the boat got ripped up pretty good. They were able to make it to Miami, but the boat was going to take a couple of months for repairs. Nadine's curiosity got the better of her and she wandered off to check out the Florida Keys. She ended up in Islamorada, of all places, and never left. Of course, this was where I met her. It's incredible how life works.

Nadine knows a lot about boats and the ocean, and she's proven it to me a few times when it counted. Most people freak out on the ocean when the weather gets rough, but Nadine was never scared.

I really liked being around her, even when we argued. I pulled her close and gave her a squeeze. "Hey *niña*, looking good, like always."

"Thank you, Kiki, and you . . . you look like you just got up."

"Thanks. You're sharp like always, with a keen eye for the obvious."

"You need to get an AC on this boat, Kiki. It's summer. You're going to die in there one day if you don't. I came by last night. Did you see the note?"

"Yeah, I saw it. I was at the Mutiny last night; El Mono invited me there."

"Who?" she asked.

"Banco Morales, the Fat Man," I told her. "Not a lot of people know him as El Mono, that's from his younger days and he doesn't really like it anymore."

"Oh, that must've been interesting, knowing Banco in his younger days."

Nadine had worked with me on a job I did for Banco off Largo about six months before. She got to experience Banco in all his glory.

"Yeah, you won't believe what he wants me to do. If I look worse than normal today, it is because I couldn't sleep a wink thinking about what that crazy bastard wants to try. He wants to pull treasure out of Cuban waters."

"Cuba sounds fantastic, Kiki. It's virgin territory, and mysterious. It sounds like a good job."

"You don't understand. You don't just dive wrecks in Cuba. Only Cuba does. Anyway, Banco doesn't want to dive a wreck, he wants to heist a stash of stolen treasure that now belongs to the Cuban government."

"What?! Are you thinking about doing it?"

"That's the crazy thing; I am thinking about it. I don't have enough information yet though, so I don't know. Banco is supposed to get in touch with me soon and show me what he has in mind. It should be interesting, to say the least. I'll see what's up then."

"Okay. In the meantime, I'm going to clean the hull on the *Lean Back*," Nadine said. "If we're going to the Tortugas to fish, I'm going to have her ready for the trip."

Nadine stood up and wiggled out of a pair of shorts, revealing a sexy black bikini bottom. She then took off her shirt, revealing the rest of her long, slender but ample-in-the-right-places body. She was definitely eye candy.

Nadine stood on the edge of the *Quest*'s deck and dove into the crystal clear aquamarine water. When she surfaced, I raised my cup of coffee to her in appreciation of the view, with a smile.

"Do me a favor and hand me down the cleaning tools in the bucket, Enrique." Nadine was like others who knew me well; when they wanted to call my attention to something or reprimand me they used my first name instead of my nickname. I smiled.

She was going to have her hands full with the *Lean Back*; there was a lot of boat to clean. I had the *Lean Back* built to spec. She was a 32' Pantera open fisherman. Three 250-horsepower Mercury engines made her real fast. She had a T-top and comfortable bolster seats that kept you snug even in rough seas. She held 200 gallons of fuel and 50 gallons of freshwater. She had long-range capabilities and I often took her out deep to catch the big fish. The *Lean Back* provided for my business and pleasure; she was my fishing, diving, salvage, and all-around boat. I loved that boat.

Nadine worked on the *Lean Back* for the better part of the afternoon while I sat around looking at ocean charts of the lower Keys and Cuba and wondering about Banco's plan. It was late afternoon when I heard footsteps coming down the dock. The sounds of the footsteps on the dock were those of heeled shoes. It wasn't anyone local; they would either be barefoot or wearing sneakers. I walked up on deck to see Banco's men. The tall one said: "Mr. Morales would like to know if he could come to your boat tomorrow and talk to you, Mr. Logan."

Where did Banco get these guys? They looked like rejects from Central Casting; they looked too much like goons to play goons. The tall one looked like he could crush a cue ball with his bare hands if his brain could figure it out. Still, I wouldn't want to get hit by him.

"Tell Mr. Morales he is welcome at my home," I told the big magilla.

He turned around and didn't say a word as he stomped his way like Frankenstein back down the dock to a waiting car. The almost normal-sized guy followed him.

Meanwhile, Nadine had made a day of it working on the *Lean Back*; she had her cleaned up and looking good. After the goon squad left, Nadine climbed up on deck and stood there soaking wet a few feet in front of me. She looked even better wet, with her bikini bottom sagging a little low on her hipbones from the weight of the water.

"I'm hungry Kiki; let's go get dinner somewhere, *oui*?"

"OK, *niña*. Let's go to South Beach, to Puerto Sagua. You like that place."

"The Cuban place?"

"Yeah, that's the one."

We drove to South Beach and had a great dinner. Unfortunately, we somehow got into an argument after dinner and the night was over quickly. It was probably my fault. I couldn't get the idea of trying to heist the Beard's treasure off of my mind, and I felt like telling Nadine much about it would spoil my thinking process. Nadine asked me a few questions and I brushed her off. That didn't go over well. So she said a few words I had never heard before in French and I was pretty sure I didn't want to know what they meant. After I dropped her off, I drove back to the *Quest*, where I fell asleep to the New York Jets beating up on the Dolphins again. Well, good for them. I hated the Dolphins. Beat them up good.

The next day brought more of the usual – beautiful weather and beautiful scenery, another day in paradise. About mid-afternoon a big Mercedes pulled up and Banco emerged. He walked down the dock to the *Quest* with a long roll of papers in his hand. They looked like maps of some kind.

"Come on up, Banco." I reached down and gave him a hand as he stepped onto the *Quest*.

"*Buenos dias*, Kiki. Are you ready to see what I have?" he asked with a huge smile.

I opened the galley door and walked down the steps with Banco close behind.

"*Madre mia*, you've got to get some AC on this *lancha*, Logan. How in the hell do you stand this heat?"

I smiled at him and shrugged. A bead of sweat ran down his temple.

I could tell the Fat Man was used to more plush surroundings.

I cleared off the table and Banco took his rolled up papers, unfurled them on the table, and pinned the top corner down with the bottle of Bacardi. Ocean charts of the Florida Keys Cuba and the Bahamas were laid out before me. There were also computerized aerial photos of the north coast of Cuba.

"Damn, Banco, you weren't kidding."

I looked at him with a smile; he looked up at me with a sarcastic look on his face, as if he was wondering why I doubted him.

"Kiki, *mi amigo*, this one has its danger, but if we score, you won't regret it."

Banco sat straight up on his stool, reached into his pocket, took out a big Cuban Cohiba and lit it.

"You know Cuba has been pretty much a mystery since Castro. That bastard doesn't really let anybody know what's going on. The people stay in misery while he lives like a king," Banco said while shaking his head. "But it's my homeland and I love it."

"You know I go to Cuba a lot and I do business there. I've developed some contacts; I hear things now and then. Everyone thinks Castro was just some mountain mercenary, a guerilla fighter, but few people know that he loved the ocean and he loved to dive. At one point it was even an obsession. Remind me later to tell you the story of how he evaded arrest by Cuban gunboats while trudging three miles through the mosquito-infested mangrove swamps. When he was still a student at the University of Havana he got involved with some Dominicans trying to take over the DR, and if it wasn't for Castro's knowledge and awareness of the ocean, they all would have died. That little adventure planted the seed of his revolutionary fervor.

"Anyway, as the years went by, his time was taken up by matters of state, but his love of the ocean and sunken treasure didn't diminish any. That *hijo de la puta* sent small fishing boats with experienced divers all over the Caribbean. He had access to the royal records of the treasure fleets kept in Seville and Madrid. He sent undercover agents there and he got the info he needed. So he knew where the best and most accessible wrecks were. He didn't give a shit that they weren't in Cuban waters; he sent people anyway and pillaged many sites. God knows how much he took."

Banco wasn't wrong about Cuban fishing boats being all over the Caribbean. I had seen then as far north as Bimini and as far south as Trinidad and Tobago. I'd heard stories from other people, just like the ones Banco was telling me, but the Fat Man had taken it to another level.

Banco took a picture from his pocket and threw it down on the table.

"Take a look at that, Kiki," he said.

I picked it up. It was a picture of a gold crucifix with inlaid emeralds.

"A private collector in Romania sent me this picture. He asked me if I knew of any more pieces like it on the market. He researched the piece; it came from the Spanish galleon, the *Concepción*, that sank off the Dominican Republic in the early 16th century. The crucifix was on the manifest and; the relic was headed for the church of Spain, straight to the Archbishop. The Romanian says he bought it through a connection with a Cuban diplomat in Bucharest. One and one is two, Kiki; it always will be. I found out where they've got it stored: Caibarién.

He waited for the response he knew he would get from me. Not wanting to disappoint, I showed my surprise.

"I thought that might spark an interest, Kiki," Banco said with a smile.

Banco knew a little bit about my Cuban history and he knew my family was from Caibarién. My father was a representative for a large sugar importer from New Orleans and he spent a lot of time in Cuba. My mother was the granddaughter of the sugar baron, Don Baldomero Braceras. My parents met at a company function in Santa Clara; they fell in love and were married. My father moved to Cuba permanently and continued to work as a representative for the U.S. branch of the sugar company.

Things were turbulent in the 1950s. Fidel was in the Sierra Maestra mountains near Santiago, raising hell and doing a good job of it. Families like ours were the first casualties of Fidel's revolution as he and Che Guevara swept through the provinces of central Cuba and took everything on the way. The sugarcane plantations and the sugar mills were their main targets, since Cuba's economy depended on its sugar production.

In the process my family lost everything. We moved to the family home in old Havana that was owned by my grandmother. It was 1959 and everybody was trying to get out of the country. It was crazy. I remember the feeling, even though I was only four. Everyone was talking about how the Revolution had gone bad, how Castro was becoming Batista, or worse, a communist. A bad feeling back then, bad memories. I cried a lot. My father told me to be strong, that we'd pull through. I guess he was right, but he was also wrong. A crying shame, a fucking shame.

The Catholic Church had a mission in Havana and it arranged flights for children to Miami, where they were housed at the Freedom Tower downtown on Biscayne Boulevard until their families could join them. This exodus of children was dubbed "the Peter Pan flights" and these children became known as "*Los Niños de Pedro Pan*," or "the Peter Pan kids." I don't know why they were called that, but I was one of them. Eighteen months after I left Cuba, my family was able to get a plane out and we were reunited in Miami. Eighteen months is a long time for a kid. Fuck Peter Pan.

Banco knew how I felt about Castro's revolution and what it had done to Cuba and its people—and what it had done to me. He felt the same, though I never talked with him about his story. But they were almost all the same in the end. Anyway, combine all this with the lure of Caibarién and the fact that I had this almost sacred memory of the place, and the whole thing started to look more than interesting to me.

I began to pay a little more attention to the Fat Man and his plan.

"I don't know what's there, or how much of it there is. Most of it probably won't be identifiable to the extent of determining what ship it was on, but it doesn't matter; it's priceless. Especially to private collectors," Banco said.

He reached over and secured the corners of the satellite imagery photos laid out in front of us, before pointing to the north coast of Cuba. He put his finger on the plantation town of Caibarién, with its old docks and warehouse compound. Before the revolution and for a number of years after, that was where the freighters were loaded with sugar before departing for different ports, mainly those in the United States with sugar refineries, and later of course in the Soviet Union. All of this sugar trafficking was long gone by the 1990s. Whatever production Cuba was able to muster never met quotas, but the good old Ruskies would always bail them out.

"That's where it is, Kiki, right there." He tapped the square shapes that represented the warehouses just off the point in Caibarién. The photos were taken from space and clearly showed the buildings, the docks, and the surrounding terrain. How Banco got them, I don't know. Like I said, Banco is very well connected. Not much goes on in Cuba that he doesn't know about.

"My people on the inside tell me it's in there, Kiki.

"There are some big companies doing salvage work in Cuban waters now. They're using a lot of divers who worked for the Beard in the old days, some of the same ones who brought back the stolen gold.

"I was able to track some of them down by spreading the word and some greenbacks around. You know you can get a lot done in Cuba with the almighty dollar."

Banco was getting excited. He sat back on his stool, took a big puff of his Cuban Cohiba and said, "What do you think, Kiki? How do you like my plan?"

"What plan, Banco? This sounds more like an idea, not a plan."

"I'm an ideas man, Kiki. You know that. The plan is to use your knowledge of that area, your contacts in and out of Cuba, and my information, and then we heist the fucking Beard."

I sat back on my stool opposite Banco. I was on my second cup of Cuban coffee and I was buzzing.

"Enrique, I'm not going after this if you aren't in. On the other hand, I don't want to throw you under the bus. I have to tell you that this one is tougher than anything we've done before, and your life may be in the balance. I don't need to tell you what they'll do to you if they catch you. But I also know you'd like to pull at least one whisker out of Castro's beard," Banco laughed.

"Banco, look, I need to think this over and check out the odds with some people. Give me about a week or so. I'll be back in touch. If it's a go, I'll tell you."

"Fair enough, I'll wait to hear from you."

Banco stood up and went topside. As I followed him up I noticed that his nice guayabera shirt was soaking wet from the heat in the galley. Up above he fanned himself and gave me a pitying look.

"*Hombre*, you have to get an AC. They're going to find you dead in here one day." A big smile and then a typical Banco guffaw, and he even bent over and slapped his knee. I guess he was still kind of giddy from talking about his crazy scheme. Ah, Banco, how could we not love you for it; it's so fucking Cuban.

I raised my cup of coffee to him and waved goodbye as he hurried off to the air-conditioned comfort of his waiting Mercedes.

As I watched Banco's tail lights recede, I planned my next move. I needed to see Charlie Alvarez and find out more about Spanish galleons that sank in the Caribbean and see what he knew about Castro pillaging the wrecks.

CHAPTER 3

Charlie Alvarez was my father's best friend until my father kicked the bucket, or as the Cubans say, *"Hasta el final llego."* They met in Cuba back in the fifties and they stayed close. They both had ties to the CIA and the Cuban anti-revolutionary group Alpha 66. A lot of Cubans had ties to the CIA back in those days. Or at least all the ones my family knew. My mother was against my dad's involvement with the guerillas. She thought we'd be run out of the U.S., but she was also confident that Castro couldn't last and we'd be back in Cuba within a year. My dad respected my mother but he couldn't just sit around and do nothing.

My father got involved in intelligence gathering and reconnaissance on the Castro government and he and Charlie got real close. They both hated what Castro's revolution did to Cuba and they taught me to hate it too.

Charlie was hell on wheels when he was young; back in the day; the son of a bitch was ready to die for the opportunity to kill Castro. Shit, I still thought he would shoot him if he ever got close enough. Charlie moved to New Jersey from Miami in 1960 and my dad soon followed, with us in tow. My father's and

Charlie's activities were not known to me as a child, but it all became clear when I got older. Charlie headed up a large group of Cuban expatriates backed by the CIA. They played war games in the Jersey hills, forty miles outside New York City, preparing for an assault on Cuba.

Up in the hills of northwest New Jersey there was a little town called Hope. The town was so small you didn't know when you were in it or when you had left it. My father was up there a lot, and he often took me with him. I used to run around wearing camouflage and carrying a B.B. gun. I could still hear the soldiers laughing at me while urging me on. To me it was all a big game; I couldn't wait for the weekends so I could go play soldier. My father enjoyed watching me join in. He talked to me about Cuba all the time; my love for Cuba—and my anger at what it had become—began at a young age.

The men in the New Jersey hills weren't having Boy Scout meetings, though; they were serious. I'm talking about full armament, .50 caliber machine guns, everything needed to start a war, and that's exactly what they had in mind.

Charlie was a top CIA operative for years, until the New York press caught wind of what was going on in the Jersey Hills and the CIA closed up shop. They didn't end it though; they just left New Jersey.

They took their whole operation to Florida, just outside of a little town called Clewiston, on the edge of the Everglades. The CIA set Charlie and his men up there in a hunting preserve called Montura Ranch, where Charlie passed himself off as a hunting guide. The operation grew and prospered for years, but then began to die off in the late seventies. I swear, though, to this day they were still in the Everglades training, and they were still backed by the CIA.

Charlie eventually got into business and he faded out of the day-to-day of the counter-revolutionary world. I knew he still hads contacts though; they were just political now, not cloak and dagger. He also played the game differently now—with money—but he still played. He was a Cuban at heart. What could I say?

After Banco left, I knew I needed to go see the man. If anyone knew what the Beard was up to back then, it was Charlie Alvarez. Charlie and I had grown apart in the last few years. He didn't agree with my way of life and I didn't subscribe to the fucked-up-young-Republican mentality, but he still treated me like a son, lectures and all. For my part, I understood where he was coming from; the circle of businessmen and politicians he associated with didn't want to hear my views.

Charlie used his connections well; he parlayed them into a real estate empire in Miami-Dade County. He had political clout in Washington and he was a patron of the arts, especially Caribbean art. He gave generously, and graciously, to charities. The son of a bitch didn't miss a beat; he knew how to play the game and he was setting himself up to get a piece of the pie when Castro was gone. That's what pissed me off about Charlie. He turned into what he started out fighting against. He became just another shark in the water, waiting to get a piece of Cuba. Castro came to power because of sharks.

I picked up the phone and called his number.

"*Si dime.*"

"Hi Charlie, its Kiki. How have you been?"

"Well, look who decided to call and say hello..."

"Yeah, it's been a while. I was wondering if I could come by and talk to you."

"No problem, Enrique. Come by my office tomorrow around eleven am. I can't wait."

The next morning I got up and had some coffee. I got in the 308 and headed up to see Charlie. Tiger Enterprises was located in the Dupont Plaza on Dupont Circle in downtown Miami, right on the water. The offices had beautiful views of the city and the aquamarine water surrounding all of the little islands that made their way across the bay to Miami Beach and the big blue of the Atlantic beyond.

I arrived a little early. Charlie must have been waiting for me, because his secretary showed me right into his office.

He was sitting with his back toward me, in a big plush leather chair behind an oversized mahogany desk that looked more like a dinner table. He was looking out a huge window that framed a beautiful view of the bay and those nice little islands, the bay full of boats, all of it drenched in so much glinting sunlight it had a surreal look.

Charlie turned in his chair with a big cigar in his mouth.

"Enrique, have a seat. Would you like anything to drink?"

"No. No thanks, Charlie."

"It's been a while, son. I hope everything is going good for you."

Charlie was trying his hardest to be nice to me. If it weren't for our family ties, he probably would have punched me in the face by now.

"Everything is fine, thanks; I see you're doing as well as ever. Is that a real Cuban you're smoking?"

Charlie was a little uptight, and I enjoyed busting his balls. He was one of those right-wing Cuban-American Republicans who continued to support the embargo, despite all the evidence of its ineffectiveness. He enjoyed the finer things in life, though, and that included fine Cuban cigars. So despite his support of the embargo, he didn't let it stop him from getting Havana-made Cohibas. I always knew when he was smoking a really good Cuban cigar because he removed the ring label. The bottom line was that I really didn't care what he did or didn't do. Hell, I often did many of the same things, just with a different taste and style, that's all.

Charlie was tightly wound; it was easy getting under his skin, and I couldn't help myself in those situations. I got under his skin.

"You came here to see me and be a little asshole? Come on, Enrique, you're getting too old for this bullshit. What is it you wanted to see me about? You know what? If it weren't for your father, I wouldn't give you the time of day. He was my best friend, though, and I promised him I would always do whatever I could for you. But you live your life wild and crazy like a beatnik and a beach bum, and if you keep it up you won't be around for much longer, boy. So, let's get to the point."

Charlie stood up from his plush chair and walked around the big desk to where I was sitting. As he hovered over me I knew I needed to stop playing around with him or he'd kick me out. I needed the information that I thought he could provide. "What do you know about this, Charlie?" I asked him as I showed him the picture of the crucifix Banco had gotten from his client in Romania.

"Looks like a nice piece, but I don't know anything about it. Where did you get it?" Charlie asked.

"I don't have it," I told him. "I just have this picture. It is in the hands of a private collector in Romania who says he got it from a contact of his working with a Cuban diplomat."

"And what's so strange about that?" Charlie asked grinning.

"The collector had the piece researched and it was on the manifest of the *Concepción*, which was headed for Spain before it sank in Dominican waters in 1641. I was just wondering how it got into Cuban hands."

"Maybe it was bought by the Cubans from the Dominicans. Their relations aren't as strained as ours."

"But why a private collector? Wouldn't it command more at an auction, handled by Christie's or Sotheby's, stir up more interest, create a bidding war?"

"Yeah probably, but what's the point, what are you getting at?" Charlie asked as he settled into the chair next to mine.

"I want to know if you know anything about Cubans diving old wrecks around the Caribbean—*outside* of Cuban waters."

Charlie looked at me, with no sign of surprise on his face at all.

"A lot of people know that, Enrique, including me, but there's no proof. There have been instances of Cuban dive boats being chased out of Bahamian waters and other countries' territorial boundaries. But they've never been caught; no one has anything on the Beard.

"Face it, treasure is hot these days. We're in a time of hyper-awareness when it comes to salvage and ancient artifacts. Ever since Mel Fisher brought up the *Atocha*, archaeologists and museums have been getting a lot of press. There's a lot of interest in these relics–not only because of their value, but for the treasure trove of historical information they provide.

"The Beard is real careful though; I don't think he's going to open himself up to criticism from the world over stolen treasure. He can't be robbing his neighbors while trying to look like a poor, beleaguered little boy being abused by the U.S. It just won't fly," Charlie said firmly. "Can I keep this picture?" he asked. "I have some friends in the I.N.A., the Institute of National Archaeology, who can probably tell me a lot more about this crucifix."

"Yeah, you can keep it, Charlie. I can get another if I need to, but to tell you the truth, I have no need for it."

Charlie sat back in his chair, looked at me and asked, "What are you chasing down, Enrique? You better be careful if you're messing around in Cuba. Fidel will cut your *cojones* off; he's done it to bigger and better hombres than you, *amigo*."

Evidently, Charlie knew me a little better than I thought; he had a stern look on his face as he watched me. Then he stood up, walked over to his office door and opened it. "I've got a busy afternoon, Enrique. If I find out anything about the crucifix, I'll let you know," he said. In no uncertain terms, he was letting me know the meeting was over.

"Thanks, Charlie." I shook his hand, walked out his office, down the stairs, and out of the Dupont Plaza, back out onto Biscayne Boulevard.

I thought about the meeting with Charlie. He had pretty much confirmed it: Cuba had been pillaging foreign waters. There was no proof, but if anyone knew, it would be Charlie. This job was becoming more interesting to me every day. Now if Charlie confirmed the provenance of the emerald-encrusted crucifix with his friends at the I.N.A., then I was on solid ground as far as establishing that Cuba had a cache of looted treasure.

I called over to Hawk Marine, hoping to see the Miami boys before going back to Islamorada. DK, Jony, and Jorge came to Miami during the Mariel boatlift in 1980 and they had done pretty well for themselves. They worked hard, pooled their money, and bought a rundown old marina on the Miami River. They had worked day and night to rebuild it.

Dry dockage, wet storage, dry storage, mechanic's service– they had it all there now. The center of the marina was the dive shop, though, and all three of the boys were master scubadivers with reputations for solving tough salvaging assignments.

Naturally all three of the Miami boys were fanatics about the water, but most of all Jony. DK handled the business and Jorge took care of the technical part. Jony was the gregarious front man and master diver; everybody liked Jony. The boys were making great money with their set up.

The secretary told me the boys weren't around; they were out celebrating a contract they had just gotten with some European group. The job was diving the Bimini Wall and examining its formation.

According to the great mystic, Edgar Cayce, known as "the sleeping prophet," that was the lost city of Atlantis. Cayce had predicted that Atlantis would begin to rise off the coast of Bimini and be found in 1968. Sure enough, in 1968, a small plane was flying over Bimini and the pilot saw a strange underwater formation no more than 100 yards offshore. Dubbed the Bimini Wall, it has been a subject of discussion and controversy ever since.

I knew the boys were going to make some good money on this one if they were out celebrating, and I had a hunch where they would be: Porky's. They were probably enjoying a few beers and some Russian female entertainment.

Porky's was a strip joint owned by a Russian expatriate who everyone knew as "Tarzan." Tarzan was a Russian Jew with ties to the Russian mob. He was a big, muscular, imposing figure, but he always had a smile and something nice to say. On the other hand, he was known to make people disappear if things didn't go his way.

Tarzan was hotter than a smoking pistol. Both the local cops and the Feds were interested in him. The word on the street was that Tarzan's ties to the Russian government and the

KGB could get you anything you needed. The word was that he was for real, no bullshit.

Miami lent itself to a lot of bullshit. It was an international, multi-cultural place and its underworld came from all parts of the globe.

A lot of scams went down in Miami; there was always someone who thought they could pull a fast one and make some quick money before running. They didn't usually get far, though; they ended up in the trunk of some car, decomposing and stinking up some neighborhood. Miami's underworld was largely freelancers, with no organized power structure, no center. You fucked up and you died. There was no meeting of crime bosses, or "capos," to decide if you could be hit. You just turned up dead and that was it; no questions asked. Miami had more than its share of Tony Montanas, and they played for keeps.

Tarzan had managed to get his foot in the door of the Miami scene, but now he was branching out, going beyond the drug trade and the stolen art business; he had begun talking nuclear. I heard he was trying to sell a nuclear submarine from the former U.S.S.R. Since that kind of deal carried a terrorist label with it, the Miami underground didn't want anything to do with it. They knew better than to shit where they ate.

I walked into the dimly lit club; the strobe lights were flashing on the beautiful women up on the stage. I let my eyes adjust a little and took a look around at the customers, not the women. I felt a tap on my shoulder and turned around; Tarzan was standing there with a big smile on his face.

"Hello, Kiki! It's been a while since I've seen you. What's the matter, you don't like Russian women?"

I laughed, and the big burly man grabbed me and gave me a comradely hug.

"Oh, they're beautiful, Tarzan. I love Russian women. But it's a rich diet, these girls. Would you eat caviar every day?" He laughed and slapped me on the back.

Tarzan had approached me a few times about some work in the Cayman Islands, and I had always declined. I had never even asked what it was; I didn't want to know.

"Whenever you want to make some big money, Kiki, you let me know. The word on you is good," Tarzan said.

We talked for a few minutes, and then he pointed to the table where the Miami boys were sitting.

"Are they who you're looking for?"

I walked over and before I could say hello, Jony jumped up and gave me a big hug. The boys were in a good mood. I thought that maybe this would help my cause. If I did this job, I would need them. They had always been my safety valve in the past. DK looked up at me and shook my hand.

"Porky's on a Tuesday night? What's up, Kiki? You feeling okay?"

"I'm doing well, boys, and it looks like you are too. Your secretary told me the good news. Congratulations."

"Have a drink with us, Kiki," Jorge said, and he poured me a big glass of beer.

I sat down and we caught up on what was happening since we last saw each other. They told me about the contract they had landed in Bimini. It would stretch out over a couple of years and would still give them all the time they needed to run the marine shop.

"Guys, I don't want to break up your good time, but I'm headed back to the Keys and I wanted to know if you could come to Islamorada tomorrow. I've got something important I need to talk over with you." I looked at each of them, smiled, and said, "Large. Very large."

I stood up and shook their hands.

"See you tomorrow, guys? I'll be waiting on the *Quest*. I promise, at the very least, it will give you a laugh and we can drink a few *mojitos*."

"Hmm. Large huh, Kiki?" Jony said, smiling. "*Valla*. We'll be there, *hermano*."

I said goodbye to the boys, and then Tarzan. Then I walked out of the club and into the warm, muggy Miami night. Tarzan had my 308 out front and the valet refused a tip. Whenever I came here, Tarzan took good care of me. He hadn't given up on the idea of me working for him, but he should forget that. I had enough bullshit in my life without bringing Tarzan and the Feds into it.

I got into my car and worked my way around Miami International Airport, where Porky's was, and onto I-95 southbound, heading for US-1 and away from the city, to the peace of the Florida Keys. I hadn't talked to Nadine since our argument at dinner. Nadine could really piss me off, but I always felt at ease when I was around her. I knew that sounded crazy, but that's how it was. I called her to see how she was doing. Typical of Nadine, she had forgotten about the whole argument and was only interested in how I was doing. Nadine was selfless; it made me feel like shit sometimes. Her concern for others honestly came from her heart; she seemed to see only the good in people.

"Can you come by the *Quest* tomorrow, *niña*? I'd like to see you; we'll have some lunch, talk about our trip."

"Ok, Kiki. I'll see you there. *A demain.* Tomorrow," she said, and hung up the phone. Once again she made me feel like shit by not even acknowledging the problem, but at the same time it relieved me to know she had forgotten our argument. Now at least the drive to the Keys wouldn't be consumed with how to make up to her.

It was early evening and the sun was almost down, creating those outrageous Florida pastel colors in the sky. I felt like I was driving through a beautifully painted picture, balmy weather, not a cloud in the sky, palm trees swaying in the humid breeze, and my woman had forgiven me once again. All was well in the universe. I punched the gas pedal down on the Ferrari and left cars in my wake as the Master himself, Bob Marley, belted out the truest Reggae song ever recorded, "No Woman No Cry". Everything was beginning to have a feel to it, and it felt right.

The next day was overcast; the normal early morning blazing sun was obscured by clouds and the summer thunderstorm looming on the horizon. I heard a noise outside the *Quest* and looked out the galley window to find Nadine on the boat, storing some gear.

"Hey *niña*, good morning."

"*Salut*, Kiki. *Ça va?*" she asked.

"I'm good, baby. I'm coming up. I have something to ask you."

I had some coffee made. I walked up on deck, gave Nadine a cup, and sat down.

"What's up, Kiki? You look a little serious."

"I think I'm going to do the Cuban job for Banco. I need to talk to the Miami boys and make a call to Cuba. If everything checks out, I'll take the next step. I'll go to Cuba, and see the situation over there."

"Are you sure about this? You want me to be cover for you?" she said.

"That's part of it," I told her. "But I also need someone who is good with boats. We're going to be on the water for a while; it's too much for one person. I need a partner I can trust."

She looked at me with a suppressed grin—dimples and all—then stood up, walked over, and extended her hand to shake mine.

"Partners," she said.

"Partners," I told her and reached out and shook her hand. "Whatever we get, we share equally."

"*Bon*. When do we leave?"

"Hold it," I said.

"Why?"

"You said '*bon*,' right?" I asked, and I began to break up laughing. I couldn't help it. My mind works in weird ways sometimes.

"Yeah, so? I always say *bon*. I'm French, remember?" She knew I was fucking with her head. "I'm not a cracker, I'm not a Cubanito like you. I'm a froggie." She tried to make some croaking noises.

"No, you don't get it. Bonnie and... bonnie and....?" I stood up and made those hand motions you make in charades. I knew this was way beyond her.

"First you make my '*bon*' 'Bonnie,' now it's 'Bonnie Ann.' Are you trying to tell me you have someone new? I think it's time to leave. *Tant pis*, I thought you were such a nice boy." She got up and pretended she was leaving.

"Bonnie and Clyde, don't you get it?"

"Oh you silly *garçon*. *Merde, t'est vraiment fou*." She shook her head in mock dismay. "Well, I see your point. Let's hope we don't end up like them at least. Are the Cuban police as mean as Elliot Ness?"

"A lot meaner, *mucho* meaner. Anyway, to answer your question, I don't know. Maybe a week, maybe sooner. It depends on us, and then Banco's go-ahead."

I clapped my hands together and made a serious face. "So let's get going on this, Bonnie. I need you to go to West Marine and pick up some charts of the lower Keys, the Cay Sal Bank, the southern Bahamas, and northern Cuba. The Miami boys are coming over this afternoon and I want to look over a few things with them. Plus I need to make a few phone calls; and the mechanics are coming over to fine tune the Mercs on the *Lean Back*."

I gave her the keys to the 308, and some money for charts, and she was on her way to Miami, but only after giving me a kiss and saying she had an appointment with someone named Clyde that night on a dreamboat called the *Quest*.

I was still smiling when the mechanics showed up 10 minutes later. They were done with the *Lean Back* in 45 minutes. They went over the lower end units to make sure they weren't dinged up, changed the oil and timed the engines. I knew they wouldn't have much to do. I stay on top of her; my life would depend on how good this boat ran.

My dog Bentley came running from the forward deck of the *Quest* when he saw Calvin coming down the dock.

Bentley was a 145-pound Rottweiler. He was pretty impressive; he looked like he could eat you alive. His face was ebony, with two little tan marks, like eyebrows, above piercing brown eyes. His dark, shiny eyes gave the impression that he missed nothing; he was fully aware of his surroundings. He scared the hell out of people sometimes. As my live-aboard pal and watchdog, he did his job, but in reality he was a big teddy bear. Like his namesake, Bentley the butler, the gentleman's gentleman, he was usually well mannered and proper.

Although he never left the *Quest* without me, he was very well known. Everybody at Bud and Mary's loved him. But then, they had never seen him when he couldn't get back to his sleeping spot under the galley table. He loved that spot and his pillow. The only time I have ever heard him growl is when someone messed with him when he was trying to get to his spot or when he was in it. Just the day before, he growled at Nadine because she was blocking him from getting to his spot.

I'd had Bentley since he was two months old, and he had never known anything other than life on the water and our home at the marina. He always went fishing with me, and I took him on the small, easy salvage jobs close to home. Lately though, Bentley had been lying low. The poor guy swallowed a piece of plastic and needed an operation. He just got home from the vet's a week ago and he'd been cooped up on the *Quest* ever since.

He knew he was going to get off the boat when he saw Calvin. I always left Bentley with Calvin when I went on a job where I would be away for a few days or more. If I didn't come back, I wanted Calvin to have Bentley. Calvin loved Bentley, and Bentley liked Calvin a lot too.

Bentley sat at my feet on the aft deck and looked at me with his head cocked like that dog Nipper from the old RCA Victor ads. Bentley looked over at Calvin approaching and began to wag his nub tail, which had the effect of wagging his whole ass end. He knew I was leaving, but clearly he looked forward to his time with Calvin.

"Hey Bentley, what's up big boy?" Calvin said as he stepped up onto the deck of the *Quest*, squatted down, and began to pet Bentley. After a bit he looked up and said, "Hey Kiki, how are you doing?"

"Not bad Calvin. Why the long face?"

"It's nothing. Some fucking crackers swerved their car at me on the road when I was riding my bike down here, calling me "nigger" and shit; you know how that goes, man."

He smiled down at Bentley, and continued to pet him. He knew the dog held no prejudice; Bentley licked his face.

Calvin Rolle was a good kid. He'd never been in jail, but the way he was going he would have been there sooner or later. Young, and black, with no job and no prospects, he was from Coconut Grove's ghetto. Living there, his days were numbered. He made his money selling dope on the streets for the local dealers, but he eventually developed a crack habit and ended up essentially working for free. The dealers owned him when he was only 16 years old. Thank God for his parents, who moved out of Miami just to save their child.

Calvin's parents, Roosevelt Rolle, or "Roozie" as everyone called him, and Beverly Rolle, came from good stock. The Rolles; were one of the oldest and largest families in the Bahamas. A branch of the Rolle family had been in Coconut Grove since the early 1900s. They were one of the original black families who settled there. Roozie made a living as fisherman. As with every prime area near the ocean, though, properties in Coconut Grove became very valuable and the original settlers, the Bahamian blacks, were being pushed aside. The black section of Coconut Grove, the West Grove, was nowhere near the water.

In Coconut Grove you could see one of the most unbelievable class contrasts, between the mega-rich mansions of the white Grove and the ultra-poor shotgun houses of the black

Grove. You could literally stand in the back yard of a ten million dollar home and all that separated you from a sixty thousand dollar home was a seven-foot fence with appropriately high hedges to hide the view. I wondered who appraised those properties.

The older residents could stand in their end of town and look onto the enclaves of the rich and famous, watching them go in and out of the Hard Rock Café, or the glitzy, super-rich Mayfair shops on property that was worth millions upon millions of dollars and was bought and sold by the square foot. Yet when you walked fifty or a hundred yards down the road and cross that invisible line, the money is gone. It was the same story everywhere; it repeated itself in different times and eras, but it was still the result of the same old shit: racism.

The Rolles moved to Islamorada a while ago. Roozie worked in the agricultural fields for a co-op in Homestead, but there were times of the year when he was out of work and the money was tough. Beverly picked up odd jobs cleaning homes for the wealthy islanders. They barely made ends meet, but they had Calvin back in high school and he seemed to be doing a lot better. I gave him work to do around the *Quest* to keep him busy, even when I didn't need it. It kept him out of trouble.

Islamorada was a small place; stand still and you would eventually see everyone there. I met Calvin at the grocery store; he was in front of me in the checkout line. Calvin was a good sized kid, about six feet tall and muscular. He could look imposing, but once you looked at his face and into his hazel-green eyes you saw that he was still just a kid.

He was at the checkout, trying to pay, but he was fifty-three cents short and the checkout girl wouldn't let him slide. His edgy city side, from having grown up in the Grove's ghetto, came out and he began arguing with the girl about cutting him a break. The poor girl got scared and promptly called the manager, who asked Calvin to leave. I looked down at the counter to see what he was buying, and it wasn't frivolous stuff. It looked like regular groceries and it wasn't much, only about fifteen dollars worth. I knew the manager casually from shopping there once in a while. We would cross paths and say hello with a nod or a smile; he didn't seem like bad guy. When I offered to cover the fifty-three cents, he accepted graciously.

Calvin glanced at me, barely making eye contact, with his head half bowed, and softly said "thank you." It wasn't a perfunctory "thank you," intended to get things over with; it was a humble "thank you." Calvin took his bagged groceries and with his head still half bowed, he walked out the automatic doors of the store.

I paid for my groceries and the manager thanked me with a smile as I walked out the doors and into the parking lot. Outside, I looked to my right and saw Calvin putting his grocery bag loops on the handlebars of his bike. I thought about what I'd seen inside and wondered if maybe he would be interested in making some money. I was going on a fishing trip to Bimini on the *Lean Back* and I needed her cleaned up, inside and out. I walked over to Calvin and asked him if he wanted to make some money cleaning my boat. His eyes showed interest and he said yes, before quickly looking down again. I told him to meet me at Bud and Mary's the next day and he did; ever since then, he worked for me two to three days a week. When I was gone, he took care of Bentley.

I looked at Calvin as he petted Bentley; the forlorn look in his eyes told a sad story.

"Don't let those motherfuckers get to you, Calvin. They're just stupid rednecks."

"I know, man. I know," Calvin said, still petting Bentley and still smiling.

Calvin knew I was Cuban, and he knew how I felt about discrimination. In the time that I had known him, I had tried to console Calvin a few times when racial discrimination affected him. Calvin considered me to be Cuban, not American, kind of like blacks of mixed race who are considered to be black only. Yet I didn't look Spanish, and unless I told someone, they don't know. So I could only imagine what it must be like to experience bigotry and racism on an almost daily basis.

Mainstream society had made minorities gunshy, and reactions like Calvin's at the grocery store when I first met him were common. Whether or not we admitted it, racism was alive and well and it affected everyone, including those who are disgusted by it.

I felt sorry for Calvin, but I didn't want to give the topic life either, so I let it drop. I didn't forget, though.

"So how long are you going to be gone for, Kiki?" Calvin asked. He was smiling, with the thought of the rednecks behind him and the prospect of spending a few days with Bentley ahead.

"I don't know, little brother. Two to three days, maybe a week. Can you handle the big baby for that long?"

"Hell, yeah. If you die on some crazy job though, he's mine, so don't have one of your friends come looking for him."

Calvin was laughing, in a much better mood.

"No problem, little brother. He's yours if I don't come back," I said smiling. "But I'm coming back."

Calvin stood up and Bentley stood right with him. I handed Calvin fifty dollars for dog food.

"If you need to spend more, go ahead; I'll pay you when I get back. Take good care of him."

Calvin walked off the *Quest* and Bentley followed; he knew he was going. I threw Calvin the leash and they headed down the dock toward Calvin's waiting bicycle. Bentley turned around a couple of times to look back at me, but went willingly. I turned around and walked down into the galley of the *Quest*.

I needed to call Serafina in Miami, to see if she could get hold of David in Cuba.

David was my Cuban contact; Serafina was his aunt in Miami, my telephone go-between for communicating with David.

I called and Serafina answered the phone.

"*Digame.*"

"*Como estas, señora? Es Enrique.*"

"*Bien. Bien, mi hijo. Y tu?*"

"*Bien. Gracias.*"

Serafina was a wonderful lady. She came to Miami with her late husband, Ramon about 10 years ago. Her nephew David brought them over. David often transported people from Cuba. Serafina loved him like a son and she worried that he'd get caught one day.

As easy as it would have been for David to leave Cuba, he always returned from his fishing trips; his wife Sara refused to leave Cuba. David was one of the few men in Cuba who was allowed to fish commercially. Although he had that privilege, his actions were still watched; however, being out at sea for twenty, thirty, or even forty days at a stretch, he found time for diversions.

I met David in Bimini in the early 1980s. He was docked at Weeche's Marina; his boat said "Caibarién, Cuba." Because my family was from that town, I walked over to the boat and met David, and we'd been good friends ever since. He'd worked for me in the Bahamas a few times, down on Ragged Island on the Columbus bank. I paid him $50,000 cash one time; when I paid him, he couldn't believe he was holding that much money. I remembered him saying that it was more money than his whole family combined had seen in the last fifty years. For Banco's job, David was important; he was experienced and from the area where the treasure was stored.

"Serafina, I need to talk to David. Can you place a call for me?"

"*Sí*, of course. Call me tonight and I'll let you know when he'll be home. I'll try and set it up for tomorrow, *mi hijo*," she said.

"*Gracias, Serafina.* I'll call you tonight."

As I hung up, Nadine pulled up to the dock in the Ferrari, with a big smile on her face and the nautical charts in her hands.

"*Mon Dieu,* that car attracts the boys and the girls; you can really get in trouble with it."

She walked up on deck and handed me the charts. I had a pitcher of *mojitos* ready, overflowing with fresh mint. I poured her one.

We were enjoying the tropical breeze and our *mojitos* on the back deck of the Quest when the boys pulled up in their big Ford F-350 Dually with salsa music blasting. Jony jumped out of the truck and began dancing his way down the dock to the *Quest,* smiling the whole way. DK and Jorge got out of the truck. They looked at Jony, shook their heads, and smiling, they followed him to the boat.

We walked down into the galley; Nadine had the charts laid out on the table and I poured everyone a *mojito.*

"Large, baby, large; I couldn't sleep last night thinking about what you were up to," Jony said.

"I see whatever it is, it's down south," DK said, staring at the charts.

DK was obviously the most serious of the three "boys" and their de facto leader. Whatever they did, they decided together; but DK felt free to speak for Jony and Jorge.

Like a lot of Cubans, the Miami boys had some common links: their belief in their religion, Santeria, was an important one; love of the ocean was another. They went to see a Santeria priest before buying the old run-down marina and he had told them they would only succeed together. Ever since then, they relied on each other for everything; they were like brothers. It made you wonder, but I said, to each his own, it's a big world out there.

"The job is in Cuba. It's not salvage, it's a heist," I told them.

I wanted to get right to the point and there was no other way to say it. I couldn't softsell this job to anyone. It got their full attention.

"*Alavao!* You mean, as in 'robbing?'" DK asked.

"Hey, anything I take from Castro, he owes me, you, or someone else. Anyway, it's black market merchandise in the first place, that he's stolen. It's anybody's who can get it. Right now it's his; I want to make it ours."

"*Este hombre esta loco,*" Jony said, looking at DK and Jorge. "But I love you, Kiki," he said, turning to me and starting to laugh.

"Go ahead, we're listening," DK said.

I went over the treasure story with them, and then the maps, including the aerial photos Banco had left with me.

"I've got a contact in Cuba who I need to meet with, to make sure it's possible. I don't think we have a big window on this one, so I plan to try and meet him in the Cay Sal Banks in the next day or so. If he thinks it's doable, we have to be ready to go from there. It's a fifty-fifty job. Banco sells it off; we get half, no commissions."

"What's the take?" DK asked.

"I don't know, maybe $20 to 30 million, Banco said."

"Mi Madre… DK, Jorge, we have to take a look," Jony said.

Jony was ballsy and loved any kind of adventure on the ocean. I had known he'd be up for it.

DK looked over at Jony and Jorge, then back to me and said, "Sounds good so far; let's take a look. So, what's next?" DK asked.

"I've got someone I need to go see first; then I need to talk to David. He's my Cuban contact. You know him, right? I'll tell him to meet us in Cay Sal. In the meantime, we need satellite phones and some small and not-so-small arms. Banco is covering the expenses, so get the best."

"I'll handle that," Jorge said.

"I'll call you in a day or so. Be ready to go," I told them.

After another *mojito* the boys said their goodbyes and left. A few minutes later, my phone rang; it was Serafina, David's aunt.

"Buenas noches, señora, como estas?"

"Bien gracias, Kiki."

She switched to English. "I spoke to Sara, David's wife; he wasn't home but he will be in tomorrow afternoon at one. You can come over here and call him then."

"Gracias, senora. I'll see you tomorrow."

I hung up the phone and immediately, it rang again. It was Charlie Alvarez.

"Enrique, I had that picture checked out by a friend of mine at I.N.A.; he confirmed that the crucifix was on the manifest of the Concepción. Listen, son, I don't know what you're up to, but be careful. That crucifix was never confirmed found, nor has it ever been seen on the market before. Stay away from the Beard, Enrique; it's not worth it."

"Thanks, Charlie. I appreciate it; don't worry about me, though. I'm a big boy."

"Yeah, that's what I'm worried about," he said and hung up the phone.

Nadine got her things together and decided to go home for the night. Clyde would have to wait. But tomorrow she was coming back to stay on the *Quest* until we left for the Cay Sal Bank. And tomorrow I would talk to David and then go see my old friend, Maxi Betancur. After Nadine left, I found some things to do on board and called it a night early.

I woke up full of energy and I couldn't wait to get on the water. It was 7:30 am and the galley of the *Quest* was already steamy. The rays of sunlight coming through the window illuminated and brought to life the particles of dust floating around in the room. There wasn't a breath of fresh air anywhere.

Maybe Banco and everyone else were right. I needed to get an AC for the place. They were going to find me mummified in there one day.

I had heard Nadine arrive at about 7:00 am; she was cleaning the *Lean Back*'s deck and sides, swabbing off the overnight dew and salt residue. She knew I wasn't much of a morning person, so she left me alone in the below deck. The heat would drive me out soon enough, and she knew it.

Meanwhile, she was passing the time swabbing the deck and talking to my neighbor, Crazy Mary, who's docked on the other side of the *Lean Back*. Crazy Mary earned her name because she was always half cocked; sometimes she was even fully cocked. The lady loved her vodka. She was harmless, though. The worst thing she ever did was put on her bikini and walk around topside. That bikini revealed more information than I or anyone else needed to know.

Mary must have come from money or married it. She didn't strike me as the type to have made her own money. She had a big home in Miami but she spent all of her time on her 42-foot Hunter down in Islamorada. It was immaculate; she always had somebody working on it.

But she was a good neighbor. She minded her own business, and watched out for the *Quest* and the *Lean Back* when I wasn't around.

"Good morning, Kiki," Crazy Mary greeted me from her boat as I walked topside.

"Good morning Mary, how are you?"

She raised her glass full of vodka, with just a splash of orange juice for color, and let me know she was doing fine. It was 8:00 am and Mary was already slamming them down. The crazy thing was that Mary would look no worse for wear at 8:00 pm that night, and she would still be slamming them down. She had to be pickled.

Nadine came on board and started stowing her gear.

"*Niña*, would you mind doing some shopping for provisions for the trip?"

"No problem, Kiki. How many days, do you think?"

"A week will be good," I told her.

That's what was great about Nadine and made her a good partner. She knew exactly what to get, and in what amounts for trips out on the water. It wasn't easy. Most people who had boat problems on the water–aside from sinking–miscalculated their rations. Nadine, however, knew how to stock a boat and prepare it for a trip.

"I'm going to see Serafina; I'm talking to David from her house today."

She nodded and went back to work. I finished my morning coffee, cleaned myself up, got into my 308 and headed up US1 to Little Havana.

I got to Serafina's at 12:30 and knocked on the door of the tiny house on the corner of SW 12th Street and 10th Avenue, smack in the middle of Little Havana. All the homes here were tiny and well kept. This was old Miami. When you looked around the neighborhood here, you thought you were back in the 1940s or '50s.

"*Entra, mi hijo.*"

Serafina opened the door and showed me inside. There were religious artifacts here and there throughout the house and a small statue of "Our Lady of Charity," Cuba's patron saint,was on the mantle with a candle burning in her honor.

Serafina brought me some fresh Cuban coffee and setting it down, said, "You're just in time to make the call, Kiki."

She picked up the phone and dialed. Usually, I could call China and get through easier than I could to Cuba, but we got lucky. It took a few minutes, but she got through, and after speaking for a few seconds, she handed me the phone.

"*Buenas, mi hermano. Como estas?*"

"*Bien bien, David, gracias.*"

David and I chit-chatted for a minute or so and then got down to business.

"*David, los perros sies dias, es posible?*"

"*Sin problem, nos vemos,*" David said.

That was the end of the phone call. David never lingered on the line; he didn't trust the communication. We had agreed to meet at Dog Rocks in the Cay Sal Bank in six days.

I handed the phone back to Serafina and said my goodbyes.

She stopped me at the door, made the sign of the cross on my forehead and said,

"*Que Dios te cuide,* may God watch over you, *y cuidame ha David.*" She gave me a look. She knew something was up. A phone call from me to David from her house wasn't just to exchange pleasantries.

I had called Maxi Betancur earlier in the day and he was waiting for me at his office in North Miami. I drove up US1 and took in all the glorious sights that were everyday views in Miami. Tropical balmy breezes blowing tall majestic palm trees, beautiful scantily clad women, and expensive cars filled my eyes all the way to Maxi's office.

His office was in a three-story building, very distinct and plain looking. He was C.I.A through and through, and some really big, really covert decisions were made in that building.

Maxi was an old friend; our families were friends. I wasn't the only little boy running around in camouflage in the Jersey hills back in the 1960s. Maxi's father worked in intelligence for the CIA, focusing on Cuban matters. His family lived in Elizabeth, New Jersey, a real Cuban enclave. Like my father, every weekend Maxi's father took him to the encampments. That was how we met. Being the only children out there, we developed a friendship that was strong to this day. Together we learned a lot about Cuba, and the Revolution, and developed a hatred for Castro.

When the press blew the camp's cover in New Jersey and the CIA pulled up stakes and moved their operation to the Everglades, Maxi's family moved to Miami.

His father was an important figure in the CIA and he was needed in Florida. My family stayed in Jersey. I would see Maxi now and then on summer vacations. We never lost contact; we stayed close. We both had a vision of going back to a free Cuba one day.

When the CIA pulled out of New Jersey, my life changed. There were no more weekends playing soldier, no more sitting around with the guerilla fighters listening to stories of Cuba and how beautiful it was. I quickly blended into my new environment, and like any other little boy, I became distracted by other things. My mother would still tell me stories of the old Cuba. Even though my life was completely American, I still enjoyed listening to the stories.

Maxi, on the other hand, never stopped living a counter-revolutionary life. He spent every spare minute he had in the

Everglades with the CIA and the Cuban resistance fighters. He graduated from high school with honors; he was active in the R.O.T.C., the whole nine yards. He graduated from the Citadel with honors, also. There was no question of what he wanted to do and what direction he wanted to take.

He went to work for the government right after college, and with the help of his father's contacts stretching all the way to Washington, it wasn't long before he was in the CIA. He called me the day before he got hired, right before he went to Langley to begin his training. He said it was the happiest day of his life, what he always wanted.

Maxi was the chief liaison in South Florida for the Caribbean. He was the man who got grilled by the press when shit went wrong. There was nothing secret about what Maxi did; his position was well known. It's what he knew that remained unknown. As a result, he could get things done; people paid attention to Maxi. He was no bullshit, a company man through and through.

I walked into the building and up to Maxi's office. Very few people knew that the CIA had an office here and its seemingly easy access could fool anybody. But the place is wired to the hilt. Maxi had shown me. This was the fucking Hotel California: you could check in, but if they didn't want you to, you didn't leave.

The secretary showed me the way and I knocked on Maxi's office door.

"Come in."

"Kiki, how in the hell are you, man?" Maxi said. He stood up and gave me a hug. "I can see you're as relaxed as ever. Do you ever get out of a pair of shorts and into pants? You've got the life of Riley, man." Maxi really didn't agree with my lifestyle, but he was like my brother and it didn't matter to him that I chose a different path. "So what's up, kid? I haven't seen you since last month, when I beat your ass at the poker table. Remember that royal flush? God, are you bad at poker or what? Charlie called me up; told me you went by to see him. That man loves you, Kiki, but you sure can get under his skin. He thinks you're up to something involving Cuba."

Since I knew that Charlie had probably told him everything we had talked about, I wasn't going to go around and around with Maxi on this.

"I have a lead on some treasure that's been stolen by Cubans. I just wanted to know what the coastline of Cuba is like lately. I haven't been down there in about a year and I was thinking of going. I wanted to know if it had changed any as far as patrolling goes."

"Things haven't changed any. You know the Cubans let boats in from the States; they don't deter them. They want the money. Now, whoever gets caught by the U.S. will be fined heavily, and may even have a chance at jail time. But you know how that is, Kiki. The ocean is huge; it's like the needle in a haystack. Chances are slim to none that anyone gets caught and slim just left town.

"As you know, Cubans don't stamp U.S. passports; once you're twelve miles out, you're in international waters. Who's to say you were in Cuba? It's a catch-22 for the U.S. But I can't believe you're considering this craziness, man. Banco is going to get you killed one day."

"Who said anything about Banco?"

"Charlie told me. You know he doesn't like Banco and his way of doing business."

"I know Charlie worries about me a lot, but he needs to lighten up. I'm not going to change, and I'm not going to become a Republican."

"I know Kiki, but he's old school, so cut him a break," Maxi said with a smile.

"Maxi, I'm going to see if there might be some more pieces like the one I showed Charlie. There's a collector who will pay big money for them in Romania. Banco knows I've been to Cuba a few times and he wants me to ask around, that's all."

I couldn't tell Maxi that I wasn't going, but I also couldn't tell him what I had in mind. I would never hear the end of it. When Maxi and I talked, it was always off the record. The truth of what I was planning, though, might have made him react differently. I changed the subject as quickly as I could.

"How are those crazy revolutionaries out in the 'Glades doing, Maxi?"

"You know how the world changes, Kiki. I doubt there will ever be an invasion of Cuba; the embargo has kept Cuba in check all this time, and that's good enough for the government. We funnel money out to them and keep them afloat, just to keep the politicos in Miami happy. I go out there once a month and give them a pep talk. They're still a good source of info on Cuba and its underground resistance."

I knew he hadn't forgotten what I came for, but I had at least got him off of the subject. "I know you're a busy man, Maxi, so I'll let you go. Tell your mom and dad I said hello and I'll drop by to see them soon."

Maxi walked me to the door and I said goodbye, got in my car and drove back to Islamorada.

I called Banco on the way and told him I'd come by tomorrow to see him at his office.

When I arrived at the *Quest*, Nadine was already asleep and I could see the boxes of provisions for the trip on the table of the galley. Nadine was in the main berth and I fell asleep like usual on the couch in the galley.

I woke up early the next morning as I needed to go see Banco and call the boys and have them meet me that night. Everything was a go. I planned on leaving the day after tomorrow.

Nadine came out of the main berth, looking a little tense. Zero hour was nearing and she was feeling it—I could see it in her face. I offered her some coffee and she gratefully accepted.

"Are you okay?" I asked.

"*Oui*, I'm fine. I have been working hard and getting little sleep; this coffee will help."

"Is there anything I can do?"

"I'm just a little anxious. I'll be fine."

I left her alone; she had to get through it on her own. The reality of going to Cuba and attempting a heist was weighing her down, as you would expect from someone who'd never before experienced violence in any form, aside from a belt-strapping from her *desgraciado* stepfather. No doubt about it, that was a legitimate fear. Even I was a coward about it, at least in anticipation, even though I'd seen my fair share of blood sport. Until I took the first steps and enter the arena, I just couldn't calm down. I was an old veteran of having a too-active brain and the only solutions I had ever come up with were to either get busy, or to numb the brain with alcohol and pot. So in this case it was a matter of getting busy.

Nadine went right to work, reviewing the checklist, storing gear and readying for the journey that was ahead.

"*Niña*, please take the *Lean Back* to the marina and fill the tanks, take four extra ten-gallon containers and fill them also. I'll leave you the money on the table."

She looked up at me from the deck.

"*Oui*, no problem Kiki," she said and continued her work.

Busy work was good right now; it would keep her and her mind occupied.

I walked onto the dock and made my way to the 308. I wanted to catch Banco before he went out on one of his two-hour lunches. He had a little unassuming office in a plaza on Okeechobee road in Hialeah not far from his home. Not many people knew where Banco lived. A few more knew where he worked. He kept his family very private, and he was pretty cagey with the business too. If you wanted to see Banco, it was here or the Mutiny. I got to Banco's office and he greeted me like usual, with a hug and a smile. He was in a good mood, as always.

"Come on in, Kiki. Do you want some coffee?"

"No thanks Banco, I've had two today already and I'm buzzing on that rocket fuel."

"Sit down, Kiki, sit down. Tell me something good." Banco pulled out a wad of cash and laid it on the table. He stood up and closed the door to his office. "There is a hundred grand there Kiki. That's for expenses."

"How do you know I'm taking the job? You're awful sure of yourself."

"Because you're here. If you weren't going to do it you would have phoned me instead."

Outside Banco's office, in the outer room, some of his gophers were hanging around. The place was messy and loud, but Banco was in his element when things got confusing. He thrived on living on the edge.

"You see those guys out there, Kiki? The ones goofing off, waiting for me to throw them some crumbs now and then? Some of them are *balseros*. They thought it was better to risk their lives in the Florida Straits and try to reach paradise rather than to stay starving in Cuba. They think they're rich, with what I throw them. And here we are, throwing a hundred grand on the table like it was lunch money. It is a shame that ninety miles off of our coast there's misery on a grand scale. There are few options in Cuba, Kiki. Doctors, lawyers, educators, are taking jobs in all the tourist areas, in Habana, Santiago and Cienfuegos as waiters and *jineteras*, just to afford a pair of shoes or a little food on the table. It's a shame when a country's best and most promising are reduced to menial labor to survive. Something's wrong with that, Kiki, and I know you think so too. That's why I knew you would do it. You hate him as much as I do, and giving him a little headache and something to think about attracts you as much as me."

"I'm leaving the day after tomorrow and the hundred grand is non-refundable," I told him. "My people are set up and whether we succeed or not, we have to put people and equipment in motion. If you hear from me in Cuba, we're moving ahead."

Banco reached over and handed me a name and number.

"That man is a contact of mine in Cuba, Sergio De La Rosa. Call him once you're on the island and he'll help you with anything. The man has a lot of connections. He's not my source of info on this job, but he has a lot of pull and can help you get around. Keep him on a need-to-know basis; don't trust anyone there. People in Cuba are truly scared of the government, and if they get squeezed it could be trouble."

"I appreciate it Banco, but I've got my own people in Cuba."

"Well, just in case you need it, hang onto his number."

"Right now I'm going to have lunch, Kiki. Would you like to come? South Beach, your pick."

"No thanks, Banco. I need to get back to Islamorada and finish up some things."

Banco walked me out to the parking lot and told me about delivery on the merchandise. He had private collectors ready to go, cash in hand. We'd be paid quickly.

This bothered me a little. I'd worked a lot with maritime historians and archaeologists and I understood the historical value of those priceless relics. I believed salvagers should get their share—after all, we were the ones who risked our lives to retrieve it, but I thought historical treasure belonged in museums for all to enjoy and profit from.

I got in the 308, put the stack of money in the glove compartment and drove back to Islamorada on another balmy summer afternoon. I called DK on the way. The Miami boys would be at the *Quest* at 7:00 pm.

When I arrived at the *Quest*, Nadine had stored all the gear and provisions for the trip and was sitting on the back deck of the boat enjoying the cool breezes coming off of the ocean.

"Bonjour Kiki, Ça va?" Mental and physical fatigue showed on her face.

"Ça va, niña. You look tired; you'll sleep good tonight. By the way, the boys will be here in a little while; we need to go over the plans."

"The charts are on the table in the galley. I've been checking the weather reports and it looks like we're going to have good weather for the trip."

She was being cautious about preparation, making sure everything was in order. I knew anxiety was getting to her, but she was focused on the task at hand and kept moving forward. It was a good sign; she was controlling her demons.

It was about 7:15 when the boys pulled up in their big truck with the beautifully painted name on the side, 'Hawk Marine.' They walked down the dock and boarded the *Quest*. Jorge had a briefcase with him.

We went down into the galley, and I opened up the charts of Cay Sal Bank on the table. I pointed to Dog Rocks on the northern edge of the bank.

"I'm meeting David there the day after tomorrow. I need you guys there one day after that."

"David, right. The guy you mentioned before. Is he your main contact?" DK asked.

"Yeah, he's the one. We'll plan accordingly from there, depending on what David thinks. I'm betting he knows everything we need to know about the warehouse we're hitting, since he lives in the same town. Nadine and I will make our way into Cuba after that. I need you guys cruising the coast between Cay Fragaso in Cuba and Ragged Island in the Bahamas. Make yourselves noticed somewhat because I'll need the distraction once we hit."

"We fish Ragged a lot, so we know the area well. We've got some friends in Duncan Town," DK said.

Ragged Island was about 20 miles off the Cuban coast and was a great place to be near Cuba, to fish and to observe the coast line.

"Don't make any contact at Dog Rocks; keep the *Hawk Marine* at a distance, one-eighth to one-quarter of a mile," I said. "Jony, you know what to do, nighttime swim to me. Don't let anyone see you. I'll be waiting for you to come to the *Lean Back*, then we'll both swim over to David. He worries about being watched when he's out of Cuban waters." I turned to Jorge. "Did you bring the phones?"

Jorge picked up the briefcase at his feet and put it on the table. He opened it and took out two satellite phones.

"There are three numbers on the back of the phones. The top number is that phone's number; the other two numbers are the two other phones. We have the third phone. When the time comes, ditch the phones in the ocean. They're untraceable, but they'll turn up hot in about a week. So after a week get rid of it or they'll pinpoint you." Jorge said.

He reached back into the briefcase and pulled out a .380 caliber Pietro Berretta semi-automatic handgun equipped with a six-inch silencer.

"I knew this was the one you liked; I got it just for you," Jorge told me.

The gun was easy to conceal and fit the hand perfectly. Maxi introduced it to me years ago. Jorge pulled out another just like it and set it on the table along with a hundred rounds of ammo.

"This one is for making people pay attention quickly," Jorge said. He reached back in the briefcase and pulled out two Uzis, each with a six-inch silencer like the .380s had. They had 35-round clips and he had bought two hundred rounds of ammo for them.

"All four of these are compliments of Tamiami Gun Shop. The silencers I tooled myself. The guns are probably already reported missing, so don't bring them back to the States, especially the silencers. I think it's ten years for just having one, even without a gun."

I looked at the firepower. I hoped the first shot would never have to be fired. I reached into the cupboard, pulled out twenty-five grand and put it on the table.

"That's for your expenses, boys. If we pull this off that will be play money. DK, I'll call you before I leave to let you know it's on. If anything comes up before then I'll call right away."

Up on deck I said my goodbyes to the boys as they got in their truck. Down in the galley, Nadine was staring at the guns. Needless to say, she didn't look very happy.

"I guess the ante has just gone up," she said.

I'd had a long day and really didn't want to get into it over the guns.

"They're mainly for protection on the water, *niña*, don't worry about them."

She looked at me through squinted eyes, smacked her lips and walked into her berth.

"*Bonne nuit* Kiki, I'll see you tomorrow."

She knew there was adventure involved; now she knew there was also danger. I lay down on the couch and fell asleep to the water lapping against the hull of the *Quest*.

Nadine and I spent the next morning checking things over, then went to the Tiki Hut for some lunch. It was difficult for her to tell me how she felt, and our lunch consisted of idle chit chat while sitting there in the steamy afternoon. It was stinking hot in the galley when we returned, and we whiled away the afternoon on the aft deck of the *Quest*. I paid some bills and made some phone calls that had to be made, some that I wanted to make. I had a good talk with my friend Dreamer in Bimini. Nadine read a mystery book she said she had become engrossed by, just flipping those pages. The wind whipped up and some thunderheads rolled in, the typical Florida afternoon thunderstorm, so we went down to the galley and made dinner. By the time it was ready, the storm had moved on and we ate on the deck. The air was fresh and the sunset gorgeous. I felt good, ready for the trip. I was looking forward to this heist.

"Do you want to talk about anything, *niña*? You look a little preoccupied." I'd had a bit too much wine, since Nadine poured herself just a half a glass and I had the rest to myself.

"No I don't, Kiki. I don't know that there is anything that can be said." She was visibly upset. "I'm going to bed." It was only 8:30, but we had to get up early the next morning.

I wondered why she was upset. I followed her into her room. I had all intentions of letting her know that I wasn't the source of her anxiety and she should lighten up and get over it. I found her lying on her side, still in her shorts and shirt. The heat in the room had caused her to sweat, and droplets rolled down her temples. Things were mentally rough right now on all of us, and I changed my mind when I saw her lying there. She turned and looked at me. "Do you want me, Kiki?"

I was tempted to take advantage of her vulnerable state, but instead I felt sorry for her. It was a momentary weakness on her part, a half-hearted attempt to try and blur her mind of what she signed up for. I understood, but I had feelings for her that went beyond the satisfaction of physical pleasure and I took offense at her willingness to compromise them.

"If you think I need the affections of a woman to shade my fears and anxieties, you're wrong. I can get a grip on my emotions and obviously you can't. And if it was just a matter of getting off to calm me down, well then I can get laid anywhere and most anytime."

"Kiki, Kiki, I didn't mean it that way," she said as tears began to flow.

"Go to sleep, *niña*. Tomorrow is going to be a long day."

I lay down on the galley couch to see if I could forget the day and get a good night's sleep. I turned on the TV to try and mesmerize myself into a state of sleepiness, but to no avail. I had the news on and was bombarded by the evils of society, with just a smattering of weather to fool me into thinking I lived in paradise. It was too much. With the thoughts running around in my head and the wonderful evening news, I felt like Chicken Little, like the sky was really falling. I had been rough on Nadine and I felt like shit and couldn't get her out of my mind.

I got up and walked to the kitchen, reached into the cabinet and pulled out a bottle of rum, Habana Club. I had it left over from one of my trips to Castroland and was saving it for a special occasion. Well, tonight was special. I grabbed my private stash of most excellent Jamaican weed and headed topside to the aft deck, to induce sleep through self-medication. I took a seat at the helm, rolled myself a big fat spliff, opened the bottle of rum and took a swig, then lit the joint and took a mighty pull.

I leaned back in my seat and waited for magic. A light breeze blew from the southeast, as was usual for this time of the year, and it provided a cooling effect as the wind raced over the water before reaching me. Lights flickered throughout the marina and in the distant horizon from passing boats, and with the pungent aroma of the salt air mixed with pot and the ever-so-light rocking of the *Quest* I really began to relax.

It was an active night in the marina, as captains secured their boats and checked their gear and the locals and vacationers mingled on the docks and on shore, enjoying the tropical breezes, such a relief from the torturous heat of the day. Little by little the effects of the rum and weed began to take hold, and for a blissful half hour I forgot all my troubles. Music came from several boats, and now the sweet smell of grilled fish wafted my way. A smile came to my lips as I let the sounds and lights and hustle and bustle of the marina wash over me and push away all the negative thoughts. I was glad I hadn't slept, because I had gotten to where I wanted to be in my head. I was right smack dab in the middle of paradise, and being there helped me see not only that all the danger and risk was worth it but also that I had to be as calm as I was now, in this place of beauty, in all the worlds I ventured to.

Yes, but that was a tall assignment. I thought about how for the last couple of days I'd been having pangs of anxiety, dealing with my demons. Could I really have induced this sense of tranquility yesterday and the days before? I went *loco* before every job that had its share of danger, and now look what we were attempting to do. Not an everyday thing, and Christ, I hoped a never-again thing. I was even hoping we'd actually live through this one, so it wasn't that easy to be calm.

A group of people strolled up the pier and back down and as they walked by the *Quest* they smiled and waved. Some, recognizing the aroma of good weed, smiled even more and gave me the thumbs-up sign, which I returned with an acknowledging smile. Even if they only came here on vacation or to escape, they were true Parrot Heads, free spirits with a love of the ocean and a sense of adventure. I wished them well.

So the basic story was that I got all tense and then I mentally beat up on Nadine. She had been steering clear of me the last few days, and she knew I wasn't myself. She had been choosing her words carefully, not asking any questions pertaining to "what if." She knew the time would come for that, just before the shit hit the fan. I felt sorry for her, not looking me in the eyes, having a totally different posture around me— one of submissiveness, as if I'd fly into a rage if she bugged me in some way. But she knew I was deep inside my thoughts, and she gave me a wide berth so I could focus.

It was just the day before that Nadine realized we were going on a very dangerous trip. I think instinctively she knew that I, being an old pro and pretty damn sure of myself, could save her ass if things got out of control. So she was going to trust me, trust my judgment and my abilities. I appreciated her for that, for understanding how important it was to get things right on a job like this. It showed me that she knew that her place was as one who follows, like a good lieutenant. But it also showed that she wanted to learn, and that meant she believed in what we were doing. Or did it?

Was I just bullying her into my own way of being, my own way of thinking? Maybe she wanted to earn my admiration and was doing what I thought she should do, what she thought I considered the good and honorable thing for any man or woman to do and accomplish in this world even though it wasn't her own cup of tea. Now that I thought about it, I had no idea about what she believed in. When I first met her and we started going out, I thought she was perfect, not only as eye candy, but also as this incredibly innocent waif who had a boundless sense of adventure. She was pretty much clueless about where she was heading but she was sure she had to get away from where she came from. She hit the road so she coud experience everything, at least once, and she wouldn't and couldn't settle down. She was bored by the prospect of all the old bullshit—the middle-class jobs and the middle-class homes and the SUVs and the kids. She wasn't interested in finding a man who would take care of her, she was looking for someone to share adventures with. I fit the bill.

But the fact was, we were totally different. I might have been an odd-job, boat-dwelling Parrot Head, but I was far from carefree. I had always known what I wanted and what direction I wanted to go in. I was set in my ways and I didn't let anyone or anything deter me from reaching my goals, as strange as they might have seemed to the average yuppie. So we were like yin and yang *vagabundos*, one totally uptight and one with stars in her eyes. Yet I could see that the way I approached adventure, the way I planned things out, and also the way I counted on taking the plunder that was mine–I could see that these traits were influencing her and I was beginning to wonder if that was a good thing.

What a beautiful innocence. There were too few people in the world like her, and I wasn't going to be one of those people in our society blindly telling other people who marched to a different beat to change, to be a damn sheep. No way, no fucking way. Why should I make her risk her life for a hatred of Castro that she didn't have? That said, there were two kinds of assholes in the world: those who didn't know they were assholes, and those who did. I was the latter. I would chastise myself for days until I laughed and realized that life had a balance point, and that's where I needed to be. So I guessed she was in for something different, and who knew, maybe she would like what I had to offer her. That is, if we were both still alive to enjoy it.

The marina was quieting down, just like the breezes. In the distance, probably in the parking lot of Bud and Mary's store, some drunk was singing "Mack the Knife," of all things. Other than that, the only sound was the clanking of swaying masts. It was getting late and my attempt at self-medication had worked very well indeed. The little attempt at meditation had had a nice outcome, but the mindnumbing effects of the rum and weed were even nicer. I could hardly walk down the steps to the galley, but I made it to the couch and my familiar position and quickly fell asleep to an old rerun of *Father Knows Best*. How ironic.

CHAPTER 4

It was seven am and I was having coffee in the galley when Nadine came out of her room. I could tell the night's sleep hadn't washed away the heebie-jeebies. We had a quick breakfast, and finished making all the preparations on the boat. We were gassed up and had added extra fuel in ten-gallon containers, which were strapped tight to the side walls. All set to go, we locked the *Quest* and said goodbye to the old girl. I tapped her twice on the teak railing and said, "Stay afloat baby, you're my home sweet home." We both jumped down onto the dock at the same moment and smiled at each other. Then we walked over to the *Lean Back* and jumped on. I looked everything over to make sure we were ready. Being a bit superstitious about the ocean and my boats, I knelt down, put my hand on the deck, and said, "Don't fail me now, sweetheart, do your job and do it well. I need you on this one more than ever." Then I stood up, took a big deep breath, and looked at Nadine, "are you ready?"

She looked sheepishly at me, and in a low voice said in her native French, "*Merde!* We're really going through with this."

"What's the matter?" For a split second I could see reluctance in her big blue eyes. Her body lost the poise with which I was used to seeing her carry herself. Her beautiful stride, hips swaying back and forth, her confident look, that proud awareness that she was a treat for the eyes—it was all gone for a brief moment. She reminded me of a young child who had been separated from her mother at the mall on a shopping trip, and was being pulled along by an elderly security guard who kept reassuring her everything would be all right. But in the child's face, you could see a scared little person who was not quite sure what was going on, and not quite convinced by the fatherly figure of a security guard.

She shook her head and made a face. When I realized what was happening, I turned over the three 250 Mercs on the *Lean Back*. It was go time, and I didn't want her changing her mind. I needed to get underway quickly before her mental demons began to talk to her. I asked her to undo the lines, and then we made our way out of the marina. From my new point of view, she was just being self-indulgent. We had made plans, many of which I would need her for. No one was backing out of this motherfucker; it was too late to start crying or having second thoughts. She'd had a chance to say no. She knew what was happening and where we were going. If she backed out now, everything would turn to shit; I would have to postpone departure and find someone else to take her place. No way! Not now! Anyway, if my instincts were right, she would get over her anxiety and have what it took to be part of this.

I shifted forward, entered the main canal serving the marina and brought the *Lean Back* up to 15 knots. I was in a hurry to hit the ocean but I had to be cautious not to cause too much of a wake. Since Bud and Mary's Marina was on the southern side of long, narrow Upper Matecumbe Key, you didn't need to pass through a channel like the boats that used the marinas on the north side have to go through. You just went straight from the canal and into the Straits of Florida, but getting out of the canal took a while, so you had to be patient. I stole a glance at Nadine now and then as we puttered along. She sat in the bolster seat, long hair streaming in the wind, arms crossed, body tense as hell, and I knew she was still bothered by this shit even though we were already on our way.

I looked over at her for something like the fourth time, and her head jerked in my direction. Her face had a defiant look, but it was also a pained look; her lips were pursed, her pupils seemed dilated. She almost seemed like she was about to scream.

"Now's not the time sweetheart," I said. *Tant pis*, as she likes to say. Tough love, it was true, but I knew it had a chance of bringing her round.

As we made our way to the end of the canal and prepared to hit the open ocean and make our way south along the Keys, I passed the last "No Wake" sign and the last of the far too many "Slow for Manatees" signs that pissed off every boater down here, not to mention the guides who made a living on these pristine waters. I punched the throttles on all three 250 Mercs. The transom sank in and the engines thrust the 36-foot

Pantera forward until she lunged up on plane and began to scream out into the ocean.

Now that I was out beyond land, I trimmed the engines out. She was running smoothly even though there was an offshore breeze, which made the ocean rough, about three- to four-foot waves. The sun shone and the wind blew strongly into us as the *Lean Back* did about 50 mph. I needed to pay attention to what I was doing and this cleared my mind of anxiety.

I looked down at Nadine and realized that I'd forgotten all about her since we'd left the canal. I waited for her to return my stare. She looked back at me with a huge grin as if with the rush of the wind and the speed, and once in a while a good hearty thump of the boat, she'd made up her mind to not worry and to let all that anxiety slide away like the Key behind us and to enjoy the ride, with as much enthusiasm as if that little lost child had found her mother and the world was all right again. I winked and nodded back toward the engines as I trimmed them up and shot back a rooster tail at least twenty feet high. She laughed, then put the seat part of her bolster down and stood in the detachable seat with her back against the cushion with the padded arms of the bolster hugging her waist and keeping her in place. I trimmed the engines back down, pulled back on the throttles and kissed Nadine on the cheek.

"You okay now?" I asked.

She looked at me with disdain in her beautiful blue eyes, which could burn a hole in you, and merely said "*oui*," almost daring me to continue a conversation, which might not be in my ears' best interest.

She turned her head away from me, and once again in French said *"Parles a mon cul—ma tête est malade."* Talk to my ass—my head doesn't feel good. I had known her to use this expression before, if she didn't like a situation or a person. It sounded a little crude coming from such a beautiful woman, but it showed she had an edge that could cut you. We both began to laugh out loud. It was just what we needed to break the tension.

She looked at me, and in a French accent that was like honey to my ears, said, "Let's go, Kiki Logan."

I eased back on the throttles and brought her to a nice little cruising speed of about twenty-five to thirty mph, just enough to keep her on top of the light chop we were running in. The wind had died down and the wave action had settled as well. We were riding the *Lean Back* on an easy plane and with the sleek, bullet-like design of Pantera boats, she looked like she was eating up the ocean, majestically thrusting forward with her roaring engines saying power to spare, no time wasted, destination in mind. To me it was always an instant high and it was always the only way to go.

Nadine, who loved the idea of sails in the wind, shouted to me over the noise of the engines. "We should be on the *Quest* right now."

"If we had the time, I guess we would be," I shouted back. "When we finish this trip you'll probably come to appreciate instant power at your fingertips when you want it. We've got to be able to outrun anybody—any boat out there."

She looked at me and curled her lips. "Maybe so. When I buy my boat someday I'll take you on a cruise and teach you the pleasures of sailing."

"That sounds great to me girl. I think we'll both need it by then. But right now we need speed."

I had lied to her. I could never be patient enough to be able to just putter around in a sailboat, trimming sails, tacking, coming about. To me a speedboat with big engines was the only way to go for the work I did, and for my fishing habit I needed range and speed. If I couldn't get there quick, when the bite was on, I lost. The other thing was, salvaging on the open ocean wasn't easy. Once in awhile, you had to get up and go in a hurry—hence the *Lean Back*, gone in a hurry and at my fingertips. The *Quest* was a house, a place to hang my hat. I wasn't much of a landlubber, so being on a nice live-aboard sailboat always on the water was perfect, and if I wanted to leave for a while I could take my house with me wherever I went. I spend a lot of time on other islands.

Nadine was gazing ahead, and without even turning around, she said, "Can you believe the job Mother Nature has done with the Keys? The colors are just so unbelievable. Look at that." She pointed to the shifts in color. "It's like every shade of blue and green you can imagine. And the water is so clear, it's like looking through glass; fifty feet, a hundred feet down, amazing. Those guides call it gin-clear water, and it is."

She had that right; you could see it in magazines, postcards, and movies, but until you saw it in person, actually touched, smelled, and completely let your senses enjoy it and form a big, beautiful sensual stew, you'd never really know what it was like. For the fortunate few who lived down here and for those who had been here and continued to return, no explanation was needed. This was truly like living in a postcard.

I looked to the west and the Keys. I could see the beautiful houses of all shapes, sizes and colors. What a jumble: no symmetry, no noticeable regular pattern, and so unlike all those damn developments in the city and its outskirts. Billionaires, millionaires, and nine-to-fivers, all living together and enjoying not dealing with the rat race of the city—even if it was only for a short stay.

Now Nadine was all caught up in boat-gazing and she let me know which ones she liked and didn't like. Then she was looking over the side rail of the boat down into the water when she was suddenly startled by a dolphin crashing through the surface ten feet away.

"Kiki, *attends, attends! Regards*, there are dolphin swimming along with us!"

"There are two over on this side," I called out.

A small school of dolphins had joined up with us and they were swimming and diving along to the rhythm of our boat, once in a while darting in front and trying to tease me into thinking I would hit them. I didn't bother swerving to avoid them, since there was no way I would ever come close to them even if I tried.

"*Cono*, they're taking us to the fish, Nadine," I said to her, smiling at all the excitement around us.

"They're good luck, Kiki. You know that, right?"

"An old wives' tale," I blurted back.

"We have to believe in something other than ourselves sometimes, Kiki; something that can help get us through when we fail and can't carry on. *Tu vois?*"

I smiled back, not wishing to engage in conversation. I had my own view of things, and believing in luck, other people, or a giant dolphin in the sky was not part of my master plan. I lived my life believing in myself and making my own luck.

We spent the next twenty minutes or so just enjoying the dolphins swimming with us, splashing around and enjoying their easy life in the ocean, and obviously enjoying each others' company as well as ours. Maybe I should have taken a lesson from them and been more accepting of others. But not yet. I had to get somewhere in my head first, get to that point where I could sit back on my throne and laugh at the jester, put up with all of the crazy fuckers in my royal court. Because if I wasn't the king I just couldn't take it. That's right, I was stubborn, and when you went for the gold and the royal purple you could only have the most loyal people close to you. Nadine could be like that, I guessed, but she could never help me get over that hang-up of needing to be in charge and to not take shit from fools. I would have to be king, and she would have to be my loyal queen. Oh well, first things first. If we could work together on this gig, then maybe we could hook up for good.

We were both still pushed up against the bolster seats as we ran just inside and to the west of the Gulf Stream, between the

Keys and that big dark-blue water. I had been carefully watching the water for floating debris, a weed line or some birds flying overhead that would indicate the edge of the Gulf Stream and therefore some good fishing. More than likely at this time of the year we would find the eating kind of dolphin—the Mahi-Mahi—the best eating fish in the ocean, in my opinion. If we came across some we'd have a nice dinner.

"Kiki, look south, southeast. I think there must be something out there. See the birds circling?" As she finished saying that I noticed the bow crossing what seemed to be the beginning of a huge weed line.

There were only three boats out there and that told me that the word about the weed line had not spread to the rest of the fishermen in the area. The bite was on, and we had stumbled across it before everyone else. Maybe there was something to be said about dolphins being good luck.

I gave Nadine the wheel and told her to steer toward the southwest edge of the weed line, which I'd estimated to be about a mile long and 200 to 300 yards wide. I knew that before long the word would get out and everybody out here would call their buddies to come out and enjoy the bonanza that was about to kick off. It was Mahi-Mahi time.

The weed line was all sorts of seaweed that got pushed to the side by the Gulf Stream, and once it was there it acted as protection of sorts for the baitfish, which in turn, attracted bigger fish, and so on and so forth until you had a feeding frenzy. The great thing was that you never know what you were going to catch. You just had to be ready for whatever took your bait.

When Nadine put us on the edge of the weeds, I could see through the breaks in the seaweed. The water was teeming with fish, all darting about nervously as if realizing that they've just been discovered and there was no way out.

Gulls and terns flew frantically overhead, positioning themselves to have a go at the free buffet. They began to dive, kamikaze style, with precision and accuracy like no Japanese hero ever could, disappearing for a split second in a splash and then soaring back up with the greatest of ease, prey firmly clenched in their beaks. Nadine brought us around into the right spot as I stood on the bow, balancing myself, a hand full of bow line attached to the forward cleat, directing her to where I thought would be a good position to catch some Mahi. We wouldn't be anchoring off, we'd be drifting along in the current following the weed line until we had our fill of it, or it became too crowded.

As I prepared our fishing rods, boats began to show up. We weren't as early to the bite as I had thought. You could tell that all of us had the same sense of excitement, and that was all about the hope of eating some Mahi tonight.

"Getting a little crowded," I said to Nadine.

"Can you blame them, though? A catch here today will be better than anything they can get at the top-notch restaurants in Miami—and much fresher," she replied.

There was a fishing spot just off Key Biscayne called the Cuban Hole. It was a huge, blue hole that just dropped off into the deep. People went there to do some really great fishing. The problem was that it could be so crowded—sometimes up to five boats deep—that you couldn't get near it. When the bite was on, people were going to come and come, and it would get crowded. This weed line was going to become a moving Cuban Hole.

I got the poles ready and pulled out my vast array of artificial baits: Tsunami, D.O.A., Yuzuri. These artificials looked so real that when in the water you couldn't tell they weren't. I always caught more fish on artificial than on live bait. We hadn't come prepared for a big fishing trip, so the rods we had were lightweight. Throwing lightweight line in on a feeding frenzy was chancy at best; you didn't know what the hell was going to swallow that baby up. This was going to be fun if we didn't get our equipment torn up. I handed Nadine her pole and went out on the bow, then made a cast about forty feet out and quickly had to retrieve it. Those damn birds were hitting anything and everything in the water and there were about five of them in the water between me and my lure. Lucky for those birds that they didn't get hooked or I'd have had to reel their asses in.

I changed my mind and decided to use a top-water lure. This would provide for the best visual when the fish hit the lures, though it might also have spelled even more trouble with the birds. Top waters would be a whole lot of fun, providing our ten-pound test lines would hold up to some of the bulls I was hoping to tie into.

Nadine had put the engines in neutral and made her way to the back of the boat. She made a beautiful cast out into the middle of the frenzy and looked as ready and prepared and professional as any guide running these waters. Sunglasses on, knees bent in an athletic stance, bent over a little at the waist as if peering through a knothole in a fence, she watched her lure as she slowly retrieved it, hoping and waiting for the moment when the fish would crash through the surface, take the bait, and run for it. At that precise moment she would set her hook and the fight would be on. I watched her, ignoring what was happening to my own line as I reeled in on autopilot. I was surprised at her and could only remember one fishing trip with Nadine in the distant past. You could tell she had picked up a lot of knowledge from the locals in the Keys, and I didn't doubt for one second that she would be successful when the time came.

She looked my way for a second. The smile was gone, her blue eyes were hidden behind Costa del Mar sunglasses, which gave her an ominous look, and I could see the intent in her posture and look. Beautiful women, independent, strong, outdoorsy, and feminine as the day was long, turned me on. I stood on the bow of the *Lean Back*, rolled my tongue—which had been hanging like that of a panting dog—back into my mouth and prepared myself to do some fishing. I couldn't let her have all the fun.

Keeping my eye on the birds above, I cast out to where I had seen some nice bulls feeding on the easy pickings the weed line was providing. No sooner had I begun to retrieve my line than there was a loud crashing of water at the surface, and instantly my lure disappeared into the blue beneath the froth. I pulled sharply back on my rod to set the hook in the big fish's mouth and felt it dig in. The fight was on.

Remembering that I had lightweight equipment, I was careful not to get overly anxious. Shit could happen, and would happen, so when my line went slack, I thought I'd lost this bad boy. But then I realized that he had turned and was running toward the boat. I began to reel the line in as fast as I could to take out the slack. All of a sudden I saw color and then the big fish saw the boat. He changed course instantly and made a run back into the deep blue. The line was being pulled out at an incredible speed. He was big and he had a lot of fight left in him.

This back-and-forth scene of me gathering in line and the big bull stripping it off my reel and making it sound like a humming bird in flight would be repeated several times over until one of us came out victorious. For now, he had the advantage of twenty to thirty pounds of gold dolphin against a ten-pound test line. But I had modern technology, Shakespeare, and Shimano on my side, some of the best equipment money could buy, and I hoped a good amount of patience also. Either way, the fight was on and it was going to be a lot of fun.

"Don't let him go, Kiki," Nadine yelled. "I'll cook him up tonight. Or are you so impatient that you'll snap the line?"

"Nadine, you clever, clever little girl; what the devil do you mean by that?"

"I know how hot-tempered you are! You're going to spoil a wonderful meal just because you always blow your cool. *Tant pis.*"

Her mockery got my full attention, and I lost my balance for second. She laughed and then returned to her chore of catching a fish herself, just in case I did fail.

I yelled back at her, "Don't worry sweetie. I've got my eyes on the prize and I'm just trying to figure out the best way to land her—I mean *it*."

She got my play on words, and I saw the smile in her half-turned face. That surprised me. She'd just been teasing me like a boy in grade school. I had become accustomed to dating Cuban girls who still had chaperones, even if they were twenty-four or twenty-five. When you went to pick them up at their homes, you were inspected by the whole family. When you went to a party with her, the whole family was there, from eight to eighty. In Jersey, you'd even be put under the microscope for being Latino. The Wasp and Italian and Jewish and Irish parents almost seemed like they were about to hire detectives to follow us around. It was nice to see the openness and freedom of a woman who was just reacting to being on a boat in a stiff breeze on the high seas.

I sometimes allowed my past, the racism that I'd witnessed and experienced, cloud my judgment of people, especially the whites in the U.S. They didn't seem to understand that there were white people in the Spanish-speaking countries also. Hell, I could still remember my mother saying that she didn't know she wasn't white until she came to this country. To them, you were just another Latino, and that meant you're brown. It was an easy thing to say, but until you walked in those shoes you'd never know how fucked up that behavior was. The people in the U.S.

had a convenient label for everything, and if they didn't like something they declared war on it with labels, and those labels were hell.

Nadine was now in a full-blown battle with a Mahi of her own and was not paying much attention to our little banter. I had been in a struggle with the bull I was trying to land and at the same time trying to pay heed to our mental joust. I hadn't noticed Nadine was doing better than I was at landing our supper. It was weird, but I suddenly heard thrashing going on in the cooler box and took a look. Damn, she already had a nice one in there, a beautiful gold and green dolphin, about ten pounds. I wondered how she had managed to do that so fast. She was presently in a *mano a mano* with another beautiful fish that she was intent on landing. She motioned to me to close the top of the cooler box.

"We don't want to lose our dinner, just in case the luck runs out and I turn out to be the only provider," she teased.

I closed the box with my foot and continued to fight my fish. "What am I, your servant? I've got my hands full, girl."

"That's okay, Kiki; I think I can handle this job. Just sit back and watch how it's done."

I began to laugh and said, "It's on, girl, the race is on."

I finally landed my Mahi and put him in the cooler. He was a beauty, a good twenty-seven pounds, I estimated. But Nadine managed to land three more good-sized dolphins and get them all in the cooler too. They were smaller, but good fish nonetheless. She must have been in a hot spot.

She looked at me and said, "I told you I can handle this job. We'll be eating well tonight—island style."

We had been on the weed line for about forty-five minutes and had had great success. Now it was time to leave. Word had finally gotten out to everybody, and the weed line had now become one big mass of boats floating along with the current. They sort of reminded me of the birds—obsessed with the big bull dolphins just as the gulls were obsessed with the baitfish.

We pulled up our rods stowed them away in the rod storage bins. I secured the *Lean Back* for the rest of the trip. Nadine and I got back in the bolster seats and prepared to put her back on course for Cay Sal. Nadine took the wheel and spun the *Lean Back* around till she picked up the right heading on the compass. In only a few seconds we were pulling away from the drifting mass of boats. A lone tern on a long-distance migration, abandoning its flyway companions.

"Hold on, *mon ami*," she said as she punched the throttles, then brought her to a plane and eased her back to a nice easy cruising speed that had her skimming along the water like the dolphins that had been swimming with us earlier. We had a long trip ahead of us and we had to conserve fuel—we were going to need it later. Another hour or so and we would pick up the new heading, toward the southeast, and point her to the Cay Sal Bank, then Dog Rocks.

The colors of the water flashed by us and ran off into the horizon and melted together into a picture-perfect painting. It was definitely the season down here; everywhere I looked I saw boats with people enjoying the great weather and the good fishing. I looked over at Nadine and she gave me a big, happy smile. What a woman! *Que rica esta.* And we'd worked things out and now we were a team. But premonitions quickly seeped into this pretty picture and an image of hurt and harm crossed my field of vision.

CHAPTER 5

The *Lean Back* was running strong and I could tell that my little talk with her back at the pier before leaving had done some good. She was eating up the ocean and she sounded great. I knew I was a little superstitious and quirky, but she had a soul and feelings, as far as I was concerned, and you had to let her know you care. I took good care of her and she took good care of me. Not to mention that Pepe Pantera knew how to build a boat. He was one of the big-time offshore racers and had a bunch of world records to bolster his knowledge and boat-building ability. Miami to New York, Miami to Nassau, Miami to Bimini, to name a few of the records. I was a little superstitious, like I said before, but I wasn't stupid; I knew a good boat when I saw one. I tried to cover my bases and for what I did, Pantera covered them all for me as far as boats were concerned.

We were dead center in the Straits of Florida, and I could see in the distance a cruise ship that looked like it had a heading for Mexico, probably Cozumel, then on to Belize and the Panama Canal. I saw that our paths were going to cross, and since I knew their courses from spending a lot of time in this area I knew this ship would maintain its course straight and steady. When you came across a cruise ship or a freighter out here and your paths were going to cross, there were two things you could do: either cut back on your engines and let them go by; or be foul and cut in front of them. If you chose the latter you had to hope you had plenty of boat under you and that you did it with plenty of room to spare. Those giants moved faster than you think and there ain't no brakes. Get it? Crunch! Bye bye...

The *Lean Back* was plenty of boat with power to spare, but I figured this wasn't the time or place to be getting our kicks. I'd done it a few times before, running up on a freighter just like the dophins did with us a while back, and suddenly darting in front of them. It was an adrenaline rush like you wouldn't believe. When you got close to these massive ships you felt miniscule, and you could sense their power ready to engulf you if you made the slightest mistake. That sucker could have swallowed me up in an instant. Murphy's Law was tapping me on the shoulder and saying, "Be careful, shit can happen around here," like the asshole diver who goes out on a dive and doesn't anchor his boat off good and when he surfaces his boat's gone. Murphy's Law: be careful, if shit can happen, it will.

Nadine eased up on the engines and idled the boat while we awaited the approach of the behemoth; she passed close enough for us to pick out details. I always found it amusing how these midwesterners—clad in flowered shirts and Bermuda shorts, legs so white they could light up the night—enjoyed being cooped up for a week or two getting ridiculous sunburns and gaining twenty pounds. How could that be fun? They needed to come down here, feel it and smell it, not watch it from high above in a passing ship that stops at a port only to let the passengers go get liquored up and then be taken in by peddlers. To each his own misery, I guessed.

She was close enough for us to start making out the faces of the human cattle being hauled from port to port. They waved to us excitedly as if it were the first time they had ever seen people in a boat. I thought it was a reflex action, waving at people on other boats when you're on a boat; anyway, we waved back, causing more excitement on the gargantuan deck.

I could feel the force the giant emitted through the water, pushing and pulling at us and causing a wake that rocked the *Lean Back* a little too much for my liking. The force of one of the waves hit us hard and completely soaked Nadine. She gasped as water ran down her face and into her wide-open mouth, making her exhale immediately. She grabbed the wheel, spun the boat around, punched the throttles and moved us away just enough to get out from under the breaking water, wiping her face with her free hand all the while. "*Merde!*" she sputtered.

"I told you, pay attention around them."

I was laughing at her and she wasn't liking it too much. She caught the brunt of that wave, and I happened to be standing behind her and didn't get nearly as wet.

The soaking had elicited a raucous round of laughter from all the pasty-legged cruisers on deck who had so much sunscreen on their faces they looked like mimes, especially since we couldn't hear them. Nadine looked up just in time to realize that she had just made the start of their cruise memorable, possibly the only part they might remember, considering the drunken stupor they had just embarked on. She realized how silly she must look and she began to laugh.

I was cracking up myself, and to tease her a little more, I said again, "See, I told you to be careful around them."

She replied, "*Ferme ta bouche, tête de merde.*" *Shut up, shit head.*

"*Tranquila, linda, tranquila,*" I said and smiled, shaking my head. This seemed to relieve the tension even more.

It was starting to feel like a weekend fishing trip to me, as if I'd be making my way back to port soon with a boat full of fish, ready to cook a beautiful dinner and make beautiful love in my own bed tonight. I caught myself for a moment, realizing that was far from the reality, but I couldn't really help what I did next.

I walked over to Nadine, asked her to move and I slipped into the bolster seat; Nadine sat next to me, still wiping her face dry.

"What are you going to do?" she asked.

"I'm going to put her through some paces."

"What paces?"

"Just sit back and hold on."

I pointed the *Lean Back* away from the big cruise ship. I hit the throttles on the three 250 Mercs, she sprang up and shot out a spray of water, putting distance between her and the big ship. I began to put the boat into a turn, little by little bringing her around and heading straight for the wake the monster was leaving behind. Nadine was in full concentration mode, every once in a while glancing at me. With her eyes wide open and a smile on her face, she realized what I was about to do.

"You're going to jump those waves aren't you?" she asked me with excitement in her face.

"Yeah, hang on, *niña*."

We were now screaming toward the ass end of that huge boat doing about sixty miles an hour, with water spraying up and causing a commotion that brought all the people on the ship back to the railings. When they saw what we were about to do, they began to cheer and clap, something we would have heard this time but for the *Lean Back*'s engines.

I positioned the boat so I could catch the waves at the correct angle to not get tossed on our asses. I caught the first wave at a bit of an angle and the force of all that water bucked us sideways slamming Nadine and me against the sides of the bolster seats. Thank God for these seats. Built for racing boats in particular, they did their job beautifully and held us snugly in position as the *Lean Back* went airborne. Nadine let out a shrill screech that would have made any preschooler proud, and she hung on tight. I pulled back on the power once we were airborne and you could hear the big twenty-four-inch propellers screaming to get their traction. Instantly I readied myself to come crashing back down in between two huge waves being left behind by the cruise ship.

This was a crucial moment; I had to punch the throttles just as the propellers hit the water to give me the power we needed to thrust us through the next wave. If I miscalculated we were in deep shit; it would be like hitting a wall doing sixty miles an hour, without power to push us through. I would bury the nose of the boat right in the water. End of trip.

So much for not getting my kicks. The big Pantera corrected her position as we slammed down on the water. I punched the throttles and the big Cleaver props again found their traction and dug in, shooting us right at the oncoming wave. I caught the next wave perfectly, catapulted over it, and again we were airborne. This time, we landed with the precision and grace of an Olympic freestyle skier going through his run and sticking the landing.

I looked back at the route I had taken and smiled at our near-perfect performance. Running along the south side of the big ship, I could see that our audience was not gone; they had again gathered at the railing and they were whooping and hollering—now we could hear them—like Sunday afternoon at a football game. I thought I even saw a high five.

We were laughing as we waved back to the cruisers. I eased back on the engines and once again picked up our course. I leaned back in the bolster and relaxed.

"Nice ride, right, *niña*?" I said to Nadine.

"*C'etait incroyable, magnifique. Merci,*" she said with a big grin on her face.

Ever since I was a little boy I had felt refreshed by the ocean, the smell of its saltiness, its immensity, the power and force it could emit at the blink of an eye, and the calmness it could induce, making you feel free and at peace and also completely energized. It was always exhilarating to me. It always caused me to think about all aspects of my life, past, present, and future and somehow, even if only for a split second, I thought I understood it. If only for a split second, it was worth it. That's why I came out here as often as money allowed. That feeling was special, real special.

Nadine looked at me, catching me in my thoughts, and said, "Beautiful, isn't it?"

"It sure is," I said without hesitation, letting her know that I was in total agreement with her thoughts.

"When I was growing up in Martinique I always felt safe around the ocean," she said, "like if I needed to escape from anything I could run to her and hide and no one could find me. It always offered somewhere I could go, somewhere I could be alone with my thoughts. The answers to the questions that confused me always seemed to come to me when I was by the ocean."

Changing her train of thought, Nadine suddenly said, "It's not always nice though. I've never told you this story because it still gives me the creeps. I was on a trip in a sailboat, a beautiful 50-foot Gulfstar, going from Martinique to Miami. The weather suddenly got real nasty and the water churned up like I'd never seen it do before. The clouds were totally black and the rain became just torrential. It was incredible. The stupid *conards* who were on the trip with me thought they would be safe by going below. Imagine that! There was no helm below, nothing.

"Before I knew it I was all alone topside. A huge whirlpool suddenly appeared in front and slightly to starboard. It was pulling the boat closer and closer to it. It took all my strength to keep the boat from being sucked into that huge hole and as we got closer, I didn't think I would be able to skirt around it. We came real close and I could even see down into the giant eddy, which seemed to drop off into nowhere. In the meantime the wind was blowing so hard it had torn our main mast down, and it was dragging in the water, still attached to the boat by all the ropes and rigging. A blessing from God. I think the mast dragging in the water acted as a rudder and I was able to hang on just long enough to narrowly escape the whirlpool. It was like nothing I ever experienced before and never want to again. The funny thing was that as quickly as this massive wall of black clouds and torrential rain appeared, it disappeared. It was really strange. I think that was my first experience with the Devil's Triangle, which I didn't believe in before that moment. There are some strange things that happen out here, don't you think, Kiki?"

"I've never had anything happen to me out here other than seeing some strange lights now and then, but I've heard some really weird stories from some very upstanding people who have no reason to bullshit anybody. So the answer to your question is yeah, some really strange shit happens out here."

"Anyway, that's how I got to Miami and I never left, and we met just shortly after that," she said smiling, but with her dread of the storm and whirlpool still etched in her features.

I could see how she got her sea legs; a lesser person would be another statistic of the Devil's Triangle right now, adding to the growing number of missing people that had never returned home from the fabled waters in the triangle between Miami, San Juan and Bermuda.

I personally believed that bad weather did most of these people in. Bad preparation or just bad luck, whatever you wanted to call it; when the ocean got riled up she had no mercy. To Nadine's credit, it wasn't the first time I had heard of giant whirlpools swallowing up ships. On the other hand, a lot of the disappearances attributed to the Triangle did have explanations other than bad weather. For hundreds of years these waters had been breeding grounds and grazing grounds for pirates and smugglers. Modern-day pirates were downright evil, and if they caught you off guard you wouldn't live to tell about it. They took no prisoners. Smugglers kept to themselves, and they weren't murderers; nevertheless, if you did come across them you might have had a bad experience.

When you flew over the south side of south Bimini you could see what looked like an airplane graveyard, planes everywhere, clearly visible in five to ten feet of crystal clear water. The people on the island didn't even know how ninety percent of them got there or who they belonged to. No one seemed to care much either. They were probably smugglers who never made it to their destination . When you asked someone, all you got was, *"Me no know Mon, why you wanna know anyway, Rasta?"* Those poor bastards who ditched in the water would never even make it to the statistics list.

We were moving along at a good clip, about fifty miles per hour in a southerly direction, talking about some of our experiences on the water, which made the time pass quickly. I looked down at the compass and corrected my course for the

Cay Sal Bank. It was time to cross the Gulf Stream and get into shallower waters on the other side, and finally to the Banks.

The water was beginning to take on a different shade of blue; we were nearing the Stream. Before long we were in deep, blue-black water the color of a navy pea coat. We could no longer see through it, and it would scare the hell out of anyone, if they let it.

Today was a little different, though. My eyes were drawn skyward, toward cloud formations so unreal that we couldn't help but watch them, changing shapes as they billowed higher and higher, becoming thunderheads bursting into pastel colors as the sun reflected its late afternoon light on them. We were in the heart of the Stream and all was well. The weather was great and it seemed that we would have some company down in Cay Sal; there was traffic headed that way. It was actually a good thing that we wouldn't be alone there and stick out like a sore thumb, in case we were being watched. Nadine looked up.

"Color change up ahead, maybe 300 meters. Is that the Bank?" she asked.

"Yep, that's it."

Crossing the Gulf Stream to the Cay Sal Bank went without incident, considering we were in the Devil's Triangle, and before we knew it we were there.

CHAPTER 6

I looked for a place to anchor among the scrub rocks they called Cay Sal, or as some of the Cubans in Miami who came down here fishing called it, *Los Perros*, or "The Dogs." Dog Rocks. These rocks jutted a few feet into the air out of pristine water, and when glancing over the whole area it looked beautiful and serene—and it was, to the unsuspecting eye viewing from a big luxury yacht or fishing boat. But for those who knew, this area spoke its share of misery.

I couldn't help but think of how many people running from Castro's grasp had taken to the open ocean on makeshift rafts or rickety old boats, only to meet the Grim Reaper on these rocks. They took to the ocean by the thousands. Some made it, some didn't—but that didn't deter thousands more from trying. Many ended up stranded on the rocks as their rafts fell apart and their boats finally sank. In most cases they ended up swimming there, or paddling with a board or innertube, shouting and screaming to their panicked family members to swim for those rocks just ahead. Once there, they might have got lucky and been seen by someone, then reported, with the Coast Guard picking them up. However, this was not so lucky—they were returned to Cuba for all their troubles, and God knew what awaited them when they get back to the island Gulag. Unfortunately, most of those who were stranded here also died here. There was blood on those rocks, and it came from Castro's hands.

What typically happened was that they were unprepared for the elements, and little by little they died from exposure, starvation, and thirst. But there was another kind of luck that wasn't so lucky. They were often spared the agony of a slow death by Cuba's henchmen, who frequented the Cay Sal Bank via patrol boat and fighter aircraft and killed any *gusanos* they happened to find. *Gusanos,* that's what they call them: worms. Anyone who was against the Government got the nametag.

With all the beauty of the Banks, there was a lot of ugliness and evil; it couldn't be seen—it could only be felt in your heart. Many people died here, and all they wanted was a chance at a better way of life for their children and themselves. Hell, I knew for a fact that most Cubans would have stayed peacefully in Cuba if that same chance were afforded them there. Unfortunately, Cuba and the Cubans had been subjected to a tyrant who had systematically depleted its resources and its people for almost 50 years. He had brought a beautiful island and its people literally to their knees. Some wished to stay, not wanting to deal with leaving their loved ones behind for an entire lifetime. I couldn't blame them one bit. I'd witnessed firsthand what separation had done to many Cuban families. Others took to the ocean in their rafts and rickety boats.

The blame needed to be shared. That wonderful U.S. embargo on Cuba had also been very harmful to the Cuban people. Shit, they were a small island nation to begin with, so the American solution was to deprive them of the necessities Cuba needed to support its economy and maintain its people. Fucking stupid, if you asked me. How was that endearing to the people? The Americans should have figured that out long ago. Fifty years was long enough to understand that a policy wasn't working. Castro had everything he needed and more; what did he care about an embargo? It only hurt the people.

Enough was enough. All the right-wing Republicans sitting in their fancy offices toasting Pepe Fanjul, and the old Cuban guard in Miami enjoying their freedom and the luxuries of the free world, should have begun to think a little more about the Cuban people, the little people who had taken the brunt of this nasty fifty-year ass kicking. It just made me want to pull off Banco's little job even more, and stick it up the Beard's ass as far as I could.

It must have been our proximity to the "Pearl of the Antilles" that got me caught up in my own little misery. Nadine called out to me. "Hey Kiki—is this a good spot to anchor? What do you think?" I came back to the reality at hand.

"Yeah—right over by the dark patch to your right." I pointed to the spot.

Nadine threw the anchor in and we were hooked solid on the first try. The current was pushing our boat to the north, northeast; this was going to give us a beautiful view of the sunset. Nadine reached into the cabinet under the center console of the boat for a bottle of wine, cups, the little stove, a frying pan and some dishes. She opened the bottle and passed me a cup while I prepared to get the *Lean Back* ready for the evening.

The *Lean Back* was built to go off shore and had long-range capabilities, but she wasn't prepared for sleepovers or comfortable overnights. I did the best I could and had a little cover made for her, which draped it from the bow back to the center console. At night I would lay the seat cushions on the deck, put the cover on and get a decent night's sleep. I spent many nights on her, and while it wasn't the Holiday Inn, it wasn't all that bad either.

I tied down everything that needed to be tied down, checked the batteries, turned them off, went over the engines and checked the props for any obstructions. When I was done I sat down and leaned back. Nadine was next to me working on her cup of wine, typically French, and gazing at the magnificent sunset. We could almost see the ocean bubbling and the steam rising as the sun sank further and further into the horizon. Seeing an open-ocean sunset was very different from seeing one from land. Our view was completely unobstructed, with no unnatural-light interference. To witness the explosion of colors as the sun set on a clear night was something else. The night's show was spectacular. Then the colors faded to gray and everything began to disappear into darkness and it all became the blackness of night on the water, but this was when the stars came to life to provide us with an encore. It was so much better even than being in a planetarium.

There were five other boats with us out on the Banks that night. Once in a while we could hear music and laughter carried over the water, fading in and out with the breezes. Million-dollar boys enjoying their million-dollar toys. They probably just came from Cuba and were doing the mandatory, "Oh we were just on a fishing trip in Cay Sal" routine in case the Coast Guard questioned them as to where they had been.

I lay there for a while, looking up at the millions of stars in the sky, feeling a little bit worn out from the trip, and the wine was starting to have an anesthetic effect on me. Nadine sat up and touched my forearm with her hand. "It was a good day, Kiki. Are you okay? You look a little tired."

"I'm okay, *niña*; the wine got to me before I could get my legs back, but I'm doing fine."

It was that goodness in her that sometimes worried me; she was always concerned more about other people than herself. She was a fighter, but she tended to think with her heart instead of her head. I caught myself staring into her eyes; she noticed and smiled. I pulled myself up into a sitting position next to her.

"It was a great day, *mi amor*, but right now I think we should grab another bottle of wine and get our stove ready. Remember, you promised me Mahi-Mahi island style tonight and I'm holding you to it."

"That's right, I did promise," she said. She jumped up to her feet, and pulled me to mine.

I made my way to the back of the boat, reached in the cooler and pulled out one of the medium-sized dolphins. I rigged a spotlight to the side of the boat so I could see what I was doing. I gutted and prepared the fish and gave it to Nadine. We were beginning to attract some sea life with the spotlight and the guts and this created a small chum line leading back to the boat. That was going to attract larger fish; I thought we might get to see some of the Bank's local residents.

I checked the boat over one more time; on the ocean I never just check once when I can check twice. I finally felt at ease enough to relax a little and made my way to the back of the boat, where Nadine had uncorked a second bottle of wine and was pouring herself another cup.

She had the stove set up and ready to go, and with a cup of wine in one hand she prepared the Mahi with the other. I wondered when she was going to fall on her ass. She wrapped the fish in tinfoil with a little bit of salt and pepper and a pat of butter and put it on the stove. Absolutely right, island style; you didn't mess with the flavor of this great fish. True to her blood, every once in a while she would unwrap the foil and add a dash of wine.

The fish was wonderful and I almost wished we had cooked two of them. I was hungry from a long trip without a bite to eat. We had a great meal considering the seating conditions. Simple was sometimes the best. I just sat there savoring the Mahi and the wine and looking out on water as calm and smooth as a pane of glass. I had an eerie feeling that it was enticing me to sleepwalk on it.

Nadine walked over to the center console and put her wine down. She leaned back and looked out toward the open ocean. I got up and started to walk by her, when she put one leg up to not let me pass. This surprised me a little, never having seen her so playful before. I put my hand on her knee and she put her other beautifully tanned leg up and caught me in between both of them. The skimpy little bikini she had on didn't exactly deter my enthusiasm.

She meant more to me than just a couple of bottles of wine and a quick romp. I was somewhere in between letting my natural urges take over and enjoying what the good Lord had put in front of me, and keeping her comfortable in her head by not going too far and getting wild on a small, open deck. I thought that in the long run she might not want to literally rock the boat that way. She could see my hesitation.

"I'm a big girl, Kiki," she said. "Let's enjoy the time we have." It was a clear-cut invitation—not that the other advances had flown over my head, but I was still a little reluctant to do anything that would jeopardize our plans.

So much for our plans.

Before I knew it we were locked in a passionate embrace, me between her quivering thighs, both of us sliding down to the deck. In our deep, sensual kiss I could taste the sweetness of the wine on her mouth, and I felt the roundness and softness of her milky-white breasts as I caressed her body. She arched her back as my wet kisses crept down her face and then to her neck, and she moaned softly in French, things I couldn't understand, but that weren't hard to figure out.

I had been thinking about too many other things lately, and had forgotten what the love of a good woman really felt like.

We lay there in each other's arms for a while, just enjoying the safety we felt.

Exhausted, I slowly got to my feet and drew Nadine to hers. With little beads of pearly sweat rolling down her face ever so slowly, she put her head against my chest and gave me a light hug.

"Is that Cuba?" she asked, looking into the night.

I hadn't noticed before, but off in the distance to our south, southwest, the lights of Havana glittered like little stars on the horizon.

"Yeah, that's Havana," I said. "Poor bastards. They're lucky Castro hasn't diverted the power elsewhere tonight. It's probably the tourist part of town; they always have power. The Beard needs his American greenbacks—screw the people, love those tourists," I said sarcastically. It was getting late and we'd had a long day. I turned to Nadine. "We need to get some rest. Tomorrow's a big day and the Miami boys and David should be pulling in."

We made our way under the protection of the boat cover, lay down on the cushions and drifted off to sleep in each other's arms.

CHAPTER 7

The next thing I knew Nadine was waking me up. It was around seven a.m. I lay there a second, still a little groggy from the wine the night before. I wasn't much of a drinker; I was actually a lightweight, to tell the truth. I enjoyed the taste of a good wine now and then but I couldn't handle the alcohol, so I stayed away from it.

I stretched, still lying on the cushions under the boat cover, and took stock of the sea swell, which was strong enough to give the *Lean Back* a good roll. Yet when I looked out I saw that we were in for another sun-drenched day. This meant heat and humidity and I wasn't so sure I wanted to get up yet. We were going to be in that heat all day, and the coolness trapped under the boat cover felt really good.

"We had some company show up overnight," Nadine said, pointing over the bow. "I think it's an old Bertrand, and I mean *old*. Due east of us, and it must have come in during the night sometime. I saw it anchored when I woke up. *Señorita Inez* is her name. Is that David?

"Yeah, that's him if that's the *Inez*," I told her. "Good old David." I smiled at Nadine, still lying down and in a full stretch.

"Here, take a look," she said, passing me the binoculars. I propped myself up with a groan. "There are two guys on board and they look like they're having engine problems."

"The *Inez* with engine problems? Hmm, I doubt it." I waved away her offer of the glasses and continued to stretch. Boy, was I stiff. "Whenever David's away from Cuban waters and he anchors, he always fiddles with the engines. In case he's being watched, they'll think he has a legit problem, and he won't be asked what he was doing anchored in that area. These boys are like the Green Berets or special ops guys; they cover their tracks just as well, if not better."

That fuzzy, unawake feeling in my head was all mixed up with a dream I couldn't quite remember. Something to do with being on a train with my mother. "You know, *niña*, David once told me that he never knows when he's being watched, and believe me, he's right—everyone is being watched. That's why Cubans are so leery about everything, so overly cautious. My mother visited Cuba a few times, and on one of her trips she told me that her brother Hector wanted to *speak privately with her*." I made quotation marks with my fingers and laughed.

"He took her into the bedroom, sat her on the bed, and then he sat down and pulled the blanket over their heads before he began to talk. Unbelievable huh? She still can't believe it. She loves to tell that story; she thinks it's hilarious."

There was a little bit of a breeze as the day warmed up, and Nadine put a scrunchie around her hair to keep it from blowing in her face. "She must have been like that too, though, before she came here," she said.

"No, no, she left too early to really experience anything like a police state. They left right in 1960. Castro didn't get the intelligence agency, the G-2, up and running until '62. Much too early."

My head was feeling better and I was enjoying this little history lesson. "It was different way back in '59. There was still a lot of freedom, and there was food, all the supplies you can get in the States. Now, though, with the new Cuban arrivals in Miami, boy, you can tell they've been through hell. If they're in a store they'll look around in amazement at everything on the shelves and wonder if it's okay to take it. They'll ask if it's a tourist store because there's so much. And I've noticed when they talk sometimes they'll look around to see who's listening. Can you imagine living like that your whole life, while Radio Free Cuba and Radio Mambi in Miami are constantly telling you how great things are just 150 miles north of you? And then you think of your family members who are living there. *Ave Maria!* Shit, I'd go crazy myself."

I finally worked my way out from under the cover. The sun was already intense. I stretched my arms, in a futile attempt to get the kinks out of my body, and I glanced over the bow. I turned while still stretching nonchalantly.

"Yeah, that's David. I don't know who's with him, but I trust his judgment."

Nadine was preparing a cup of Cuban coffee, and the aroma was wafting through the air and mixing with the salt air; it smelled great and I anticipated a nice buzz. She handed me a shot of coffee, I sipped it down as I looked toward the *Señorita Inez*. I saw David acknowledge contact with very low-key body language. I knew he probably couldn't make out a head nod but I nodded anyway, and smiled. It would be good to see him again.

David knew the *Lean Back*. I had taken him for rides before, when he showed up in the Bahamas. He loved it—the sleek look, the speed, jumping waves. He would say, "Kiki, with a boat like this in Cuba, I would become a rich man." I told him he could have it if he wanted and he'd think about it for a minute, then smile and say, "It wouldn't do any good, Kiki. Castro would take it away and it would go to ruin like everything else he has ever touched." And then he would start laughing. "I'll take you up on that when the Beard is gone, okay Kiki?" We always got a good kick out of our little joke. And it always stayed the same because Castro was always still there.

Nadine handed me another shot, and I knew I would be more than buzzing soon. Cuban coffee was strong, like liquid speed.

We sat around for a while, finishing our coffee and looking out on the water. Something caught my eye on the southern horizon and I grabbed the field glasses. It was a Cuban patrol boat about five miles away, too far to make out details, but I could tell it was Cuban navy. The Cubans were able to acquire a lot of American boats during the Mariel Boatlift, when the Cubans in Miami flooded down to Mariel in every craft known to man. Many of those boats were confiscated after they had mechanical problems and weren't able to make it back to Florida. This one looked like an old shrimp boat. Its course of travel, from east to west, made me fairly certain that it was a patrol boat since that was against the current, which I guess added an element of surprise when you were stalking your prey. They used them to circle the entire coast of the island, and usually one of them passed the Cay Sals every three or four days.

"Who are they, Kiki?" Nadine asked with concern.

"Well, I'd bet you dollars to donuts there's a Cuban sailor on board that's looking at your tits *ahora mismo* with Russian-issue binoculars. That'll make his day. And be sure to smile! No, just kidding. Act like everything's normal—we're a couple from Florida on a fishing trip."

"They can see all this way?" she asked with a fake smile on her face.

I laughed. "*Niña*, those glasses are as strong as they get. I'm sure they can even see that little mole on the inside of your left thigh."

"Oh, Kiki, you know you're not supposed to talk about that," she said, pouting. "I'm cleaning the dishes. I'm not too interested in giving some horny sailor a peep show so he can have a story to tell his other little horny friends."

There was a long day ahead of us before the nighttime rendezvous, and we were going to need to stay busy and not look out of place. What would the tourists do? Fishing, scuba diving, the usual. Nadine was right on cue.

"I'm going to take a dip and wash up, Kiki—would you like to join me?" Before I knew it, she had stepped up on the side railing of the boat and dived over the side. When she surfaced, she called out, "Wow, nice. It's really refreshing! Come in!"

It did look inviting. We were in about twenty to thirty feet of water, and it was gin clear. I could clearly see a school of yellowtail Snappers swimming on the bottom. The offer was too good to refuse, so I did a quick scan for shark fins, stepped up on the railing and joined Nadine in the 82-degree ocean-sized bath. Even though it was a salty bath, it felt good to clear the cobwebs.

I scrubbed my face and rubbed at my body. Then I swam over to the back of the boat and used the engines as a ladder to step back up on the *Lean Back*. I toweled off still covered with salt water. We had fresh water but drinking water is more important than bathing water, so you make do and skip the freshwater rinse.

I sat down, lit up a joint, and watched Nadine do her water-ballet act. I loved seeing her splash to the surface, then roll and prop those long, tan legs way up in the air, and then slide gracefully down into the depths. She was like a mermaid, or a dolphin. I laughed and pictured a dolphin with Nadine's face, catching and eating the yellowtails beneath the water.

It was almost noon and the sun was blazing. The glare on the water was painful to the eyes. DK and the boys still hadn't shown up, but I wasn't worried, not yet. When they got down to business they were pretty serious dudes, even though they sometimes seemed like a circus act. I guessed DK-the-ringleader maintained discipline.

I was feeling peckish and thought about lunch, then a nice nap out of the hot sun. If I could catch a couple of big yellowtails – flags, they called them– then we could have a nice fresh meal. We'd save the Mahi for another time.

I got out my rod and baited the hook with a piece of yesterday's Mahi. Some of the fishing shows on TV back home made me laugh. What incredible hype. Compare those to the old boys teaching you skinny-water fishing, basically shallow-water fishing, down here. It was true there was a technique to skinny and it was best learned with a pro. But I'd skip the commercials, thank you.

Anyway, here it wasn't skinny but fairly deep, just like open ocean fishing, or mainland coastal fishing or like on the Marquesas banks west of Key West. You didn't need lures, just bait. And everything hit your hook. Drop a hook in the water with any bait on it and you'd catch fish. You didn't need a whole lot of technique or knowledge, just patience and will. I had seen some of the old boys back in the Keys make a better cast with a spool of line in one hand, weighted, hooked and baited line in the other, swinging it around their head like David with his sling, eyeing down Goliath. Let's see those so-called professionals catch as many fish.

As I cast my line I kept an eye on the *Señorita Inez*. The two men really did seem to be tinkering with the engine. Yet I seriously doubted there was anything wrong with the boat. All those beautiful antique Chevys, Fords and Chryslers they always showed when you saw any images of Cuba—well, 90 percent of them ran on Russian Lada parts. Open the hoods and you wouldn't see Chevy, Ford or Chrysler anywhere. Necessity was the mother of invention, and when it came to necessity the Cubans had cornered the market. Poor bastards, they needed everything. They couldn't just make a phone call and go to the auto parts store and get a hook-up for their '56 Chevy Bel Air. So all those Ladas that came to Cuba during the revolution just became customized parts for all those antiques that people throughout the world oohed and ahhed at when they saw them in those beautiful brochures that promoted an island paradise.

The point is, Cubans were incredible mechanics. Those beautiful relics were put together with spit, bubblegum, band-aids and sheer genius. Two years ago, David took the *Inez* to Bimini and we brought over a brand new Volvo Penta with a Mercruiser Outdrive. David's boat is only 32 feet long and that engine got her up and going real quick. There wasn't shit wrong with that old *Señorita*. She might look like shit, but she was strong and could run like hell all day long!

I felt a tug and set the hook. I reeled her in and found that I had a beautiful four-pound yellowtail on the line. I repeated the process two more times and got about eight pounds of snapper. We had enough for lunch, dinner, and to feed the fish in our private aquarium that we called the Cay Sal Bank.

I roused myself from my nap around 4:00 pm. It was still blazing hot and the wind was gone. Nadine had gotten up earlier and was reading her novel under the protective cover of a big floppy hat.

"*Que carajo*, what the hell is that music?" I asked Nadine, slightly annoyed.

"Well it's not me singing, *mon petit garçon*." She smiled and pointed. "Take a look."

There she was, just due west of the *Lean Back*. DK, Jony, and Jorge in their 52-foot Hatteras named *Hawk Marine* after their marina in Miami, and she looked majestic in the water. Tuna tower glittering in the afternoon sun, rocket launchers loaded with rods ready to take on the ocean. She sure was pretty, sitting there anchored about two hundred yards away and bobbing in the rolling ocean water.

The current had pushed her so her stern was facing us. I could see someone in the lower deck by the transom; the *salsa* music could be heard faintly and the person was dancing and laughing.

"Look at Jony dancing," I said.

She glanced over, noticed Jony, looked back at me, and with those long legs she shook her hips from side to side. Still wearing that revealing bikini, she shuffled her feet in a hot *salsa step*.

"When we get home you need to take me *salsa* dancing, Kiki."

"No problem, *niña*," I replied. "*When* we get home."

Anyone who didn't know the boys would think they were a bunch of yahoos with big money and a big boat. To underestimate them would be a huge mistake. They were the real deal when it came to boats and the ocean. You couldn't find any better.

As Jony continued his dancing and partying, I couldn't help but think how different the Miami boys were from David. The boys were outgoing and David was quiet. I wondered if, given the opportunity to live as free as the boys do in Miami, David would open up a little. Probably not—that way of life is all he'd ever known and we were all products of our environment.

At that moment David was probably thinking, "Who are those assholes?" We would all meet soon enough, and I knew, considering what we were about to do, that they would end up with mutual respect for each other—even if their personalities were total opposites.

It was cooling down, and the sun was melting into the horizon, right on cue. The people at Malloy Square in Key West were probably gathered, waiting for the sun to do her nightly thing to a raucous round of applause.

My sunset would be spent pondering other events, those of the coming days.

I prepared some yellowtail and we enjoyed a good meal. I needed to relax a little before we got together with David tonight. I was going to be taking a long swim in the middle of the night. After the meal I lit up another joint, but knew not to ask Nadine if she wanted to share. For me it's calming, for her it's too stimulating. She had a glass of wine instead.

Nadine went to bed early and set an alarm for two AM; she would wake me up shortly before Jony's arrival. I joined her after straightening up, and struggled to sleep under a sliver of a moon and a blanket of stars. You'd think such a beautiful setting would have a calming effect, but I couldn't help but go over and over in my mind what the next week or so would turn out like. Would I be able to have my Cuban coffee and rum on the *Quest*? Would I be able to go *salsa* dancing with Nadine? Would I see Bentley again? My life was in the balance and I knew it. On one side was money and satisfaction; on the other, jail or death. I had a choice, but I made it a long time ago. This job chose me as much as I chose it.

CHAPTER 8

"Kiki, Kiki, wake up. Jony should be here soon."

I sat up and glanced over at the *Hawk Marine*. She looked quiet, and only had one light atop her tuna tower. No sooner had I turned my eyes back to the *Lean Back* than I heard some light splashing between two of the engines. I made my way closer, only to see a head pop up. Jony had a wetsuit hoody on, and his diving mask was still on his face. He held onto one of the engines with one hand and with the other pulled his respirator out of his mouth and then pulled the diving mask to the top of his head.

"*Oye, oye,* Kiki. Are you there?"

Jony hadn't noticed that I was crouching down about five feet away, watching to confirm that it was him.

"Jony, it's me, Kiki. I'm right here."

He shifted back, startled by my voice coming out of the darkness.

"*Estupido, come mierda!* You scared the shit out of me, asshole."

I almost let out a laugh, but to avoid noise I held it in. I helped him up on the boat and we embraced, then he kissed Nadine.

"Well, let's get going," he said. "I want those millions."

I pretended to lecture him. "*Tranquilo hombre, no cuentes antes que cobres.*"

Jony had already secured his scuba tanks to the engines in the water. Now he grabbed my tank, looked it over and then hung it overboard, securing it to the engines. Nadine brought my wetsuit and I put it on as Jony waited, telling me what a great trip they had down here. Jony found everything great; he had a glass-half-full attitude all the time, never half-empty.

We slipped into the water quietly between the engines and secured our tanks and masks. I looked up at Nadine, who was on her knees at the transom of the boat.

"Wait up for me," I said. "I should be back in a couple of hours. Stay low."

Jony and I submerged to about ten feet below the surface and began to swim toward the *Inez*. The beautiful gin-clear water of the day had become as black and menacing as the deep blue of the Gulf Stream. Jony knew our heading, which was basically directly east, and he kept us on course as we swam along. It wasn't going to take us long to get there, about fifteen to twenty minutes, but every minute felt like an eternity with the fear of some hungry shark cruising the shallower waters of the Bank for a little nighttime meal. My heart was in my mouth the whole way there.

We finally made it. I could see the dark, shadowy hull of the *Inez* about 10 yards in front of us. Jony grabbed my arm and pulled me upright, then pointed to the shadow and turned his palms up as if to ask me if that was it. I nodded my head, then motioned that I would go to the surface and make sure. I surfaced slowly, and under the cover of darkness and the blackness of the water, I poked my head through the surface. I immediately recognized the boat, and painted in blue against a white hull I saw the name, *Señorita Inez.*

I submerged to the waiting Jony, put my thumb up, and we swam to the stern. We hoisted ourselves up onto a small underwater dive platform that stretched across the beam of the boat and was positioned over its out drive. We took off our tanks, secured them to the dive platform and breached the surface only to find David kneeling and bent over on the upper part of the platform, reaching out.

"*Bienvenido,* Kiki, it's been a long time."

He pulled me up where he was and I crawled over the transom as he helped Jony up and over onto the *Inez.* All three of us sat down on the deck for a second. David made his way over to me, gave me a strong hug.

"It's been a long time, *hermano*; it's been a long time."

David motioned to us, and we crawled our way over to the cabin and made our way in. He had brought Anibal with him. I had met him before in the Bahamas with David, on a little job we did down in Ragged Island one time. Anibal was quiet and a little withdrawn. He had spent some time in Cuba's prisons and was definitely anti-Revolution. Like David, he preferred to stay in Cuba and help his family as much as possible.

Chino had also come along. He was a smallish man, very thin, with a perpetual smile. They called him Chino because of his Chinese descent. He was incredible in the water, like a fish. Whenever there was a problem out on the water with the out drive or prop, Chino was your man. He wasn't scared of diving and fixing the problem—even in the middle of the ocean.

We were sitting on the floor getting our greetings out of the way. Anibal started spreading the charts out.

"Well, Kiki, what brings us all here?" asked David, thinking we were going out on salvage. "Where are we going?"

I hesitated as David looked up, waiting for my answer.

"To Cuba."

"Ok," said David, "but we'll have to be careful; I'll have to fish while we dive the site and we can't stay too long. There are plenty of patrol boats..."

"It's not salvage, David," I said, cutting him off in mid-sentence. "We're looking for some salvaged treasure that the Beard has been bringing up for years and storing somewhere. My information tells me it's on the north coast in some warehouses. We need to find out where, and then hit it."

"*Este hombre esta loco!* Hit it? You mean steal it. You're crazy."

Jony had been sitting in the corner quietly, hardly noticed, when he began to laugh softly. "Yeah, that's what I said. But he talked me into crazy, too."

"Who are you?" David said abruptly.

I stepped in quick. "David, I'm sorry, this is Jony. He's a good friend and he's going to work on this job with us—that is, if you decide to do it. You know I can't do it without you," I said with a wry smile.

David turned to me, looked me in the eye for a second and said, "Fuck you, Kiki." He sat there for a moment, and began to laugh. Anibal, Jony, and I joined in. Believe me, it was very nervous laughter.

"Kiki, we know exactly what you're talking about," said David. The laughing ceased. "It's in a warehouse in, get this, Caibarién. Right in front of our noses. We first found out that there was valuable treasure being housed there a couple years ago. Some people from Santiago somehow got word that it was there. They broke in, killed a guard and stole part of it. That happened about five years ago. Needless to say, they were caught. Two of them made national news, against Castro's *Paredón*—the firing squad wall. The three others were never heard from again. To make a statement of defiance, Castro left the treasure in the same warehouses. They beefed up security for a year or two and then it slacked off again. Lack of money and personnel, no doubt. No one goes near the warehouses, and some people won't even look that way. The problem is, there are quite a few warehouses over there and no one even knows which one it's in. Kiki, *tu estas seguro?*"

"Yeah, I'm sure David; this might be the end of us all, *mi hermano.*"

"Well, what's next?" he asked.

I opened up a waterproof bag that I had brought with me and took out $20,000 and handed it to David.

"I need you to hook up the torpedoes on your boat, like back in the Bahamas," I said.

"You mean the smuggling torpedoes?"

"Yeah."

Torpedoes were a smuggler's tool, a *clabo*, a hiding spot; they were aluminum cylinders about twelve inches in diameter that were secured under the boat. Smugglers would put contraband in the torpedoes, so if they were boarded by the Coast Guard or Marine Patrol and searched they would come up empty, because the contraband would be under the boat in the water. Lately, the authorities had caught on. That said, I didn't think there was much use for torpedoes in Cuba, so the patrols there wouldn't be looking for them.

"David, with some of the rest of the money I need a safe house in Cuba, near the warehouses. It's got to be someone you really trust; keep the rest of the money for you guys and your families. On the back end of this job, if we succeed we'll all make some real money, and that includes you guys."

I told David I would make contact with him in Santa Clara in three days at the Parque Vidal, at the monument of Leonicio Vidal, the park's namesake. I handed David a sat phone and explained about the three different phone numbers.

Jony and I got ready to leave. We said our goodbyes and made sure once again that we were all in agreement. We made our way to the back of the boat, slipped over the transom onto the dive platform, and then back into the water. We secured our fins, tanks, and masks, waved, submerged, and made our way back to the *Lean Back*.

Nadine was happy to see us. Jony and I spoke for a minute about our lines of communication and his waiting point just off the northeastern part of Cuba, just outside of Cuban territorial waters, in between Cuba and Ragged Island, Bahamas. I had given them a contact on Ragged in case they had problems.

Jony made his way back to the *Hawk Marine* and Nadine and I got a few more hours of sleep. We would be Cuba-bound in the morning. The couple of hours of sleep I got were intermittent, with waking thoughts of all our plans and how they would work out.

When Nadine woke up I already had the coffee made. We sat there silently for a few moments.

"I'm ready, Kiki, what's next?"

"Hemingway. Do you know what you have to do once we separate there?"

"Yes, stay on the boat and make my way back to Cay Sal Bank where you will contact me on the satellite phone within twenty-four hours. Assuming everything is okay and plans haven't changed, I'll make my way back to Hemingway Marina. When enough boats have noticed me and I blend in, I'll work my way east along the coast. I'll stay far enough out to sea to avoid all the cays along the northern coast and I'll only travel under the cover of darkness. About a hundred miles east following Cuba's coastline is Cayo Fragaso. I'll check my time for distance, but Cayo Fragaso will be a set of cays that are much bigger and longer than any of the other cays that I pass.

Anyway, I'll judge my traveling speed for distance. When I'm there, or I think I'm there, I'll call you on the sat, anchor off, and wait for David. He'll be on the *Inez*." She pointed to the *Señorita Inez*, which hadn't left yet, and said, "And I'll identify the *Inez* by her nighttime profile, which I'm eyeballing as we speak. If I have any problems, or I'm being approached by anyone other than the *Inez*, I punch the three Mercs, point the *Lean Back* north and run like hell, catch my bearings, head to Florida and call DK and Jony to let them know what happened. But assuming things work out ok, David will take me and the *Lean Back* and hide us in the mangroves on Fragaso. Did I get it all, Kiki?"

"You got it, *niña*" I replied. "Just one more thing, Nadine, you know that Uzi that's in the *clabo* on the boat?"

"Yes."

"Use it if you have to." She looked at me and nodded. "Remember DK, Jony, and Jorge are going to be east, northeast of you, just southwest of Ragged. Their objective is to draw attention and divert, so use them if you have to. Stay in contact, *niña*. Remember, if I don't hear from you, I'm assuming you ran or something worse, so stay in touch. Oh, and be careful on that water out there; remember because you're alone and it'll be dark, you'll be vulnerable, so pay a lot of attention to all your surroundings. Okay?"

She looked me straight in the eyes and said, "Yes, Kiki. I'm ready."

At that moment, I felt better about Nadine. She was controlling her demons and her anxiety quite well. Her mind was sharp and her body posture was confident.

We got ourselves ready to go, cleaned up our gear, checked the boat over completely, and hoisted anchor.

"Are you ready?" I asked.

"Yes," she replied, confidently.

I throttled down on all the Mercs and the *Lean Back* sprung up on plane. I pointed her west southwest, toward Havana.

CHAPTER 9

We zipped along over a calm sea and under beautiful skies, and I couldn't believe I was returning to Cuba. I was totally psyched. I hadn't been to the island in two years, since a few friends and I fished the Hemingway tournament in 1985.

We hooked into everything that year—wahoo, yellowtail, more sailfish than we could count, but we never even sniffed the elusive marlin we had come down to hunt. Needless to say, we got skunked in the competition but had a great time fishing, drinking, smoking, and chasing pretty *señoritas* around Havana.

We would pick up sight of Cuba in about an hour, and we should be at Marina Hemingway in one-and-a-half to two hours, depending on our speed. Since it was a clear day, spotting land wouldn't be a problem. Next stop, Papa's Marina, Cuba.

When we were a couple miles off shore and tracking west toward Havana we began to see plenty of boat traffic milling about and fishing along the cays that dotted the northern coast. As it was late July, fishing off the Cuban shore was at its peak. There seemed to be more and more fishing tournaments in Cuba every year, and plenty of boats from the States were always there. People didn't give a shit about the embargo or American law when it pertained to Cuba anymore, and they traveled here in their boats whenever they pleased. I'd been here quite a few times with buddies on fishing trips.

Cuban immigration didn't stamp your passport if you were American and came in on your private boat, or flew in indirectly from a third country, like Mexico or the Bahamas. They knew a stamp could cause problems for U.S. citizens, because of the embargo and the law limiting travel. So to encourage return and discourage reprisals by the U.S. they conveniently "forgot" to stamp the passports.

Keep the greenbacks coming, gringos. That's really what they meant to say, and it worked. The U.S. Customs couldn't tell where you'd been without passport stamps to prove it. A marriage of convenience; one that I was willing to take a chance on and be a part of. Not so much for the fishing, even though it was great, but because I considered Cuba my homeland. And I didn't like the idea of the government telling me I couldn't get some quality Cuba time—especially when the rest of the world was coming here. And besides, most Americans thought the embargo was a relic of a past era.

We soon passed El Morro, the old fort guarding Havana Harbor, and then the Malecón, the famous sea wall stretching west to Vedado, where families gathered and lovers strolled. After a couple of days of nothing but blue, I was happy to see all the reds and oranges and purples and browns of Old Havana.

Another twenty minutes and we approached Marina Hemingway. It looked like it was packed. I pulled the *Lean Back* in at idle speed up to the gas pumps, which was our first order of business. Fill up.

It was obvious Nadine had never been to Cuba. She stared at almost everything. "It's not so pretty around here, considering how it's such a big deal," Nadine said in a low voice.

"Yeah, it could use a large infusion of capitalism," I responded.

"Mr. Logan; *Oye,* Mr. Logan," I heard a voice call. I looked toward the pump dock and recognized Raúl, who had been the dock master here for a couple decades. He took good care of me whenever I came here, because I took care of him. And by that I meant I brought him all the necessities he couldn't really get—enough to last him six months at a time.

"Hey Raúl, how are you?" I called back.

"Fine, Mr. Logan, fine."

"I see it's Mr. Logan around here for you," Nadine said.

"Just a game, *niña,*" I replied, "just a game."

Raúl took our lines, tied us off and began to refuel the *Lean Back.* I stepped up to him and shook his hand.

"I have some things for you on the boat, Raúl," I said softly.

"*Gracias,* Mr. Logan, *gracias.* I'll come back later on and pick them up when the time is right. You know what I mean, Mr. Logan."

"Sure, Raúl, sure," I told him as I patted his back.

Nadine, Raúl and I walked toward the marina restaurant. I never really knew whether to trust him or not. With all the contacts he had developed over the years, I was sure he'd had many opportunities to leave Cuba. I knew he had family in Miami. But he was still here, getting his take, and I was sure I wasn't the only one who brought him goodies. Maybe through his contacts he was able to stay in a country he loved and live rather well. Or maybe he really was a government plant. It made sense: This place was always full of foreign boats, especially from the U.S.

For obvious reasons, Castro didn't allow his people to own pleasure crafts. Everything at this marina was foreign or government. What better way to keep tabs on what was going on?

That's why I kept on Raúl's good side and tipped more than the average gringo. So even if he was a spy, he might cut me a break. And if he didn't, well then, I could get my ass locked up forever down here. I would never see Islamorada again. Keep Raúl happy and dumb—that was my motto with him.

"Go to the restaurant, Mr. Logan, and have a *mojito* with your lady; drink to Papa."

Everyone in Cuba knows what someone meant, or who they were referring to, when they said "Papa"—Ernest Hemingway, of course. Other than his namesake, this marina has nothing to do with Hemingway himself. There were a couple of overpriced eateries and a duty free shop, but other than the cigars, it was all a rip off. The annual marlin tournament, held in Hemingway's honor, was actually based at Tarara's Marina, east of Havana.

Most tourists wouldn't know this unless they were diehard fishermen.

Nadine and I walked over to the restaurant and were shown to a nice table overlooking the marina docks. There were two other couples there enjoying an over-priced lunch. They were speaking in a language we couldn't recognize, Eastern European, I think. We ordered *mojitos, minutas de pescado* and *fritas* "papas." We dug into the *mojitos* and fish sandwiches when they arrived, eager to get our land legs back after two days at sea.

"It feels good to be on land again," Nadine said.

I smiled; I could see the fatigue in her face. Two days sleeping on a boat deck wasn't exactly comfortable.

"We'll finish our lunch straight up and put the *Lean Back* in a slip, then take care of Raúl and head to Havana," I told Nadine. "We'll get a room at the Nacional tonight, enjoy Havana a little, and try to make contact with Sergio De La Rosa, Banco's man there."

"The Nacional!" she said, excited. "I've heard of that place. It dates back to the days of the American mafia in Cuba. The forties and fifties."

"That's right *niña*; it does have a little bit of history," I replied.

"Is it in Old Havana?"

"No, not at all," I corrected her. "It's in Vedado, the suburb to the west of the old city. It's pretty amazing there: big wide avenues and parks and promenades. Beautiful houses, and still in relatively good shape, at least compared to Old Havana.

Really stately. In fact, guess where Castro set up his first headquarters after Batista fled the city?"

She pondered the question a moment. "Well, maybe Batista's mansion, if he had one there?"

"No, the Nacional, on the sixth floor. He didn't move the government to Havana until early 1960."

"Can we go to, what is it, the Bogedita del Mayo?" she asked.

"Ha! That's Bodeguita del Medio, you know, like 'little bodega.' Why not." I said, happy to indulge her with my homeland's famous landmarks.

At La Bodeguita del Medio we would be in a real Hemingway haunt this time. The man spent a lot of time there, quenching his alcoholic thirst and being a pain in the ass who everyone seemed to like.

Nadine and I finished up our lunch and walked back to the pump dock. We got back on the *Lean Back* and prepared to put her back in her slip.

The marina was set up for tourists; the docks and boat slips were as nice as anywhere in the U.S: lighted walkways, electricity, water for every slip, and well maintained. The restaurant was modest, but as nice as any marina restaurant in the Keys. The duty free shop was also modest yet everything was costly. The staffers at the marina were always very nice, prompt and courteous—as they should have been. Their jobs were envied by everyone in the whole damn country.

When a waiter or staff member of any restaurant in the tourist districts of Havana could make more money in tips than a doctor or any other professional, then something was well and truly fucked up. And I didn't mean just a little more money, either. Doctors made about thirty bucks in U.S. currency a month. A waiter might make that money at one table in a night.

And the *jineteras*—oh my God—the *jineteras* came from all over Cuba to Havana to sell their wares, which were bought up by all these fine gentlemen that came from all over the world. Just to fuck Cuban women. Goddamn assholes. Back in their own country they couldn't get laid in a ten dollar whorehouse with a twenty dollar bill. But Cuba was a matter of pure economics; there were no jobs for the people. Like anywhere else in the world, people would do what they had to do. In most cases it wasn't a matter of choice, but necessity, thanks to one of the world's worst economic situations, which owed its present state of disarray, mental and physical, to a revolution and a government that failed its people a long time ago.

On the golf courses in Miami there was a joke: When someone left a putt, a turn or a roll short of dropping into the cup, they called it a Cuban putt; it was in need of one more revolution. That was really funny for me because the joke was true. This place did need one more revolution, and it couldn't be worse than the last one.

We pulled into the slip Raúl had selected for us. Nadine grabbed the line as I maneuvered the *Lean Back* into place. She jumped onto the dock, pulled the boat in and tied us off. I climbed up on the dock to a waiting Raúl. He came close to me, took a quick look around.

"I'll be back in an hour, Mr. Logan, to pick up my presents, if that's okay *señor.*"

"Absolutely, Raúl," I said. "It'll take me a while to clean up and put things away here. I'll see you when you get back."

I always brought plenty for Raúl, from toilet paper to toothpaste. They needed everything in this country. The only way to get the things we took for granted in the States was to be able to shop in the tourist sections designated specifically for tourists. That was a no-no that could bring jail-time ramifications. Any extras that you got in Cuba over and above the government's allotment through their *libretas*, a form of Cuban food stamps, came from the black market or theft—and by the way, theft in Cuba could get you 30 years in one of Castro's gulags. Cuba's jails were full of common thieves who claimed to be political prisoners, and they were. Living under a government that couldn't take care of its people and turned them into thieves and *jineteras* was political. Castro called them vermin, but what he forgot was that he was Dr. Moreau, and his mad plan failed on this island.

Nadine and I straightened up the *Lean Back*, put her front cover and engine covers on. We got Raúl's goodies ready for him and secured the rest.

"*Niña, por favor*, check the *clabos* and make sure the Uzis and ammo are secure, then seal the *clabos* back up. If they catch us with them, our stay in Cuba will be a little longer than we want."

Nadine checked them as I went over the *Lean Back* to make sure we were ready for more ocean. Time went by quickly, and before I knew it Raúl had returned with his son Andre to pick up the packages.

"*Como estas, señor* Logan?" Raúl play-acted as he asked to come aboard the boat, while simultaneously jumping on. Rude son of a bitch, I thought. I didn't pay much attention as I shook Raúl's hand.

"You remember my son Andre, *Señor* Logan? *Esta cresiendo, no?*"

"Yeah, Raúl, he must have grown six inches since the last time I saw him," I said. "Is he a *pelotero*, Raúl?" I asked, seeing a potential baseball player in him.

"No, he prefers the sport of chasing women. He's going to end up just like everyone else in Cuba. Four children and a shitty government apartment—*estupido*," he sputtered with disgust.

"Here are your presents, Raúl. I hope it's enough." I handed him the goods.

"You're very generous, *Señor* Logan, *gracias.*"

As Raúl and Andre carried the packages to their car I noticed that the customs and immigration agents were standing by the dock master's cabin. They greeted Raúl and his son with big smiles, offering to help out with their load. Raúl accepted and the two officers helped them to their car.

I always brought two to three times more for Raúl than he would need. I knew he would have to spread the wealth to *maricones* like that.

They all joked and laughed while Raúl and his son got in Raul's 1957 Chevy Nomad. The car was a sweet ride; it took good American greenbacks to get one of those relics looking and running right. They were rust buckets with a fresh coat of paint to hide the blemishes. However, Raúl's Nomad looked good and ran well. He must have gotten everything from Mexico and Jamaica on the black market, because this baby was original and clean. It took money and connections to pull that off in Cuba.

There were probably a hundred suckers who brought him goody bags all year long. Nice little setup, but he sure had to grease palms.

CHAPTER 10

"Hotel Nacional, *por favor*," I told the taxi driver.

"*Si, señor*," he replied and put the Russian Lada in gear.

The ride from Marina Hemingway to the Nacional was along Cuba's famous Malecón. It was a relatively calm day, and the waves that sometimes crashed as high as thirty feet in the air over the sea wall created only a light spray wafting up every now and then as people strolled along.

Nadine shook her head. She was still a little incredulous about how smoothly the interview with the customs agents had gone. What she had witnessed was the infamous Cuban "passport pass."

"I can't believe what I just saw. Do they do that with all Americans?" she asked.

"Yeah, all Americans who don't travel here from the U.S."

"Well what about me? I have a French passport; I'm only a resident in the U.S."

"They saw you were on a U.S.-registered boat that legally is not supposed to be here, so they afforded you the same courtesy. They're not stupid," I told her.

"If you can't beat them, join them, right?"

"That's right, *niña*; get it while you can."

The two agents had been all smiles as they made their way to the slip where the *Lean Back* was moored.

"*Como esta, Señor* Logan?"

I wasn't surprised they knew my name, even though I had never seen them before.

"*Bien gracias,*" I replied.

"May I come aboard?" said the customs agent. He couldn't have been more than 25 years old, about six feet tall, dark complected and heavily muscled.

"*Si, bienvenido,*" I said.

He stepped aboard the *Lean Back* and shook my hand.

"Welcome to Cuba, Mr. Logan," he said in near-perfect English, with only a slight accent.

"Thank you."

He glanced around, but he wasn't paying much attention to what was on board. He seemed to be admiring the vessel's design.

"She's a beautiful boat, Mr. Logan," he said with a big smile. "I bet she's fast."

"Yeah, she has plenty of speed," I said smiling back.

"Everything seems to be okay here," he said. Still smiling.

Sure, why not, I thought. He's one of the palms Raúl will be greasing later.

"If I could see your passports, Mr. Logan, I'll give them to Miguel. He's the immigration officer on duty."

I handed him our passports and he handed them to Miguel, who was still standing on the dock. Nadine sat quietly in the boat seat at the center console. She looked at me with a question in her eyes, as if to ask if she were about to witness the passport pass. I smiled and nodded my head.

Miguel was the opposite of the young customs agent: short and heavyset, with a ruddy complexion, he looked like he'd been at his job for such a long time that he just didn't give a shit anymore. All he wanted was to have his share of the take and carry on with his meager life.

If Miguel was hardened to this racket by now, the young customs agent was relatively new and just beginning to get his share. He still put on the smile when he saw pigeons like me.

Miguel glanced at the passports, closed them back up and handed them to the young officer.

"*Todo esta bien aqui,*" he said.

He turned away and slowly strolled to the restaurant, where he would probably get a Cuban coffee for free. Not much different than the States, I had thought, except for the doughnut. Everybody's got his hand out.

He never put an entry stamp on the passports, just like I had said. As long as the U.S. government stayed the same in its dealing with Cuba, this would be one of the ways Cuba would deal with the U.S., to still be able to attract our dollars, which, even though officially contraband, were Cuba's main currency. The peso has not been accepted by the world community and has no value, and it ain't worth shit in Cuba either. The dollar rules.

The young customs agent handed me both passports.

"*Gracias,* Mr. Logan. I hope you and your friend have a nice stay in Cuba and catch plenty of fish."

The funny thing is that he fucking meant it; he wanted me, and others like me, to keep coming back, so he could stay ahead of the shitty system he had to live in. I took the passports from his hand and smiled.

"*Gracias, señor.* We always catch a lot of fish, and I'm damn sure we'll be coming back."

"*Gracias* again *señor,*" he said. He turned around and followed Miguel to the restaurant for his coffee, grinning as he went.

The taxi ride was quick as there was little traffic. July and August were normally down months in Cuba. Too much heat and humidity, just like south Florida.

As we drove eastward along the Malecón we looked at the buildings and houses on our right. There were stately palms and lush greenery among run-down, decrepit mansions.

"*Aquí estamos, señor.*" The taxi turned into the long driveway leading up to the Hotel Nacional. This large American-built luxury hotel, which was constructed in the Vedado in 1930, reminded people of The Breakers in Palm Beach. If anything, it was grander than The Breakers.

"*Gracias, hombre, cuanto de debo?*" I asked.

"*Diez dolares,*" he replied.

I noticed he said dollars, not *pesos*. I handed him a twenty and said *"Gracias hombre."*

With a big smile, he took the twenty and looked at me. I realized his request. *"Para usted, para usted,"* I told him.

"Gracias, señor" he said and drove away with the smile still gleaming. Why not? I thought. I made his month.

Nadine and I stood at the entrance of the Nacional. She looked in awe at the elegance of it. "This is beautiful," she said.

"Sure is, thanks to good old Meyer Lansky, Mafia money and his view of a new Cuba. With gambling and prostitution all controlled by him, with Batista's blessing. But don't let all this elegance fool you. Calle O y 21 Vedado, Habana. Hotel Nacional is only different in one way than most of the rundown mansions we saw getting here."

"What could that be, Kiki?" she said a little sarcastically. "I know you don't like Castro, and neither do I, but give it a little bit of a break, won't you? This place is beautiful."

"You're right, *niña.*" I put my hand on her shoulder to comfort her. She looked at me and smacked her lips. *"Niña,* the Nacional is like an old, old lady who has had plenty of facelifts, and that's where the differences end with all the run-down mansions we saw. The facelifts don't help. Her guts are just as rotten as those in the buildings we saw along the Malecón. Old, shoddy, inefficient—disasters waiting to happen. You'll see. The power will go out every now and then, especially in these hot summer months. The plumbing is shitty, so be careful when you go to the bathroom. You might make us both sorry, if you know what I mean. Every building in this city probably needs to be gutted out and refurbished."

We walked inside to a beautiful lobby and were greeted at the desk by a gorgeous *mulata*, with light-cocoa skin and big green, almond-shaped eyes.

"*Buenos dias,* how may I help you, *señor*?" she asked in good English, showing her beautiful white teeth.

"*Un cuarto, por favor.*"

"*Si como no,*" she replied. "We have a beautiful room overlooking the Malecón, *señor*. Would that be okay?"

"*Si, señorita,* that would be fine."

"*Cuarto* 323 on the third floor, *señor*. Enjoy your stay at Hotel Nacional." Nadine and I made our way to the elevator, she still admiring the wonderful decadence that was El Hotel Nacional.

The room was elegant, much like the rest of the place, with a beautiful view of the Malecón and the ocean beyond. Nadine, fearing that she wouldn't be able to wash up, checked the bathroom right away.

"Kiki, we have water," she said, laughing. She walked out of the bathroom and over to the king-size bed. There she flopped down, exhausted, closing her eyes. "I don't know about the rest of Cuba, Kiki, but this is heaven."

I let her enjoy the moment, knowing she would be spending a few days alone on the boat without any comfort at all.

It was about eight, and we hadn't eaten anything since the marina. The food was so-so here, also geared toward the tourist trade. We would eat at the hotel tonight and then go to the Cabaret Parisian, also located in the hotel.

"Nadine, I'm going down by the pool for a few minutes, to call Banco and have a drink. I'll be back in a few."

"I'm going to take a shower and enjoy the view while you're gone, Kiki. It's stunning isn't it?"

"Yeah *niña*," I said. I grabbed the satellite phone and made my way downstairs and out to the poolside bar.

"*Un mojito por favor,*" I asked the bartender, who wore a tuxedo uniform that made him look very 1940s.

"*Si como no,*" he replied. He started to prepare my drink.

Mojitos always seem to taste better in Cuba. I thought it was the nostalgia of it all that made me savor them more.

"*Aqui esta su mojito, señor,*" he said, putting the drink down in front of me. I left the money for the drink and tip on the bar and took a seat off in the corner by the pool.

When I walked down here from the room I went through the hotel's main bar. It was amazing to see pictures on the walls of all the famous people who used to frequent the Nacional. Frank Sinatra, Eva Gardener, Errol Flynn, Clark Gable and others I didn't recognize, but you could tell they were famous because the pictures were always of someone shaking their hands and posing for the shot. This place sure has got history, I thought. What if, I wondered, what if? What if they'd shot Fidel at Moncada, or when they caught him afterward on the run? Cuba would have become the 51st state. It would be just like Florida, only better.

I took my satellite phone and dialed Banco's number. When I looked up after dialing, I saw a nondescript man take a table two tables away from me. He pulled out a newspaper and began to read.

To my surprise, Banco answered right away. I got up and walked to the pool as he began to talk.

"Kiki, I'll be at the Nacional tomorrow at six PM. I'm flying to Merida, Mexico, tonight and on to Havana tomorrow around four-thirty," he blurted out before I could even say, "Hello, fat man."

"Slow down, Banco, slow down. What the hell are you talking about?"

"I'll be in Cuba tomorrow around six," he repeated. "Don't worry, Kiki, I've got business in Havana. Don't call De La Rosa. I'll talk to you when I get there." With that, he hung up. Banco wasn't much for phone talk.

I went back to the table, grabbed the *mojito* and gulped the rest of it down. Then I took a deep breath. What the fuck is going on? I wondered. This wasn't in the plans, and I wasn't sure I liked new twists this late in the game. It definitely took me by surprise and left me a little numb and nervous. I walked past the guy reading the newspaper and back through the lobby to the elevator.

Back in the room I found Nadine with the window wide open and a light breeze blowing in. She had a thick towel wrapped around her head, and another wrapped around her body. "I'm going to enjoy this while I can," she said.

"Banco will be here tomorrow around six. I just talked to him on the phone," I said, not paying attention to her enthusiasm. "I don't know what he's up to, but I don't like it. And he told me not to contact his man down here, De la Rosa. What the fuck is that about?"

Nadine stopped in mid-step and crossed her arms over her breasts.

"What do we do now?" she asked.

"Now we wait," I told her. "Now we wait. We have to wait, but we don't have to wait in here, *niña*," I wanted to lighten the mood again. "I'm going to take a shower and get this saltwater off my body. Then we're going to the restaurant to get ourselves a Cuban meal. Remember though, this is Cuba and this is the Hotel Nacional; the food will be expensive for our Yankee asses, and probably very mediocre."

"There you go again Kiki Logan, the optimistic soul. The water is working, though."

"All right, all right, I get your point. Half full, not half empty." We both laughed as I walked off to the shower.

Nadine was waiting for me and didn't say a word. I got ready and we made our way to the elevator, down to the lobby and to the restaurant. The walk was eerily quiet. The waiter showed us to our seats and I half expected Nadine to make another observation on the elegance of the Nacional. Instead the first thing out of her mouth was the thought I had in my head. "I wonder what Banco's doing."

"Yeah, we have to be careful, watch our step and wait to see what he has to say."

"I guess you're right," she replied, sounding slightly edgy.

The waiter had been standing there a few seconds for us.

"*Halgo para tomar, señor?*"

"*Niña*, what would you like? A *mojito?*"

"That sounds good, Kiki."

"*Por favor, un mojito y una Cuba libre.*"

"*Si señor, como no.*" He made his way over to the bar and was back in a flash with our drinks.

Like I said, in late July there weren't many people around, except for the fishing crowd. The restaurant was barely a third full. I listened to the people around us and heard Spanish. I could tell by their speech pattern and the words they used that it was Cuban Spanish. Cuban tourists, from Miami, they probably hadn't been out of Cuba more than a few years. For some reason the newer immigrants to the States were the ones that returned to Cuba most often to see their families, and ironically these same Cubans you saw in the tourist areas—where there was anything and everything they always wanted, spending their U.S. dollars—weren't even allowed in these areas before they became *balseros* and made it to the States.

The waiter came to take our order. We weren't really hungry after the news of Banco's trip down here, though the drinks were starting to take the edge off the anxiety.

I said to the waiter, "*Un sandwich Cubano y una media noche por favor.*"

"*Como no, señor,*" he replied.

We ordered the regular everyday fare you could get just about anywhere in Miami. A Cuban sandwich and a midnight sandwich, they were both ham and cheese and sliced, roasted pork sandwiches, one hot and toasted, one not—on different types of bread. We really couldn't go wrong with this simple order.

Tourist food seemed to suck in Cuba; for the most part the best food was had in private homes. But if those entrepreneurs were caught trying to make a dollar cooking for tourists, they went to jail. The government controlled everything, and that included deciding how to milk the gringos. So no private kitchens.

"I wonder what the hell Banco is thinking. Doesn't he realize that he could jeopardize everything? Fuck the job; it's us he could screw up," I said. "Nadine, we have to be really careful when we make contact with him tomorrow; we can't let anybody see us with him."

We finished our sandwiches just as Cabaret Parisian was getting started. The club had one of the best shows in Havana.

But my head was too cloudy from the combination of drinks, being on the ocean for three days, and the news of Banco coming to Cuba, to have anything to do with a cabaret show.

Nadine and I walked out of the hotel lobby and crossed Avenida Washington onto the Malecón. The sun had set about forty-five minutes before, and there was a half moon in a sky full of stars that shone on an eerily calm ocean. Not so much as a mist of spray came up over the sea wall. This was one of those nights when you instantly understood the famous allure of the Malecón.

All the locals were there, everywhere up and down the broad sidewalk, escaping the heat and humidity of an air conditioning-less July in Havana. Families, lovers, vendors, improv *salsa* bands and *jineteras*—it seemed that the heat brought everyone to the Malecón.

We walked for about an hour, enjoying the feel of the real Cuba. The salt air, the stars, that gentle breeze, the mingled voices and music, it all wafted over us like a pleasant dream. The lure of a comfortable bed kept calling us, though, and so we headed for the hotel, filed through the lobby past the beautiful *mulata* with big green eyes, over to the elevator and up to room 323.

"I'm really, really tired," Nadine said, "and that bed looks delicious."

She didn't wait for a response. She was talking to herself as she walked over to the bed, undressing on the way. The bra came off and the thong stayed on, but that made it all the sexier. She pulled back the covers, lay down, put a pillow between her legs, turned on her side and covered herself.

"Goodnight, Kiki."

"Goodnight, *niña*," I said. So much for the breasts, thong, and all that sexiness that I was just about to tear up.

I looked out the window for a while, over the great sea wall out onto the ocean, going over the sequence of events that brought me to this point and how they might change after Banco's trip. I would find out tomorrow what was up with the

Fat Man. I lay down next to Nadine, and it seemed that no sooner had I closed my eyes than it was morning.

I awoke to sunlight streaming in through open windows and open curtains.

"Shit, its ten o'clock. I could sleep all day," I said, more or less talking to myself. "I've been up for hours, I couldn't sleep," responded Nadine.

"Don't think about it, *niña;* we'll know soon enough." I wasn't listening to my own words; I couldn't stop thinking about Banco. "We should go to the boat and check her out— make sure she's ready. We might have to leave soon, and we don't want any hesitation."

I got up, dressed, and we gathered our things, went downstairs and called a cab.

"Marina Hemingway *por favor.*"

"*Si Señor, como no.*"

It was a busy day at Marina Hemingway. The big fish were running in the Florida Straits and so the money boys with their big-time fishing machines had come here in droves to see if they could catch a monster.

"*Como estas, señor* Logan?"

Raúl had been tending to a new arrival at the marina—more goodies for him, I was sure. The new suckers were in a beautiful Egg Harbor fishing rig. It must have been at least sixty feet. Plenty of cash there, the boat alone must have cost a million or two. Raúl would have a little bit more money to put into that '57 Nomad of his.

"*Como estas, Raúl?*"

"*Bien*, Mr. Logan. Your boat is secure, *señor;* I watched out for her."

He smiled as he shook my hand, but his attention was clearly on the new arrivals in the Egg Harbor. I didn't want him paying too much attention to me anyway.

I slipped him a twenty. "*Gracias, Raúl.*"

"*Gracias ha usted*, Mr. Logan."

"Raúl, we'll be here for an hour or so. I want to check the boat and have some lunch, and then I'm going back to Havana to show my lady the city. I'll probably be back tomorrow, and then we're going out for a day or so of fishing."

"Okay, Mr. Logan, I'll make sure she's fine. You can count on me."

With that, he was on his way back to the Egg Harbor and into a big hug from some asshole from Minnesota or Ohio or somewhere, letting everyone know he had money. Dumb fuck is lucky I'm not a thief, I thought, or I'd hit him for everything he has on that boat, including the boat. Get him, Raúl. He deserves getting raked over the coals.

"Let's get to the *Lean Back*, make sure we still have our gas, top off the fresh water, empty the cooler and the fish box, clean her up a little and cover her back up," I said.

When we'd completed our tasks we got a taxi and were back at the Nacional in no time. We went up to our room, put our bags down and got cleaned up.

"*Niña,* lets go to the Bodeguita."

"Hemingway's hangout?"

"Yep, the very same."

"Boy, Hemingway was all over this city, wasn't he?"

"Yeah he was a real *jinetero* in Havana; everyone knew him. The old man raised some hell down here in his day. Even Castro respected him."

"What kind of food do they have there, Kiki?"

"*Niña,* I already told you, tourist food sucks in Havana. We're going for a *mojito,* that's where it was perfected. La Bodeguita started out as a grocery store—hence its name. But in the 1940s the Bohemian set started going there for a bite to eat while they read their galleys from the print shop. After that, the owner started serving drinks and it became a serious scene for writers, poets, and painters. It was Hemingway's favorite hangout. There are graffiti and autographs all over the walls at La Bodeguita from everybody who was anybody back in the forties and fifties," I told Nadine. "Nowadays it's pretty much just tourists and *jineteras,* but the *mojitos* are legendary."

It must have been the nostalgia, but that place made you feel the history. Papa's ghost was in there, I was sure—that drunken bastard.

"Okay, I'm ready," Nadine said.

With that we were out the door and out of the hotel. I hailed a taxi, which were plentiful at this time of the year.

"*Ha* La Bodeguita del Medio, *por favor,*" I told the driver.

"*Si señor, un mojito eh?*" he said.

Our little tourist act seemed to work on the driver. He immediately assumed we wanted to drink a *mojito* where Papa drank his, like all the tourists. He was right; I wanted to drink my *mojito* where the big man drank his. But this ain't no tourist trip Dorothy, I thought.

"*Si, posiblemente dos*," I told him. He laughed and pointed the taxi toward the Malecón.

"*Por favor doble aqui y coje la rampa Calle 21.*" I asked our driver to take a different route instead of cruising along the Malecón again. I had a funny feeling, like someone was watching me. The driver glanced back momentarily in the rear view mirror smiled and said, "*Sin problema, senor*". If someone had been watching they already knew where we were staying. I just wanted to see if my hunch was right. The driver made a right onto Calle 21, drove a few blocks and once again I asked him to make a turn, a left on Avenida L, to go around the University of Havana, and then to take Avenida Neptuno to La Bodeguita. I told him I wanted to see something of Havana other than the Malecón. He shook his head in agreement and did as he was told, either not noticing my jitteriness or not caring.

"What did you ask him?" Nadine wondered.

"I just asked him to take the back route instead of the Malecón. Thought it would be nice to see even more squalor than you'd see along the waterfront."

Nadine pointed at the University of Havana. "That's not so bad."

"Yeah, well they keep the university spruced up. Just wait till you see Old Havana."

We turned off Avenida L onto Neptuno. At that point I looked behind us. I sure had a hunch about something, but saw nothing out of the ordinary.

As we passed from Vedado into the old city, the lawns and trees disappeared. We were in a proper city now, but one from the colonial period. The architecture was incredible, but it was still a slum, and a very primitive slum at that. Cuba had more 16th, 17th and 18th century colonial buildings than anywhere in the Americas. To their credit, they were still standing after hundreds of years of hurricanes and weathering. But they looked like they really couldn't take much more. Most of them looked like shit, incredible architecture or not.

"You hear so much about what a beautiful place Cuba is to visit, enjoy the beaches, explore Havana, smoke a cigar. The brochures are gorgeous, but this—this is ridiculous." Nadine was talking out loud to herself.

"Yeah, they need to put some of the tourism money back into the country. Probably all of the money. These people are way below the Mendoza Line," I replied.

Soon we caught a glimpse of El Capitolio, the dome of which towered above the ruins along Neptuno. Ironically, the building was designed to be an almost exact replica of the U.S. Capitol. Now it was where the communist government did whatever they did. Certainly that didn't include representing the people.

In a few minutes we were rolling down Calle Empedrado and pulling up at the Bodeguita.

As we entered, Nadine scanned the room. "This is quaint. Dirty, but quaint," she said sarcastically.

A waiter without much of a smile showed us to our table.

"*Gracias, dos mojitos por favor,*" I told him. He turned away with the same forced smile and made his way to the bar. I wouldn't have much of a smile either; they served *mojitos* all day long here. He returned to our table with our *mojitos* full and topped with fresh Cuban mint. They smelled great, and tasted even better.

"To Papa," I said, lifting my glass.

"To Papa," Nadine repeated. She downed her drink, tequila-shot style. I obliged her and did the same, and we ordered two more. That got a bit of a reaction from the bedraggled waiter as he went to get us two more *mojitos*, only seconds after having delivered the first. I had to laugh.

My mood changed when I glanced toward the bar. What I saw was a man looking at me. He turned away quickly.

I leaned toward Nadine and whispered, "You see that man in the khaki pants leaning on the bar? Be discreet when you look." She picked up her drink—to sip this time—and stole a peek.

Without missing a beat, she put her drink down and said, "Yes, and what about him?"

"I saw him earlier at the bar in the Nacional and now here, both times I caught him looking at me."

"Now you're getting paranoid, Kiki. He looks like a peasant, probably trying to make some money off the *turistas.*"

"Sure, like all Cubans here don't look like peasants. Don't underestimate them because of how they dress. This is a very poor country, and remember they've been raised under the threat of an American attack for decades; they're very adept at espionage. You're damn right I'm paranoid."

The mystery man had now gotten up and was walking out the door of the Bodeguita. Once outside, he turned left.

"Stay here, I'll be right back."

I went out the door and made a left, looking up Empedrado back toward the Capitolio. No sign of the man in khakis. I went back and paid the bill, then we grabbed a taxi.

In the car I explained my strategy. "I want you to go back to the hotel and wait in the lobby for Banco. Find out what room he's in. I'll be down by the pool, so as soon as you know come and get me. I don't want him to see either of us, but there's less of a chance he'll recognize you. Anyway, if something *is* wrong, I guarantee you he's being watched and followed. So try to figure out the floor he's on, but watch out for the people who are following him. You have to play it cool and not let anyone pin you. If they're on him, they'll spot you if you're not careful."

"Don't worry, Kiki, they won't see me."

Banco had said he would be there by six, and we arrived at twenty of.

I hurried through the lobby and back to the pool area after seeing Nadine settled in on a bench in the big garden right outside the hotel entrance. She had her novel and seemed pretty together. My biggest fear was that she would start turning those pages and forget all about Banco.

Nearly an hour later I looked up and saw Nadine approaching. She gave me a big smile and I smiled back with relief.

"Kiki, he's in room 427. He got in about fifteen minutes ago and checked in. It didn't look like anyone was following him so I went up in another elevator and saw him enter the room. I was very careful."

"Is he still there?" I asked her.

"As far as I know."

"We check out of here tomorrow," I told her. "I don't want to be here if the shit hits the fan. Let's go up and pay the Fat Man a visit; I'm anxious to hear his story."

We walked back through the lobby and over to the elevator. I was careful to take notice of who was there in case Banco really was being followed. It might have been hard to spot Cuban secret service at the Bodeguita, but not at Havana's only luxury hotel. It didn't seem watched to me as I discretely scanned the lobby. Then we got in the elevator but only went to the third floor just in case. We went to our room and then I walked alone up the stairwell to the fourth floor.

CHAPTER II

I knocked on the door to room 427.

"Come on in," I heard through the door. I entered.

"Put it over there," Banco said, mistaking me for room service.

"I hope you fucking tip well," I said. Banco turned quickly, caught by surprise.

"Kiki, you son of a bitch, I was waiting for your call."

"You told me you'd be here tonight, right Banco?" I said. "No need for a phone call—here I am. I just want to know what the fuck you're doing here. Have plans changed?"

"No, no everything is fine. I'm here on something completely unrelated. I just didn't want you talking to De La Rosa until I talked to him. I need to talk to him about some other business ventures first and then feel him out about the heist. I didn't want him to know what you're up to yet. I understand these people, Kiki. Believe me, it can't hurt."

Banco sounded very confident. For the time being, I would regard his trip to Cuba as a mere coincidence.

"I'm meeting up with him tomorrow. You carry on with your plans and we'll talk by phone afterwards," Banco finished.

"No problem, Banco. But if you don't mind me asking, what are these unrelated business ventures?"

"Well I do mind, Enrique; it's none of your business," he said.

"Let me tell you something, motherfucker," I snapped. "What we have is a working relationship. And when I'm on a job for you and my life is on the line, and suddenly you show up on the work site and the plans didn't call for you to be here, I make it my business to know what the fuck you're doing. This ain't Kansas, I ain't Dorothy and you're not the Wizard of Oz. Okay, Banco?" I was pissed as I pointed at him and barked my disapproval.

"Easy, Kiki, easy," Banco said. His perpetual grin disappeared when he realized I meant business. "It's not a big deal. De La Rosa's people needed a connection for some contraband—probably cocaine, or some artwork out of Colombia—and they wanted my help. I thought I could come for a few days and enjoy Havana, killing two birds with one stone. Our original plans, and then their using my connections, all for a nice fee," he said.

"You're telling me that the Cubans don't have a connection out of South America? I find that hard to believe."

"Not really," Banco said. "They've always been able to use major ports and airports because of the involvement of the higher-ups, especially in Colombia and Venezuela. In Colombia they dealt a lot with the guerrilla factions, especially F.A.R.C."

I paid enough attention to know he meant *Fuerzas Armadas Revolucionarias de Colombia*, known friends of the Cuban government. Banco kept talking. "The problem now is that the U.S. involvement and their constant pouring of money into the drug war, and Colombia's own government fighting back to rid their country of the guerrilla factions and the cartels, has made things increasingly difficult."

Banco paused for a moment and smiled, then continued, "You know, Kiki, the world is much smaller than it used to be and Uncle Sam's arm keeps getting longer. The pressure the U.S. puts on these countries is incredible. And Venezuela, let me tell you, is being watched like a hawk because of leftist friendship with Castro. Maracaibo was a hotspot because of its large ship and airplane traffic, but since all the kidnappings, assassinations, skyjackings, and bombings building up from the late seventies till now, and then with the recent U.S. reaction, well, no more baby, no more."

"Okay, Banco, that tells me what might be a minor hitch for them. But what the fuck—if they can't get it done, how the hell can you?"

Banco sat in a finely upholstered, high back, art deco chair by the big window overlooking the Malecón, leaned back with contentment. "Kiki, *mi hijo*, years ago I had some problems trying to get out some uncut Colombian emeralds. It ended up costing me half of my stones. They told me that pressure from the U.S. and the central government was getting unbearable and it cost them much more to transport and the higher ups demanded more because of the added risks and pressure. Right then and there I decided to find another way. And that way was the Guajira," he said.

"You mean La Guajira, that peninsula north of Santa Marta in Colombia, next to Venezuela?"

"The one and only, my boy, the one and only. Back in the day, and still today, it was hard to get to La Guajira from Colombia. You would start seeing a lot of army patrols around Santa Marta, as you traveled along the Caribbean coast toward Riohacha, and then on to the peninsula of La Guajira. They had good reason to warn people about that area. Even the Colombian army wouldn't go there. The indigenous people are a proud people who don't believe in Colombian or Venezuelan authority over them. They believe that their land had been left to them by their ancestors thousands of years ago. And who were the Colombian and Venezuelan governments to impose land borders on them and make them carry travel papers whenever they crossed those borders? Needless to say, problems arose, and continued to arise, even though not as frequently anymore. The governments of Colombia and Venezuela have, for the most part, left them alone. It is an uneasy peace, but peace none the less. When you see Guajiros you immediately think of National Geographic: bowl haircuts, thongs, almost naked, women bare-breasted and suckling infants while other children run around them."

Banco went on. "The National Geographic similarities end there. These little pricks aren't carrying bows and arrows and blowguns, no sir. They're carrying AK-47s and AR-15s and they love to use them. Just give them a reason and they'll kill you as quick as they look at you.

"For years the Guajiros, because of the location of their land at the tip of northern Colombia on the Caribbean, have been involved in black market and drug trade. They formed an alliance with the cartels. The cartels would overland their merchandise to La Guajira, and the Guajiros would allow them to use their land. Sometimes there would be 10 to 15 planes up on the peninsula waiting to be loaded with contraband. In the early days there would be DC 3s there all year long carrying 10,000-pound loads of some of the sweetest Santa Marta Gold Ganja that you could ever want to smoke, straight to Bimini. They used to unload two to three planes a night in Bimini. Forty-seven miles off the U.S. coast. How sweet was that? Then the U.S. paraquated the Santa Marta Mountains and fucked everything right up. Soon after that you didn't see reefer coming out of Colombia, but the cocaine floodgates opened up and the rest is history. They kind of brought the onslaught of the cocaine cowboys upon themselves. The cartels now had a jumping off point to the Caribbean and the U.S. and Bahamas, saving themselves thousands of miles of air travel or ship travel which could easily be picked up by radar. In turn the Guajiros were paid, and handsomely. Thus the acquisition of AK-47s and AR-15s among other modern niceties they would acquire. Can you see where I'm going with this, Kiki?" Banco asked. "I had a Venezuelan friend. Julio Ruiz—he's gone now. I heard he'd been taken in for questioning by the Venezuelan secret police and no one has seen him since. That was about ten years ago.

Julio was from Maracaibo and he had contacts in Los Fulidos, also in Venezuela. That's the southern point of their territory on the Venezuelan side where the Guajiros have their Guajiro Market. It's the only place other than the wild upper peninsula where you can see Guajiros in the Guayacos, a cross between a diaper and a very short sarong. It's unbelievable. You go back in time when you're there. The National Guard warns you about even being there, let alone further north. 'Border problems and drug trafficking,' they quote. Julio got me in with the Guajiros and ever since we've had a working relationship. Just don't fuck them over or you'll never be able to go there again. They don't forgive and they don't forget and if you fuck them over and they get their hands on you, their justice is quick and lethal—you're dead. I was up in the peninsula one time setting up some transport for PreColumbian artifacts that I had just acquired in Baranquilla and there were about twelve to fifteen planes, all of them with engines running and waiting to be cleared for take off by the Guajiros. There was every kind of plane you could imagine, Piper Aztecs; Cessna 310s, Cessna 421s, even a Cessna 210, a goddam single-engine plane. I was talking to one of the *jefes,* when suddenly one of the Guajiros who was directing the planes and wasn't watching what he was doing backed into the propeller of a plane waiting for clearance. Needless to say there were body parts flying everywhere. It was the goriest thing I have ever witnessed in my life. Without even showing any concern for his fellow Guajiro, the *jefe* ordered two men to the plane whose propeller had accidentally hacked his countryman to death and ordered them to fire on the two men in the plane, who were still in shock about what had just happened. The two Guajiros opened fire with their machine guns and killed the two pilots instantly. Without even blinking, he ordered the plane pushed off the runway and into a ditch, and waved the next plane into position. I freaked the fuck out. It scared the living shit out of me."

Banco sat there for a second as he thought about what he had just told me. He looked as if he had shocked himself silly with his recounting of the incident.

Kiki didn't quite see how this connected with the problem the Cubans were having. "So you mean to tell me that the Colombians or the Venezuelans can't use the Guajiros anymore?" I asked. "After all, you just told me they had the connection for reefer, and then the cartels had the coke connection through there. What happened?"

"Medellin has been losing power to the Cali cartel and they've been forced to work with the guerilla factions, mainly F.A.R.C., and the Guajiros don't trust them. They're just another government to them. And the Americans' unending war on drugs is slowly but surely disintegrating that link, the one between Medellin and La Guajira. But I, little old Banco, I still have my connection with the *jefes* in the Guajira. They seem to like me and I pay well."

"So if you have the hookup in South America, why here, why now?" I asked. "Why fool around with the Cubans when they're not major players in the game?"

"The Cubans *are* major players. Cuba is a perfect mid point for transshipping, like it has been for eternity, so I need to please the Cubans as well. This is a crazy world; sometimes when people ask you to jump you just need to say, 'How high?' So here I am, Kiki. Anyway, like I said, a few days in Havana will do me some good. It's not that I planned it this way. I just got the call and I had to come. I know how you must feel, Kiki, but believe me, everything is fine. I'll be gone the day after tomorrow."

Banco had a smile on his face once again, as if the story he had just told me was supposed to make me feel better about his sudden trip to Havana.

"No problem, Banco," I said, looking at him seriously. "I'm going to call you the day after tomorrow to give you a progress report, so you'd better be in Miami."

"That's good, Kiki. Call me the day after tomorrow, in the evening, and I'll be at Versailles on Eighth in Miami, having some Cuban coffee."

I turned toward the door of Banco's hotel room.

"Let me know about De La Rosa when I call you. I'll stay away from him until then," I said.

"Everything is fine, Kiki; call me the day after tomorrow." Banco got up from his comfy chair, walked over to me waiting by the door, shook my hand and said, "Good luck, *hermano*."

Banco had a way of making you feel at ease with whatever he wanted you to do.

I smiled at him and said, "Go home *amigo*, I'll take care of this."

He laughed a loud laugh and patted me on the back, and with that I walked out of his room and took the stairs down to my room, being careful to make sure I wasn't seen.

Nadine asked me what Banco was up to and I just couldn't get into the whole thing right then. I told her I would explain it all later. We decided to stay in and order room service, as our anxiety levels were more than a little high and I didn't want to be out and about in a paranoid state, always looking over my shoulder.

I ordered a bottle of rum from room service and asked them to bring a menu up. Rum would have to do since I didn't have any weed. They were quick and we picked out some things from the menu and placed the order—just a few Cuban empanadas, some pastelitos and a bottle of cheap white wine for Nadine. The bellhop left and I poured out a shot of Habana Club on the rocks for Nadine and a big glass, neat, for myself. We clinked glasses and Nadine took a sip. I took a gulp. Nadine didn't really like rum and was being a good sport.

I wasn't much of a conversationalist just then, as I thought about what Banco had told me. But Nadine needed to know and her questions were inevitable.

"Will everything be all right, Kiki? Is the game still on?"

"I don't know, *niña*; I don't really know what's going on right now. We'll have to play it by ear."

"But what is Banco up to? Why is he here?"

I tried to explain Banco's Cuba connection, the deals he had going on with the Venezuelans and Colombians.

The bellhop arrived with the food and wine. We tried to make a nice little meal at the table but I couldn't get more than a couple of bites down, so I turned back to my rum and let the thoughts run through my head while Nadine contentedly ate her meal. How deep was Banco's connection in Cuba? I wondered. How high up did his people go? Were these powerful government officials or black-market crooks? Even if they went all the way up the ladder of power, there was still trouble in this Cuba connection. And even if Banco's Colombia job had Castro's sanction, it nonetheless meant he was patting Castro on the back with one hand and stealing from his pocket with the other. Banco was fucking crazy!

I turned back to the bottle of rum and this time took a big swig right from the bottle. I got up with the bottle, walked over to the window and looked out over the wide-open expanses of the Florida Straits. Big billowy clouds followed by towering thunderheads were speeding across the darkening sky from west to east.

I opened the window and a strong, humid wind blew through the room. Standing there in a pair of shorts, no shirt, with a half-empty bottle of Habana Club in my hand, I let the wind caress my body and my mind as the affects of the rum were slowly but surely taking over.

I looked back at Nadine and told her I was sorry.

"Kiki, if I don't know you by now, I'd better give up. This is how you solve problems. I've seen it a million times before."

"Well it's not working this time, *niña*. I haven't figured anything out. I just know we're in deep shit. End of story."

Nadine poured herself another glass of wine and joined me at the window, putting her arms around me in a noble attempt to comfort me. "If that's true, Kiki, then let's enjoy our last day on Earth."

I threw one arm around her bare shoulders while the other hand clung tightly to the bottle of rum. We stared out the window as the impending summer storm began to blow harder and heat lightning spidered across the sky, lighting everything up brighter than Carnival time. But the light only showed the emptiness of the old Malecón, the palms thrashing in the wind and the drizzle that was quickly becoming a downpour. The wind carried sprinkles of rain through the window that pricked our faces and arms. The air and rain were magical and we left the window open as we hugged each other tightly

Time went by and the anxiety melted away. As my mood changed my attitude to the situation Banco had created also changed. That feeling of comfort and security in one another's arms made me see the looming danger differently. I felt a kind of stoicism, or more than that, a sense of nobility. I was acting on principle and this was an important cause, maybe the most important thing I had done in my life. One had to take a stand, one had to take risks. If harm and pain followed, then so be it. It would be worth it.

I turned to Nadine and smiled, not saying a word. With my other hand still clutching the bottle of Habana Club rum I slung it over her shoulder and embraced her in a passionate kiss.

She gazed into my eyes and said, "Let's not think about it any more, Kiki. Tonight we have each other, and many more nights to come."

I laughed a slurred laugh as she led me to the king-size bed in the comfort and splendor of El Hotel Nacional.

"Tonight is ours and we're not going to waste it."

I knew she was giddy and excited with her fear of the mystery that lay ahead of us. If in the storm and the rum I had found my noble cause, Nadine had now had a vision of danger and adventure that she had only experienced once before in her life. It was that time the whirlpool nearly dragged her down.

"We shall defeat the whirlpool!" I slurred in a mock toast with the bottle.

Her eyes lit up when she saw the connection.

"Oh, Kiki, you really are my hero," she said laughing.

She took the bottle of rum out of my hand—which took some doing since I had begun to consider it as my safety blanket—and lay me down on the bed for a blissful night of exhilarating sex that made me forget everything. It was so good I even forgot my name for awhile. The one thing I did remember was that all was now well.

CHAPTER 12

The knock at the door woke me up . Nadine had tossed and turned all night and had gotten up early. She had ordered coffee and it was the arrival of room service that made me jump to attention.

Dealing with the hangover was the first order of business. I sat in a chair overlooking the Malecón and added the last bit of rum to my cup of coffee. I wasn't above a little hair of the dog.

The day was sunny and clear and I was trying to focus, looking out over the old seawall at the beautiful blue water beyond. It seemed like an abstract painting, given my condition.

By this time Nadine had gotten back in bed and was trying to snooze, getting a little of the sleep she hadn't gotten last night. For me the situation was improving. My special medicine seemed to be working. The rum had gotten rid of the headache and the coffee was waking me up.

It was very quiet out there this morning, as it was a Sunday, and it was probably already getting hot. Everybody was staying in and enjoying the remainder of the night's coolness in their rooms.

Looking out the window, I noticed Banco standing by the Malecón talking to three men. I watched casually for a minute, not really thinking much of it; he was here to meet some people, so I thought that was them. But only for a moment.

I suddenly jumped up. "SHIT!! Get up, *niña*, get up! We have to get the hell out of here! Come on! Come on!"

"What's the matter, Kiki? I'm so tired I can hardly move," she said as she hazily got out of bed.

I grabbed her by the arm, stood her up and shouted, "Banco's been snatched!"

"What?!" she gasped, wide awake now.

"I was just sitting at the window, right there in the chair, looking out at the Malecón, and I noticed Banco talking to three guys. They were pretty much by themselves, nobody around. I was watching for a minute or so, not really thinking much of it, when all of a sudden two of the men grabbed him and the other man and forced them into a Mercedes that was parked there. I hadn't noticed the Mercedes before, but they had a driver in the car waiting for them. Banco probably knew they had him when he saw the setup, but it was too late by then. Let's go, *niña*, we have to get the fuck out of here."

Nadine didn't say a word. The surprise I just gave her woke her up better than that liquid cocaine they call Cuban coffee.

We grabbed our things, tried to calm ourselves, got in the elevator and walked through the lobby to the desk. I did a quick scan and didn't see any trouble. We checked out and looked for a taxi at the hotel's entrance. Nothing. We ran down to Avenida Washington and tried to hail one.

While we waited, the thought of Banco being abducted kept running through my head like a bad dream, only it was Nadine and me in his place, being shoved into the car and driven away, probably to be beaten halfway to death and tortured.

I tried to figure out a plan. We could take a taxi to the marina but we'd have to get out before we arrived there and figure out how to look over the place in case the Secret Service was watching the *Lean Back*. If we could check in to a nearby hotel we'd have a base for reconnaissance. Or maybe we should just run for it, hop in the boat and gun the engines.

A taxi approached, and I tried to flag it down but the driver turned his head away and pretended not to see us. Suddenly a car appeared, speeding toward us along the avenue. It was nondescript by Havana standards, a Russian Lada, except for the telltale sign of heavily tinted windows, a sight not seen in Cuba. Probably G-2, Cuba's equivalent to the Gestapo, who answered only to Castro himself.

It screeched to a stop in front of us and two men jumped out, one from the passenger side, one from the rear. Without hesitation, they grabbed us and pushed us into the rear seat of the car. It all happened so fast, but I did manage to yell out at the two people on the sidewalk. There were more along the Malecón across the avenue. They just kept walking as we disappeared into the Lada. They would have seen scenes like this before. They avoided eye contact and went about their business.

The two men quickly got back in the car and we sped away heading south along La Rampa. I looked in the rear view mirror of the car and immediately recognized the driver. It was the same man I had seen in the bar at the Nacional and at La Bodeguita, the man in the khakis. My paranoia was right. We were being watched, and now they had us.

I looked at Nadine and there was terror in her eyes. She was hyperventilating and shaking, and looked like she was going to pass out. She grabbed my hand and I pressed it firmly. I nodded to her as much to say that we would be all right, that things would work out. It was a lie, I was certain of that.

No one spoke as the car sped and wove through the streets of Vedado heading south out of Havana. The driver worked his way to the *autopista*, drove for about five minutes, then turned onto another road and drove to what seemed to be a junkyard with old cars and scrap metal lying everywhere. The driver parked the car behind a makeshift fence. Hastily he and the two men got out of the car and escorted us to a small house in the midst of all the junk and debris strewn about the property.

Inside, an elderly woman prepared Cuban coffee in the tiny kitchen. A table, a few chairs and a weatherbeaten couch adorned the one-room shack.

The driver of the car was definitely the man that had been watching me at La Bodeguita. He pulled up two chairs.

"*Sientese por favor*, sit down please, Mr. Logan. Would you like some *café Cubano*?" We sat down on the chairs and waited.

"Don't worry Mr. Logan, we're not G-2, we're not with the

government. You're lucky you have a brother who loves you and is worried for your safety. My name is Nestor Martin."

My brother, I thought to myself, has no idea I'm down here, nor does anyone else.

"Maxi Betancur called me and alerted me that you might be coming to Cuba with some foolish ideas. The fat man, whom you might have noticed was taken into custody, was being watched from the moment he landed, and if you have anything to do with him I suggest you leave Cuba right away, señor. We may have just saved your lives."

I couldn't believe our luck. "Maxi, that wonderful son of a bitch. I'll have to thank him when I see him," I said. Maybe he did save my ass. It wouldn't be the first time.

Nadine hadn't said a word during the whole ride. She was still shaking and quivering. I put my hand on her shoulder and told her everything was okay, that she could relax. She finally seemed to understand and let out a deep breath she had been holding for what seemed to be an eternity. Still, no words came from her. A slight smile crossed her face and she reached across and held my hand as she looked into my eyes. I smiled back, if only for a second.

The old lady finished making the coffee and brought us each a cup. Neither she nor the other two men with Nestor joined the conversation.

"We are Anti-Castro revolutionaries, Mr. Logan, taking time to save you from your foolish games, in a country that doesn't like gringos. We have a country and people we care about and fight for on a daily basis. I respect Maxi very much, Mr. Logan, but I won't be doing this favor for him again, be sure of that.

"You have put us in danger, and by being here now you're putting this community in danger. You must leave and you must leave right away. Your boat at Marina Hemingway will be picked up and taken to Cojimar. You'll pick it up there, and then you must leave Cuba, Mr. Logan."

"My boat? Who's going to be fucking with my boat?"

"You can't afford to worry about that. Your lives are at stake. Just know that your boat will be at the marina at Cojimar tonight, and you will not be in Cuba tomorrow."

The old lady who had served us coffee had left and now returned with a bundle of clothes in her hand. Nestor took them from her and put them on the old table in front of us.

"Here, change into these clothes. You look like real *turistas* in your sandals and new T-shirts advertising the wonders of America."

He pointed to one of the men who had been our abductors. "Miguel will drive you back to Habana. From there, go to Cojimar, but don't arrive until after dark. You will find someone waiting for you at the marina with your boat. Once Miguel drops you off you're on your own, Mr. Logan; we won't be able to help you any further. Now hurry up and get changed. You must leave here *rapido*. This place is getting hotter by the second, and everyone is in danger as long as you're here."

Nadine took that as a direct order. She stood, walked to the corner of the room and began to undress down to her panties and bra. Nestor and his two partners turned their backs to

Nadine, giving her some privacy. She had completely caught them by surprise with her brashness, and I could see in their faces surprise at her reaction to the orders.

"*Que guapa, una mujer con fuerza y actitude, asi me gusto, com conviccion.*"

The old lady stood there and commented as she watched Nadine expose herself without self-consciousness. A strong woman with attitude and conviction, she had said.

I shrugged my shoulders and said with a guffaw, "Don't worry about her, she's French."

They looked my way and smiled, half nodding as they acknowledged the uninhibited ways of those unique beings, the French. They must have gotten an eyeful of some French *turista* honeys exhibiting their curves on the beach before.

I quickly grabbed the clothes on the table and walked to the corner where Nadine was changing and began to do likewise. She had on a tube top and a pair of culotte shorts that were straight out of the early seventies, while I had a pair of pants that were older than dirt and a retro Miami Dolphins T-shirt. I vaguely remembered the old Dolphins logo. I was a big New York Jets fan, and I hated the Dolphins, but for some reason I seemed to remember more about the Dolphins than I did the Jets. Our shoes were also traded in for a pair of the raggediest kicks I had ever seen. At least we wouldn't be mistaken for *turistas*. Nestor ushered us to the door and a waiting car with Miguel ready to take us back to Havana.

"*Valla con dios mi amigo.* " Nestor reached out to me. "You must leave Cuba, *señor*. Things are not safe for you here now."

I shook his hand. "Maxi's man in Havana," I said. "*Gracias* Nestor, I owe you my life. I'll say hello to Maxi for you."

With that I turned and Nadine and I got into the car with Miguel. Another Russian Lada, only this one was rundown and common. No nice interior or heavily tinted windows or fine-tuned engine. Just what the doctor ordered. We had to blend in—or else.

We drove out of the yard strewn with all its junk and onto a small street with tall trees and lovely old houses. A sign read "*San Fransisco de Paula, Museo Hemingway, Finca Vigia.* We were driving by Papa's old homestead, where he lived the better part of his life. A couple more turns and we were soon on the *Autopista Nacional*, heading back to Havana.

Miguel glanced back at us and smiled. "Señor, do you know Havana? I mean, the streets. Do you know your way around?"

Miguel looked like Cuba's revolutionary poet hero, José Martí. Medium height, thin torso, receding hairline, and like Martí, he had one of those pencil-thin drooping mustaches. He looked like a Boston Blackie from the 1940s.

"I am going to drop you off here, at the cemetery." He pointed in front of us and we saw a vast necropolis in the distance.

"The best way for you to not stand out is to be on the street, walking. If you stayed in one spot you would end up talking to people, and they would discover you're a foreigner and then assume you're a spy. So I'm dropping you off at the cemetery because it's a couple hours' walk from Cojimar. Do you know the way to Cojimar from here?"

I was pretty sure where we were. "We're near the Plaza de la Revolucion, right?"

"Yes, señor, that's right over there," Miguel said, pointing. We could see the top of the tall modern monument in that plaza a couple blocks away."

Miguel pulled over and stopped the car. "You'll be safe if you just keep moving." Go into the cemetery and make sure you're not being followed. Then leave the cemetery and take the route to Cojimar, always moving. Be sure to arrive in Cojimar after dark for your pick-up, but don't be too late. *Suerte señor.*"

We got out of the car and Miguel drove off.

CHAPTER 13

We stood in front of an arched stone entrance marked "Cementerio de Colon." People strolled in and out, most wearing white, with Santeria beads draped around their necks.

I shot Nadine a questioning look. She replied quickly.

"Well, this is as good a place as any," she said. "And it's probably very interesting too. It looks like whoever built it went out of their way to be extravagant and gaudy. Let's go have a look." She took my hand and we passed under the stone arch.

"I don't mean to be morbid, Nadine, but we have one foot in the grave as it is. I don't want to put both in just yet." I said jokingly.

"*Ferme ta bouche,* Kiki, let's go."

It was definitely an eerie place.

"You know Kiki, they took Banco. We were probably next. Nestor and your friend Maxi probably saved our lives."

"But it's weird, *niña.* At least from what I could tell we weren't being followed. Nobody seemed to suspect us. Think about how many Americans come down for the fishing and end up spending a night at the Nacional just for the fun of it."

"True," she said. "But there's one thing you haven't thought of. They could make Banco talk, use torture to make him spill his guts and talk about the plan."

"Yeah, that crossed my mind. If that happens, we're screwed. They'll start a manhunt. Good thing they moved the *Lean Back*. If they do an all-points bulletin, Raúl at the marina will see it and will probably squeal, spy or no spy. He'd save his neck."

"With the boat gone, maybe they'll think we already left the country," she said tentatively.

"No, because if Raúl talks, he'll say it was someone else who took the boat, that it wasn't us. They'll know we're still at large in Cuba."

"Kiki, we just have to follow the plan and cross our fingers and hope for the best. It's all we can do."

"You're right, *niña*. No creative thinking, no new strategies, I promise. Just stick to the plan."

We continued on our way through the cemetery. There seemed to have been a competition to see who could outdo the other in family tombs. The result was a decadent, morbid atmosphere, something straight out of a Stephen King film. I half-expected someone to jump out from behind one of the macabre statues with a blood-drenched knife and attack us. As we continued our walk through the array of Grecian temples, urns, columns, Madonnas, crucified Christs and angels of mercy all watching diligently over their deceased, I noticed once again the abundance of people wearing Santeria beads and praying or performing ritual ceremonies at crypts and monuments.

We walked past a mausoleum with a large statue of San Lázaro with a faithful dog lying supine at his feet. In front of San Lázaro stood an elderly lady in a long white dress and a white scarf around her head. She was heavyset, and couldn't have been more than five feet tall.

As we walked past, she slowly turned to us. I noticed she had many sets of beaded necklaces around her neck, all white and red. We drew closer, and she gazed into my eyes with a steady stare, not once looking toward Nadine. Her eyes were jet black and deepset in their sockets. She didn't move a finger. It felt as though she could see into my soul.

Suddenly she uttered the words, *"Cuidate, mi hijo."*

She had a little burlap sack, embroidered with beads, in her hand, and she raised it and shook it three times in front of my face. Then, as calmly as she had faced me. She turned away and continued her chanting and praying at the feet of the life-size statue of San Lázaro and his loyal dog.

Nadine tugged at my arm to continue our walk and asked, "What did she say, Kiki?"

"She said to take care of myself."

"That was spooky, Kiki."

It didn't surprise me that Nadine would find that behavior a little strange. I don't think Western Europeans are well-versed on the spiritual world of the Caribbean. To them Santeria is all voodoo and zombies.

It was around 6 o'clock and I wanted to get going. We needed to get to the docks down on Calle O'Reilly where we could catch a ferry to a little town across Havana Harbor called Casablanca. From there it was only about a half hour walk to Cojimar, where we would, we hoped, pick up the *Lean Back*.

We left the city of the dead and began our walk through West Havana toward Habana Vieja, enjoying the architecture and smell and feel of the city. The whole time my head was on a swivel, watching out that we didn't get taken for another car ride, this time a deadly one.

An hour later we'd made it by the Plaza de la Revolucion, the stadium and finally down O'Reilly street to the docks and the ferry. The boat would carry us across the harbor and out into the bay to Casablanca, all for only ten *centavos*. Ten centavos, that was unbelievable. If you were a foreigner, it was almost like they were paying you for the ride instead of vice versa, and from what I'd heard of these rickety boats they should have paid you for riding on them. The dockworker who handled the ferry told us it would be about half an hour before the next trip. We sat down and waited in the cool breeze coming off the bay with other patrons of the ride, who all seemed to be Habaneros, not a *turista* among them that I could tell. I was hoping we blended right in.

Ten minutes went by and I couldn't stand the tension anymore. And anyway, Miguel had told us to keep moving. We wandered over to the ancient square right behind the docks, called the Plaza de Armas. We strolled about, admiring the gardens and the venerable facades on the periphery of the square. As we walked about we were surprised to find that we were avoided by the street vendors and *jiniteras* working the tourists. It was nice to know the costumes worked. And it was interesting to be on the other side of the equation. I had to laugh when I thought about the $40,000 I carried in my pocket.

Before we knew it, it was time to head back. As we approached the docks we could see the ferry coming in. When we got there we found the ferry entrance thronged with people waiting to board—about fifty passengers trying to squeeze on this tiny boat. What if we couldn't get on? Were there more ferries? Would we miss our connection for the *Lean Back*?

Everyone was shoving and pushing as the entrance gate opened up, and we were no exception. We made our way up the ramp, paid our fare, stepped onto the rundown old boat and found a spot at the stern. People continued to board and push back toward the stern and at one point we became afraid we'd get shoved over the railing. Some passengers were in fact stepping over the railing and standing on the little ledge beyond, holding on for dear life.

Finally the pushing stopped and the boat whistle blew. We chugged backward and set course for Casablanca. We were uncomfortable, but at least we could relax. Nadine and I didn't speak for fear of being overheard and identified as non-natives. But we communicated with our eyes, which Nadine continued to mischievously roll. This crowding would definitely be a violation in the States, and there was not a life jacket in sight. It looked exactly like the public bus system in Cuba, and its alternative transportation system, the trucks and cars that pick up people hitchhiking, something that always seemed comical to me. The ride across the bay and it had all the potential of a disaster just waiting to happen.

The other passengers seemed unaffected. They talked, laughed, and some even sang. Many people began to drop little pieces of paper in the water on our ride across the bay. I couldn't figure out why but I didn't ask. Everyone except Nadine and I knew what was up, and if I asked we would have stuck out like a sore thumb. I later found out that it was a Santeria ritual, ridding them of bad luck and giving them better luck. Luck is something I thought we needed. I couldn't wait to get off that death trap and back on my own boat.

Soon we pulled up to a dock on the east side of the bay, in the ramshackle little town of Casablanca. There were balconied houses along the waterfront, and it exuded a sleepy, laid-back air. But what was different was that dominating the bay was a big statue of Christ, carved out of stone. I didn't think there was one town in all of Cuba that didn't have some kind of religious artifact at its center. This was ironic, given the fact that the Revolution outlawed religion nearly from the beginning. You would have thought that the communist party would have torn them down and gotten rid of them, but there they were, everywhere you looked.

The ferry tied off to the dock and the mirthful passengers crowded off the boat, everyone still talking and laughing, seemingly unaware of their brush with danger. I was just glad to get off that leaky raft with an engine that they called a ferry.

We walked through the small colonial town, making our way toward Cojimar, which lay three miles away. It was about eight-thirty, and the midsummer sun was getting low on the horizon. I noticed a group of people waiting on the side of the road, and I asked a young woman holding her infant son by the hand where they were headed. They were waiting for a flatbed truck to catch a ride to her hometown of Cojimar, and sure enough, a truck pulled up as we were speaking. Nadine and I climbed aboard the flatbed with the others, and once again we were on an overcrowded ride with people hanging from the sides. This time, we rode an old beat-up truck that could do no more than twenty miles per hour. Nonetheless it was a short fifteen-minute ride, and we were soon in the fishing village of Cojimar, a palm-fringed town with a very relaxed feel.

Getting out of the truck in the town's central square, we went down to the docks along a path Hemingway must have walked many times when coming to his boat for fishing trips. He kept his boat, the *Pilar*, moored at the docks here.

When we arrived at the waterfront, it was almost dark, the last light of the day in the sky above the wide-open expanses of the ocean to the north. We weren't prepared for the crowd of people we found. There were about thirty of them milling around on shore, all in a state of flux, scurrying about nervously, almost all of them looking out at the ocean. Some of the women were being comforted by the men as they sobbed, eyeing the angry seas.

"What do you think, *niña?* Why are these people looking out at the sea?"

"Kiki, I think it's a boating accident, fishermen probably, don't you think?

"That sounds right. I'm curious, and I'd ask if it weren't so dangerous. Maybe we'll find out."

A boat was tied at the far end of the dock. It looked like the *Lean Back*, but night was falling fast, and I couldn't be sure until we got closer. I looked around for anyone watching us. This would be the obvious spot for a trap. Nothing. We quickened our pace to reach her as soon as possible. But walking down the dock back toward us was a man who had clearly just left the *Lean Back*. If this were my contact, I knew I wouldn't recognize him—he'd just be one of Nestor's many foot soldiers. How would he know we were the Americans who owned the boat? I had to think of something. But when we came face to face I was completely taken by surprise.

"*Senor* Logan, hurry, *apurate*, come with me." He quickly turned and hastily walked back up the dock toward the boat. It was Raúl from Marina Hemingway.

"Raúl, what the fuck are you doing there?" I asked in amazement, quickly beginning to put things together in my head. "I guess you know the people who took me for a ride earlier."

"*Si, si, señor*, they are my *compadres*."

"What's up with all those people? They look worried and upset."

"They're the family members of a group of people who left on rafts for America last night, from the beach over there. It's a good point of departure for catching the gulf currents that take them north, to the Keys and mainland Florida. As you can see, the weather has become very rough out there. They sure picked the wrong time; the weather caught them. Bad weather in the summertime comes from the south, the Caribbean; this makes the currents stronger and faster. If they get lucky it'll be a quicker trip—too bad that the weather will also destroy their rickety little rafts. Poor bastards, I hope they make it, but I don't think they will. Not it in those seas. *Señor* Logan, *apurate, you must go*," Raúl urged.

We hurried to the slip where the *Lean Back* was tied, and jumped on board. Nadine undid the canvas covers that Raúl hadn't already taken off. I went over all my mechanicals to make sure everything was right. It was going to be rough out there and the boat had to be ready for what was ahead.

I saw that Raúl was untying a dinghy behind the *Lean Back*. "You think of everything, right, Raúl? Did you tow that here?" I asked.

"That's right, señor. I couldn't risk being seen passing through Cojimar. Too many eyes."

"Well, good luck in these seas with that. It will be rough out there."

Our tanks were full, water topped off, and everything looked good. We pulled away from the dock and waved goodbye to Raúl. I set a course for the Cay Sal Bank and punched the throttles.

"*Niña,* we're headed out to Cay Sal tonight to stash some provisions, and then I'm heading to Cayo Fragaso to meet David."

"What are you talking about?" Nadine asked, thinking that we were just going to make our way back to the Keys.

"I'm not leaving without at least knowing that there's no way I can help Banco. I'm on a course for the Cay Sal Banks. We're going to Elbow Cay and then to Fragaso."

The weather was rough, those three to five foot coastal seas became five to eight foot seas in the Stream. The pounding was hell. Our course was north-northeast, and even though the seas were rough we'd make good time to Elbow Cay. Elbow Cay was on the west side of Cay Sal Bank, right on the edge of the Gulf Stream. I'd been fishing there quite a few times and had climbed up on the rocks, and I knew a low-lying area on the cay where we could stash some food and water. We'd be heading back this way, and a stash might come in handy. I also felt it was too risky to hug the Cuban shore.

The seas were getting higher and rougher, and we had to keep the *Lean Back* up on plane. We were jumping from wave to wave, doing at least forty-five to fifty miles per hour, to keep from getting swallowed up by the waves as they rolled endlessly northward. Nadine and I were strapped into the bolster seats. They kept us cushioned and from getting thrown out of the boat altogether, but it was still a jarring ride. Our teeth rattled and our insides felt like mashed potatoes. Now and then we would dip in between two huge rolling waves and as we began to rise up through the oncoming wave, the bow of the boat reaching the rim of the chasm, the wave would crash over the boat, soaking us. I had white knuckles from holding on so tight and concentrating on the boat and the ocean. The only sound she made was from spitting water every time we crashed through a wave. We had been traveling for an hour or so, with the seas becoming nastier.

Finally we reached the Cay Sal Bank. I anchored off the *Lean Back* on the lee side of Elbow Cay, away from the rough weather, but we were still bobbing up and down in three to four foot seas.

"*Niña*, hand me the satellite phone. I need to call the guys. "

Nadine grabbed the phone from storage and handed it to me. I made a call to DK, Jony, and Jorge. They were between Ragged Island, Bahamas, and Cuba. They had been there since I last saw them at Dog Rocks. I told them what happened.

"I knew something was up," DK said. "We saw three patrol boats between yesterday and today; usually you don't see any for weeks."

"DK, I'm going back to see what happened to Banco. I can't leave without at least doing that. I need you to cause some commotion, get noticed—you know what I mean. I need you north of Cayo Fragaso, which is just a little west of Cayo Coco; there are always government people out there. Stay outside the twelve-mile limit, and be careful. You know they don't respect the limit."

"Don't worry, Kiki," DK said. "I'll give them reason to come check us out. And if they get too close, I'll let them meet my little friend."

"*Gracias, amigo*, just be careful. You know they play for real. I'll call you in a day or so; heads up for the call." I turned to Nadine. "*Niña*, get the dive bag that has our fins and masks and empty it, fill it with some canned goods, water, flare guns, a knife and anything you can think of that we might need, please."

I called David next, and he also knew something was up. He had been seeing strange cars and faces in Yaguajay and Remedios. He told me that he was nearly finished with the torpedo setup. That was good news, but secondary to Banco's situation.

"I'll try and find out about Banco, Kiki. Believe me, I'll do my best," David said.

"*Gracias, hermano,*" I replied.

We finished by discussing the new plans for a rendezvous tonight.

We were bobbing up and down on the *Lean Back*, anchored about fifty yards off and at the mercy of the waves. We were wet and cold, but the anxiety of events and Banco's kidnapping kept us on edge and as awake as if we each had drunk a few cups of Cuban coffee.

"Time for a little swim, *niña*. This should only take a half hour if all goes well." The seas were rough, but I dove off the *Lean Back* and swam towards the Cay carrying the dive bag with the provisions.

I cut my elbows and knees climbing up on the rocks; everything I touched was jagged and sharp. Finding my footing up was difficult, with the water pushing and pulling at me. Luckily my feet were spared from being shredded, courtesy of the dive booties I was wearing. But I fell a few times and that did real damage. I finally made it up out of the water onto solid ground, then made my way to a swale in the rocks. I found a hole for the dive bag, and in case the weather got rougher I covered it with a few heavy rocks to keep it from being washed away.

I worked my way back to the edge of the cay, waded out as far as I could on the jagged rocks without losing my balance, and then chose a receding wave to dive into. Risky, but if it worked I'd be out of there without all the tumbling around I'd experienced before. I swam back to the *Lean Back* where Nadine was waiting to help me up on board.

I was bleeding pretty badly from gashes on my elbows, knees and side. I sat down to catch my breath.

"Here, drink some water," Nadine said, handing me a glass.

"We're going to be right in the weather going back to Cayo Fragaso tonight, *niña*. It's going to be rough for maybe three or four hours. We have to make the run in the black—no running lights. DK told me he's seen beefed up patrol north of Cayo Coco. We need to make it to Fragaso tonight. David will be waiting to stash the boat in the mangroves where it won't be seen."

"Are you sure we're doing this?" Nadine asked, with a frightened voice.

"No. No, I'm not *niña*," I said. "I'm not sure Banco would come back for me; he'd probably be in Miami by now. But I'm not Banco. I saw what happened, and I have to see what's happening now, and help him if I can."

"Well I think you're wrong on this one, Kiki. We're going straight back into the mouth of trouble. You told me yourself that trouble with the Cubans means death or long prison sentences, with death being preferable," she said.

"I know, *niña,* but that's the hand we were dealt on this one, and we need to play it out. Let's get what rest we can get and head out in a couple of hours so we can reach Fragaso before sun up."

I grabbed the Uzis and the .380 Berretta and began to prepare them. The Miami boys had come through with the firepower. I had two full-auto Uzis with 35-round clips, two extra clips and a six-inch silencer. This baby spat fire. Anything you pointed it at was gone, consumed. The weapons came fitted with shoulder straps, which would come in handy. The handgun was a semiautomatic .380 caliber Pietro Berretta, with a silencer. It was a beautiful handgun, smaller than any standard issue for police work—the same size as the British secret service issued, the Walther PPKs. James Bond's gun. It fit in my hand perfectly. They were easy to conceal, easy to use, and light. They also brought me ten extra clips holding 13 cartridges, with one in the chamber. I wiped all three down and oiled them. I loaded every clip, loaded the Uzis and the .380 and put them away in my backpack.

Nadine had been watching intently while I prepared the weapons never saying a word. I had brushed off her attempt at talking me out of going back to Cuba and she knew it would be a waste of time to keep trying.

I lay down on the deck and looked into the sky. The sun was long gone and even the light in the west had finally faded. The half-moon showed the clouds rolling through. For a second

I wondered if this might be the last time I got to enjoy feeling and seeing Mother Nature's beauty and fury before I would see the moon through a tiny window at the top of one of Castro's infamous prisons. Or maybe I'd just be dead.

Nadine had dried off and prepared for the ride back to Cuba.

"Here's a towel and some dry clothes. You need to warm up; you look blue," she said.

I was so caught up in my thoughts that until Nadine brought it to my attention; I hadn't noticed that my teeth were chattering.

"*Gracias, niña,*" I said, gratefully taking the towel from her hand and wiping my face and drying my hair. "Yeah, that feels good."

I got out of my wet clothes, dried off and put on what Nadine had brought me from storage.

"We need to get going, *niña*. It's going to be a long trip into the weather to Cayo Fragaso tonight."

I pulled up the anchor and Nadine started the *Lean Back*. I secured the anchor, sat down in the bolster next to Nadine and aimed the boat south-southeast toward Cuba and Cayo Fragaso. It was a waste of time to slowly put a boat up on plane in bad weather. We had to punch it and get on top of the waves as quickly as possible, otherwise we'd be swamped under fast. I hit the throttles on the three mercury 250s and the *Lean Back* screamed as she pushed water back and jumped on plane so quick that Nadine and I were pinned back in our seats.

I had just put the boat through three hours of hard pounding in eight-foot seas and there wasn't one screw loose or any rattling, and now she was back up on plane, eating up the ocean again. No wonder Pepe Pantera won so many races and set world records back in the day. The boat was also powered right: 750 big Merc horses gave her all the power and speed she needed.

CHAPTER 14

It was about one in the morning. Only four hours of darkness left. We were running in the black. Ten minutes after putting the *Lean Back* up on plane we were soaking wet. Our trip would be a long one.

We rode waves up and down for the next three hours, through pounding ocean and darkness and howling wind. We caught sight of a few freighters steaming along to the south, but the weather was so rough that we lost their lights just as suddenly as we saw them. Like phantoms. It was an eerie trip.

An hour later we started picking up shoreline lights on the Cuban coast. Slowly we worked our way toward the lights, edging closer to Cuba and then east to Cayo Fragaso. We were absolutely soaked by the time we arrived.

David called and he said he would be meeting us in his skiff at the edge of the mangroves. He would be checking his lobster traps. This was legit, not play-acting. He usually checks his hundred or so traps every morning at five. This morning it was a little earlier, but his cover was still good if the authorities checked him out. But he wasn't about to make it easy for them; he had all the lights off and was waving a flashlight up and down every half a minute, knowing we were approaching.

We were invisible in the darkness, and quiet. The *Lean Back*'s Mercs purred at slower speeds, they didn't putter like cheaper engines. We came up on him fast, and I could tell we had caught him off guard. He was facing the wrong way, and he jerked around suddenly when we loomed up. We cut the engines immediately and David threw us a line. He slowly pulled us into a barely-visible opening in the mangroves of the cay. About 50 yards in, we positioned her for a fast getaway.

Nadine and I pulled the canvases over the boat and tied her to the roots of the mangroves, then tilted the engines out of the water. We were in about two feet, which was just barely enough, as the *Lean Back* could draft about 18 inches. She would probably go dry in low tide, which could present a problem later on.

For the next few minutes Nadine and I gathered our things and prepared to leave with David while he hacked away at mangrove branches and brush with a machete. He collected a good number of branches and put them over the *Lean Back* to camouflage her.

"Jump on my boat," David said. "We need to get out of here right away."

Nadine and I jumped onto his skiff; I hugged David and said, "*Gracias, mi hermano.*"

"*Tranquilo,* Kiki, we'll have time for that later, but right now we have to get the hell out of here."

We lay down in the bottom of David's skiff and he covered us with canvases. Then he made his way back to Caibarién and the moored *Señorita Inez*, where he tied off his skiff. We stayed put under the canvas while David moved lobsters to the bigger boat, keeping the fiction alive just in case there were eyes somewhere on the waterfront.

As I've said, Caibarién was the town of my birth. Today it was a rundown little fishing village, which was very unlike how my mother described it to me. When we lived there, it was a large port, mainly handling sugar exports, and was full of life and vibrancy, with beautiful little fishing boats all along its docks. At least that's what she said, and I believed her. She'd have been sad if she had seen it now. The wharves and warehouses all along the waterfront were the only testament to the town's one-time importance as a shipping port.

Rumor had it that Castro would be pumping a lot of money in for tourism. There were a few beaches on the point that were quite nice, but nothing like Varadero, near Havana. There was also a national aquatic base just northeast of the port. Most of Cuba's sailors, windsurfers, and kayakers came here to practice for competitions. There were always some government personnel out, taking advantage of their official status by bringing their families to enjoy the amenities.

There was also Cayo Santa Maria, which was a small cay just outside the harbor. Cayo Santa Maria used to be known as Los Encenachos. My family would vacation there, usually day jaunts. Now there was a long causeway that stretched from Caibarién to Cayo Santa Maria, and the government was developing it for tourism. But all of this belonged to Castro, not the Cuban people. Every place in Cuba that had been developed for tourism was taboo, a big fat no-no for the Cuban people.

We heard David gathering the last lobsters from the skiff. It was 4:30 in the morning and I knew that when we got out from under the cover I'd see a little light in the sky.

"*Tranquilo,* Kiki," he said. "When I tell you, get up quickly and quietly. Get on the dock and follow me." We heard David walk away on the dock and then nothing but the sound of the gentle waves lapping against the dock and the occasional cry of a seagull.

About fifteen minutes passed before we heard footsteps on the dock nearing the skiff. "*Vamos, hermano, vamos,*" I heard David say. I pulled the cover back away from Nadine and she and I jumped on the dock and followed David to his car.

The dock and the harbor were completely silent and void of life in the darkness, thanks to Cuba's rationing of electrical power. Caibarién wouldn't be seeing any additional power out her way until tourism was firmly established here. Until then the light of the sun and the moon was the only light they would get.

We got into David's rundown old Chevy—rundown, but by the sound of the engine I thought he had that old jalopy running like a top. We lay down in the car and David covered us with some old blankets. It was a short ride, and we soon felt David pull in somewhere, then make a quick left and come to a stop.

"*Todo esta bien,* Kiki, you can get up now," David said.

Nadine and I pulled off the blankets, got out of the car, and followed David into his house.

It was a modest, to say the least. He made good money on different jobs, but he spent his money wisely: on his wife, his daughter, his son and his son's wife and two children, who lived in Havana. He also helped all his neighbors, and that's why he had so much confidence in his surroundings. He made sure everyone always had food, no matter what their circumstances. And he never gave himself away by being over the top with anything. Many people thought that he made a little extra by fishing and besides, they really appreciated his generosity and weren't about to turn him in.

The house had three bedrooms, though all the bedrooms were small by U.S. standards. It was clean and tidy, but the lack of materials in Cuba gave everything a decayed look. The walls were a pale yellow that had faded to an even paler shade. It had knicks and chips and holes throughout and we noticed a patchwork of attempted repairs. A meager wood-frame sofa, futon style, and a matching wooden coffee table worn to a frazzle were in the living room. Pictures of the family adorned the walls, every one situated to hide a blemish. A TV set on a stand stood opposite the sofa and chair. I couldn't begin to think how old it was, but there were dials and no remote controls. A futile attempt at decorating the rest of the room had been made by adding vases with fake flowers and a little ceramic Christmas tree sat on the table next to the TV, even though we were in high summer. To top it off, a big white teddy bear sat on the sofa. It looked like something frozen in time. But one thing this house didn't lack was love and hospitality.

We were greeted by Sara, David's wife, with two cups of coffee in hand. Their daughter Sarita was sitting on the sofa, sleepy-eyed at this early hour. David gave me a hug and said, "*Esta es su casa, hermano.*"

I thanked him. Sara took Nadine by the hand and mumbled something in Spanish that ended in *bendido Jesus*—"blessed Jesus." She took out some towels, handed them to Nadine and pointed to the shower.

"*Gracias, señora,*" Nadine said with a smile, as Sara closed the door to the bathroom and walked over to me.

"*Y tu, te vas ha morir del frio,*" she said. She was right, since the first time we left Havana this morning I hadn't paid much attention to anything except the task at hand; now I was beginning to feel the wear and tear of the trip. The constant pounding and soaking that had taken its toll, and for the first time I realized what I must look like. I was shivering and I wrapped my hands around the cup of coffee.

"*Si, señora, gracias,* I'll take a warm shower after Nadine."

Nadine came out of the shower, tired but somewhat refreshed. I did the same and came back to the living room.

"Kiki, Sara has prepared a room for you, so get some sleep and we'll talk when you get up," David said.

"Gracias, David, that sounds very good right now."

Nadine and I made our way into a modestly furnished room with two small twin beds that were barely more than cots. The anxiousness and excitement of the day's happenings had us edgy and unable to sleep right away. We were finally able to look back, giddy because we'd pulled off a tough assignment: getting out of Havana, stashing our provisions, and then pounding our way to Cayo Fragaso. We felt a sort of nice high, but we knew the anxiety would return. We talked about the day as our bodies began to relax. The last thing I remember was lying back, Nadine sitting up and looking down at me. I must have fallen into a deep sleep, because the next thing I knew Sara was knocking at the bedroom door.

"*El café esta listo.*"

We got dressed and made our way to the living room. David, Sara, Sarita, and Anibal were all sitting there.

"*Buenos dias,*" I said to the group as a whole and they all replied. Sara and Sarita got up as if on cue and began to leave.

Anibal, joking, said to Sarita, "*Vete esta va ser conversacion de adulto.*"

She rapidly shot back, saying "*Mira tio, yo soy un adulto.*" My daddy trusts me.

Anibal laughed and said, "*Yo te quiero, mi amor.*"

Everyone had a laugh as Sara escorted Sarita out of the living room, saying, "*Vamos que tu eres una niña.*" Sarita smiled and smacked her lips sarcastically as she walked to the kitchen with her mother.

Anibal laughed, looked at me and said, "She's the next generation of anti-Castro resistance fighters."

"I hope you slept well, Kiki," David said to me, inviting me to sit down. David didn't waste any time reporting on the situation. "Chino and I should be finished with the torpedo hookup by tomorrow. I'm waiting for some welding equipment that I'm borrowing. I should have it today, and then I'll tack everything together. Chino will have them put under the boat tonight at the latest. It's a tricky job, and could take a while. They have to be balanced or the boat won't ride right."

He looked up at me. "Oh, and Anibal was over by the nautical center on the skiff yesterday pulling up some lobster traps, and he saw G-2 arrive in a white Mercedes, escorting two men in handcuffs."

"Did you see what they looked like?" I asked Anibal.

"*Si yo los vi.* One was a small man, light colored shirt and tan pants. The other was a bigger man, heavyset, and bearded. What stood out to me about him was his clothes. You can't find that quality in Cuba unless you have a lot of money. He had on a white *guayabera* and black pants. He looked like he'd had a rough night."

I turned to David. "That's Banco. Why would they bring him here?"

"Could be many reasons, Kiki. It's a government facility and the G-2 is able to operate very covertly here. Havana wouldn't be a good place to deal with a kidnap victim—too many eyes and foreign government officials around, since Castro opened the doors to tourism. This place makes sense. No tourists, only Cubans, and they stay quiet. They've seen people hauled around in handcuffs by G-2 before; nothing new there."

"Or they could have broken him down and he told them everything," Anibal said.

Then he added, "Maybe he hasn't broken yet, but is just about to. In that case it would be best to kill him, Kiki, for your sake. Banco doesn't know who we are, but you, he knows, and if they broke him they know you now too. When the G-2 gets involved the situation goes straight to the top. The Beard will send people to Florida to hit you, Kiki; count on it. G-2 doesn't play around. It seems that this Banco has some higher-ups really pissed off, some real *mallimbes*. Think about it before you make a move. As for me, I would like nothing better than to hit the Beard where it hurts, and at the same time kill a couple of those *hijos de putas*. You can count on me no matter what you decide, *hermano*," Anibal said.

I nodded my head to Anibal in gratitude, but he had me thinking about Banco now. The G-2 could break anybody down eventually. Their ruthlessness precedes them, and their reputation stretches worldwide and is well known in Miami, talked about often in places like Versailles, where many Cubans go to eat or simply have a cup of café Cubano. At Versailles, the topics *du jour* are always Cuba, Castro, and politics. The G-2 and their sordid history was a common theme.

"I think Banco has more than thirty-six hours of resistance in him. He's a smart man, he knows that the longer he delays telling them what they want, the longer he lives. Maybe he thinks someone will come bail him out some way, through contacts, but I don't think he expects us to even try. Fuck, we're not navy seals over here. I'm supposed to call him in Miami in a day; he knows that if I can't reach him, I'll know something is wrong. I'd go back to Miami and tell his people. Shit, that's what he must be thinking. I think we have about another twenty-four hours or so before we really have to worry. Banco's involved, they know it has to do with money and lots of it, but they won't kill him until they know what's up."

"Good, then," Anibal said. He threw down a set of false Cuban papers for me, which even included a *libreta*, a Cuban-government food card. Theoretically this would allow me to get free food at government-run grocery stores, which were empty anyway. And when they did have goods, people waited in lines that wrapped around the block, hundreds of people waiting for hours just to see if they were lucky enough to get something.

"You're my cousin from Pinar del Rio, if anybody asks," David said.

Pinar del Rio was west of Havana, at the tip of Cuba. Most tourists didn't go out that way, as they traveled east when visiting Cuba. No casinos, no Las Vegas-style shows, but it did boast a beautiful landscape and the best growing soil for the worlds most famous cigars.

David continued. "You and Anibal will check out the warehouses and the station where the G-2 has Banco. You'll go out on the skiff and set some traps. You won't look out of place."

"David, there seems to be a lot that I don't know about what goes on out here. Yeah, I know, there's the treasure and the Canadians and the salvaging operations, but why would they bring Banco here?"

"A lot of shit goes on in that compound. I don't know what exactly, but there is too much military movement going on there to make that just an area where the Canadians do their salvage operations. I've never seen locals around there and they don't let too many people near it. We have our opinions of what's there, but we don't really know about much more than the treasure they find and what they brought up before the foreigners got involved with the Beard. And that's all local lore because no one has ever seen it. The big rumor is drugs, and no one talks about that too much."

Drugs made a little more sense, especially with the U.S. tabloids loving to pound that theory to death. It was all beginning to fit together. Banco's knowledge of the treasure and other underground dealings he'd had with the Cubans led me to think that Banco probably knew more about this compound than he admitted.

"Kiki," David said, "do you remember a few years ago when a Cuban Mig sunk a Bahamian defense force boat off Ragged Island?"

"Yes, I do," I replied. People were wondering why, and everyone knew it wasn't because of coming within the territorial space or the 12-mile limit that Cuba claimed. Hell, there were always Bahamian boats in Cuban waters and vice versa.

"The Beard had some salvage boats near Ragged Island in Bahamian waters," David went on. "They had found a famous wreck and were bringing up all kinds of good shit: gold, jewels, religious artifacts that were headed back to Spain, you know, all the shit the Spanish stole from the Incas. They say it was the best salvage ever; the treasure is supposed to be priceless. Anyway, then the Bahamian defense force stumbled across them. They chased the Cubans, and had a good chance of catching them. But then the Cubans called in the Migs, and they took out the Bahamian boat. The Bahamian officials were never found and only bits and pieces of the boat were ever recovered. Castro made it a border claim.

"We know that's all bullshit, Kiki. They brought that loot to those warehouses out on the point where the Canadians are, and the Canadians themselves probably don't even know its there. Too tricky letting them know, because of the Migs. That's my opinion. But obviously they're in on all the other loot Castro's collected, all that treasure from the 16th, 17th, and 18th century. That's the Canadians' expertise—salvage and catalogue. It's all there somewhere, *mi hermano*." David leaned against the sofa's backrest.

My mind was racing. Every salvage diver from here to Cartagena had heard of the Golden Madonna and dreamt of finding it one day. The problem was that it didn't show up on any manifest anywhere—ergo, myth. Every good salvager knew that most of the good stuff on a sunken ship never made it on the manifest. That was why myths like the Golden Madonna would always stay alive. Hell, no one believed in Troy until they found it. Could it have been that this is what Banco was after? Knowing that sneaky prick, it probably was.

"Well, if I'm going to try and get through the hands of the G-2, the Beard's personal ruthless pit bulls, then taking some gold and jewels should be easy," I said.

Anibal and David both laughed and I laughed along with them.

"Okay then, let's do this," I said.

"Good," David said, "I'm going to the docks to meet Chino and work on the torpedoes. You get ready and go with Anibal. We'll meet here later tonight for supper."

"*Sin problema*, David," I told him. "First I'm going to make a call. We might need some backup if we get away with this, and I have a friend that can help us. I just hope he can pull the strings I think he can."

CHAPTER 15

"Kiki, is that you?" the voice on the other end of the line said.

"Yeah, it's me, Maxi."

"I didn't recognize the number," he replied.

"I'm out of town right now. I'm on a sat."

"Where are you man?" he asked.

"Don't worry about that now, Maxi. I'll see you soon and tell you all about it then. But right now I need a favor from you, if you can pull it off."

"Anything I can do, within my limits, you know I'll do for you, Kiki. What do you need?"

Maxi was a true company man. No wasted words, straight to the point.

"I'm in up to my whiskers," I told him. The reference was not going to be lost on Maxi; he knew exactly what I meant. He shot back without hesitation.

"What the hell are you doing there Kiki? You know the consequences here—and there. Are you all right?"

"Yeah I'm fine, Maxi, thanks for the opportunity to meet your man in Havana. He scared the living daylights out of me."

"So what are you still doing there, Kiki? Weren't you told to get out? You run your life the same way you play poker—you don't seem to know when to hold or fold."

Maxi and I were close; his concern for me was genuine, but I knew how he felt about Castro and the Cuban situation, and the question I was about to ask would go against everything that was Maxi Betancur, let alone what was humanly possible.

"I'm all right, Maxi, I'm all right," I assured him. "Listen, I don't have time for all that now. I might need your influence in arranging some things for me. I hope I won't need it, Maxi, but right now things aren't that good."

"Okay, what is it?"

"I might have to leave in a hurry, and if I do things are going to get hot and I'll probably have a tail on me. If they do get froggy and jump, I'll be lucky to get to the Bank. I'll owe you big time, Maxi."

"You still owe me two hundred and thirty bucks from last month's poker game, Kiki. If you can't pay me that, how the hell are you going to take care of anything else?"

"Maxi, if they come after me I'll be headed for the Cay Sal Bank. I figure a two- to three-hour run—barring problems; I'll be lucky to get that far. I need to use your influence and call in some favors with your flyboy *compadres* at MacDill Air Force Base. If the Migs are on me and you can pull this off, when they see your flyboys in the area they'll pull back. Maxi, I'll owe you big time and I'll pay you the money I owe."

There was no sound on the other end for a few seconds.

"Are you fucking crazy, Kiki? Do you know what that takes and what kind of explaining I'll have to do if there's a fuck up? It's my ass, Kiki, it's my ass. They're going to want to know what the fuck I need that for. What do I tell them then, huh? Oh, I have a friend who has a problem with the Beard and he wants to borrow one of our planes. Is that what I tell them, Kiki? Son of a bitch, man, is it that bad? Is the heat that hot? I suggest you get the fuck home, *hermano*."

"I can't Maxi; the situation is like quicksand. I'm up to my hips and the only way out is to relax and lay low, or you won't ever see me again."

"I don't know what the fuck you're up to, Kiki. I'm sure we'll get some headline news from this. For the record, I'm against whatever you're up to. As a brother I have to be honest and tell you I can't make any promises. Good luck, *hermano*, you dumb shit." And with that the phone went dead.

Maxi wasn't very happy with my situation. But then again, he never agreed very much with the things I got into. He had helped me out before, with the Coast Guard, down in Andros when I had a problem with some Bahamian pirates. Modern-day thieves are what they were. Maxi called in a favor, and before I knew it I had a Coast Guard cutter coming to my rescue. What I needed now was not a Coast Guard cutter out on patrol, diverted a few miles to assist a U.S. citizen. This was getting F-14s, 15s or 16s—whichever ones, and getting clearance to put them airborne and flying to a certain area. I wasn't sure he could pull this one off. I knew he had the contacts, but that didn't mean anything. If he could pull something like this off it would be David Copperfield-type shit. And I mean the magician, not the Dickens character. I wasn't sure what would happen, but I just had to make that call. I wanted someone to know where I was, and who better than Maxi? I cut off the phone and walked back into the house, to a waiting David and Anibal.

"Let's go," David said. "Chino and I have a lot of work to do yet."

David, Anibal, and I walked out to David's jalopy, got in and drove down to the docks.

It was a beautiful, sunny day and the town was quiet. Considering the lack of all that was infrastructure in Cuba, Caibarién had its charm. Small homes with front porches, streets lined with royal palms, all roads leading to the town's once vibrant waterfront. Everything a little beaten up, a little dusty, a little faded.

An oxen-drawn cart ambled down the road. It had an old car axle with a makeshift platform made of wood. The sides of the cart were wooden poles, spaced about six inches apart and six feet high, braced together with rope and a few poles crossing.

The yokes on the oxen were what really threw me. They were made of long wooden poles about six to eight inches in diameter and about six to eight feet long, all thatched and strapped together with rope. From there the ropes attached to ox horns with the tips sawed off. The ropes then ran down to a nose ring, forming the steering mechanism. Absolutely incredible. You wouldn't see that on I-95.

I expected to see something like it in a National Geographic article on some South American country's uninhabited regions, not ninety miles off the U.S. coast. There was potential all over Cuba, in its people and the land itself. But the more I saw of it, the more I saw all this potential going to waste, thanks to a mismanaged revolution and a tyrant who lied to his people and became communist after his coup succeeded.

Modern Cuban society was an oxymoron, and the more the outside world saw what was going on, the more of a moron they'd see Castro is. Oxen-drawn carts in the middle of the road in Cuba. I guessed U.S. influence and its wholesale exportation of prosperity and democracy could reach the other side of the world but somehow couldn't make the short jump to Cuba.

We pulled up to the docks in David's Chevy. Totally empty. There were no tourists to take fishing or on boat rides, and it being late July, the Caibariénos were all out setting or retrieving their *nasas*, their lobster traps. The fisherman went out on month long trips, so except for the lobstermen the docks stayed mainly empty until early autumn.

David parked and we got out, walked to the dock, and down to the *Señorita Inez* where a hard-at-work Chino was in the water, with the boat jacked up on one side. He was just finishing welding in the first torpedo on the exposed side of the hull. On the opposite side Chino had wedged an inflated inner tube to raise and bolster the boat, allowing him to install the torpedo.

David and Chino had installed torpedoes on the *Señorita Inez* before, on a job we worked together on in the Bahamas. It was tedious work, but they knew what they were doing. The bitch is taking them off without tearing the hull apart.

"*Como esta,* Kiki?" Chino said.

"*Bien,* Chino," I replied.

Chino was a tiny man, around 120 pounds soaking wet after a heavy meal. He had a bronze tan and brownish hair, just beginning to show signs of gray. He was absolutely unafraid of the water. I had seen him dive into a pitch-black ocean in the middle of the night to work on a broken propeller for an hour with a flashlight in his mouth. He never got cold, and he never complained.

We were diving one time off Great Isaacs Light in the Bahamas, north of Bimini, and Chino was going down 120 feet to spear fish, which took time—they weren't just sitting there waiting for you to catch them. He would come back up nearly three minutes later, not even winded. When Chino dived, we would start the boat up and at a minimal speed, we'd turn the boat in a tight circle, causing the water at the rear of the boat to get very calm and clear, allowing us to see through the water as if we were looking through a glass-bottomed boat. We would see him spear a fish that looked small to us, but when he surfaced it would weigh 90 pounds. It was nearly as big as he was. That Chino could really dive.

"We should be ready to use them by tonight," Chino said.

"Good, Chino," I replied. "Just like the old days."

Sitting on a bench next to the *Señorita Inez* was an older looking man, maybe mid sixties, salt and pepper hair, dressed very much like a peasant.

Anibal called to him. "Tomás, *ven aca hombre.*"

The man stood up and walked over to us. "*Mucho gusto senor, me llamo* Tomás," he said.

I reached out, shook his hand, "*Mucho gusto, soy* Kiki."

He was medium height, with broad shoulders, and his face was tanned and leathery, like that of someone who has spent his life on the water. He had thick forearms and his hands were as rough as sandpaper and looked like they had been the main tool of his occupation. He slouched a little and had a forlorn look with a half-forced smile.

"Tomás is an old friend of ours," David said. "When I was a young boy, Tomás taught me how to dive. We used to go off the point out there where the Nautical Club is now; it used to be called the Yacht Club before Castro. My mom wouldn't let me go out any further than her eyesight, so when Tomás had time he would take me out there and we would fish and dive for lobster. He taught me a lot," David said.

Anibal continued, "Tomás used to work for the Cuban government on dive sites all over the Caribbean. He helped them bring up a lot of gold, silver, emeralds, and pearls, and it was all brought back to Cuba."

CHAPTER 16

Tomás stood up, as if on cue. "We were simply *pescadores, señor*, but the government knew that we knew the ocean and boats and they hired a lot of fishermen to support the manpower for the dives and extraction of treasure. We worked very hard and were paid very little. We were constantly told it was for the *Revolucion*.

"*El problema* was that the *Revolucion* wasn't taking care of our families. We were fisherman and we always had food on our tables; they were never empty even though *el dinero* was scarce. Now we were working for nothing and we were away from our families for months at a time. We used to steal gold coins and silver coins; we would swallow them and bring them home. Sometimes we had to swallow them a few times because trips home were delayed." He paused for a moment, obviously remembering the discomfort. "They didn't give us anything; we did what we had to do. We worked like *perros* for a long time, and then the Canadians, French, even the South Africans came.

"Los South Africans son *descarados, hijos de puta*. They abolished apartheid they say, *pero* here in Cuba they made friends with Castro, who permits apartheid. Look at the *turistas*. They have the best Cuba has to offer and the Cuban people get *mierda*. That's apartheid, tourism apartheid, no matter how you look at it, and these so-called salvagers, they piss on it all for money, and it's all blood money, *sangre*. That treasure came from the Spanish raping the people and the land in the colonies, and now a lot of it is back in hands that are also covered in *sangre*, and those hands are the hands of Castro, *descarado, sin verguensa*.

"When the foreign salvagers came, things changed," he continued. "Castro stopped his pillaging and began to concentrate on Cuban waters only; he let them pay the cost of operating and then take their share of the wealth." He laughed once again and said, "Do you know how they split with *el Barbudo*? I was not a part of the negotiations, you understand *señor*," he said as he laughed. "But I did spend a lot of time with the Canadians who had hired me to work for them as a diver. I was told by *el jefe* cataloguing what we brought up that they split fifty-fifty first, then from their fifty percent they subtracted their expenses, and then they had to make a further split with the Cuban government. He never knew himself what the other split was. I used to tease him and tell him that *el Barbudo* had put it up in them and broken it off. Right up in there, *ping pang*," Tomás said, making a shoving motion with his right hand.

Tomas laughed so hard he began to wheeze and cough. When he recovered, he looked over at me and said, "I has a sixth grade *educacion* and I coulda made a better deal."

David, Anibal, and I laughed along with him. The Beard was fucking them good. But if they wanted to play, they had to play by the Beard's rules, and the Beard's rules were, "What I want, when I want it, how I want it, or go the fuck home."

Tomás continued, "They pay us better and there were benefits. The Canadians treated us *bien*. The problem was that our pay went straight to *el govierno*, who in turn paid us. Castro wasn't just fucking them, he was fucking us too, *cacho de Maricon*."

"Who were you working for on these dives—I mean officially?" I asked.

"It was *el govierno* who got me my job. I worked for the Canadians, like I was saying," Tomás said, "but the Cuban government oversaw us."

"Do you still work for them?"

"No, *señor*. About a year ago we were on a dive, I was down about fifty or sixty feet, and we were diving with the air supply being pumped down to us through a hose by a how you say, *compresor*. I was searching the bottom, where we had been bringing up gold chains, gold coins, silver coins, *mucho oro y mucha plata*, and all kinds of gems and pearls. It looked like someone had robbed a jewelry store and smashed everything and left it all laying around. There was *tesoro* everywhere. I swam around a little coral formation and as I pulled the hose it got wedged in between two rocks, cutting off my air supply. I went for air and realized something was wrong. I grabbed the hose and followed it until I found the kink and undid it. A couple of minutes had gone by and my air was running low. I swam back up to the boat with very little air left in my lungs. I reached the surface and grabbed onto the ladder on the dive platform of the boat. Naturally, I was out of breath.

"The crew came over and heard me gasping for air, asking *que pasa que pasa* and if I was ok. I told them everything was fine and explained about the hose getting stuck. It had been cut badly as a result, and was leaking all the air, so I had to surface. The Canadians didn't think anything of it, but apparently one of the Cuban crew members on the boat reported the incident. Two days later, *me votaron*, I was off the job. They told me I was *un viejo*, getting too old to do this work anymore. They told me I should be proud of the years I had put in *el servicio de la Revolucion*. They were feeding me *mucha mierda*. The Canadians tried to help me out, but the government had made its decision and I was back here with nothing to show for it except my *libreta*, so I can go and stand in a line to get a loaf of bread," Tomás said.

"So you haven't worked with them for about a year now?" I asked.

"*Sí, señor*, that's right."

"Where did they take all the treasure after it was brought up?"

"Before the Canadians, French, and South Africans came, we stored it all in those warehouses *allí*," he said and pointed to the warehouses along the waterfront. "They still store it there; I've seen different dive groups dock there and unload."

I was thinking about Banco and how spot-on his information was, and how ironic it was that they were now holding him prisoner, just like the treasure he so eagerly sought, in the same warehouses.

"Who's in charge of all the treasure they find?"

"*Todas las companias* work under contracts that allow them concessions to explore different parts of the sea around Cuba, and they all have to take *ordenes* from Geo Mar, the Cuban government department that oversees all the *tesoro*. They have their own people working at the warehouses that track and store everything that comes in. Some high-ranking officials oversee them. I've even seen military people checking up on Geo Mar, some colonels and generals."

This was getting interesting. "Who were the colonels and generals?" I wanted to know.

"I didn't know all their names, but I did hear of some. There was a General Ochoa and a General Blanco. I didn't see them. But I did see Colonel De La Guardia at the office. He was only there once *una vez, posiblemente dos*, that I know of, and for a *mallimbe* of his stature to personally oversee something, there must be *halgo muy importante* there, something of great importance in it."

"De La Guardia, he is a personal friend of the Beard and is said to be like a favorite son. He works for the Ministry of the Interior—the headquarters of Cuban intelligence. He is one of their top *hombres* and a very powerful man in Cuba.

"So Geo Mar runs the show but it's all overseen by the Ministry of the Interior," I said. "It seems a little strange to have the Cuban equivalent to the CIA watching closely over salvage operations. How is the security situation over there?"

"The salvagers have their own security 24 *horas al dia*, but from midnight till eight they only leave two guards who watch the doors and monitor the cameras. Those guards bring *jineteras* there once in a while to pass the time. They probably figure, who in the hell is going to do something around there when they're backed up by the Cuban military? Patrolling the whole warehouse area nightly are *cuatro guardias en dos jepes*, regular military green army uniforms, *tu saves*?" Tomás said.

"You've been busy Tomás; you have a lot of information."

"David didn't bring me here to meet you por *nada, señor*. Anyway I think the *Revolucion* owes me a little more than they are giving me."

"I know what you mean, Tomás. I think the *Revolucion* owes a lot of people a little more than they are giving them. *Gracias* Tomás, I won't forget you like the *Revolucion* did, *mi amigo*."

David wrapped up the discussion. "Kiki, I have to help Chino. You and Anibal need to make your way out to the traps and see what you can see, and bring us back our dinner." He made his way onto the *Señorita Inez* and began to help Chino finish the torpedo hookup.

Tomás walked away with his hand in the air, waving goodbye. "*Buena suerte señor. Valla con dios.*"

Anibal jumped on the skiff and started its ancient little Johnson Seahorse 25-horsepower outboard, and I undid the bowline from the dock cleat. I jumped on and we were on our way to the point by the Nautical Base and the warehouses.

CHAPTER 17

Anibal talked as we rode the skiff out of the harbor. "They say there is *mas* than three trillion dollars worth of treasure on the bottom of the Caribbean, and a good part of that treasure is in or near Cuban waters, because a large part of the Spanish colonial wealth came through Cuba on its way back to Europa. *Piratas*, storms, reefs and bad navigation caused many of the ships to go down around Cuba and the Bahamas."

"Cuba is right in the center, the logical route for all ships headed to Europe, and it's the starting point for the Gulf Stream," I said.

"Those big salvaging companies know that the Beard doesn't have any money or technology to do any quality salvaging. And he knows that they know. But one thing everyone knows is that we do have excellent divers," Anibal explained. "But it's true, it's not just the opportunity for them. We really do have some amazing wrecks in our waters. And it's not just shipwrecks. There have been stories going around for a few years now that a very big Canadian company has found a lost city underwater, just off the western tip of Cuba. They say it's in deep water, and they have been taking pictures with all the special equipment they have. I was told that they have found what looks like *pyramides*, roads, and buildings, but they're keeping it as quiet as possible. Shit, the lost city of Atlantica *otra vez*," Anibal said, laughing.

I'd heard something along those lines from salvage people up in Florida. "Well that will tickle the Beard's ass with a feather, the thrill of his life," I told him.

"He'll make it an amusement park and charge the tourists twenty times what they charge at Disney World."

We were getting close to the point, and could see some of the warehouses. "So, Kiki, what do you think about this idea that Castro is smuggling drugs? I've seen a lot of trucks coming into the warehouse area being escorted and driven by army personnel. To me there is more going on there than just salvaged treasure. There has been talk about drug smuggling with the Colombianos, into Florida from Cuba."

"I wouldn't put anything past the Beard. He needs money any way he can get it, and if it means sending drugs into the U.S., so be it," I told Anibal. "He'd love nothing better than to keep Americans in love with drugs. In Miami the people and the government are convinced that he's allowing the cartels to use Cuba as a jumping-off point for shipments to the U.S. I guess Cuba's location as a central point for transfer of contraband hasn't changed in 500 years. First the robbing of the New World for its gold, silver, and gems, and now the robbing of people's minds through cocaine—all for money, blood money."

We were out off the point now, on David's lobster-trap line, pulling them up, taking the lobsters out, re-baiting the traps and throwing them back into the water. The traps were full and the work was hard, but we would be eating well tonight. The day was crystal clear, bright with a blue sky and not a cloud in sight. The water was clean and clear, but it seemed to have a lot more sea life in it than I was used to. It made sense; these waters were relatively unfished. If this were the Keys there would be fishing boats dotting the water as far as you could see. These were virgin fishing waters and our lobster haul so far was bountiful.

As Anibal and I pulled up the traps, we kept an eye on the waterfront by the warehouses to see what we could pick up. We could also see in the distance the Nautical Base, where the Cuban athletes came to practice. It was busy with sailors, windsurfers, and kayakers plying their trade, in hopes of becoming part of Cuba's athletic machine. Cuba was respected worldwide for its athletic prowess and Olympic viability. But Cuban athletes had different motives than most Olympians. They were seeking a better way of life, not gold, silver and bronze medals. If Cuba's athletes performed well in international competitions they would be granted a privileged life in Cuba. That didn't mean much by world standards, but in Cuba it meant you and your family would live a little more normally than most Cubans do. There were no delusions of grandeur with the Cubans; theirs were dreams of a better pair of shoes or pants or more food on the table.

I once asked Alexis Vila, a Cuban wrestler who was an Olympic silver medalist and a two-time world champion and

Pan-American gold medalist, what his incentive was and how is it that he had so many athletic accomplishments at such a young age. His answer was simple and to the point. "I either performed at a high level or somebody would take my place, and I would be back cutting sugar cane and standing in long lines for my food," he said.

In the U.S. he'd have been a hero with opportunities galore, in Cuba he was a means for promoting the revolution. Alexis defected to the U.S. after the Atlanta Olympics.

The Cubans incentives were the bare essentials of life. It was no wonder how an island nation of ten million people could compete with the U.S.'s nearly 300 million people. They trained for life, not gold.

It was nearly four and the day had turned out hot. There was hardly any breeze now. The sailors and windsurfers had gone. Anibal and I had spent the better part of the day hauling up lobster traps, and I was worn out. But it was worth it. We had seen what we needed to see at the warehouse.

We had noticed a few cars and vans pulling up to the warehouses and then leaving after cargo was unloaded. We took notice of where the men entered and how many people were watching or guarding. So far, what Tomás had told me was right on. It looked as if they were doing casual work, something they had done so many times that it was just routine.

"That's a main storage area right there," Anibal said. "Every week the cars and vans show up—one day, maybe two days a week. They stay for a while then *se van*; security shows up, then all is back to normal. The whole situation is very relaxed, no one there worries. Fuck, you're in Cuba. Half the people here are *soldados* or spies. You're the only *cabron* crazy enough to rob the Beard, Kiki," Anibal said, snickering, "and now you've talked me into it. If I get out of this alive, I'm going to Miami. No more Revolucion-viva-Che-Guevara *mierda* for me. It's going to be Calle Ocho and South Beach from then on."

I laughed as I listened to Anibal. He never broke stride; he noticed everything around him, and carried on a conversation and hauled lobster traps all at once. He grew up knowing nothing but hard work. Multitasking was something Cubans learned to do at a young age. It was preparation for their mere survival.

"You see those offices there?" Anibal asked as he made a gesture without pointing. "That's where the *'mallimbes,'* the big boys, go. Tomás has seen De La Guardia there. I think that's where they are holding Banco; no one has seen him since they went in there two days ago. What do you think, Kiki? How long can your man hold out before they come looking for you?"

"I don't know, man, but no one holds out long with those guys. We don't have long, I know that much."

I had memorized the whole complex and its setup. There was one way in and one way out. A wooden barricade at the entrance acted as a deterrent for anyone tempted to enter. According to Anibal, the barricade was pulled aside during the day and replaced at about seven at night. The only other way out was the ocean. Other than kayaks and windsurfers, the only boats around were those coming in from salvage jobs, and then they were there only for a day or two before retuning to work. And we were the only lobstermen working these waters. There were others who passed through on their way into the harbor, but this was David's turf and they didn't come near his buoys. Right now the ocean side of the warehouse complex was devoid of boats. When the time came, we'd stand out like a sore thumb. This was starting to look more and more like a suicide mission.

We arrived back at the dock where David and Chino waited. We tied up and unloaded the lobsters. Sara was there, waiting for the catch of the day. She took about a dozen lobsters, made her way back down the dock to a waiting Sarita, and walked home with her to prepare dinner.

David and Chino had finished rigging the torpedoes under the *Señorita Inez*. From the surface, they were completely invisible. The only way to know they were there was to jump in and dive under.

We had brought back a good five-dozen lobsters and so we spent some time transferring the remaining ones to a holding tank on the *Señorita Inez*. David helped everyone in Caibarién, and true to his principles, he would give the rest of the catch to neighbors and those in town who needed food.

We secured the *Inez* and the skiff and drove back to David's house to what turned out to be a Cuban feast. Nadine was waiting for me there, eager to tell me how she had helped Sara and Sarita prepare the meal.

As in all Cuban homes, I was asked to eat and enjoy. Food was a great part of Cuban hospitality, which was ironic considering the lack of it in Cuba. But with the simplest of foods, Cubans can create a feast. The table was set with white rice, a Cuban staple like potatoes in the U.S. There were fried sweet bananas, fried plantains, yucca, a sort of fibrous potato, black beans and a lettuce and tomato salad. Sara had prepared the lobsters we brought in a light tomato sauce with a medley of onions, green peppers and traditional Cuban spices. Luckily for David and his family, his boat provided them with the bounty of the sea.

It was a fabulous meal, which we all enjoyed sitting at their modest kitchen table. To top it off, Sara had made a beautiful flan. In all my life I couldn't remember having had a better one. Sara, Sarita, and Nadine cleared the table, cleaned up and made coffee. David, Anibal, Chino, and I went to the living room and sat down.

"Well what do you think, Kiki? Are we going to try this craziness?" David asked.

"I think I've come too far to go back now, David."

"That's not my question, *hombre*," David came back. "Are we going ahead on this one?"

"The place is slack, so getting in won't be a problem. It's getting out that bothers me," I said.

Pleasantly full from the beautiful meal, I had said this almost jokingly. Now David set his jaw and gave me a look that said only a fool plays games with fate.

"You're *loco, hombre*," he said, "but I guess I'm with you. I've already got my boat rigged and ready, there's no going back now. I believe if we don't get your friend out somehow they will come looking and snooping around here and that puts *toda mi familia* in the line of fire and I don't like the sound of that at all." David looked at me with a stern and convincing look on his face. His jaw still set and now even somewhat clenched, he glared my way. I looked into his eyes and I understood that I couldn't fail now, there were innocent lives involved. I sat quietly as the seriousness of the situation permeated my every fiber.

CHAPTER 18

David, Anibal, Chino and I were still sitting in the living room talking about the plan for tomorrow. It was around nine o'clock and the last of the twilight had left the two living-room windows. Sara and Nadine came in with a tray and demitasses of coffee.

Nadine sat down and Sara put the tray on the table and handed the cups to everyone. Then she took a cup, turned and walked to a corner of the living room where there was a makeshift altar with small religious statues, candles, glasses of water, old plates of food, rosary beads and photos of the deceased. Everything was arranged in tableaus on several shelves, and the largest statue, that of Santa Barbara, stood on the floor. I didn't need to think twice about what this altar represented; I had seen the same sort of thing in many Cuban homes, both in Miami and in Cuba. These were David and Sara's Santeria icons that they gave offerings to and prayed over. The statues of saints also represented Santeria gods, known as *orishas.* Sara set the cup of coffee down on a shelf just above Santa Barbara and crossed herself as she walked away.

I looked over at David and he made a mock bug-eyed look, then smiled.

I had been in Miami for a long time and in and out of Cuba a few times, and I could tell you for sure that Santeria was not just a religion to the believers, but a way of life. Every time I was in Calle Ocho, Eighth Street, Miami to replenish my cigar stash with some fine, well-rolled cigars, I was sure to see a few initiates of Santeria. They were always dressed in white and wore different-colored beaded necklaces, each one representing an *orisha.* These initiates adhered to a very strict code of conduct and they underwent a year-long communion with their *orishas.*

How ironic that the Christian religion looked at Santeria as barbaric and paganistic when Christianity and Judaism had the many sacrifices found in the Old Testament. This was about as far as my thinking went on the subject of Santeria. They were victims, and the Christians were fucking hypocrites. But I always had a strong sense of what Santeria could do for its believers. It was like putting on a bullet-proof vest and having angels as your bodyguards.

Sara looked back at David and said, "*Cuando tu estes listo mi amor.* Whenever you're ready."

David looked at his old, beat-up Timex. Seconds later there was a knock at the door and he smiled at me and nodded in satisfaction.

Sara answered the door and let a smallish man with snow-white hair and deeply tanned skin enter. He was dressed in white and had four strands of beaded necklace around his neck that draped over his shirt. The strands were yellow, red, green, and blue.

He entered the living room, bowed his head slightly and said, *"Mucho gusto, me llamo Erasmo."*

Nadine and I stood up and shook his weathered and worn hand.

"Este es Erasmo, el es el babalawo," David said.

My mind had been on other things and this took me completely by surprise. But now I put all the pieces together. David and Sara were very religious and Erasmo was the Santeria priest, the *babalawo*. We were about to have a Santeria ritual to keep us safe and clear our path for our upcoming journey. I realized now that they wouldn't make a move without first being blessed by their *babalawo*.

David and Sara cleared the small living room of furniture and asked us to sit down on the floor. They turned the lights off and Sara lit a single candle next to the statue of Santa Barbara. Erasmo finished his coffee and thanked Sara. Then he walked over to Santa Barbara and sat on the floor facing the statue.

Like I said, I had developed an interest in Santeria when I first got to Miami. Not as a believer, but as a Catholic Cuban who had grown up in New Jersey and who had a sense that the Cuban coffee was a little stronger in Florida than in the North. It was fascinating for me because it was about my roots. But not literally, because Santeria was always more African than white, more rural poor than the middle class. Yet since 1959 the isolation of the island had created a hothouse environment for

Santeria and the religion had spread among the "comrades," while in Miami the focusing of Cuban culture within the larger Anglo society had had the same effect. So in a sense Santeria had become a pan-Cuban phenomenon and if I wanted to think about my Cuban roots then Santeria had become part of what I had to consider.

That didn't mean I had to believe in it; I simply respected its practitioners and was fascinated by the strange gods and rituals and ceremonies. It all went back to the African slaves in Cuba, Haiti, Jamaica, Barbados and other plantation islands in the Caribbean.

The religion was known generally as Santeria, but to the believer that was an insult. The name Santeria was derogatory to its practitioners. It was called Regla Ocha or Regla Lukumi. Those names came from the beliefs of the Yoruba, a people of West Africa, the dominant ethnic group of slaves in the Caribbean.

In order for the slaves continue to practice their African religions they disguised their gods in the garb of Christian saints. There was Chango, the fiery god of dance, passion and lightning, and represented by Santa Barbara. The colors red and white and a double-headed axe were also part of Chango.

The top dog in Santeria was Olofi. He was the spiritual energy that made up the universe and everything in it. Olofi interacted with humans through lower gods, the *orishas*. Kind of like the Christian God sending Jesus to deal with humankind. Only to the Yoruba people, Olofi sent hundreds of *orishas* to help in every aspect of life and every force of nature. Ten to fifteen *orishas* were seen regularly in the pantheon. The rest were a mystery to me, known only to true devotees of the cult.

A commonly known goddess in the pantheon was Oshun, the goddess of sweet waters, love and fertility. Oshun was represented by Our Lady of Charity, Cuba's patron saint.

There was a *boveda* in front of Erasmo, one of the shelves that was the ancestral altar, and this was covered with photographs of those who had died. Off to one side was a statuette of Eleggua, the guardian of roads and doors. Eleggua stood at the crossroads of the human and the divine. Nothing should be done without his permission.

Personal communication with all these *orishas* was through offerings, but more importantly through blood sacrifices of chickens, goats, and lambs. Sacrifice could only be performed by a *babalawo*. They were priests indoctrinated into the rites of Orula, the *orisha* of knowledge and wisdom. Erasmo was a *babalawo* who was around seventy years old, more or less. He had probably been a *babalawo* most of his life.

I had witnessed these rituals before, but for Nadine I knew it would be a first. She looked at me with questions in her eyes and I looked back calmly, letting her know everything was all right. She was visibly uneasy with what was going on and I was pretty sure she was aware that Santeria entailed animal sacrifice, among some other very strange rituals. All I could do was hope she could take it—and also hope there wouldn't be too much blood.

You might have thought that the sacrifice of animals was a huge price to pay in a country with so few resources, and you would have been right, in a sense. But hope was worth more than a little lost blood. The Revolution was an elaborate human ritual of despair; Santeria was its flip side, an elaborate human ritual of longing and hope. And then of course in Cuba you got the sweet and simple outcome of that latter elaborate ritual: you also got to eat the sacrificial lamb—or goat or chicken—for dinner. It was about making do with limited resources while you prayed for a better future.

In Cuba, women used the cardboard inserts from toilet paper as rollers for their hair, and there were businesses that took old keys and made new ones using old key copying machines from the 50s. Another made new eyeglasses from old frames; coffee grounds became fertilizer; old CD cases became picture frames; drinking glasses were cut down from old rum bottles; at a bakery the flan puddings were sold out of old soda can bottoms; and some people made a living out of refilling disposable lighters. They did it by injecting lighter fluid using an old aerosol can that once held god knows what. They washed and dried plastic bags—you could see them hanging on clotheslines everywhere. It was absolutely amazing, some of the things you saw that were not supposed to be happening. Most people outside the Cuban community had no idea what is going on.

The progressive, liberal, left wing assholes around the world who still thought Castro and Che were heroes would call the Cubans masters of recycling. More like saving themselves, survival, not some obscure eco-craft they had mastered. The Revolution hadn't brought them anything but heartache and misery. And all those simple little things that they were deprived of could be bought in any tourist shop in Cuba right in front of their noses, but not by Cubans. Something was wrong with this picture.

In a nation where salaries averaged fifteen dollars a month, necessity ruled, and the necessity of this animal that was probably going to be sacrificed to the *orishas* in our honor also dictated that it would become a needed meal.

We had been sitting there in the dark for a while and all that time Erasmo had been sipping away at some Cuban *aguardiente*—a liqueur made from sugarcane—and playing a small set of *bata* drums, kind of like Conga drums. He was working himself into a trance little by little as he played and bobbed back and forth, like the Jews did at the Wailing Wall.

David, Sara, Anibal, and Chino all sat quietly while Erasmo chanted and played the *batas* and the candlelight flickered over his lined face. Their belief was strong; they were completely captivated by the ceremony. And there did seem to be something growing and moving about in the room; an aura, a presence. But it was clear that Nadine hadn't sensed this spirit, or if she did, she felt it to be dangerous. She was squirming like a little kid who had to go to the bathroom. Sara noticed her anxiety, reached over, and took her hand. This seemed to calm her down. She looked over at me and gave me a faint smile.

Erasmo was now in a full-blown trance, or so it seemed to me. He had some pieces of coconut shells, which he had pulled from a small burlap bag with a leather drawstring decorated with beads of different colors. He tossed the shells on the floor, and began to point at them, and speaking emphatically in a language I didn't understand, sometimes breaking into song, addressing each shell as though it were a person or animal. While speaking to the shell he would look up, skyward, and lift his arms as if he were appealing to the judgment of a greater power above. He got up from his position in front of the Chango Santa Barbara and began very slowly to dance around the room, all the while continuing to talk and sing like he was speaking in tongues.

Still dancing, talking and singing, Erasmo lit the twelve candles set up around Chango, Eleggua and Oshun. He lit a cigar and offered the smoke to them, then laid the burning cigar at their feet as an offering. He offered *aguardiente* to them by pouring small amounts at their feet. There was a bowl of fruit, oranges, grapes, mamey, and papaya and Erasmo offered each and every one individually while he said prayers to the *orishas*.

There were other things there also. He took a honeycomb, fully drenched in honey, out of a small bowl and dripped it across the various statues. He came over to us and gathered pieces of clothing—scarves, coins, handkerchiefs, a hat—and brought these back to the altar.

Erasmo looked fully immersed in his trance; his eyes were usually rolled back in his head and when they did lower they were unfocused and set in an intense stare. He was still sipping at the *aguardiente*, which couldn't help but keep him in a trance. He was dancing vigorously, his white clothes soaked in sweat, as if he had a hose turned on him. But there was no stopping him; he seemed to be gathering strength and energy as he continued a ritual that had been going on for two hours.

Everyone was totally enthralled with the ancient ritual and no one seemed to mind the heat and stuffiness of the little living room on that sweltering summer night. We were all sweating and had been sitting in one position, but no one seemed anything but fully absorbed in the ceremony. Even Nadine had calmed down, though she still held Sara's hand.

I had been through Santeria rituals before and I took it all in stride. Everyone had their beliefs and I respected them all, just as I expected others to respect mine. Even though I had never practiced Santeria, I understood it and knew why people held onto it so strongly. It gave them a magical feeling of being totally protected. No harm could come to them while being protected by their gods, their *orishas*.

Back in the day, I was rebellious, angry at society and how it looked at the human race, labeling some majorities and others minorities. What the fuck, I thought, we were all human, how could one be a major and another a minor. We were all from planet Earth.

Back then I didn't give a shit about what society considered right or wrong. I was determined to make my own way and write my own rules, and what better way to do it than on the open ocean. Once you were beyond the twelve-mile limit, you were in No Man's Land. Only the strong survived there.

I ran a little *ganja* from what we called the Yard, meaning Jamaica, and a little *marimba* from Colombia. Many smugglers were involved in Santeria ceremonies before going on their adventures on the high seas. And if they refused to take part in a ceremony for ritual cleansing, the owners of the merchandise would not let them work. You either partook or you stayed home. There were large dollars involved, so you just shut up and went along with the ceremony. Personally, I didn't give a shit. It wasn't going to change my beliefs, and the Benjamins at the end of the line were awfully enticing. It was baptism by fire and Santeria.

The only things I didn't think about back then were the consequences if I got caught. Well, I saw the consequences hit a few people upside the head, and that's when I decided to bow out. All the money in the world wasn't worth my freedom, which is what I was searching for anyway.

That's when I took to salvaging and fishing. You couldn't get more freedom than that on this planet. You lived in unison with Mother Nature and she provided for you.

I learned a lot about the ocean, the Caribbean in particular, which is how I came to know Banco Morales. Through mutual contacts he heard I could handle tough jobs, big ones, and then he found out I got jobs done, and was trustworthy. So I'd worked a few salvages with Banco before, but nothing like this.

This job reached down deep inside of me, not for the greenbacks but for my soul, my homeland, my people. This was a crime of Cuban passion. I wanted to stick it to the Beard, that was all. Just fuck him.

Erasmo stopped dancing and slowly walked over to the statue of Santa Barbara. He knelt down and bowed his head as though praying, or even resting. The drums were silent. It was a pause and I wondered if the ceremony were over. Could there be a full ceremony without a blood sacrifice? My question was answered when David stood up and walked to the kitchen. He came back with a blindfolded chicken—a red and black banty rooster—with its feet bound together. I knew what was about to happen. I looked at Nadine and saw that she realized it, too, but other than a wide-eyed curiosity she remained calm, with Sara's help.

Erasmo stood up, took the drums and began again to pound them and dance. After a couple minutes he approached David, who offered the victim to him with both hands. David knelt slightly, clearly projecting humility. Erasmo stopped the drumming, and bowed his head in thanks as he took the rooster. Then he started in again with the dancing and chanting.

The *babalawo* raised the sacrifice above his head with both hands. Facing the statues of the *orishas,* he began to speak to them, concentrating on Eleggua, asking favors in reverence and respect.

He knelt in front of them and lowered the sacrifice to the floor, where there was a makeshift altar that looked like a kitchen cutting board. He laid the rooster on the board. To my amazement, it wasn't struggling. It was performing double duty, as a sacrifice and tomorrow's dinner.

He held the rooster in his left hand and with his right picked up a knife that lay next to the board. He looked at the ceiling, then toward Eleggua, continuing to speak in tongues. He reached down with the knife and quickly and efficiently sliced the rooster's neck, severing it completely.

Still there was barely a struggle from the blindfolded, bound and confused animal. Blood spattered Erasmo's white shirt and pants as the bird's pulsing heart spewed blood everywhere.

The *babalawo* stayed kneeling in front of the *orishas,* offering the blood of the freshly sacrificed animal. He waved the slain fowl back and forth in front and over the *orishas* as blood spilled over the statuettes and at their feet. He continued his chanting, which I knew were prayers on our behalf.

It was at this precise moment in time that I chose to believe in everything about this ancient ritual and in the powers of Erasmo, the wise old *babalawo.* Maybe it was irrational, but I knew I was in deep and I knew luck would have to be on our side. The pure, beautiful belief in the faces of David, Sara, Anibal and Chino gave me a sense of security and serenity. I felt more secure than I had at any time since we ventured onto the island.

Erasmo turned to us, holding the sacrificed rooster in both hands. The animal was still dripping blood. The *orishas* were drenched and Erasmo's hands were as red as if he had dipped them in a can of paint.

His face had blood on it and his white clothes were covered. If not for the ritual that we had just seen, I would have taken Erasmo straight to the hospital. He looked like the victim of a multiple stabbing.

Erasmo began to dance and chant again, praying and asking favors of the *orishas* on our behalf as he held the sacrificed bird in front of us so blood would drip on our knees.

He asked for the sun to always shine on us, for the night to hide us and keep us safe, and for all paths that we chose to open and become clear for us. From your mouth to God's ears, I thought, as Erasmo continued his prayers. I'm going to need them and all their powers.

Erasmo turned to the *orishas* once again and gave thanks to them for listening to his pleas. He laid the now bloodless sacrifice on the altar and turned to us again.

He came to where I was sitting and knelt in front of me. With his blood-soaked hands he took my right hand in his left and with the thumb of his right hand he made the sign of the cross in blood on the back of my hand, in between my thumb and forefinger. He then bent over and whispered in my ear. "*Buena suerte,* Joel Enrique Logan."

I jerked my head up and looked in his eyes. I was shocked to hear what I just heard from the old *babalawo.* He called me by my full name, Joel Enrique Logan. No one knew my first name, especially in these circles. I never used it.

Not David, nor anyone else in this house—including Nadine—knew my first name.

I looked at the old *babalawo,* my mouth half open, and he looked straight into my eyes. Seeing my amazement, he said, "I always know who I am blessing—my *orishas* tell me."

Then he smiled and said, "*Buena suerte, mi hijo.*"

The ceremony had come to an end after five hours or so. You could see the weariness and fatigue in the *babalawo*; he was slowly coming back to merely kind old Erasmo.

Throughout this long and enchanted night of *Regla Ocha* rites, rituals and sacrifices I had come to admire the old *babalawo*. I admired him for his strong beliefs, I admired him for his knowledge, I admired him for his endurance, and I admired him for staying true to himself.

Erasmo began to stand up and I helped him, and as we rose he put his bloody hand on my shoulder—not so much priest and acolyte as older man and younger man. We stood there, looking at each other for a moment. I was eager to communicate that I understood, that I'd been enlightened, that in a strange sense I'd been converted and believed in what he'd expended so much time and sweat and energy on. Yet I also wanted to be polite. It wasn't my place to validate what he'd done; I merely needed to be grateful. So I thanked him for his time and energy. But in my mind I also thanked him for the magic and mystery of it all.

It was three o'clock in the morning. We all stood up. I was a little bit cramped but I felt good considering how long we had been at this. Erasmo gathered his things as Sara helped him on with his coat for his trip home. He made his way to the door, blessed us one more time, and said goodbye.

David, Anibal, and Chino were cleaning up the blood. Sara walked over to the altar cutting board and grabbed the sacrificed rooster. It would be dinner for someone in the neighborhood who needed it.

"I guess we wait another day to go ahead, David?" I said.

"I knew this ceremony would take a long time, Kiki. It is a very serious matter we have undertaken, and we can't take it lightly," David replied.

David's belief in his *orishas* was strong and it gave me a sense of ease to know he took the job so seriously.

I helped clean up the rest of the mess and put the living room back in order. Nadine was in the kitchen with Sara, cleaning up and washing herself. She walked back into the living room, gave me a hug and whispered in my ear, "*Mon Dieu.*"

"We'll get some good rest now, Kiki. Tomorrow we'll eat well and relax, and tomorrow night we'll put a fire in Castro's ass," David said as he laughed quietly. It was past four in the morning and we needed all the rest we could get. The next evening when the sun went down, the game would be on.

CHAPTER 19

It was late morning when Nadine and I finally walked into the living room. Sara had Cuban coffee ready. David was sitting on the sofa reading the local communist party newspaper, which I guess he read for laughs. I figured he'd normally be out on the *Señorita Inez* on a fine morning like this, but what with all the planning he had to stay here at headquarters.

We had another day before we made our move. The weekend was a better time to execute our plan; there would be more people milling about during the day and it took the guards' minds off of the usual.

"I think I'll go for a walk with Nadine. Where's a good place that's nice and quiet and not too public?" I asked David.

Sara jumped in and answered, "Walk the railroad tracks; you'll see some beautiful trees and flowers and you'll be alone. It's very pretty and peaceful."

We had a full day to kill and sitting around was just going to cause me to think and rethink. I didn't want any ideas creeping in and causing me to second-guess myself. That was how big mistakes were made.

Sara pointed the way and Nadine and I walked out of David's tiny house on the outskirts of town and onto a beautiful little street lined with royal palms, all regal and majestic, standing tall and reaching a hundred feet into the cloudless blue sky. They looked like a row of soldiers guarding and maintaining the sleepy colonial village. The proud royal palm was Cuba's national tree. The tears of the Revolution hadn't been able to diminish its beauty.

We walked down the quiet street. It was hot and humid, but the light ocean breeze made it comfortable. Warm weather, plenty of rain, and humidity kept Cuba very green. We got to the tracks and walked east toward Yaguajay; a little town in the middle of the vast belly of Cuba's sugar cane fields. Everything was overgrown, the bushes and trees reached the edges of the train tracks and the only trimming they received was when the train came by, which by the looks of the overgrowth wasn't too often. There were *polimitas*, Cuban land snails, everywhere; in all colors, white, yellow, orange, striped, spotted. They crunched under our feet as we walked the all but abandoned tracks that once supplied Cuba's bustling economy. Another catastrophe of the Revolution.

It was a beautiful walk and we made small talk as we noticed all the flowers, butterflies and birds. Cattle egrets poked around in the scrub and hobbled across the tracks as they searched for insects. Turkey vultures soared in the sky without so much as batting a wing. They showed up every year in South Florida around October and were known as the Cuban Air Force. They were everywhere down here all winter long, and evidently Cuba was no different when it came to their numerous and hideous presence.

I stopped and picked a flower, a butterfly jasmine. It smelled wonderful. I put it in Nadine's hair, just like Cuban women wore them to symbolize their patriotism. She held my hand as we continued our leisurely walk down the tracks. It brought back memories of my childhood; a time long ago, with no worries or hurries.

I was seeing everything through Cuban-colored glasses; all was right in the universe. The sun was shining and the birds were singing. We walked about a mile and came to a big ceiba tree. It created a huge nimbus of wonderful dark shade. This ancient tree had its origins in Africa and was an object of reverence among peoples in the Old World and the New. There was said to be a stately ceiba in Havana that dates back to early colonial times.

We circled the tree, gazing upward. Birds sang and flitted from branch to branch, as though the tree were the extent of their universe. When they lit on its huge, hand-shaped, web-fingered leaves, it seemed as though the branches were catching them, holding them. The girth of its massive bole covered a wide area and the trunk tapered as it reached to the sky. Cottony fiber hung from its limbs to complete the look of the eerie shadow this magnificent giant cast. A pair of hummingbirds, stationary in flight, plunged their needlelike beaks into beautiful red flowers growing around the base of the ceiba.

I sensed a feeling of peace in the presence of the old tree, but also of power and mystery. It seemed as though all of nature came to the tree to pay tribute.

This was not only my own impression. Around the ceiba's base were half-spent candles and other offerings from Santeria ceremonies. Unlike Erasmo's ceremony, which was a blessing, an endowing with positive energy, these offerings to the *orishas* were about casting out the negative; they were cleansings intended to rid believers of evil spirits. The ceiba's craggy, angular trunk provided many nooks and crannies and I could clearly see in them additional remains from religious gatherings. The big tree commanded respect and all of nature recognized its supremacy.

I was startled by a shrieking noise coming from the heights of the ceiba, piercing and loud. Its suddenness made us crouch, as if ducking something that had just been hurled at us. We laughed when we realized it was the cry of a bird. It shrieked again, half-startling me once more. I turned quickly in the direction of the piercing sound. Ten meters away, perched on a limb, was a very conspicuous-looking parrotlike bird. But it wasn't green or yellow. It was red, white and blue, standing out like a sore thumb against the greenness of the surroundings.

Its big pagoda-shaped tail fanned underneath it and the bird stood proud and alert on the limb. His quiet sanctuary violated, he arched himself up, stood tall, raised the crest on his head and glared at us, as if to ask what we were doing in his domain. He stared quietly for a few seconds and again shrieked that piercing cry. "To-co-roro. To-co-roro." It was hideous; it grated on my nerves; it made me squint my eyes and cringe and cup my ears with my hands. I felt like I'd been hit by lightning, zapped by a thousand volts. It turned my stomach and yanked me in the guts. I felt sickened, and this feeling somehow conjured up within me an ugly vision of the future. I felt as though I'd seen death, here under this beautiful tree in the midday sun on a tropical island.

The bird glared at us once again, quickly turned and flew off, screeching his horrible cry.

I walked nearer the tree, leaned my back against its grayish trunk and let myself slide to the ground. I wrapped my arms around my knees and drooped my head. I was mentally exhausted, and no matter how hard I tried, I couldn't keep my mind off our ugly reality. The shrieking bird had chased all calmness and peace from my thoughts.

I was on a beautiful island, with a beautiful woman and all wasn't well. I was scared, and I felt alone.

Nadine knelt down next to me, reached out and clasped my hand in hers. I looked up and gave her a half-hearted smile.

"I have an idea," she said, "I think the compound…"

I cut her off in mid-sentence. "I don't need any ideas right now, Nadine. Anyway, it's not about getting on the compound, it's about getting out." I stood and walked a few feet away from her. I was truly scared; I felt my life was in the balance.

She rose and walked toward the tracks. "*Parles à mon cul, ma tête est malade*. Again right, Kiki. You didn't even know what I was going to say." She hurried by, visibly angry. She began walking at a quickened pace back toward David's house.

"Nadine, Nadine, wait!" She wanted nothing to do with me. I hurried after her, asking forgiveness, but no, nothing doing. She began to run, and I could hear her crying softly as she disappeared down the overgrown tracks.

I slowed my pace. She wanted to be alone. She was right, I didn't know what she was going to say, I just blew her off. I thought about her the whole walk back. I arrived at David's house; Sara looked at me with a half frown and nodded her head to the bedroom Nadine and I were staying in.

"*Esta llorando, llevala suave.* She's crying, go easy on her," Sara said.

I walked to the bedroom, opened the door and entered. I tried talking to Nadine to no avail. She wouldn't say a word, no matter how much I coaxed. I guess she needed her space and time after I'd beaten her up; I understood that. I had really been inconsiderate, on what had been a tranquil and beautiful day before tomorrow's craziness, the calm before the storm. Now the storm had begun.

I left the room, defeated, and crashed down on the sofa, mentally exhausted, next to the teddy bear. I lay there as motionless as that ridiculous bear for a good half hour.

"*El puerco estuvo aqui.*"

I looked up and saw David standing in front of me, a worried look in his eyes. The statement caught me by surprise but had my attention.

"What pig?"

"Capitan Molina, the top cop in Santa Clara who has his fingers in everyone's pocket that has a government business license. He's always fucking with the fishermen at the docks. Always looking for handouts and handing out threats in return if you don't pay up. His threats aren't empty; he runs everything in the entire province of Las Villas. He shows up unannounced and makes our lives miserable. You do what he wants or he pulls your license. That would be my death. He was at the house this afternoon asking questions, wanting to know who my houseguests were. I told you Kiki, the Beard has many eyes. Someone told him we had people here, foreigners. Sara has a government license to rent out the room you're staying in, and I have a license to take tourists fishing, so *el hijo de puta* wants a cut. He looked a little suspicious, though; and there wasn't anything routine about it. He had two other cops with him, and he's usually alone."

"That's bad. Did he ask where we were?"

"Yeah, I said you were out sightseeing but were coming back. Then he looked in the room you're staying in. I almost shit, but he only looked in for a few seconds, nodded his head and closed the door. He said, '*no me olvides,* David, don't forget me David,' and then he was gone."

Thoughts of Banco crashed into my mind. Had he talked? Was I the target of Molina's interest? Small-time cops like him were always looking for a gold star from the communist party, and in doing so they created a lot of bad faith with the people. They had to hope the *politiboro* held things together, because the day the Revolution went south, they were the first ones the people would hang form the majestic palms and the mystical ceiba.

Other than squeezing the already poor people in true Marxist style throughout the province, I would have thought that when he turned to harassment, he could find enough poor souls in his own city of Santa Clara. A provincial capital, it had about 200,000 inhabitants, beautiful parks and *parroquial* churches, lots of tourists and history—and Che. Santa Clara was where his decisive victory against Batista took place. It had a lot more going than David's north coast, with its sleepy little villages.

He'd had two other cops with him; it didn't seem like a routine black-market squeeze to me either.

"I know you're thinking about Banco, Kiki. He didn't search the house or the room, or he would have found the guns. He went to a few other houses too, and down to the docks. I think he's looking for something, but he doesn't know what yet. And if it is about Banco, he can't tie me to it; we've never laid eyes on each other. I don't know, I just don't think it was routine. *Cuidado*, Kiki, we have to be careful and we need to move fast. That *hijo de puta* is greedy and evil."

David plopped down in the living room chair. I could see the wheels turning in his head. I tried to gather my thoughts, too. Things were edgy enough without a goddamn communist cop snooping around trying to earn some stripes. He must have had results, though, to have those stripes to begin with. Capitan Molina must have distributed some serious abuse to people through the years.

Many a Cuban cop has rethought the Revolution midstream, good and bad, but mainly bad. They didn't just up and quit the force. That would have been like trying to leave the Mafia. There would have been consequences, and that usually meant they would be done away with. They were typically cowards who disappeared into the bowels of Havana's seedy, run down, decrepit neighborhoods and waited for their chance to become *balseros*.

During the Mariel Boatlift in 1980, hundreds of cops disappeared among the throng of 125,000 that made their way to South Florida, mainly Miami.

When you had suffered the hardships and ridicule of the Revolution, and you risked your life in one of the most treacherous necks of water on earth to escape the poverty, misery and abuse Castro had offered you, you didn't forget the faces of your tormentors, the bastards who abused their positions in order to abuse you. No matter how much you mixed and melded into South Florida's Latin community, at the end of the day the world was a small place and South Florida even smaller. Sooner or later you ran into someone you knew or who recognized you. Water didn't wash under the bridge so easily for some. Just because they were out of Cuba doesn't mean they had forgotten. And many exact their revenge on the scumbags who preyed on the weak while draped in a revolutionary flag.

Many of these cowardly cops had met their demise at the hands of those who refused to forget. They ended up fertilizing some wooded area in Miami's outskirts and were never heard from again.

The ones who decided to go and take their chances had to hide real well. Maybe China, or Burma. There were thousands of Cubans who possess a pure hatred for Castro, or anyone who agrees with the Beard. They were dangerous; they lived to see Castro dead. Anti-Castro sentiment was as strong in Miami as anti-American rhetoric had been in El Comandante's long-winded, pompous three and four hour speeches through the years.

The more I thought about Molina, the more pissed off I was getting. Captain Molina's day would come. And soon.

"Kiki, Molina usually comes once a month. If he's back in a day or two something is wrong. We have to move tomorrow."

David was right, and he felt it came close to home. I understood his concern. His wife and daughter would become involved if they tied him to Banco through me.

There was a loud knock at the front door, and I stood quickly. My heart was pounding and my nerves were on edge. David ushered me into the tiny bedroom. I thought of Molina at the door—had he come back knowing I had returned? I reached into my bag and pulled out the .380, slipped in a clip and jacked a bullet into the chamber. We might all be leaving for Miami in a hurry. I readied myself for the worst.

Nadine sat up quickly, eyes wide open in worried surprise. I put my finger to my mouth. "Don't say a word." I whispered.

There was a knock at the bedroom door sooner than I expected. "Kiki, it was Chino at the door," David said.

I walked out of the bedroom and saw an agitated Chino milling nervously about the kitchen, drinking some Cuban coffee that Sara had just made. The coffee wasn't going to help his hyped-up state.

"*Que paso*, Chino?"

"Molina *estuvo en el muelle, miro a la* Señorita Inez," he said.

Molina was at the docks searching boats, the *Señorita Inez* included. That didn't sound good. Why now? That son of a bitch knew something, or he was getting close by luck. Either way, it made me very nervous.

"What did he want, Chino? Did he ask any questions?"

"Fucking money or food if you ask me. *Hijo de puta;* always looking for a handout. No Kiki, he asked the usual shit. Where are you going, where have you been, are your licenses in order? The same shit every time he picks our pockets. He had a little smile on his face like he knew something. Everybody got questioned and he boarded a few boats. Silvio Gomez got it the worst. He had just gotten back from a fishing trip and Molina and his men went over his boat with a fine-toothed comb and found nothing, but walked off with a sack full of lobsters. *Maricon*."

"What about La *Señorita*, Chino—do you think he noticed anything?"

"Hell no, the only thing he could have noticed were the torpedoes and he would have had to jump in the water for that. That pig wouldn't chance ruining his cheap Russian-issue footwear. They get a pair every two or three years; those pieces of shit fall apart easily enough without soaking them in salt water. Besides, he's too lazy. He'd rather steal from us than do his job. You can't see the torpedoes from the water line. He boarded, looked around and asked me when David was due to go out again. I played slow and stupid. I'm just a working slob, I told him. He looked at me, nodded his head, and walked off."

Chino sat down nervously, the Cuban coffee now coursing through his system. The contact with Molina had the little man pretty well jacked up.

I couldn't put Molina and De La Guardia together. Two different levels. There was too much government in between them. Maybe Molina heard something. I was sure he had some spies, and he was from the provincial capital, the top cop. Maybe he was being used as a bird dog to see what he could flush out, sent on a mission by the higher ups without their letting him know what was up. Or he was acting on his own, trying to get some political recognition. Who knew what that prick was up to, except that something wasn't right.

Either way, if that son of a bitch tripped over us, we were screwed. We had to be careful and we had to move fast.

"*Gracias por todo,* David. I owe you big time."

That night dinner was a quick affair. Nadine didn't emerge from the bedroom to help Sara, and she didn't join us for dinner either. Anibal and Chino came, though, and after dinner the four of us met in the living room and talked about the new developments. We talked about what we would do if we received another visit from Molina tomorrow, or if any of us were raided by his men during the night. If it was just Molina snooping around again, everyone would play it cool, and I'd lay low so he couldn't interview me. If it was a real raid, the plan was to take them all down, get to the boats and head for Ragged

Island, each of us taking a separate route. Once we made it to Ragged we'd park the *Señorita Inez* and I would smuggle David, Sara, Sarita, Anibal and Chino into the Keys. That is, if we were still alive.

Anibal and Chino left and David, Sara and I turned in early, each of us anxious about what tomorrow would bring. I went into our little room and it was all I could do to get undressed and lay back on the tiny cot-like bed. Nadine and I hadn't had much time together since the morning. Nadine was awake, but she remained on her little bed. Neither of us could muster up the strength to talk, or even say goodnight. There had been a lot of excitement, and I drifted off to sleep letting it all go through my head again like a movie.

I heard knocking at the bedroom door and I sat up quickly out of a dead sleep. Nadine was not in the room. I heard David's voice calling me.

"*El café esta listo,* Kiki. *Vamos levantate.*" David was urging me to get up.

I got up, got dressed, and walked into the living room where the ceremony had taken place the other night. David, Anibal, and Chino were all in the living room waiting on me.

"*Donde esta* Nadine?" I asked.

"She went for a walk early this morning," Sara replied as she walked into the living room with a tray holding our demitasses of Cuban coffee.

I sat drinking my coffee, thinking about Nadine. This was not a good time to be wandering around.

"Do you know where?" I asked Sara.

"She was headed toward the waterfront," she responded. "But she didn't take the main road into town first. She went straight to the water, right across the way over there," Sara said, pointing to the front of the house, and thus meaning across the street and across a field between the house and the water.

"There's a beach there," David said. "And it's also close to the Nautical Base," he added.

"I told her just go to the water, and don't wander east or west from there," Sara said.

"Let's hope she took your advice," David added.

"Tonight we make our move," Anibal said, changing the subject. I nodded my head in agreement.

"David, we have to figure out the best way to get on the compound without being noticed. If we can do that, then we're in the game," I said.

"Anibal and I have a way, we think." David said.

"I'm all ears, *hermano*; tell me what you've got," I replied. I listened to David as he laid it out as best he could. I knew there would be a lot of improvising once we got inside the compound. Hell, no one knew what we'd find there.

"The compound is on the waterfront. The whole area is fenced off, but only with a simple chain-link fence and I don't think it's alarmed or hot-wired. The front gate is always open, and at night when they close it there's no guard. There are civilians and athletes there all the time. The Canadians are constantly in and out. Some Canadians live on the compound and at night they have a security guard out there, Cuban military, but only one. We don't know anything about who or what is inside the warehouses, or how the buildings are alarmed. That's what we have to figure out when we get there. So far, so good, Kiki," David said, smiling. "The waterfront is open. No fence—no nothing, just the seawall where the sugar was loaded in the old days. The wall is pretty high off the water, but there are re-bars bent into a ladder shape and imbedded in the seawall here and there for climbing up and down."

"What kind of night lighting do they have?" I asked.

"Very little," David replied, "it's pretty dark out there at night. Other than some individual bulbs over some doors on the compound warehouses, the lighting is in our favor."

"It sounds like everything is in our favor," I commented.

"This is Cuba, Kiki, and just like Uncle Sam has the long arm of the law, Castro has a thousand eyes out there. Nothing is easy in Cuba; don't you know that yet, *mi hermano?*" David said as he patted my shoulder.

"I guess I'm finally beginning to realize that. Anyway, you're thinking we should have two teams and one should go in via land, the other via water, right?"

"That's right," David said and smiled. "You guessed it, Kiki. This way we have two escape routes, so we double our chances. Of course we also double our chances of giving ourselves away, but we'll end up doing that anyway, I'm sure of that. Somebody somehow will see us. It's really all about how big our window is before they see us and we have to either get out of there or kill everyone."

"I assume the boat should go in first, right?" I said.

"You got it. Get in there first and find Banco, and let's hope the treasure. The rest of us arrive from the front gate and provide cover when the shit will probably hit the fan. What do you say, twenty minutes, a half hour earlier for the boat?"

We both looked at Anibal and Chino.

"A half hour or more," said Anibal.

"Let's make it a half hour," David said. "All right with you, Kiki?"

"Fine by me."

"Ok, I think that will work then. You'll have to scramble in order to find them in that maze in that a time period, but I don't want to make the window too big because that means you're without reinforcements. I'm just going to count on you being lucky." David said.

I looked at him and smiled and said, "I'd rather be lucky than good any day, *mi amigo.*"

It was noon and Sara was preparing lunch for us as we sat in the living room reviewing the logistics, even preparing some of the equipment, though each item had to be brought out from hiding one by one in the event Molina and his men showed up.

There was a knock on the door and Sara answered it. A small, middle-aged woman in a loose, full-length dress was at the front door. Sara spoke with the woman for a few minutes, then said goodbye and closed the door. She walked into the living room toward David, holding her hands to her face.

"Nadine was wandering around the front gate of the Nautical Base and my friend Miriam saw a soldier escort her back to one of the offices at the warehouse." Sara said, then slumped down on the couch.

"What?" I said, standing up quickly.

David walked over and said, "*Tranquilo, hermano*, we'll get her back. Maybe she just talked her way in, posing as a tourist."

My heart was pounding hard. It seemed like everything was changing day by day. First Banco, then Molina showing up, and now Nadine being taken. There were only four hours left until sundown and tonight was do or die.

Sara and her friend Miriam went to see if they could find or see Nadine, but Sara returned a short while later, alone. She shook her head and quietly went into the kitchen. I sat in the living room with David, Anibal, and Chino. My mind was racing; I had to focus or I was going to snap. I began to lay out the plans as I saw them based on this new development.

The plans were simple enough. Getting in wasn't going to be much of a problem. The problem was getting in and getting Banco and Nadine out of there. The gold and treasure had become secondary. God and all the *orishas* are going to have to be on our side for this one, I thought.

Night was quickly approaching and there was still no sign of Nadine. I gathered my things and put them all in my backpack. My guns were ready and loaded. I gave David the other .380

Beretta that I had, and Anibal the other Uzi. They were locked and loaded, ready to go.

Anibal looked at the Uzi. He had a sinister smile on his face as he caressed the gun as if it were his favorite lady. No words were needed. I looked at David and Anibal and they nodded their heads and at that time I knew it was on.

I thanked Sara for everything she had done.

"*Valla con dios, mi hijo*," she said.

She turned to David, gave him a hug, and then walked off to her bedroom. I felt sorry for her. Her life had somehow gotten turned upside down over money and I'm the one who brought it all to her doorstep. Anyway, it wasn't all about money.

I looked at Chino and he nodded my way with a smile.

That's right, I thought. This is for Chino and Sara and for the Cuban people and a lot of others who have felt the sting of Castro's Revolution. I felt bad about the circumstances, but I knew I was justified. I knew I was right.

CHAPTER 20

We walked to the front door of the little house; no more words were said. David and Anibal got in David's old jalopy and in a moment they were gone. Chino and I walked down to the docks and got into a small dinghy. I sat in the prow and he took the seat with the oars. I cast off and we were soon on our way to the old sugar-loading docks by the Nautical Base. That was our point of entry, God willing.

When we got out into open water I realized the weather had become rough and stormy again, and rowing over wasn't going to be easy, but happily necessary if we weren't going to be heard or seen.

For a small man, Chino could sure row his ass off. He kept us close to the sleepy village, a couple hundred yards out. Caibarién was unlit and the shore seemed like an abandoned coast. It was eerily quiet and dark, a ghost town.

I felt my heart pumping faster and stronger as we approached the docks, as if it were warning me of the upcoming danger, but something kept pushing me forward with a calmness and alertness that I had come to know and welcome as a close friend in dire times.

I was close enough to see that one of the patrol jeeps with the two Cuban guards was making its rounds and it was nearing the docking area where we were going to climb up at the Nautical Base and warehouse complex.

"Chino, *mira.*," I said. Chino stopped rowing and turned around to look at the docks. The jeep came to a stop at the docks facing the ocean. The two men got out, walked to the front of the jeep, leaned against the grill and both men lit up cigarettes. They had left the lights on on the jeep and we could easily make out their silhouettes. When they took a drag, we could see the embers light up and it created an aura-like effect around their faces.

It all looked like something out of a World War II black and white movie—the guards making their rounds; the thieves hiding in the shadows; the camera going back and forth; the calm before the storm.

I sat there quietly with Chino as we bobbed up and down in the pitch black and stormy night. We were no more than fifty yards away from the guards and their jeep. We were completely invisible to them and they had no idea that we were sitting there watching them.

"*Come mierdas.* They work for the government and take advantage of their positions and the people. They think they are bulletproof, *hijos de putas,*" Chino whispered. He was pointing the .380 Beretta I had given him in their direction. "I should shoot those *hijos de putas* right now."

"Easy, Chino," I put my hand up on the silencer of the gun and pulled it down. "We're going to hit them where it hurts."

"*Si*, Kiki, we're going to take their fucking money."

"No, Chino, we're going to hit them in their communist tough guy pride. The Beard has the world thinking he's got everything under control in Cuba and look where we are right now. I just want to tear down some of that curtain of invincibility that he thinks he has. Fuck him and his Revolution."

"Coño! I want the money. I'm not staying in Cuba, Kiki. I'm going to Miami," Chino said. "I was always afraid of going to Miami. Not because of the water, shit, I think I could swim there," he smiled and continued. "I'm not an educated man Kiki. What would I do in Miami? It scared me to think what would happen, what would I become? I'm not young, it still scares me. At least here I'm with people I know. I have no family in Miami, and all my family in Cuba is dead. The only thing I have is my country, *mi patria*, so I stay. But if I can get some money to go to Miami with, I would have a good start. Get a little apartment, some nice clothes, and eat good everyday. That is all I want. I don't think it's too much. If I could have that in Cuba I would stay. Am I wrong, Kiki?" he asked sincerely.

"No, Chino, you're not wrong. That's what every man wants."

"Well then, this Revolution owes me, and since it's not paying up then I'll take what's mine and go to Miami," he said.

We had been bobbing up and down in the water for about ten minutes waiting for the guards to leave. They finally finished their cigarettes. One of the guards walked over to the dock and flicked his cigarette into the water as he looked out onto the ocean. For a second I thought he saw us; he was staring right at us. I could tell by his body language that he didn't see anything. The ocean is a very dark place at night, even at fifty yards away. The guards walked back to their jeep, got in and continued their rounds.

Chino quickly grabbed the oars and rowed the dinghy to the docks. While he rowed I made sure I had all my equipment and put on my backpack. The wave action was rough against the high walls of the old cement piers and it slammed the dinghy against it with enough force to make a loud smashing noise. We quickly grabbed onto the guidelines that were hanging there, used to balance and support the men that worked on the ship hulls when they were docked. Chino maneuvered two old tires that were already secured on the dinghy and prepared to serve as bumpers on the tiny boat. Once in place they stopped the boat from being smashed against the docks yet again. The waves kept slamming into the wall and every now and then the boat and bumper made a loud thud. But luckily with the stormy weather and the intermittent thunder I doubted anyone would hear anything.

I quickly latched onto one of the guideline ropes, balanced myself and jumped up and out of the dinghy, swinging over to the side where I was able to grab one of the re-bar ladder rungs that was imbedded in the seawall. I climbed up the seawall ladder, one rung at a time. I cautiously peered over the top of the wall; everything seemed quiet. I waved Chino to come up and he scaled the wall as if it wasn't even there.

I ran as fast as I could across the 30 yards of concrete with Chino hot on my tail and we hid behind the first set of warehouses. It was dark and the back of the warehouse was only a few yards from the chain link fence that surrounded the compound. We crouched there and caught our breath.

"Was there anyone around?" I whispered to Chino.

"No, I didn't see anybody; the weather probably has anyone who is here inside."

"I hear someone, Chino."

"I hear it too."

I unlocked my Uzi and pointed it at the corner of the warehouse where I heard the noise. My eyes had gotten accustomed to the darkness and the lack of light at the compound made it easy for me to see who or what was coming. It was David and Anibal; they came around the corner of the building and quickly squatted down, but without seeing us.

"Psst, psst, *olle* David, Anibal, *aqui*," I called.

They were startled when they heard me call and before I knew it I had two guns pointed at my head.

"*Tranquilo*, Anibal, es Kiki," I said. They were both a little winded. "What happened?" I asked.

"That son of a bitch jeep almost saw us," Anibal said. "It was so fucking easy jumping that fence and it was so quiet that we didn't expect that jeep to be coming around the corner. Fuck

I've never run so hard in my life; I thought I was going to have a heart attack. *Pero los come mierdas* didn't see shit."

"That's why we're early," David said. "We never thought getting in would be that fast."

I sat there for a second and thought about what to do next. The mystery about where everything was on the compound kept me from thinking about it too much. It had to be played by ear and the time had come. Everyone was a little winded and my heart was racing. If we got caught on this compound we'd be doing a long stint in a Cuban jail.

I stood up and looked around. The rear of the warehouses had intermittent midsized windows all along the back side of the long, stretched-out building. I crept along the back wall until I reached one of the windows. These were old buildings, dating back to the late 1930s and 40s. The alarm system back then was probably nil and the system they had on the buildings now were probably put in back in the 70s.

It was that aluminum tape that was pre-wired and applied along the edges of the windows and along the windowsill. There is a connection at one point and if you open the window the connection breaks and the alarm goes off. Simple, but effective. One switch inside will turn the whole thing off and no one will be the wiser. I didn't want to chance breaking the window and climbing in for fear of noise. I didn't know what was in there.

"David, there is a roof entrance up there somewhere; we have to get up there and find it."

"There is an old truck at the end of the building, maybe we can get up over there."

"Come on, let's go." I said.

We crept along the wall of the building to the old abandoned truck about 50 yards away. I could see light in some of the sections of the old warehouse. Now I heard one of the jeeps in the distance. It was undoubtedly the one with the guards and they were probably still making their rounds. It seemed as though they were slowly driving along the front of the buildings. The outside of the compound was quiet, except for the waves hitting the dock and the wind. We got to the old, rusted-out truck and crouched down. I looked around in the muggy tropical night.

"Chino, climb up there and see what's up. Be careful and look for a roof door down into the warehouse."

Chino climbed up on the truck and leaped up over the edge of the roof onto the building.

"I hope it's as easy as that little spider monkey just made it look," I said.

The adrenaline was pumping, but watching Chino jump up on the roof of the warehouse was funny and I had a good snicker. He was up there for about a minute before he peered over the wall's edge down at me.

"*Una puerta en al techo.* One door on the roof," he said.

David, Anibal, and I climbed up on the old wreck then onto the roof of the warehouse. Not as easy as Chino made it look, but we made it.

CHAPTER 21

We sat back against the rim wall that circled the entire roof of the warehouse. It was about three feet high and provided good cover from anyone down below. I looked out over the roof and onto the ocean. It was an eerie night and there were a lot of intermittent big black clouds, with heat lightning flashing in the background. The ocean was rough and white capped, growing angrier with the oncoming storm. The sapphire waters of the tropical paradise that was usually drenched in sunshine was feeling a jolt from Mother Nature. I had respect for the power and mysteries of the seas, and this was becoming a night that demanded respect. Cuba had long been in the shadows, but no matter how much wind and rain comes her way, she would soon enjoy her day in the sun.

I walked, stooped over, to the roof hatch that Chino had found. The flooring on the roof was old-style tar and gravel and made a crackling noise when I walked. We had to be very cautious. I waved Chino, David, and Anibal over.

"Good deal, no alarm," I said.

"What did you expect, modern electronics? This is Cuba, a communist island, who in the fuck is going to rob this place?" Anibal said, patting me on the back.

"Thank God for communism," I said.

I lifted up the hatch door slowly and peeked down into the building. There were no lights and the area seemed quiet. I took my backpack off and pulled out a thirty-foot rope I had packed. The drop from the roof hatch to the floor inside was about twenty feet. I tied one end of the rope around the big hinge of the roof hatch. I gently opened the hatch door all the way and lowered the rope. Feet first, I went through the hatch, and descended into the warehouse.

I crouched, with my Uzi aimed at anything that might appear out of the darkness. My eyes were beginning to adjust more and more and I realized that there were cars in this part of the building. I couldn't tell what they were, probably military vehicles.

I called for them to come down. I looked around, but it was darker in the warehouse and my eyes hadn't adjusted. I couldn't see a damn thing. David, Anibal and Chino made their way into the darkened building.

"Let's separate and take a look," I said.

I walked around using the vehicles as cover. We seemed to be alone, but where the hell were we? There wasn't any uniformity to the vehicles in the darkened warehouse.

"David, everything okay?"

"*Si*, this place is empty except for all these cars," David replied.

"Yeah, what are they? They all seem different."

This area of the warehouse seemed secure. I took a lighter out of my pocket. I wanted to see these vehicles. I thumbed the lighter and brought it closer to one of the cars for inspection. To my amazement I was looking at a canary yellow 1950-something Cadillac—a relic in mint condition. I went over the whole car, inside and out. It was mint. Boyd Coddington would envy the craftsmanship on this beauty.

"Do you see what I see, David?" I asked.

"*Alavao*! Fucking Beard has a warehouse full of beautiful cars."

"No David, not just beautiful cars. Beautiful, priceless cars, relics. These cars, in this condition, are worth hundreds of thousands of dollars to collectors in the States."

The Barrett-Jackson Auction would make world history with this fleet of antiques, especially since they probably belonged to the Beard himself. Holy shit.

I was totally blown away by what I was seeing. There must have been at least thirty of them. I walked around and looked. Cadillacs, Fords, Chevys, Chryslers, all from the forties and fifties—Cuba's heyday.

"Fucking amazing, David, this is a fortune in motor and metal," I said to him.

I walked to the corner of the northern wall and got my bearings. "There's a doorway at about the middle of the wall. Let's take a look."

I opened the door slowly, just a crack, and looked through into another large area. It seemed quiet; nothing moved, no one there. A faint light shone under a door on the far wall that I suspected led to yet another large warehouse area.

I called the boys. We walked in, guns already unlocked and aimed. We slid into the large cavernous room and crept along the wall for a few feet, crouched down, as we looked around. There was equipment stored here. I motioned the others to stay put and made my way to the light coming out from under the door. A radio played softly, but I heard no one talking. I walked back along the wall to where David, Anibal, and Chino were still crouched down.

"I don't know if anyone is in there or not," I whispered.

"Spanish or English?" David asked me.

"What do you mean?"

"*La radio*, Spanish or English?" he repeated

"It was English."

"They're Canadians. If it were Spanish guards there would have been Spanish *salsa* music and loud talking," David said.

Everything in the room was diving equipment. There were scuba tanks lined up and put on racks and various pieces of electronic equipment with rolls of wires and cable. The one piece of equipment that was easy to recognize was the mini sub. Castro wasn't kidding with his attempt to bring up lost treasure. These Canadians were loaded for bear. There had to be millions of dollars in equipment in here.

"All this fucking shit and those cars and I can't feel good with a nice home and a plate of food in this fucking country," Chino grumbled. "This is wrong, and I want mine."

The problem with a lot of people in Cuba, and a lot of Cubans in Miami, was that they lived with this deep hatred and envy of Castro. My father told me when I was a kid that to live with hatred and envy was like taking poison and waiting for the other person to die. It made no sense.

"I'm through with it all. I'm going to get mine and fucking leave this hellhole," Chino said.

"*Tranquilo hermanito, no te apures.* We don't have shit yet," Anibal said.

I noticed an enclosed area, an office or an inner storage of some kind. The door was padlocked and had a big sign. I held up my lighter. Written in red letters against a black background were the words "*Halto, entrada proivido. Por Departamento de Estado Cubano Officina de Geo Mar.*"

Geo Mar, as Tomás had told me, was the Cuban state-run head of all recovery and salvage done in their waters. Technically, they were the Canadians' partners.

"*Oye,* David, Anibal, Chino, come look at this."

"Departamento Geo Mar, these are some big boys, Kiki. These are the same guys who hired divers like Tomás before the big companies got into business with Castro," David said.

I checked for any kind of warning systems or alarms. But just like Anibal said, this was Cuba, and a little pre-wired tape on the windows and padlocks on doors were good enough. The alarm systems here were as old as dirt; the Beard had the whole country scared, and that was an alarm itself. With this system in Miami, these warehouses would have been empty. The walls might have even been gone by now. The Canadians weren't going to take anything or go where they shouldn't. I was sure they were well-informed on Castro's infamous jails.

"Anibal, Chino, go by the door where the music is coming from, in case someone comes out of there."

I waited until they were by the door. "David, shoot the lock off."

David fired two shots with the silenced gun. The lock fell to the floor in pieces.

I could barely hear the gunfire, but the lock made a clanging noise when it hit, and we crouched, thinking it might have been heard by whoever was in the other warehouse section. But all remained quiet.

I opened the door slowly; it was pitch black in there. David followed behind me and I motioned to him to close the door behind him. My lighter illuminated an officelike room, maybe a little bigger than twenty feet by by thirty. I saw a desk with paper work on it, and quite a few boxes stacked in another corner. I motioned for David to see what was on the table and in those boxes. I took a look at one of the boxes on top, prying it open with my hands.

"*Cojones mira,* David. I can't believe this!"

David looked inside the box while I held the lighter close.

"*Madre mia,* that's a lot of American greenbacks." David said.

I pulled out one of the money packs from the box. They were twenties, fifties and hundreds, packed and stacked together in neat little cubes, all wrapped and vacuum packed in airtight plastic.

"Sweet little packages, eh, David?"

"Real sweet, Kiki. This is the treasure, and already in cash, *que rico mi hermano*," David said, wide eyed and grinning.

I knew my money bundles. "I'd guess there must be about fifty to eighty thousand in each stack. And there are four stacks in every box, if they're all like this one. David, that is millions of dollars."

We stood there for a few seconds looking at each other in amazement. I lifted the lighter and scanned the rest of the room; there was a big, armylike duffle bag in one corner. I walked over to the duffle bag and tugged at it. Heavy. I balanced the bag on its end and it stood straight up. Whatever it was, it was solid enough to hold the bag's shape. I untied the drawstrings on the bag, forcing it open. I reached in and grabbed a small package. At first I thought it was more money, but it were much harder than money packs. Under the dim flare of the lighter I held the package in my hand and read a name written on it. It said "Danilo."

I knew what it was right away; I reached in and pulled out another package, and another and another. They all had different names on them, sometimes the same name on three or four of them: "Danilo." "Chispa." "Mosca," and a few others.

They were kilos of cocaine. I cracked one open just to make sure there was no mistake. You could see loads of the neat little packages all over the news every few days in Miami, from all the busts they made.

I cracked one open and the white powder spilled all over the floor in big, hard, chunks that just flaked off. This was the real deal—chunks of flaky rock cocaine that glistened even in the dim light of the lighter. It was top quality stuff.

I touched it to my tongue and a second later it was numb. David had been looking over my shoulder and saw the white powder hit the floor.

"*Asi que es verda.* I never doubted the rumors, but now I can see for myself,"

I counted them.

"There's a lot of yeyo here *mi hermano*," David said.

"Yeah, sixty-five *quesos* baby. That's a lot of cheese."

"*Ese cabron*, I knew his hands were dirty. And he talks on TV and denounces drugs and the United States' appetite for them," David said.

"These are small potatoes, my friend. If the head of a country gets involved in drugs, he doesn't do it for sixty-five keys. He does it for three thousand, four thousand, ten thousand keys. Castro might be involved in the drug trade like his buddy Noriega was, but not for sixty-five keys. This smells like a side job. The Beard's do-boys are stealing a little bit for themselves or they're doing side jobs on their own. In either case, it won't fly for long."

"But why keep this shit here in the warehouses with the Canadians?" David asked.

"It's fucking perfect, it's like having your own little bank secured by the Canadians, who don't even know it's here. If it gets to the wrong ears or hands, the Canadians become the scapegoats, they'll take the fall."

"Didn't Tomás say that Colonel De La Guardia has been seen here a few times? I'll bet you he's the son of a bitch with his hands in the cookie jar."

"Honor among thieves, my ass. Dog eats dog, and it seems like De La Guardia feels like a big dog."

"The Beard has eaten bigger dogs for lunch. I'd be careful if I were him."

"Let's go man, let's get as much of this money as we can in the duffle bag. This shit's ours now."

We emptied out the coke from the duffle bag.

"David, grab one of those kilos and put it in the bag," I said.

"Don't tell me you like to do a little yeyo, Kiki?" David said.

"When I was younger I used to do a little toot, but I got tired of waking up on the floor. I want to show some friends what Mr. Castro likes to do on his days off, when he's not managing the Revolution."

"*Si*, he is probably filling up his private banks accounts in El Salvador, or Nicaragua, or Venezuela with his arrangements with the cartels and all his off-the-record cocaine deals. If you're right that this is what some of his *mallimbes* are stealing from him, I can only imagine how much he has for himself, *ay mi madre.*"

"I know it won't do shit, and I'm not saying or showing anything that everyone who needs to know doesn't already know, but I'll get personal satisfaction from it. Get Anibal and Chino back here."

He went to the door and opened it, peered into the cavernous warehouse, and called to Anibal and Chino. They came into the office quickly.

"*Que encontraste?*" Anibal asked.

"This is what I found, *hermano*," I said, opening the duffle bag and showing its contents.

"*Cono de pinga, una fortuna.*" Chino's eyes were as big as cueballs.

"*Y eso en el piso? Es perico?*" Anibal asked.

"*Si*, sixty-five *llaves, mi hermano*," I told him.

"*Yo lo savia.* I knew it, too many happy military motherfuckers around here."

"Son of a bitch, *y yo comiendome un cable*," Anibal said.

I blurted out a little laugh. That was a Cuban saying, meaning things are so hard that they're choking. Cubans were sarcastic as hell. They also said that God never chokes you out; he just stops you from breathing every now and then.

"We need to go back to where the cars are and go to the back door; we'll find the alarm switch there. Let's go."

We all grabbed a corner of the duffle bag, walked out of the inner office, closed it back up and made our way out to the area with all the antique cars.

I saw the door and, no surprise, there was a switch with all the wires visible, running to the windows and doors.

"Let's hope this shit hasn't fucked up over the years and brings everyone down on us."

I hit the switch. Nothing. Thank God.

We went out and walked back to the corner of the building. The waterfront and seawall seemed quiet.

"Chino, you and Anibal take the duffle bag to the dinghy and come back. David and I will cover you."

We waited for the jeep to make its rounds to the ocean side of the warehouses and return up front. Anibal and Chino ran across the thirty yards of concrete back to the seawall and disappeared over it.

CHAPTER 22

With the weather setting in, I could hardly make out Anibal and Chino as they ran back. The rain was coming down intermittently, but when it did it came down in sheets, racing across the complex as blustering winds pushed it along.

I thought about all that money in the dinghy and hoped and prayed the lines were well secured. If it swamped we were not only out a couple million, we would also lose the best way to get the hell out of here.

I crept back along the wall with David, Anibal, and Chino in tow until I got to the door that I'd left unlocked. I made sure it was still clear and waved everybody in. Cautiously, we returned to the office where we had found the money and coke.

It was still empty and quiet. We went in and hid behind some of the equipment in the room. Again I made my way to the far door where the faint light and the radio music came from. I opened the door slowly, just a crack. A man sat at a desk, doing paperwork. I could hear the droning sounds of what seemed like pumps. It wasn't very loud, but loud enough to drown out other noises.

I pushed the door open further without any reaction from the man at the desk. There were a bunch of row sinks, about three feet wide and one foot deep, maybe thirty or forty feet long, all filled with water. Pumps and other tubing were attached to them. I pulled the door shut.

"There's only one guy in there. You can't afford to be seen; I'll go in and take care of that guy, then you come in," I said.

"Let's hope no one else shows up."

I opened up the door again and the man was still busy at his desk. I walked into the room and crept toward him. My Uzi was in my hands, pointed straight at my potential victim. There was still no sign that the man at the desk had heard anything.

Suddenly he turned around, still sitting, a look of astonishment and fear across his face. He fumbled around, trying to stand up and backing away at the same time. He tripped backward and fell flat on his ass. He continued to fumble around, knocking and pulling down papers from his desk while trying to stand.

Not a sound had come out of the man's mouth. It was partially open and I could tell he was in shock at what was happening to his otherwise peaceful life. I stepped toward the man, gestured to him to stay down, and hushed him. I had the Uzi aimed straight at his head. I could see the fear of God in his eyes.

It wasn't easy to point a loaded gun at anybody. One wrong move from either of us and this poor asshole's brain would have been splattered all over the walls.

"Don't kill me please, *no me mates,*" he said.

"Just stay down, I'm not going to kill you. Are you alone?"

"Yes," he said.

"How about those guards patrolling outside? Do they ever come in here?"

"Once in a while. When officials from Geo Mar come they escort them."

"Are there any Geo Mar people around?"

"I don't know!"

"That building standing alone out by the waterfront, what is that?"

"Geo Mar and government offices, as far as I know. I'm just a cataloguer. They don't pay much attention to me and I leave them alone."

"Get up, sit in the chair."

He was visibly shaking, his arms and legs quivering. I put my finger to my mouth, letting him know to stay quiet. On the floor beside the desk was a length of plastic cord. I picked it up, walked behind him, and began to tie his hands and arms to the chair.

"What's your name?"

"George," he said, his voice quivering.

"You Canadian, George?"

"Yes."

"You like Cuba, George?"

"Yes."

Old George thought I was going to snuff his ass. I finished tying him up and pushed the chair so he faced the wall.

"Stay quiet, George, and everything will be fine," I told him. I looked around and found an old rag.

"George, I'm going to blindfold you, but don't get scared, I'm not going to hurt you. But if you make any noise, the people I'm with are not as nice as me. Do you understand?"

"Yes," he said.

George was so fucking scared he was down to one word answers. David had been watching me through the crack in the door; he came in with Anibal and Chino when I pushed George to the wall.

I pulled them aside.

"Don't let him know you're Cuban. He probably thinks I'm American government or some shit. You guys take a look around, see what you can find. I'm going to have a talk with George."

I walked back to the corner where I had pushed George and his chair.

"George, what are all those long sinks?"

"Whatever the dive teams bring up is brought here and put in those basins, under water, to prevent the artifacts from deteriorating any further. Scientists and archeologists work on them until the're ready. Then the other cataloguers and I date and register everything according to dive sites."

Anibal walked up to me and motioned toward a section of the warehouse.

"George, stay quiet and don't move. Someone is behind you, watching you."

I went to where Anibal had pointed. David was there, looking into a caged area with a padlocked jailhouse-type door. I looked in at boxes and trays with all kinds of artifacts in them. All seemed to be tagged and numbered. Another cage inside that cage was also padlocked with a padlock. I walked back to George. "What's in the cage?"

"Everything that we catalogue, number, and register," he said.

"Where's the key to the cage?"

"I don't know. I've only seen my bosses and Geo Mar go in there."

"Are you sure, George?"

"Yes, yes, I'm telling you what I know," he said, despair in his voice. "Take whatever you want, just don't hurt me." George was telling the truth, he was sobbing and gasping.

"What about the cage inside the cage?"

"I don't know, I swear I've only seen as much as you have. There are a bunch of boxes in there, but I don't know what's in them, I swear," he said. "Take what's in the long sinks. They're full of valuable coins, relics, artifacts—take them. I don't know about anything else, I just do paperwork."

"That belongs to the Cuban people, George, and hopefully, someday they'll get the benefits from it. I'm not a fucking thief, I want what Castro has stolen from other places and people so it can be returned to where it belongs."

"You're not government," George said. It wasn't a question, it was a statement.

"No, I'm not fucking government; I'm just someone who thinks Castro has abused Cuba and the people for too long. And you, George, assholes like you come and help him. Don't get me wrong, I'm a capitalist at heart, but not at the expense of the people. Haven't you taken a good look, George? While you enjoy Cuba and all it has to offer, the Cuban people get shit. Or haven't you noticed the poverty around you?"

Not a sound came from George's mouth. His head sagged a little, as he heard the truth I was telling him.

"Go shoot the locks off both cages, have the boys guard the doors," I told David.

Zip, zip, zip, zip. I could barely make out the muffled, silenced .380 being fired at the locks.

I walked into the caged area and looked around. Just like George said, artifacts of all kinds: gold, silver, religious relics encrusted with emeralds—all numbered, dated and identified. It was a fortune, the greatest divers and discoverers of all time would shit at seeing this. I stepped into the inner caged area and opened up one of the boxes. More silver, more gold, more religious artifacts, lengths of gold chain five, six, seven feet long. I opened a box and it had nothing inside except what seemed to be porcelain vases, Chinese vases. I showed a vase to David. There was only one ship I knew of that had any vases of value on it when it went down. "*La Nuestra Señora de las Maravillas*," I said. "She went down off of Grand Bahama, just north of Memory Rock."

I kept opening boxes and finding more and more treasure. The only difference was that none of this stuff was numbered or dated. A box full of religious artifacts caught my eye. I noticed emeralds shining in the bottom, set in gold. I reached in and pulled out, something big. I couldn't believe what I was looking at: a flattened statue of the Madonna nearly a foot tall, all in gold and emeralds, cradling an infant Jesus in her arms with a halo also encrusted with emeralds. The Golden Madonna and Child—real as life, and in my hands.

The world's greatest diver, salvager, adventurer, and ocean historian of all time, Bob Marx, who found *La Nuestra Señora de Las Maravillas* back in the seventies, talked about a mysterious religious statue that he thought was on the Maravillas. He was the one who named it the Golden Madonna. No one believed him though; it was never found nor was it on any manifest. Everyone thought he was crazy, but here it was, in my hands. It was beautiful, mesmerizing—just as Marx described it.

It all made sense. The vases, the Madonna, all from the *Maravillas* in the northern Bahamas. This was proof that the Beard had pillaged sites outside of Cuba. I walked back over to George, pulled off his blindfold.

"Have you ever seen anything like this before?" I showed him the vase.

"No I haven't."

"How about this?" I asked, showing him the Madonna.

"I've never seen that before in my life."

"This is what I want, George. The things I knew that son of a bitch was stealing." I put George's blindfold back on. "Stay still, my man, this ain't over yet,"

On my way back to the inner cage, I grabbed and emptied two big dive bags.

"Let's put as much as we can in the bags, David."

It took us a couple of minutes to fill the bags with gold. I put the Madonna on top of the bags and we left of the cage. I walked over to George.

"Stay put, and you'll be fine."

I gagged George with another rag, tying it behind his head. I had caught him by surprise. He moaned as I gagged him.

We dragged the dive bags back through the warehouse, retracing our steps through the equipment storage area and the Beard's private car collection, then cautiously out into the stormy night.

CHAPTER 23

"Let's get this shit back to the dinghy," I said. "Same way as before; you and I will cover Anibal and Chino. Chino, don't leave. Wait in the dinghy until I signal you." Anibal and Chino struggled as each dragged a heavy dive bag to the dinghy.

Everything had been easy so far, but my mind was flooded with thoughts of Nadine and Banco. Anibal came running back to the corner. There was a steady rain, and we were all getting wet.

"*Todo esta bien?* Chino is waiting for us," Anibal said.

"That building down on the waterfront is the government building," said David. "The one with the red light outside the door."

The guards were making their way back to the waterfront. The jeep pulled up to the seawall and parked. I could see the guards lighting cigarettes. They weren't getting out of the jeep this time; it was too wet outside. They sat there, puffing away.

Anibal, David and I crouched by the corner. Water was dripping down our faces, and the wind was blowing hard enough to make the raindrops sting.

"Look, the other patrol jeep is parked over on that side of the building," David said.

"Taking a break, just like the Revolution is doing. *Hijos de putas*. They take the easy way out and work for the government and even then they don't work," Anibal said.

"Let's get around to the back of that building," I suggested. "There's a window on the side with plenty of light coming out. Somebody's in there. Follow me."

We dashed across the open lot to the back of the government building. The guards in the other jeep were headed in the opposite direction, heading toward the front of the compound. We made it to the building without being seen. I crouched and carefully made my way to the window. I could see a guard in uniform, sitting at a desk. He was talking to someone, but I couldn't see who. I crouched down again and went to the other side of the window and looked in. Nothing; I still couldn't see who he was talking to. There was no way of knowing how many more military personnel were in there.

The rain blurred my view as it ran down the window. It was hard to make anything out. I could see an inner cage, like the one at the warehouse, and someone lying on the floor inside. It was a makeshift jail, a holding cell. I crawled back to David and Anibal.

"There is more than one military in there, but I only saw one. He was talking to someone. They've got a jail cell in there and somebody's in it."

"This is the place we saw them take that man I told you about, Kiki," Anibal said. "That's got to be him; he hasn't been seen coming out since he went in. You said his name is Banco, right?"

"Yeah, Banco, that's his name. I couldn't make him out, so I don't know if it really is him."

"There's only one door; up front. The guards in the jeep will see us if we try it," David said.

"Let's go see what's up with them. Come on."

I walked over to the other corner of the building along the back and peeked around the corner. The jeep faced the road. Two men sat inside it, their heads moving as if in conversation.

"Two men in the jeep," I told David, holding up two fingers. "Check your guns, guys, make sure you're ready. The fun is about to begin."

I began to walk toward the rear of the jeep. Every hair on the back of my neck was standing up. These guys were armed; it wasn't going to be like George back at the warehouse. The adrenaline coursed through my body; it was exhilarating and frightening at the same time. All my senses were heightened. I was five steps from the jeep when the passenger side door opened. Realizing I was out in the open, I ducked down and dashed to the rear of the jeep. It was parked close to the building, and I heard the door hit the wall as it opened. One of the guards had gotten out.

I was hiding at the rear of the jeep when I saw Anibal walking toward me, not concealing his movements; his Uzi was pointed straight out in front of him, grasped firmly, aimed at the jeep.

Fire spat from the Uzi and the familiar sound of its silenced barrel cut through the sound of the rain and wind.

My eyes got wider and wider. Anibal hurried toward me. He let the Uzi spit out a few more rounds, straight through the rear of the jeep. I ducked down and lay on the ground to avoid friendly fire. I stood after he stopped shooting and backed up against the wall of the guardhouse, my gun at the ready. I was scared shitless; I thought everything had gone wrong and I was in the middle of a war.

Anibal walked around to the driver's side of the jeep, like some fucking commando, with all the confidence in the world. I heard the Uzi fire a few more rounds, and the jeep door closed. Anibal walked around the bullet-ridden jeep and leaned against the wall next to me. There was a calmness about him that scared the hell out of me. This guy had just wasted two men, one of whom was bleeding at my feet.

"Let's put him in the jeep. Quick, hurry," Anibal said.

I didn't hesitate for one minute. This motherfucker was crazy.

"He would have killed you, Kiki. Do you understand? They play different here. They wouldn't have asked you to drop your gun and put your hands up. They would have done to you what I did to them. Do you understand?" Anibal asked, staring into my eyes.

"Gracias, hermano," I shook my head in agreement.

David checked to see if the excitement had attracted anyone. It had only lasted about 15 seconds, but felt like an eternity. Everything slowed down when the shooting began; it seemed like everything was moving in slow motion.

The wind, the rain, the stormy night were our allies. Everything was quiet. The weather made the guards lazy, and it cost them their lives.

I slinked along the side of the building until I reached the front. I looked around the corner and the eerie red light by the door was ten feet away. I walked up and tried the handle; it was unlocked. I waved David and Anibal on.

I opened the door slowly and I saw the guard dressed in a full Cuban military uniform, sitting at the desk just as I had seen him through the window. He wasn't talking to anyone now. *Salsa* music played from an old radio, and he tapped the desk as if playing *conga* drums along with the Latin beat.

There were old pictures of Cuban landscapes on the walls, but the one that stood out the most was the one of 'El Comandante," Fidel himself. You couldn't go anywhere in Cuba without seeing a picture of the Beard. The only one who had more pictures was Che. Egotistical motherfuckers. Maybe that's why Hollywood loved them so much.

The guard sensed something and spun around, still sitting in his wheeled chair.

"Tranquilo, no te muevas, stay still, *mariconsito,"* I said. I put the Uzi six inches from his head.

He had no idea what was going on. His eyes widened and his mouth opened. His hands went up in the air .

"*Quien son ustedes?*" he asked.

"Shut the fuck up," I said to him, and cracked him on the side of the head with the butt of my gun.

Blood spurted from the left side of his face, and he put his hand up to it. He looked at me with anger in his eyes, and I poked him twice in the forehead with the silencer, to let him know I was serious.

David and Anibal rushed into the room at all the excitement. The soldier I had at gunpoint kept staring at the bathroom door. Anibal stepped up to a door that said, "*Bano.*"

He aimed and pulled the trigger. Half a dozen shots riddled the door. David opened it to reveal another guard, slumped down on the bowl and bracing himself with one arm on the sink and the other clutching his stomach.

Anibal walked in and put the Uzi to his head. He looked up at Anibal.

"*Por favor no me mates,*" he said.

"*Mirame bien, cingado, yo soy el que te mate.* Look at me good, fucker. I'm the one that killed you," Anibal said to the bleeding man. He squeezed the trigger and the Uzi made that deadly, muffled sound. "*Maricon, mejor muerto.* Better off dead," he said.

The man's head snapped back with unbelievable force, smashing into the wall. Blood flew everywhere. Anibal walked out of the bathroom speckled with blood. He looked at no one in particular. Tunnel vision, a man on a mission, no words were said.

In the flurry of excitement, I took my eyes off the guard sitting in the chair. He came at me, reaching out to grab me by the throat. My wrestling instincts kicked in. In New Jersey I had grown up wrestling. I competed through my twenties and was kind of a gym rat, catching a workout whenever I could.

As the guard clutched at my throat I stopped short, turned sideways to him and hit him with a head lock he never saw coming. His momentum and the thrust of my headlock flipped him over my hip. He crashed down, flat on his back, with all my weight smashing into his chest. I held on and squeezed tighter.

The impact took the wind out of him, and he grunted at the pain of being tossed on his back. A headlock and hiptoss this beautiful was a once-in-a-lifetime deal, only dreamt of and rarely seen in competition. A toss this sweet would have taken out most seasoned competitors. The guard knew his life depended on being able to get away. As soon as he hit, he began to roll over and get to his knees. It broke my grip on the headlock. I mounted his back and slipped my legs between his and put him in a rear naked choke, then arched my back for all I was worth. This flattened him out on his belly, and I could hear him gasping for air. He tried to claw at my face in desperation, but it was too late; I was wrapped around him as tight as an anaconda. A few more grasps and I felt him go limp. I unwrapped my arms from around his neck and pushed myself off his back to stand up. He was out cold.

Anibal walked over to the guard, rolled him over on his back and pumped bullets into the man's chest until I heard, *click*

click click. His body had reverberated from the impact of the bullets.

One 35-round Uzi clip emptied; four Cuban military dead, and my allies were crazy Cubans with a penchant for ending the Revolution on their own. We were in deep.

Anibal said, "I told you they would kill you if they could."

David was by the door, watching for signs of the other jeep or anyone else. He nodded that all was clear. I walked over to the makeshift jail. "Look for the keys in the desk, Anibal."

He opened the top drawer of the desk, grabbed the keys and tossed them to me. I opened up the cell and walked over to where the man was lying. He was propped up on one elbow and as I got closer to him he inched away in fear. I could see it in his face.

"Banco, Banco, it's me, Kiki." He looked up at me and relief rushed through his face. He reached up with his hand and I helped him to his feet. I could see that he'd had a rough time over the last few days, he was beat to shit. His nice white *guayabera* was covered in blood. He had a deep, wicked gash over his left eye and dried blood around his nose and the corners of his mouth. He was dirty and his hair and beard were matted.

"Kiki, what are you doing here? I never expected to see you. I thought you'd be back in Miami by now."

"I saw when they grabbed you at the Nacional; I couldn't leave you. My people told me where they took you, and here I am, fat man. But don't get too excited, we aren't home yet."

I walked out of the cell and Banco followed, limping.

"These are some friends of mine Banco: David and Anibal."

"Thank you very much, I owe you my life. De La Guardia gave the order to kill me. He was here yesterday questioning me and beating my ass for all he was worth. He was sure I was here about some drug shipments from Colombia that had been lost. He thought the Cartel sent me here to check it out. They thought I had contacted De La Rosa to have the shipments investigated through who I was sending to Cuba. That's you, Kiki."

"They never asked you about the treasure?"

"Never. Every question they asked me was about coke, and they kept insisting I knew about it. And that you knew about it. I overheard them talk about you. They were afraid you'd secretly place a call to G-2 and get them involved. They were afraid the beans would be spilled and they'd be found out. They knew you were American and they figured you were headed back to Miami. They wanted your name out of me."

"Son of a bitch. De La Guardia ripped off the Cartel and now he's scared Castro will find out."

"He was going to kill me anyway. I just accepted the fact that I was going to die and said fuck it, I'm not telling him shit. I came close though, Kiki, I really did. They beat the living fuck out of me day and night for a day and a half. He was scared man. He wanted to conceal that coke deal gone bad with the Cartel. He threatened to kill those guards if they didn't get the answers he wanted."

"Those motherfuckers aren't getting any answers now; all they got was bullets."

"They took De La Rosa out of here yesterday, he was beat to hell. I know he's dead, they were calling him *gusano.* There's a girl in that back room over there." Banco pointed to a door next to the jail cell that said: "*Privado. No Entrada.*" "That dead son of a bitch over there," he pointed to the slumping dead guard in the bathroom, "brought her here early this afternoon. She seemed fine at first and then I guess he wasn't getting what he wanted from her so he forced her into that room. I haven't seen her since."

I ran to the door, threw it open and looked inside. In the corner of the room, sitting on an old steel-frame spring bed, was Nadine. She had her feet up on the bed and was hugging her knees, cowering against the wall, frightened at what had happened to her and the noise she was hearing in the outer room.

"Nadine, are you ok? It's me, Kiki."

When she heard my voice she jumped up, ran over and hugged me.

"*Pardon, pardon,* I thought I would never be free again. I thought I would never see you again," she said.

"Are you ok?"

"*Oui, oui,* I'm fine."

She stood there looking into my eyes as tears rolled down her cheek. A tiny smile came across her face. She stood there in shorts and a bra; her shirt had obviously been torn off and she looked like she had been roughed up. She became aware of her partial nakedness and crossed her arms over her breasts. I put my arm around her and walked her out of her hellhole.

"We have to move fast, there's going to be communication of some kind soon. The other guards, the phone, something. Let's go."

"We're about fifty yards from the pier, where Chino is waiting in a dinghy."

"Banco, you and Nadine follow me. When you see me go, run fast, run hard. There's another jeep with two guards out there somewhere, but we don't know where. Climb down the pier to the boat. There are a guide rope and iron steps in the wall. Be careful. Tell Chino to get you out to Cayo Fragaso right away. Get the *Lean Back* ready to go and wait for me. It's one am now. Give me two hours and if I'm not there by exactly three, take off. Get into Bahamian waters as quickly as possible, grab the satellite phone and call the Coast Guard with a mayday. Tell them you're being chased by an unknown boat. Don't tell them you were in Cuban waters."

I took a deep breath. "Don't worry about me, I'll be fine. Two hours and take off. While you're on Fragaso waiting for me, call DK and Jony and tell them what the hell is going on. They need to cause a diversion, blow something up, take the heat off of us. Tell DK we'll be heading for the Cay Sal bank, Elbow Cay, where we stashed the food and water. He needs to meet us there, if we ever make it. David, you and Anibal cover us when Banco and Nadine are on the boat. I'll come back and then we'll get the hell out of here."

"*Dale hombre*, I've got your back," Anibal said with a grin.

I walked to the front door and opened it a few inches; the guard jeep wasn't in sight. I was still rainy and windy and my visibility was low. I stepped outside the door and began a fast walk that turned into a sprint toward the pier where Chino was waiting. Nadine and Banco were running behind me and David and Anibal watched and gave us cover. I reached the edge of the dock and lay down on the concrete and motioned Banco and Nadine to do the same. I looked over the edge of the twelve-foot drop into the water. Chino was there in the small boat, soaking wet and hanging onto one of the guidelines.

"*Vamos, Vamos, apurate*," Chino said.

I grabbed Nadine by the hand and helped her over the edge. Banco was next, and the fat man went over the edge with surprising agility. They both made it into the boat without a problem. Banco noticed the duffle bag and two dive bags on the dinghy. He looked up at me and down at the bags then back up at me with his mouth half open.

"*Cabron, cabronsito*," he said, and then sat down in the boat as Chino began to row away into the windy,rain-soaked night.

I sat up and looked around. *Mierda, mira lo que viene!* I heard the sound of the other jeep coming and I was out in the open. I got up and started to run toward David and Anibal, but it was too late. The jeep came around the corner of the warehouse and the headlights caught me in mid-stride. The guards opened fire and I could hear bullets whizzing by my head. Anibal was right, these fuckers didn't question, they killed.

From out of the darkness I could hear the familiar *zip zip zip* sound of Anibal and David's silenced guns returning fire. They jammed on their brakes when they realized they were taking fire, and I heard the tires bring the jeep to a screeching halt, then gears grinding and tires screeching again. I turned to look and they were in reverse, and in a hurry.

A dark shape came at me. I jumped to the side and fell. I pointed my Uzi at the shape as it came to a stop next to me, and in that moment I wondered what the hell had gotten me to the point where I was about to die on my native Cuban soil.

The door opened and I heard David's familiar voice. "*Vamos apurate, no tenemos tiempo.* Come on Kiki."

They had taken the jeep with the two dead guards. I jumped in and Anibal punched the gas. We were chasing the other jeep, firing at it as it ran in reverse. We got closer and closer. They backed in between two warehouse units and as we drove by Anibal emptied half a clip into them. He jammed the brakes on and we came to a jolting stop. He got out of the jeep and walked to the alleyway between the two warehouses, where the guards had backed their jeep.

He aimed his Uzi from the hip and sprayed automatic gunfire into the jeep and the guards until I heard the *click, click, click* of an empty clip. He walked back to the jeep, got in and hit the gas. We headed straight for the wooden barricade at the entrance of the base.

Suddenly shots came ripping through the jeep's ragtop. I ducked down as far as I could go. Anibal looked into the rearview mirror.

"One of them must have prayed to Eleggua to protect him tonight," Anibal said. "*El Maricon tiene suerte*, he's lucky."

We crashed through the wooden barricade and onto a darkened, rainy road. We came to a stop about a half-mile down.

"You take Kiki and ditch the jeep in the cane fields. Go to the docks and take the little skiff with the old two-and-a-half horse on it, the one that belongs to Viejo Jimenez. Get Kiki on it and get him out of here," David told Anibal.

"*Enseguida,* David," Anibal replied.

"I'm going to get my car; I can't leave it around here. When Kiki is gone, you get back to the house. This place is going to be *loco* with military within an hour." David got out of the jeep and disappeared into the stormy night. Anibal hit the gas. We went about a mile and he turned onto a dirt road that led into some cane fields. Without warning Anibal jerked the wheel and slammed us into rows of sugar cane about fifty yards deep. The jeep came to a stop and Anibal opened the door and got out. I jumped to the front and followed him.

"*Vamos, Vamos,*" Anibal was hurrying me back to the dirt road.

He knew the area well and I followed his every step without saying a word. Through some old back roads and a few avocado and mango orchards, we worked our way to the waterfront without incident. At a deserted end of the dock sat Old Man Jimenez's little boat, with its ancient two-and-a-half Seahorse.

"*Dale, alli esta,* get on, *Suerte, mi hermano,*" Anibal said as he untied the boat and helped me on. "*Oye,*" he called out, throwing me the Uzi he had wielded with the expertise of a navy SEAL and the deadliness of an angry man. "I can't have anyone find this. I might get in trouble." He smiled sarcastically and said, "*Vaya con dios.*"

"Tell David if I make it I'll see him in Bimini in two weeks. I'll be at Dreamer's."

I started up the old two-and-a-half seahorse, and in the pouring rain and wind waved goodbye to Anibal. I pointed the boat towards Cayo Fragaso, three miles off of the port of Caibarién.

I could hardly hear the little engine over the howling of the wind and the spattering of the rain on the water. I shielded my eyes with one hand, trying to make out the mangrove coastline of Cayo Fragaso. Looking toward the nautical base, I saw a swarm of red flashing lights and a spotlight combing the waterfront. The patrols had already been called, and this inlet would be swarming with Cuban patrol boats real soon.

Before long, I could make out the mangroves of Cayo Fragaso. I was twenty to thirty yards away, in shallow water. I could hear the engine spatter and the tiny boat jerk whenever we hit the bottom. It must really have been shallow, three to four inches, for this little skiff to hit the bottom.

I maneuvered the boat along the coastline until I got to the eastern tip of Cayo Fragaso, then worked my way around to the northern side of the Cay on the ocean side. I knew I was close to where we hid the *Lean Back*, but in the darkness and the stormy night the only thing that I was sure of was that this was Cayo Fragaso. I turned the skiff into the mangroves and cut the engine. I sat there in the stormy night. The sound of rain, wind, and an angry sea was all I could hear.

CHAPTER 24

While Mother Nature was showing her bad side, she also showed mercy. A bolt of lightning crashed and spidered across the sky with so much force that the little skiff shook. The lightning lit the mangroves for a split-second, and I made out the shape of the *Lean Back* about thirty yards away, tucked away among the trees.

I jumped out of the skiff and headed toward the boat, trudging along in knee-deep water, tripping over mangrove roots and falling to my knees every couple of steps. Soon, I could make out the sleek lines of my baby, my prized possession. My legs were tired as I pushed the last few feet. Without hesitation I grabbed the side of the rail and pulled myself up and over and fell on the deck. I looked up and saw Banco standing over me with a gaff in his hands.

"Easy, easy, it's me," I said.

Banco heard me, dropped the gaff and helped me sit against the side wall.

"Are you all right?" Nadine was kneeling in front of me, rain dripping down her face.

"We have to get the fuck out of here right now; there are patrols all over that base."

Nadine and Banco were physically and mentally worn out. Their faces were long and somber, and exhaustion had taken over their bodies. They both slumped to the deck. They really must have gone through some ordeal. I let them catch their breath and gather themselves, but only for a moment. "Okay! Let's go! We have to leave now! This whole area is going to be crawling with Cuban military soon."

The boat was in about two feet of water and she wasn't a shallow-water craft. The *Lean Back* was built for offshore fishing—not the skinny water. The tide was just starting to come back in, but we didn't have time to wait for it.

"Nadine, you tilt the engines up. Banco you come over the side with me."

Nadine put the three Mercs on full tilt and the lower end units were now fully exposed.

Banco and I went over the side, splashing into the mangrove water below. I pulled Banco along to the stern.

"Grab the lower end units on the engine, Banco, and pull and push, up and down, and force the boat forward at the same time."

He looked a little confused, which was due to mental fatigue, but he mimicked what I was doing anyway. Nadine walked to the bow, grabbed a bowline, jumped up on the rail and started to bounce the nose up and down. This was an old maneuver used to get a boat off a sandbar. Slowly, the *Lean Back* became un-wedged. Between the three of us, we moved her a little bit at a time, to the edge of the mangroves and close to the open water.

I saw a patrol boat heading northeast with red flashing lights and a powerful spotlight searching back and forth. Bahamian waters were the closest to Cuba and northeast was the quickest shot. Choppers would be in the air soon, searching in that direction and that would give us some time as we headed toward the northwest.

DK and Jony were out there somewhere between here and Ragged Island, and if they were making themselves noticeable with a diversion, then that was where the patrol boat was headed. The weather would help them evade the patrol and that sport fisher of theirs was every bit as fast as those patrol boats.

I just needed a little more time to get the *Lean Back* up and going and put a little water between us and Cuba.

"Get on the boat, Banco, we're out of here," I said.

I jumped on the *Lean Back* with Banco right behind me. Nadine waited at the center console, in the bolster seat. I put the middle arm of the two bolster seats up and pulled Nadine close to me.

"Get in," I told Banco, "and hold on."

I tilted the engines down, being careful not to stick the lower end units and props into the sand. I turned the engines over and punched the throttles of all three Mercs as hard as I could. The *Lean Back* thrust forward and pinned us back in the seat. I could feel the hull jerking as it hit the shallow sandy bottom and I heard the propellers grabbing sand—too much of that and the lower-end units would seize up.

I felt the hull scrape bottom one more time and then sensed her settle in and the propellers seemed to grab; I knew we'd hit deeper water.

The seas were about five feet and rough; all made worse by the pounding rain. I put on the panel lights, got my heading and pointed the *Lean Back* to Elbow Cay. Then I turned all the lights off.

"Hand me the satellite phone, Nadine. And grab the wheel, I have to make a call."

In this weather the trip would take two to three hours. It was about seventy miles from Cayo Fragaso to Elbow Cay. I didn't give a shit, we were out of Cuba.

I called Maxi Betancur.

"Hello, hello, who is this, and it better be good at this unholy hour," Maxi said, in a sleepy voice.

"Maxi, it's me, Kiki."

"What do you want at this time of night? Are you going to pay me your poker debt?"

"Listen Maxi, this is serious, I'm running northwest to Elbow Cay if I can make it. I'm a couple of hours out. I don't know what could be following me, but I sure could use some cover—a little brush-back if you know what I mean."

"Shit, your old man was right Kiki, the lines are blurred for you. Must be nice to live in your world." Maxi didn't sound happy.

"Do what you can, Maxi. Remember, I owe you money."

"Yeah, yeah, yeah, like I'll ever see it," he said.

There was a *click* and the phone went dead. Maxi got right to the point. He didn't need to hear anymore, he either could or he couldn't. I hoped the Santeria ceremony the other night had a little more magic left in it.

The *Lean Back* pounded along in the heavy seas and we all clutched onto whatever we could to steady ourselves. Waves crashed over the bow and it was an all-too-familiar soaking, like a recurring bad dream. I took the wheel from Nadine and concentrated on keeping the boat steady into the waves. Time went by fast when you concentrated so hard on a task.

I was having flashbacks of the events of the last few days, and fighting the steering wheel and the ocean and rain at the same time. My mind was flooded, it was more than I could handle. To make it worse, I heard a hum in the distance. What I had wished wouldn't happen happened. The lights were coming out of the northwest and it looked like a patrol boat heading east. We were pretty far away from where it would cross our path but I couldn't take a chance being seen. I cut the engines and let the *Lean Back* drift at the mercy of the big waves while the boat passed to the north. It was really moving and I was glad to see that it didn't slow down. It was a go-fast boat, probably one of the ones that the Cubans confiscated during Mariel and they just put some patrol lights on it and called it official. They were probably headed to see what kind of disturbance the Miami boys were causing. Our decoy setup must have worked. At least it would give us a little more time to get out of Cuban waters and to the Banks.

I turned the engines back on and punched the throttles down. She jumped up on plane and we were on our way again. If the patrol boat happened to see my prop wash, then the race was on. Let 'em try, they wouldn't be able to catch the *Lean Back.*

The clouds were spacing out and I could see gaps of starlight in the sky. The rain had slowed down, but not enough to stop me from continuously wiping my face. I figured we'd made it about halfway to the Banks.

Now another problem cropped up, this one potentially much more serious. I heard the sound of a jet, and I could tell distance by the sound. It wasn't far off. I didn't know how much further it was to Elbow Cay, but I knew it wouldn't be long before the pilot of that Cuban Mig fighter jet would tag us with his radar. Minutes later we would hear the unmistakable roar of jet engines screaming overhead. The Cubans didn't have a real navy. They handled all their offshore problems with Mig fighters and they didn't care how big—or, as in our case, how small—the target was, they came in shooting. Once he tagged me that was it, game over. My only hope was the clouds, to avoid visual, but even then it wouldn't be long.

I heard the whooshing as the Mig's engines closed in and distanced themselves a couple of times, each time becoming louder and louder. It was trying to get a visual on us. Then the Mig made a pass close enough for us to see it, and the roar of the Russian-made jet fighter made us cower in the boat. We were tagged, spotted and doomed.

I pushed the *Lean Back*, and she began to dig into the water as I throttled down. She was airborne right away; the wave action was four to six feet and we came slamming down with a bang that jolted us all in our seats. The props dug in again and the Lean Back crashed through the angry ocean. We jumped from wave to wave, the propellers revving every time we caught air.

I pushed her harder than she should have been pushed in these conditions, but I had no choice. I was sure the Migs knew our position, and we would be hearing the roar of their engines again real soon.

Timewise, I put us on the edge of Cay Sal Bank, but I didn't know if we were near Elbow Cay. I steered the *Lean Back* on a more northerly course to make sure I would hit the Bank—given time by the Migs, that was.

The roar was on us again, this time right over our heads. It was close enough to smell the fuel from the engines' backwash.

The wind was blowing hard, pushing the clouds, causing them to separate, so I could see big patches of clear sky—but not enough to give me sight of any formations on the Cay Sal Bank. I pushed the boat even harder, praying as we crashed through the waves for a sign of the scrub rocks that most seamen dreaded.

Then I saw the jet veer off sharply to the south-southwest after it buzzed us. He knew exactly where we were, there was no mistaking it.

Nadine and Banco held on for their lives as the *Lean Back* powered through another wave.

"Get ready to jump!" I yelled.

They could hardly hear over the roar of the engines and the pounding of the boat. "What?" Nadine asked.

"Get ready to jump!" I repeated.

Both of them heard me that time. They stared in disbelief, but didn't say a word. They knew it was the ocean or the Migs.

I had gotten a sense of relief when we left Cuba and saw that the patrol boats were headed northeast, toward the Miami boys' position, but now, now my worst nightmare had come true.

Banco reached over his seat and grabbed a bumper, looking back with fear in his eyes, but showing readiness. Nadine grabbed my arm, her hand shaking. She didn't want to let go. I had to pull my arm away.

"I'll be right behind you," I yelled.

I could hear the terrifying shriek of the Migs rushing up and I knew this pass wouldn't be for locating us.

"Jump! Jump now!" I screamed.

They knew death was coming for sure if they didn't jump. I took Nadine by the arm and slipped out of the bolster seat, the whole time trying to keep my balance as the *Lean Back* as it surged forward. I leaped into the ocean, holding onto Nadine and hoping Banco made the jump.

We splashed into the threatening, stormy water. I was still holding onto Nadine's arm as the force smashed our bodies together and submerged us as one. I was still disoriented, half out of it from the impact, but I grabbed Nadine and followed the bubbles to the surface.

As we surfaced, the roar of the Migs whooshed by and I saw the release of a missile headed toward the water, then a huge fireball ahead of us. I held onto Nadine. She was gasping for air, as she'd suddenly realized she had surfaced and could breathe.

"Are you all right?" I asked.

"*Oui, oui, je suis bien.* I'm alright Kiki, I'm fine," she said.

They blew up my fucking boat. I loved that boat. Those pricks.

The Mig veered once again to the south-southeast and began catching air. It flew off, rising as it disappeared. Then I heard the all too familiar roar of another jet engine coming from behind and heading in the direction of the burning pile on the water that had been the *Lean Back*. I went under and took Nadine with me.

It roared over us in the direction of the Mig, gaining altitude as it followed in hot pursuit. I wasn't sure what to think. It could be another Mig and they'd be back, or one of Maxi's flyboys had come through.

The current carried us toward the burning pile and I kept watching the sky for the return of the Mig. I spun around in the water, looking for Banco in the light of the flames, but saw nothing. I heard the plane again.

"Get ready to go underwater, they're coming back!" I pushed her under and I followed.

The new fighter went over us again and the thunder it left behind could be heard and felt below. I surfaced and watched it veer off and prepare to come back around. Again I submerged

Nadine and followed her as the fighter jet zoomed overhead, and again I surfaced. This time I watched the plane head west-northwest, toward the Florida coast.

"Maxi, you sweet son of a bitch, that was one of ours."

I was sure the Migs had planned to come back to strafe the water the way they did those poor bastards down in Ragged Island. I had been certain we were going to die.

"Maxi came through, and they ran those fuckers off!"

I was yelling out of excitement, knowing the Migs wouldn't be back. Now I had to deal with what I hoped was the Cay Sal Bank in a rough ocean with poor visibility and no land in sight. Better the ocean than those fucking Migs, I thought.

"Kiki, Kiki, where are you?" I heard coming out of the darkness. It was Banco's voice.

The fat man was being carried by the current, right at us. Nadine and I swam toward him and when we reached him, Banco grabbed onto my hand and pulled himself closer.

"Thank God you're alive," I said. "I thought they blew you up. I never saw you jump."

He held tightly onto the bumper he had jumped overboard with. Banco was rough around the edges, but he immediately pushed the bumper to Nadine, who took it and thanked him.

"Let's get close to the burn pile," I said, "and see if there's anything left floating."

I grabbed Nadine by the arm and began to sidestroke to the still burning boat, with Banco in tow. We caught up to the drifting pile of junk, which was no longer burning. The *Lean Back* was nothing but splinters. One of the coolers had been blown off the boat and was about twenty feet in front of us, bobbing in the waves. I reached it and grabbed the handle, securing myself as I pulled Nadine toward it. She latched on.

My legs were wasted and I let them just hang down in the water. For the first time in almost an hour I wasn't fighting the ocean. I just let myself be carried by the current while I held onto the cooler and rested. We floated and rested at the mercy of the current, hoping it would carry us to an outcropping.

"Shit!" My mind was playing its usual games. The explosion and the fire would attract sharks. Those fuckers like a good commotion. We were floating in the Straits of Florida, and I kept thinking of those men in World War II who went down on battleships in the South Pacific. They were thanking their lucky stars they were alive and then the screams started. Yeah, sharks loved a good commotion and here we were, right in the middle of one.

It was dark, the only light from a few embers the *Lean Back*. I looked around, sure I saw fins popping out of the water, silhouetted in the amber light. My eyes were burning and I was tired. Goddamn sharks! They were on the scene already, opportunistic scavengers that they were.

I yelled out, "Sharks off to our right!"

Nadine took my hand and said, "Take it easy Kiki, we'll be fine." She knew about my close call with the Blacktips in the Bahamas, so she also knew how freaked out about sharks I got, how they could throw me into a panic. "We'll be fine," she repeated. "The water's rough and we're in a storm. They won't be active now."

I watched the circling of those fins on top of the water as we drifted on the strong current of the Gulf Stream, rising and descending with each wave as it pushed us northward, and with each second that passed I was sure that at any moment, we would become part of the food chain. It took every bit of my being to stay semi-calm, and with every little nudge or bump I felt,I reacted sharply, thrashing my limbs. I wasn't helping my cause any, but if I was going to go down, I was going to go down fighting.

My head jerked and I realized I had nodded off. I looked at the sky. Bands of light reached through the clouds being pushed along by the still-heavy winds. The sun was coming up.

We had been in the water for about two hours, and were beginning to get cold. We wouldn't survive long in our condition, without protection. I could see breaks in the color of the water. That meant shallow water; we were on the Cay Sal Bank.

I looked around, but couldn't see any rock outcroppings. We floated along with the current, not fighting it and conserving as much energy as possible.

"Kiki, look!" Banco said, pointing.

"Where? I don't see anything."

But as I was raised up by a wave I saw one of the familiar scrub islands of the Bank. "Come on," I said, "we all have to push. If we miss it we'll never be able to get back to it with this current."

We struggled hard to make it to the rocks; we were using up all our energy. If we didn't make it, once off the Bank we'd be in the Florida Straits and I didn't think we'd have a chance in hell. Luckily, the current pushed us pretty close to the rocks.

"Grab whatever you can and secure yourself. Climb up as quickly as possible, the waves will beat you up against the rocks if you don't," I yelled.

It was a struggle, but we all made it up on the rocks. I found a spot and collapsed, then lay back, so glad to be out of the water. It was still raining lightly and the taste of fresh water on my lips was good, offering relief after hours of spitting out salt water. I lay there for what must have been an hour or so, then sat up and looked around.

Banco sat up too, looked at me and said, "Kiki, it was all about the coke back there."

"What are you talking about, Banco?" I was still exhausted and didn't know where he was coming from or if I wanted to hear whatever it was he wanted to say.

CHAPTER 25

"In Cuba." He looked at me seriously, but with a half-scared face. "De La Rosa got hung up in the middle of all this shit and the poor bastard is probably dead now. The man didn't know what was happening when they snatched us up on the Malecón that morning. They questioned him the whole way to Caibarién; every time he answered they slapped the shit out of him. They didn't like what they were hearing. They asked me what shipment I was waiting for. When I told them none, they'd slap me, but nothing like they were doing to De La Rosa. I was never asked about what kind of shipment, neither was De La Rosa. They saved that for De La Guardia, that sadistic, brutal son of a bitch. By the time they put us in the guardhouse down by the waterfront we were both bleeding pretty good.

"When De La Guardia got there, the fun began. He walked in, didn't say a word, just stepped into the cell and began kicking and punching De La Rosa and me all to hell. We were on the ground; he kept kicking us until he was literally out of breath. The only way I even knew it was him was because I overheard one of the guards call him Colonel De La Guardia. When he said the name I knew things would get even worse. De La Guardia is infamous in Cuba, and is thought to have underworld ties that are more solid than the high-level connection between the Beard and the cartel.

"When he was done beating the shit out of us, the questions began. De La Rosa got it first; he kept asking him why I was there. The poor guy didn't know and the more he didn't know the more he got beat. They eventually stopped, dragged him out of the cell then out of the guard house and I never saw him again. He was half dead when they took him out. I'm sure he's all the way dead now.

"Then the prick turned to me. I guess he thought the beating I just witnessed him give to De La Rosa would make me sing like a little bird. He helped me into the chair with a smile and asked me if I had anything to say. He didn't even begin to wait for an answer. Immediately he blurted out, 'Fuck you, fuck your people, and fuck your boss. They're going to have to start to deal with me and with what I say. Pablo and his buddies in Medellin, the Ochoa brothers, everyone. And that fucking Mexicano, Gacha. That little asshole Carlos Ledher that's taking the Bahamians for a ride, using Norman's Cay as his private transport station and bunker and not paying the Bahamians. Those boys are not going to do that here. I don't care if they have direct contact with El Comandante himself and diplomats and ambassadors. I'm in charge and if they don't pay what I want I'll keep it all,' he screamed.

"Kiki, the man has been doing business with the cartel in Medellin and now he's trying to hold them up for more money. The word must have already gotten back to the cartel, because he was acting like he thought they were wondering where their loads were and why they weren't being delivered to Miami. Evidently he was holding onto some merchandise and wanted more money and has pissed some people off. He asked me if Pablo had sent me. I'm not squeaky clean, Kiki, but I had no idea what he was talking about. Of course, I figured it out. I don't have a lost load of cocaine or anything else in Cuba. I was just preparing the setup for a delivery. He was intent on making me confess to his paranoia. Like that was going to help him with the Cartel. Something was going on, something he did. He was scared.

"All the rumors about the government being involved in coke with the cartel are true, but De La Guardia is making new rules. And it's not going to work. He's got the cartel after him and now that he's killed De La Rosa he'll have the Beard after him. And he knew it. He was as scared as I was, and I was the one catching a beating. No matter how many questions he asked, he never gave me time to answer them, like they were all rhetorical, like he just wanted to get them off his chest. The man is a fucking paranoid maniac, and the guards in that building were scared shitless. He told them that if he didn't get the answers he wanted he was going to put them against the *Paredón*. The expressions on their faces told me that they believed him."

"Those fuckers don't have to worry about that anymore. Anibal saved De La Guardia the trouble," I said.

"That crazy son of a bitch spent about an hour asking me, then answering his own questions, in between beating me and kicking me senseless," Banco continued. "Then, as suddenly as he appeared, he turned to his personal body guards and said '*Vamonos.*' He looked over at the guards and said, 'I'll be back tomorrow, you better have my answers.' And with that he was out the door and gone. The guards were probably thinking the same thing I was. What fucking answers? There were no real questions. One of the guards came over, closed the cell door and said, '*Ese maricon este loco; yo creo que esta empericado*, that faggot is crazy; I think he's coked up.' They've got a big coke business going on in Cuba and De La Guardia wants more control. He's playing with fire; either the Cartel will burn him or El Comandante will.

"Anyway, Kiki, I owe you my life. He was going to kill me when he came back. He had no intention of using me as a messenger boy to negotiate; he had already made his move and was sticking with it. Now the pressure was getting to him. I'm telling you, Kiki, the man is crazy. I agree with the guards, he's getting high on his own supply. I've seen coke heads before; he definitely had that edginess about him. You know what I mean—really hyper."

Banco finished and wearily lay back down on the jagged rocks and closed his eyes, still exhausted from our ordeal during the night.

"I always believed the rumors in Miami," I said. "There was never a doubt in my mind. Too many Cuban boys in Miami driving Mercedes and they've only been in the U.S. for a few years. Maxi has also told me it's true; the U.S. is just waiting to pin it on the Beard. If they pin it on anyone else Castro will just use them as scapegoats. So they catch as many as they can coming in and bust them. Believe me, they want to Velcro that one to El Comandante, but the Beard's no fool. He hasn't been there this long because he's stupid." I stood up and looked down at Banco. "This is a pretty big rock we're on; I'm going to take a look around."

I reached down and touched Nadine on the shoulder. She had been lying next to me and was completely zonked. "Banco, watch out for her, I'll be right back. I'm going to see what's up."

"How did you do it, Kiki?" Banco asked me.

"How did I do what? What are you talking about?"

"How did you get the gold?" he asked again.

"Luck. I jumped into the wrong warehouse; it was the only entrance I could find. I didn't go back there to get any treasure; I went back to get you and Nadine. I just happened to run into it and it all worked out. There are a lot of dead people back there, Banco, and we're lucky to be alive. I maybe fucked up a family's life, I don't know. They could be all over David right now. He has a beautiful wife and a wonderful young daughter—that might be all gone, and it's my fault—and for what? Some fucking gold."

I looked out over the water. The sun was up now, shining in our eyes. I continued, "We don't have shit yet anyway, my man.

I suggest we pray for David and his family. If David comes through, he's getting his cut and the rest is going back to where it belongs. To a museum someplace where it can be appreciated by the world, not hoarded by some private collector in Europe, where it once again will be lost to history. They already have enough money to live like kings. Why do they need hidden historical wealth?

"Not this load, Banco. This one is going to the people," I said. "I'm calling Charlie Alvarez in on this if we score."

"Charlie Alvarez? That smug, self righteous son of a bitch," Banco said. "He thinks he's so squeaky clean with all his hotshot friends and political contacts. He's just playing the Cuba game exactly like all those *maricones* in Miami who are waiting to scoop up whatever they can when the Beard dies."

"Exactly why I'll call Charlie. He's a glory hound; he'll want the publicity, and that's a way to ensure the treasure will get to a museum. Besides, he's got contacts with the Florida Bureau of Historic Sites and Properties and the INA. Charlie Alvarez might be a self-righteous son of a bitch, but he's an honest self-righteous son of a bitch. I've known him all my life; he's honest to a fault."

"Yeah, well, I still don't like that *maricon*," he said. "I've got nothing to say on this one, Kiki. I owe you my life. You do what you think is right and it's fine by me."

I nodded my head at Banco in agreement. He was right. This was my call, but I respected Banco's acceptance and gratitude. Good old fat man.

I walked over to a high point on the rocks to have a look around. The weather was breaking, but the sea was still rough and white capped. I knew the Cay Sal Bank—I fished these waters often. The first thing I noticed was the proximity of the dark blue water to the scrub rocks I was on. It was the Gulf Stream. The only cay in the Bank that was right on the edge of the Gulf Stream is Elbow Cay.

I was exhausted and beat up and second-guessed myself for a minute. I looked around, but these rocks could all look the same, even when you knew exactly where you were. There was a slight ridge running along the spine of the small island and I walked up there to get a better vantage and see if there was anything I might recognize. As I came to a swale in the rocks I looked down and was amazed at what I saw. There was a group of people, all sitting closely together on the rocks. There were four men, one woman and two children, little boys, around six to eight years old.

By the looks of them, they weren't victims of a boating accident from a fishing trip on the banks. They weren't dressed for the part. These people were *balseros*, rafters, Cuban boat people who had enough of Cuba and decided to take their chances on the ocean and a freedom. These were the lucky ones; God knows how many people had drowned. At least this group got washed up on the Cay and were given another chance.

I stood there, looking down at them, feeling just as lucky. They hadn't noticed me up till now as they were all faced in the other direction, the one that pointed to the USA. Then the smaller of the two boys looked up at me and without any excitement at all said "*Mira mama.*" and pointed at me. His mother turned around and saw me. She grabbed the little boy and pulled him in close to her and did the same with the other boy as she turned and faced me. Then the four men all stood up and turned around one by one. I looked at them for a few seconds.

"*Son Cubanos?*" Are you Cuban? I asked.

One of the men stepped forward and said, "*Si, y tu?*" Yes, and you?

CHAPTER 26

"*Cubano por sangre pero vivo en la Florida.*" Cuban by blood, but I live in Florida, I told them.

"*No eres del govierno?*" he asked.

He wasn't quite sure what to think of me yet and he obviously worried about me being a government agent for Castro.

"No," I said, reassuring him. "My companions and I had a boating accident and we drifted up on the Cay."

"You have others with you?" he asked.

"Yes, two others. They're over there." I pointed to where Banco and Nadine waited.

"This place was crazy last night. There were planes flying everywhere and then there was a big explosion out there on the water," the man said to me.

I played dumb. "I saw it too," I told him. "I thought there was a war going on."

"*Si, yo tambien.*"

I knew I was on Elbow Cay as I could see the dive bag I had left here at their feet. They had helped themselves to its contents.

"Come, come, call your friends. You must be thirsty," the man said.

"*Gracias señor*, let me go get them." I waved to him, and then walked over to Banco and Nadine.

"You wouldn't believe what I ran into. *Balseros*, rafters, over there on the other side of the ridge. We're on Elbow Cay. They found our stash, Nadine. There are four men, one woman and two children. They heard the fireworks last night and wanted to know if I was Cuban government. I told them we had a boat wreck and drifted here. Don't say anything to them, okay? Keep it low. Come on, they invited us over for some of our own water."

I helped Nadine to her feet. "How are you feeling, *niña*? Are you okay?" She looked worn, but the look of distress was gone. After everything she had gone through, when I looked at her I still saw a stunning woman. She caught me staring at her and gave me a smile of approval.

"Let's go this way." I held Nadine's hand and began to walk to where the *balseros* were. Banco got up and followed.

"*Hola*, these are my friends. *Yo soy Kiki, ella es Nadine, y el es Banco*," I said to the man I'd had the conversation with.

"Sit down, please. Have some water, and there is also a little food there if you like. We found this bag with water and food when we washed up here two days ago. *Me llamo Roberto, esa es mi esposa, Clara, y mis dos hijos Robertico y Juanito*," he said.

"This is *Miguel, Santos, and Joaquin,*" he said, pointing to the other three men. "We're like family."

We sat down by the *balseros* and drank some water. It sure tasted good after all that time in the ocean.

"What happened to you? How did you get here?" I asked Roberto.

"Two days ago we left Cuba. We had made preparations for three months, but no one ever knows how the ocean will act. We left from just east of Havana. It was a good evening, calm. About twelve hours into the trip the weather got us."

These were the very same *balseros* whose worried family members were huddled together on the waterfront in Cojimar a few days ago, I thought.

"There were four groups, and we all left together. We were getting pounded by waves and we got separated. I don't know what happened to the others. I heard cries for help in the darkness but there was nothing we could do, we had our own battle. After a while it was just too much, the raft fell apart by being hit by too many waves. We were able to grab some planks of wood and one of the inner tubes from the raft and we managed to stay together in the water. The current pushed us up against the rocks. We were lucky; we wouldn't have been able to swim against it. I can still hear the calls for help from the others—the women and children crying in the dark stormy night—I'll hear their cries for help for as long as I live. I'll never forget it."

His wife reached over and put her hand on his shoulder, understanding his grief. They looked weather-worn and beaten;

their faces told a story of having cheated death once but still not knowing their fate. I had cheated death too, and didn't know my fate, yet I felt sorry for them.

I leaned over to Nadine, "Were you able to get hold of DK and Jony?"

"Yes, I told them what was happening and where to pick us up—if we made it, that is."

I hope they make it, I thought. I wondered what kind of heat they might have drawn. Chances were good that the Migs got them, or that the Bahamian patrols intervened and they had been taken back to port for questioning.

I looked at Roberto, Clara and his friends. I could see despair in their eyes. We all knew that if we didn't get picked up soon none of us would make it. Even if we found some rope to fashion a makeshift raft, the odds were against getting all the way to Florida. It was too far, the sea too rough, the Gulf Stream too strong.

Dying on these scrub rocks was easy, I reasoned. Exposure to the elements and a lack of food and water would kill us all after several days. The two little boys were unaware of the dire situation we were in, and they played with each other as if in their own backyard. Two days from now they wouldn't be able to move.

The inevitable demise of so many on these rocks was all too real. I thought about what we would need most, and without question that was water. Food, I thought I could handle. I could fashion a net with clothing and eventually snare some fish, even if small. We could eat plenty of curbs. They were little crustaceans that clung to the rocks all over these scrub islands. They were small, but there were thousands of them. Most people didn't know about them, but they were a Bahamian delicacy. We could live on them for a while, but water was going to be the big issue. If I were lucky enough to find a piece of plastic on this rock I could stretch it out on all corners and weigh the middle down to collect the evening dew. There was plenty of moisture in the air, especially in the summer. But at best this method would yield maybe a cup to a cup and a half a night. Not nearly enough for everyone here, and that was if I could find plastic. And that didn't even factor in the freaking exposure. Things were looking bleak, but I couldn't let these children see it in my face.

Curiosity brought them close, and like all little children they began to ask questions and play around. At one point they walked over to a swale in the rocks several yards from where I was sitting. They squatted down, intent on examining some new discovery they'd made on their private island playground. I stood up and walked over to the swale where they were crouching. They stood up and began swordplay with what looked like some driftwood they'd picked up. I looked in the swale of the jagged rocks down on the waters edge. The crystal clear water of the Cay Sal Bank made it easy for me to see what the boys had become so fascinated with. Trapped in between some rocks, being washed back and forth from the wave action as if in a washing machine, and constantly ripping against the knife-like edges of Elbow Cay, was a body, almost totally disintegrated down to bare bones. Pieces of flesh clung to ligaments and bone. Tiny crabs were making a meal of it, as well as every little baitfish in the vicinity who could handle the banquet without becoming part of it themselves. Half of the hair had been scraped away, and the eyes, tongue, and flesh had long been eaten off the skull by the crabs. The mouth was wide open, his desperation frozen in time.

Another one of Castro's victims, a *balsero*. This was one of the unlucky ones; he probably died at sea and was washed up here. Maybe he was lucky after all, not to die a slow, torturous death. His was probably quick and somewhat merciful. If the Miami boys didn't come through, ours would be slow and painful.

The sinewy remains washed back and forth in the beautiful aquamarine water. I stepped back and looked away. If rescue ever came, I would probably continue to be creeped out by this image for the rest of my life.

The two boys danced their way back toward me, still engaged in swordplay. When they came close enough I saw that their swords were made of human bones. I called them calmly, as if wanting to join their game. I took the bones out of their hands. Their mother was watching; she never let them out of her sight. She walked over and saw what I had taken from them. Quickly, she wrapped them in her arms and smiled a desperate smile my way, never really making eye contact. I felt sorry for her; the thoughts that were running through her mind must have been horrible, seeing death visit her children in that grotesque manner. She hurried to her husband and whispered in his ear. Roberto came over and I showed him the bones, pointed out the dead man washing up against the rocks. "*Lo reconoses?*" I asked. Do you recognize him?

"No, *ni la ropa en las piedras.* Not even the clothes on the rocks, but that doesn't matter. No one can recognize that mess."

He looked into the sky. With tears rolling down his cheeks, he took the bones from my hands gently and tossed them in the clear waters of the Cay Sal Bank. Roberto walked back to his wife and put his arms around her. The boys asked their mom why she was sad. She knelt down, hugged them and said "*Nada niños, todo esta bien,*" she assured them.

Santos and Joaquin turned to Roberto for an answer that didn't exist. We had no control of our destiny. Feeling helpless in a dire situation was a terrible feeling. I didn't want to look away from Roberto's forlorn gaze. For some reason he considered us as a meal ticket. I didn't want to disappoint him. Maybe he was right, maybe we were.

I told Nadine and Banco what the boys had found. Other than a slight gasp from Nadine, nothing was said. The situation was understood. The reality didn't have to be rehashed. I sat down next to Nadine and tried my damnedest to think good thoughts about the Miami boys. Time seemed to have slowed down. The sun felt hotter, I was thirstier and anxiety kept creeping back in. I lay back and tried to rest.

It was fruitless; sleep was nowhere in sight. I tossed and turned only to be poked, jabbed and cut by the damn rocks. I sat up in frustration. My mind wandered back to the guard shack and Nadine huddled on the bed in the corner.

"What happened back there?" I asked her.

"Back where?"

"Back at the guardhouse. You didn't look in good shape; I was really worried about you."

"It was really stupid of me, Kiki. After we had that fight when we walked along the tracks I felt really hurt, obviously. I felt like you thought my input was worthless and once again you were blowing me off. You made me feel useless, and I wanted to prove I could be of value."

She had a way of pointing out flaws in my personality that made me feel like shit. She was right; once again I had turned it into my way or the highway. But she had picked the wrong time to show me the error of my ways. She had made a bad decision. And she was lucky to be alive.

"What if they had gotten me? Where would you be right now?"

"I guess in pretty bad shape. But you see, I had been thinking we didn't know enough about the compound before going in there, you know, with guns blazing and not even knowing which building we had to get into for Banco. So I tried to figure out how I could get some information by snooping around either at the gate or even inside. I didn't think they'd suspect little old me. I figured they'd just think I was a French tourist who wanted to windsurf. So I walked to the compound, acted curious, and the guards let me in. I really did pose as a tourist and they went for it. I thought I would be out in ten minutes with a *gracias* and a goodbye, but the joke was on me. Before I knew it they forced me into the guardhouse. It's not the first time they've done this to unsuspecting women. They laughed and said how stupid the foreign women were, and if men came from all over the world to fuck Cuban women, then they were going to get their share of women tourists. There's no doubt in my mind, Kiki, that those sons of bitches kidnap women for the slave trade. Thousands of women disappear every year in third world countries and are never heard from again."

"So they just had sex on their minds? They didn't suspect a plot?"

She shook her head no and lay back on the rocks, using my body to shield her eyes from the sun. Her eyes were wide open. I could see the fear return to her face as her mind raced back to her abduction.

"Maybe it's the wrong time to ask, but I've had it on my mind since we left Cuba. Did they… were you…" I couldn't seem to get it out of my mouth.

She understood what I was getting at, and spared me the discomfort.

"He didn't rape me Kiki. Not that he wasn't going to. He just didn't get the time. He manhandled me, grabbed at my ass, grabbed at my breasts, hugged me and pulled me close. I always thought the Spanish language was so beautiful, but everything I heard coming out of that disgusting bastard's mouth sounded so ugly. I'm glad he's dead. I'm glad Anibal shot him over and over again. He wouldn't have spared me, Kiki; my fate was sealed. I would have been used, then killed or sold off. I believe that."

Her facial expression had turned from that of fear to a squinted-eye look of revenge and hate as she recalled her tormentor's death. There was no mercy in her eyes.

"Believe it or not I was saved by De La Guardia. I don't mean he stopped them. He looked into the room they were holding me in and said, 'I'll see you later.' I was saved because he had Banco and De La Rosa on his mind. In his yelling, frustration and the beating he was giving them, he forgot about me. I was sure I was next when he was done, but he left and I never saw him again. The guards never came back into the room where I was; they became preoccupied with Banco and De La Guardia's tirade. Not long after that, you came. It was the most relieved I had ever felt in my entire life."

She closed her eyes and lay there quietly.

"It's all over now," I said, trying to comfort her.

I reached down and passed my fingers across her soft and sunburned cheek. A smile came to her face. I stood up and panned my vision across the vastness of the Cay Sal Bank and the Gulf Stream. The day was getting late, the shadows long. Soon it would be sundown, time for a dinner that we didn't have.

A few boats passed in the distant Gulf Stream, and the men would get up and wave at them, trying fruitlessly to get their attention. But at the distance the boats passed, we were no more than part of the rock formations to them.

Some planes went by, but they were commercial airlines on their routes to and from the Caribbean at 30,000 feet up.

Cuba protects its airspace, but there was a flight corridor that all planes used when going over Cuba, called the Mayaguez Corridor. A lot of the air traffic headed to the States coming from South America went right over Cuba and most flights out of the States headed down did the same. Smugglers used the same path, and Cuba let them go right through, no problem. Unless the brothers to the rescue happened to be in this area on surveillance flights, there was no chance of any air traffic around here.

However, if the brothers to the rescue did find us, then we would go home while Roberto and the others would go to Guantanamo Bay and then most likely back to Cuba proper. I know that's not what they wanted, but I think they would take it.

It had been three days since they had washed up on Elbow Cay and I had only left provisions for a couple of days for a couple of people in the dive bag. Supplies were pretty much exhausted. Tomorrow I would organize everyone in an effort to gather food and water. I paced on the rocks as I thought the plan through. One group would retrieve curbs from the shore. Another would try to catch fish. A third party would search the island for plastic and anything else that might be handy. We wouldn't last forever, but maybe we could buy some time. We would survive.

CHAPTER 27

When I woke up the next morning I was amazed I had ever fallen asleep in the first place. The scrub rocks on the Cay Sal Bank were unbearably hot during the day, and after being exposed to the hot sun all day, it could feel very cold at night. There was no comfortable level; hot or cold, cold or hot. We spent the night huddled in the swale and out of the breeze, but we were still cold and there was nothing to be done except lie there and shiver. I must have fallen asleep at some point; exhaustion beat out body temperature. But the shivers started up again as we awaited the warmth of the sun.

As planned, we spent all of that day gathering food and searching the cay for useful debris. I organized everyone into teams and all were glad to be engaged in purposeful activity. It took away some of the anxiety and helped focus on our glimmer of hope of survival and rescue.

Later in the day we had a nice pile of curbs, some baitfish, mussels, crabs and even one small lobster. There was nothing to start a fire with, so we had to eat everything raw. I decided to wait until dusk to eat, so everyone would be hungry enough to be motivated, and also so we couldn't see too well what we were eating.

I figured we could survive on seafood for a couple of weeks. Food wasn't the problem now; water was. We hadn't found any plastic sheeting, only a garbage bag that had been thoroughly shredded. We would have to hope for rain, but that seemed unlikely over the next couple of days as the weather cleared. Of course there were afternoon thunderstorms almost every day in the Caribbean in summer, so we prepared ourselves for a downpour by laying clothing and rags about, and setting upright any tin can or container we could find. We were ready.

Later in the day I had also organized the teams to retrieve loose rocks and driftwood. We used these materials to fashion crude walls in the swale, which we covered with driftwood poles and then smaller driftwood and debris. This gave us a primitive dwelling, which would block the wind and retain a little heat.

That evening, we gathered by our makeshift hut for our seafood meal. The sun had just set but there was still a glow in the sky. Everyone sat around the pile of shells and crabs and fish and waited for me to begin. I handed a medium-sized stone to Nadine and she picked up one of the curbs and smashed the shell, then pried the meat out. She looked at the two boys and said, "*Mira mira*," and then she put the meat in her mouth and chewed it. She smashed a couple more and offered them to the boys, who hesitated. They looked at their mother for approval, and she urged them to eat. The younger boy took a few of the delicacies, put them in his mouth, and began to chew. He bobbed up and down, like young children often do to signify satisfaction. We all watched him and laughed, then we reached for the different little bits of seafood we had gathered and began to eat.

I was proud of what a trooper Nadine was. Not every girl could do that, but hell, she was French. She ate raw snails; curbs were a cakewalk. When I ate curbs they were usually cooked. I was no a sushi lover and I would never have come across raw curbs in the Bahamas. Anyway, they weren't too bad. Sort of like eating steamed clams, only they were cold, no steaming involved.

After our seafood meal, I had everyone go into the house to get some sleep. I stood guard on the ridge to look for passing boats. Roberto had found that the cooler, when struck with a solid piece of driftwood, made a loud drum-like noise. I figured that that noise, with shouting, was our best chance at attracting any passersby in the dark.

I sat down on the ridge and watched the lights of a jet, far above. So strange. I felt like we were in one of those movies where the dead couldn't be seen by the living. They, the dead, were always struggling to get back into the land of the living, but to no avail. The Island of the Dead. That's where we were, and that meant we *were* the dead.

A half hour later, Nadine joined me, worried that I would fall asleep on the rocks and get cold. She sat down and we put our arms around each other and chatted for a while, laughing about the evening meal. Then we both drifted off.

I was dreaming about being out on the water and there was an intense glare from the sun reflecting off the waves. Then I woke up and saw that it was still dark and that the light was a searchlight, sweeping back and forth. It came out of the northwest, about a hundred yards away and closing in. I wasn't afraid. If it had been the Cubans, they'd have been shooting by now.

We stood up, ran to the edge of the rocks and began to shout and wave and bang the drum. The spotlight streaked across us a few times before it settled on us, causing us to turn our heads from the brightness. There was a boat no more than fifty yards away. We could hear its idling engines.

Out of the direction of the spotlight I heard a voice.

"Kiki, Kiki, is that you? *Cabron*, you made it. I thought the Beard got you for sure."

It was Jony's voice, and those engines I heard were from the *Hawk Marine*, that big, beautiful boat of theirs. The boys had gotten away from the Beard. I'd almost given up hope. *De pinga, al fin*. Finally, I thought.

"Jony, you son of a bitch, am I glad to hear your voice. I was beginning to worry about you guys."

"*Hermano*, hold tight. I'll be right there to pick you up," Jony said.

Everyone had heard the commotion, seen the searchlight, and come to the edge of the rocks.

"It's DK, Jony and Jorge—they came to get us," I told them.

Nadine grabbed me and gave me a big hug and kiss. Banco started whooping and then he began to shout out the names of every restaurant he frequented in Miami—probably because food was on his mind—and how the Miami boys were going to get free dinners every night for a week. Roberto and crew were a lot quieter, but you could tell they were giddy with the thought that not only were their lives saved but that they were on their way to Florida. The two boys were jumping up and down.

Jony got close enough to the rocks with the *Hawk Marine's* dinghy and threw me a line. I secured it to the rocks and used it as a guideline. We all made our way to it and then onto the boat.

"*Cabron*, alavao! You're alive!" Jony said, giving me a big hug. "I see you brought some friends."

Without hesitation, DK, Jony and Jorge attended to Roberto and his group. They knew what they were, *balseros*.

I sure was glad to be leaving Elbow Cay. I settled into the comfort of the *Hawk Marine* and told DK and the boys what had happened. Talk turned to the *balseros*.

"Well, what do we do with them?" DK asked. "Going to Florida is too risky. If we get stopped or if they get caught and say anything, I could lose my boat and my business. Not to mention my freedom. Ten years for human smuggling. The Coast Guard has stepped up its lookout for *balseros* and human smuggling. Getting stopped is a real possibility."

"I understand, DK. They have to go to Bimini with us. I'll get Dreamer to get them to Nassau and get an immigration lawyer for them. I'll handle the cost."

Dreamer would be well respected in Nassau; his lawyer had been working for his family for over 20 years now. Dreamer was from the Smith family, out of Ragged Island. His father, Cappy Smith, started a lobster fishing business down in Ragged Island that eventually grew to a fleet of about fifteen boats working out of Nassau and supplying lobster to the hotels and casinos. They became very wealthy. The Smith boys, Dreamer and his brothers—the oldest they called Footsy, he was the crazy one, and Roots was a year younger than Footsy and Edward is the youngest—all took to Cappy's lobster business and helped run it. Dreamer lived in Bimini but he kept daily contact with the office in Nassau and oversaw the fishing fleet. He was an amazing seaman.

Footsy and Roots worked at the fish house in Nassau and handled all the distribution. Edward was the brains of the business and handled all the financial ends. The Smith boys had done well for themselves, and were respected members of the community.

For a while I wondered why Dreamer chose to live in Bimini. He grew up in Nassau, which although on a fairly small island, had a sophisticated city atmosphere. As I grew to know him, I realized that his love was the sea and the peace he felt there. The solitude, the serenity, the power and mystery that is the ocean were what formed his character. He was a man of little words, but in a pinch, he performed. The serenity and solitude of Bimini attracted him like a magnet, and gave him the peace he needed in his daily life. Dreamer was almost an introvert, until you really got to know him you'd never hear him say much. Even then he was a quiet soul.

"I think Roberto's family will be fine. They couldn't have fallen into better hands. Dreamer's lawyer knows the ropes in Nassau and he'll get things done. Hell, El Duque Hernandez got to the Bahamas and got an immigration lawyer through his agent Many De Cubas, and he won a world series with the Yankees. If it's good enough for El Duque, it's good enough for Roberto and his family."

Jorge was at the wheel. He had backed us away from the rocks and turned and pointed the *Hawk Marine* toward Bimini. He punched the throttles of the big twin diesels, and for the first time in about a week I actually felt good. All my fears and all my anxiety had vanished.

Jony was all smiles. In typical Cuban fashion, he had brought Roberto and his family towels and dry clothes and was offering them all the food and drink on the boat. The Cuban coffee was already brewing. I called Roberto into the galley, where DK and I explained to him what we were doing.

"*No importa,*" he said. "I'm glad to be off those rocks and I owe you my life. I promise, when I get to Miami I will get a job and pay you back. I won't forget."

Jony, being Jony, yelled out from the deck, "You don't owe us anything, you're my blood. When we get to Miami, you call me and I'll help you get started."

DK and I nodded our agreement.

"I wouldn't have it any other way." Jony said.

Jony showed Roberto and his family to the main berth on the *Hawk*. They were tired and needed to clean up and get a lot of rest. Without that enormous weight of life-or-death that had been hanging over their heads since they left Cuba, Clara and the boys were giving in to their fatigue and fading fast. Yet Clara kept smiling and holding her hands before her as though in prayer and thanking us over and over again.

"I've never heard *gracias* and *que dios te bendiga* so many times in my life," I said.

I walked up to the bridge with one of the boys' brews in my hand. A nice cold Beck's; they always had a cooler full and it sure tasted good. I sat down next to Jorge, DK and Jony. Jorge looked at me and smiled. "You're a lucky son of a bitch, Kiki. Was that you those Migs were going crazy over on Saturday night?"

"When I left Cayo Fragaso in a hurry," I said, "and saw the patrol boats heading toward you guys I knew it wouldn't be long before they began a wider search. I was just praying I had enough time. The weather was rough; I guess we were running for about an hour to an hour and a half, being pounded to death by waves, when I finally heard the roar of the jet engines. I knew it was the Migs. The clouds and the bad weather kept us hidden for a while, but they kept looking, getting closer and closer every time until they tagged us. The last pass they made was so close that the whole boat rattled. I could smell the jet fuel, they were so close. After that pass I knew the next one was it. We were in deep shit unless we bailed out. I heard him coming back. We all jumped. We bailed just in time, about twenty seconds before the strike. The *Lean Back* was doing about forty, so we were a hundred yards from the fireball. It was incredible; I think it was a heat-seeking missile, and you know what they can do. It was dark and stormy and I didn't know how close we were to the Cay Sal Bank, but at that point the water was better than what the Migs had in store for us.

"What came to my mind then was what happened to the Defense Force boys from the Bahamas down in Ragged Island when the Migs shot their boat up. The motherfuckers swung back around, strafed everyone in the water who had jumped overboard, and killed them all. I hoped they wouldn't come around, but no such luck. They began to swoop back around to look for us but then I heard another one coming in from the opposite direction. It was a much higher-pitched jet engine sound; I knew it wasn't the same plane. We went under just in case, and when we came up I saw it in hot pursuit of the Mig. At that moment I realized Maxi had came through. I knew he *could* pull it off, I just wasn't sure he would. Thank God for those flyboys.

"They knew what they were doing, so I'm sure Maxi called in a favor. But doing something like that was awful risky, and really disobeying orders. I complain sometimes about America's problems, its inequalities and inefficiencies, but it is still the best place in the world to live, and I've been to quite a few places. Where else could a friend call in a favor, utilize a highly skilled pilot from the air force, a multi-million dollar piece of equipment, and not hang for it? In Cuba or Mother Russia they'd be arrested and shot as soon as they landed. You can only play the Revolution's game there. Only in America baby, only in America. I guess it's not what you know, but who you know, or who knows you. Damn, I'm really glad Maxi knows me. So to answer your question Jorge; yes, that was us those Migs were going crazy over."

I took a drink of my beer and nodded my head.

"Motherfuckers blew up my boat. They took out the *Lean Back*. I loved that boat."

"We saw them crisscrossing this area, so we headed the other way," Jorge said. We didn't know what was going on. That's why we weren't here sooner. I wasn't sure we'd find you on Elbow Cay, Kiki. When the patrol boats headed our way we backtracked to Ragged Island and pulled into Duncan Town. They stayed around for the better part of a day, in fucking Bahamian waters no less."

"Those fuckers don't give a shit."

"That's when we became pretty sure they had you," Jorge said. "When Nadine called us on Saturday to tell us to pick you up on Elbow Cay, I asked her where you were, but she wouldn't say. I insisted, and she hung up the phone. That made us think you were in the Beard's hands, but we weren't sure. Then when we saw the Migs and all that the Beard had going on in Bahamian waters, well we kinda gave up hope. But DK kept reassuring us. He said he had gotten some kind of signal."

"What kind of signal?" I asked

"He said he heard the Santa Barbara that we carry on the *Hawk* speak to him. It told him you were in trouble, but alive."

"He actually heard her?"

"Not out loud, but in his head he said he heard her talk." Jony sat back and just nodded his head, as if signifying the reality of his Santeria belief. I sat back in my chair and continued. "Shit got nasty back there. Anibal killed four guys. All hell broke loose for a while."

I took another swig of my beer, and put it down empty. Jony handed me another. "But I'll tell you what, God willing, David and his boys are okay, and we have a shitload of treasure sitting in the torpedo tubes we installed in the *Señorita Inez*."

The Miami boys went quiet on me as I continued drinking my beer.

"No way," Jony said.

"Yes way, if David makes it. He's meeting us in Bimini in a week."

They sat there for a moment, and Jony let out a yell that could be heard in Miami.

I leaned up and sat on the edge of my chair. "Hey guys, I think it belongs to the people, in a museum somewhere."

DK looked at me, "You mean, give it all up?"

"You almost lost your life, not to mention the Lean Back; she's fucking gone."

I looked down the ladder from the helm to the deck, to make sure no one was around. In a low voice, I said, "We got a duffle bag full of money. It's with David in the torpedo tubes. I didn't have time to count it but I think it's around ten to twelve million."

Jony sat up. "Pesos or dollars?"

"Dollars, baby, dollars. American greenbacks, all packed in airtight plastic bags. It was in the warehouse where we found all the treasure."

Jony fell back in his chair this time, no yelling.

"If it's true, you're a lucky son of a bitch. Hey DK, Jorge, I'm with Kiki. Who gives a shit about the gold?"

I sat there and smiled as I pounded the rest of my beer and watched the Miami boys look back and forth at each other, then at me, still soaking in what I had just told them.

We all started to laugh. "Ave Maria! If David makes it, we've scored boys. *Coronamos.*"

The sun was coming up and the stormy weather of the last few days had finally blown by. The seas had calmed down and the big 52-foot Hatteras was riding the ocean like she owned it.

All the beautiful colors of the water were coming to life in the Straits of Florida and it felt good to see and smell them. We were going home.

DK, Jony and I went down into the galley and found Banco sleeping on the couch, covered with a warm blanket and snoring his fat ass off.

I pulled out another Beck's from the fridge, sat down, and began to tell DK and Jony what I had gone through in Cuba after we parted company here in Cay Sal several days ago.

"You're a lucky son of a bitch, Kiki. Just like I always said." Jony was shaking his head.

"We need to call Dreamer, let him know we'll be there tomorrow."

"I'm tired *hermano*, I'm going to bed. I'll call him tonight or tomorrow morning."

In the second berth, I found Nadine out cold on the bed. Poor girl had gone through some shit over the past few days. Relieved sleep was the best kind; she'd be out for hours. I lay down next to the gorgeous blonde, spooned myself behind her and threw my arm over her. She moaned slightly and settled into my body pressing up against her. Thoughts were rushing through my head about all the events of the past few days, but I hit the wall; fatigue settled in so hard that I was asleep in a second.

Jorge had kept the *Hawk Marine* at a steady clip and made good time to Bimini. I woke up at two am and went out onto the deck, I could see the outline of the concrete ship that had run aground just south of Bimini. I felt at home here. The old ship was purposely scuttled during WWII and used as a target on bomb training runs. There was great fishing around the old ship.

I could see the lights on South Bimini as Jorge steered the *Hawk* into the cut just off the point of the old Paradise Hotel and worked his way into the channel that led to Dreamer's property. The man had a beautiful place. Crystal clear water, 280-degree ocean view and tropical vistas everywhere you turned. I had known Dreamer for a long time and he'd been like a brother to me. It'd been about two years since I'd been here. It would be good to see him.

As it was three in the morning, we anchored in the channel and waited for dawn. Dreamer was an early riser, so at five I gave him a call. He was surprised, but said to come on over and dock the boat.

Jorge maneuvered the big boat through the last bit of channel and down to the point where Dreamer's houseboat was moored. We pulled up to the dock and a waiting Dreamer. I walked onto the bow and tossed the line to him.

"Haven't seen you in a while, brother," I said. "How's paradise treating you?"

"Everyting fine Rasta, everyting iree." It was good to hear my old friend's island twang again. "Come boy, get all your people and come to da house. Blood clot, ya look like ya been runnin from da devil, boy."

"If you call the Beard the devil, then I guess I was running from him."

"Why ya mess wit dat crazy fool, boy? Ya know dat blood clot crazy. Ya know how him do those boys down Ragged a few years back. Him crazy boy, ya know dat."

"Yeah I know, Dreamer, but this one was like a magnet. I couldn't help myself."

We secured the *Hawk* to the dock and made our way to the houseboat. It felt good to be in Bimini. I felt safe here. It was 47 miles from home, just a little jump across the Gulf Stream and I would be in Miami with Cuban coffee and salsa music—home sweet home.

I sat up with Dreamer, the Miami boys, Nadine, and Banco the rest of the early morning hours and repeated the episodes of the last few days.

Dreamer would make arrangements for Roberto and his family. He would put them on a Chalks flight from Bimini to Nassau to a waiting lawyer who would handle their situation. They'd leave the next day.

CHAPTER 28

Banco called Miami and made arrangements to be picked up at the Big Game Club on North Bimini the next day at noon. His boys would jump the Gulf Stream in about two hours, pick him up and he'd be back in Miami at the Versailles restaurant drinking Cuban coffee, and then home for the early news. Nadine, the Miami boys and I would stay at Dreamer's and pray that all of David's *orishas* were with him.

I was still tired from the trip and made myself at home in one of the guest rooms on the massive houseboat. I slept for only a few hours and awoke to the most delicious aromas of Bahamian cooking that I had smelled in a long time.

When I walked downstairs, Dreamer asked, "Ya remember dis woman?"

I looked into the kitchen and standing there was Mama Bea, a big happy woman, always smiling and ready with a hug.

"Ya don't remember me, ay," she said with a big smile.

"Mama Bea, you know I could never forget you," I said and gave her a big hug.

Whenever I was in Bimini, Mama Bea would cook for us. Her food was as good as any restaurant, and more plentiful. Mama Bea had a feast going: conch fritters, conch chowder, deep-fried grouper and peas and rice. This was going to be my first real meal since I left David's house in Cuba and I couldn't wait to dig in.

We all sat down at the big table to a magnificent feast. Mama Bea and Dreamer brought out the big platters of food. Beer and wine were flowing. Roberto and his family couldn't believe how much food they were seeing and their mouths were wide open with anticipation. Dreamer made a little speech welcoming everyone to his home and then we began the meal. But before I ate, I felt compelled to ask the higher powers of this world to be by David's side.

A wonderful dinner was had by all. My body's need to further recuperate made me extremely tired, and the huge meal I had just eaten doubled the need. I excused myself and went back to get some more sleep.

Everyone had their own little nook in the big house and had gone to bed. Nadine came to the guest room and joined me. I dozed off to the sound of dead silence and the comfort of a real bed and blanket. It was a beautiful day in paradise.

When people thought of the Bahamas, they thought casinos and babes all over the beaches. Bimini wasn't like that at all; it was just quiet and peaceful. The quaintness and quietness of Bimini made me feel like I was in another time. Of course it had its share of bad publicity, from Joe Kennedy and the rum running days to the Colombian cartels and dope running. But the people had stayed true to their own traditions and quiet and unpretentious island lifestyle.

Everyone was up the next morning, and except DK and his boys, were ready to go to North Bimini. Banco's ride would be at the Big Game Club at noon. Dreamer made two trips to the dock, where the water taxi waited. His VW Thing couldn't handle everyone at once.

The water taxi took us across the channel to North Bimini and docked at the government dock. Dreamer and I walked Roberto and his family to Chalks airlines, the seaplane airline that served the Bahamas. We got tickets for everyone to Nassau, where Dreamer's lawyer would be waiting to take care of them and hopefully get them to their families in Miami soon.

We walked back up the narrow street to the Big Game Fishing Club. The club was made famous by Ernest Hemingway in the thirties, when he portrayed it and Bimini in his novels and Esquire articles. On the way we passed his old haunt, the Compleat Angler, a bar and hotel owned by the Brown family. This place was hopping on weekends. You could rub elbows here with the rich and famous on any given night. Bimini was small and quiet—but big money came here in droves.

Banco was on the docks, impatiently waiting for his ride. The fat man had had enough of the islands and the ocean for a while, and wanted to get back to the comfort of his Miami enclave. His ride pulled into the dock in a beautiful 40-foot Donzi, a fast pleasure/speed boat with all the comforts of home.

"I owe you my life, Kiki. I'll never be able to repay you," Banco said as he shook my hand, thanked Dreamer for his hospitality and gave Nadine a kiss goodbye. "I'll see you on the next one, Kiki."

He jumped on the Donzi and they were down the channel, out of the cut and into the wide-open ocean, westbound 270 degrees. Next stop: Miami.

"Dreamer, let's go. I'll buy you lunch at the Red Lion," I said.

I sat down with Dreamer and Nadine at a table overlooking the bay and the Bimini Flats.

"Dreamer, when we hit the Beard I ran into money, a lot of money—maybe ten to twelve million dollars. David is bringing it with the treasure in the torpedo tubes. Banco doesn't know; it's none of his business."

Dreamer being a laid back, quiet man, leaned back in his chair.

"Ras clot, ya say ten to twelve. Bumba clot, ya always been lucky, Kiki. Ever since I know ya, ya been lucky."

We finished up our meal and went back to South Bimini, to Dreamer's houseboat. We spent the next couple of days trying to occupy our time and not think about David. Nadine and I spent a lot of time up at the old abandoned Rockwell mansion and its surrounding beach. It was one of the most beautiful beaches anywhere.

We hung out with each other in a way that we hadn't for quite a while. We weren't adjusting to situations, in a panic, or contemplating our imminent deaths, which was a mental relief.

And our roles were equal now. I wasn't the captain and she wasn't my faithful lieutenant. I was starting to think she could be someone I could spend a lot of time with and never feel corralled or pressured by. She was strong and beautiful.

Still no sign of David, and four days had gone by. I had too much time to think, so bad thoughts crept into my mind. On the fourth night I was out on the small balcony of the houseboat, feeding the mangrove snappers that hung around the dock, when I looked up at the channel and saw a boat coming toward Dreamer's place. Not many came down that channel, especially at night.

"Dreamer, someone is coming down the channel. Are you expecting anyone?"

"No one ever come here, mon. Ya know me private."

I stepped down to the dock.

"Dat's David, mon, me know her anywhere, dats da *Señorita Inez*. Me know her sound too, she purrin. Yes mon, dat David."

Dreamer knew boats by silhouettes in the night and the sounds of their engines. I wasn't about to question him.

As the boat pulled up to the dock and cut her engines, I could see Anibal at the bow with a line in his hand and Chino at the stern. David stepped out of the pilothouse; he had a smile on his face. I knew everything was fine. David wouldn't give a shit about money if something had happened to his family— hell, he wouldn't have left Cuba.

"*Como estas, mi hermano, todo bien?*" I asked.

"*Si gracias a dios, todo esta bien,* Kiki?" David replied.

They got off the *Señorita Inez* and onto the dock. We greeted and hugged like long-lost brothers. Tears rolled down David's eyes as he asked, "Is Nadine okay?"

"Yes, she's fine."

"*Valla.* I thought they got you that night. The patrol boats and Migs were around for two days. I didn't think you made it," he said. "It's good to see you, *hermano*, it's good to see you alive."

"David, *como esta?*" Dreamer said.

"Mr. Dreamer, how are you? The engines are running great, *no problema*," David said.

We walked into Dreamer's houseboat and began to reacquaint ourselves with the events since we left each other in a hail of fire in Cuba a little over a week ago.

"How are the torpedoes, Chino?" I asked.

"*Tranquilo.* They checked us twice; one time in port in Caibarién. Three hours and those *hijos de putas* never checked the bottom. The other time we had just gotten out of port, another two hours. It took us a few days because of the torpedoes. We didn't want to chance ripping them off the bottom of the boat."

"Did you lose anything?" I asked.

"*No creo,*" Chino said. "It was a rough ride to Cayo Fragaso and back to the *Señorita Inez.* Things got tossed around a little bit, but I don't think we lost anything."

"We need to get the gold and the artifacts out of the tubes," I said.

I had never used torpedo tubes on a trip that long before. I was wondering how much water, if any, they took on. Chino jumped in the water and opened the seals. You could see the boat sink a little deeper from the rush of water into the torpedoes when Chino opened them. That was a good sign; they had stayed dry. Chino pulled out the dive bags with the treasure and the duffle bag with the money. I reached down to the water from the dock with a gaff and hoisted the bags up one by one. I had a grin on my face from ear to ear as I walked down the dock back into the houseboat. I had one of the bags in my hand, Anibal, and David had the other two.

Once in the houseboat we laid the bags down in the living room. Dreamer closed the door and locked it behind him. We sat there for a second, just looking at the bags. No one said a word. I thought about what all that gold and money meant. A lot of lives had been lost over it, from centuries long ago to the present day.

"Let's see what we have. David, Anibal, grab a bag and open it," I said.

I grabbed the duffle bag and opened it. I emptied it onto the living room floor. It seemed like those airtight plastic bags just never stopped coming. They were piled high, one on top of the other right there in front of me, real as life. I leaned back on the sofa and smiled.

"Blood clot, a pirate's life for me," Dreamer said softly as he stared at the piles and piles of dead presidents.

Anibal and David emptied the dive bags on the floor. Even in the dimly lit room, the glint and sparkle of gold bars, gold chains, statuettes encrusted with emeralds, and religious artifacts of all kinds was truly blinding. The money made me smile, but the treasure left me in awe; my jaw dropped in astonishment at what we had gotten.

They made movies about things like this. Children dreamed of treasure hunting and grown men lost fortunes and their lives looking for it. And here it was, sitting in front of us. We all were in awe, admiring the pieces that lay on the floor.

I was spreading some pieces around to take a good look and I noticed something was missing. I pushed the plastic bags of money aside and out popped the kilo of coke with "Danilo" stamped on it.

"What's that Rasta? Ya takin up bad habits?" Dreamer said jokingly.

"*Sí*, that's what I said to him, Mr. Dreamer," David said smiling.

"We took it from the Beard. That duffle bag was full and we traded it out for money," I said. "I have a destination for it. Let me tell you something, Dreamer: the Beard is heavily involved. Cuba's letting it all come through them, for a fee. Drugs, pre-Colombian artifacts, gold, stolen treasure, they don't care, they just want money. And I think some of them are getting greedy."

But it hadn't been the kilo I was looking for. It was the Golden Madonna, and I didn't see it anywhere.

"David, Anibal, Chino, I don't see it, do you?"

"See what?" David said.

"The statue of the Madonna, I don't see it."

We couldn't find it anywhere. I was starting to wonder if I had really found it. "David, I did put it in one of those bags, didn't I?" I asked.

"*Sí* Kiki, I saw you put it in the duffle bag. I think things were a little crazy and hectic, and maybe it fell out," David said.

"Chino, do you think it fell out on the way to Cayo Fragaso?"

"I don't know, Kiki, maybe. When I left the docks with Banco and Nadine I was going to row for a while and then start the engines, but then all hell broke loose and I heard the shooting. I scrambled around, started the engines, and we took off. So I don't remember, I can't say."

I double-checked and triple-checked—and nothing. No Golden Madonna and child to be seen.

"I can't believe this. The myth of the Golden Madonna goes on; no one will ever believe I found it."

"Not even Bob Marx," said David. I looked at him and smiled. "We know it exists, Kiki."

"Yeah—us, Bob Marx, and the Beard. We all know it's real," I said.

"Maybe it was meant to be. She had been a myth for centuries and she will remain a myth," David offered.

We spread everything out on the floor and ogled it one more time.

"Let's gather it all up and get it on the *Hawk*. We're leaving for Miami tomorrow," I said. "DK, tomorrow I want to anchor the dinghy with all the gold off of Fowey Rocks. I'm going to call Charlie Alvarez to come pick it up and get it to where it needs to go. He will be real surprised."

Everything was put away on the *Hawk Marine* and we walked back to Dreamer's houseboat.

"Let's count this money and see how generous the Beard was to us."

The duffle bag was a big army-style bag. We stuffed it with 87 of the airtight bags full of money. We opened up a pack and counted it. They weren't new bills. Castro was either stockpiling greenbacks from tourists or this was a drug payoff. Either way, it was ours now. We came up with $150,000 in the bag. We counted a couple more and they were all the same, $150,000. It was twice as much as I thought and then some. We left a lot of it behind. Maybe that's what we should have taken instead of the treasure. The total take was $13,050,000. I sat back and took it all in. Damn, not bad for a couple of weeks out of my life. Shit, but I wouldn't try that again for twice this amount, I thought.

We agreed on a split: $50,000 would go to the lawyer to handle the immigration costs for Roberto and his family. If there was anything left over they would keep it. One million went to Dreamer. Without him being there to bail us out—not just this time but many others—we wouldn't be able to work in the Bahamas. I respected him as a straight shooter, and he got things done. Six million went to David and his crew. The *Señorita Inez* saved the day and they took most of the heat. They deserved every bit of it. The Miami boys got three million, and Nadine and I took four million. The next morning, I got ready to make the trip home.

David, Anibal, and Chino would stay at Dreamer's for a day or so, until they dismantled the torpedoes on the *Señorita Inez*. Then they'd go back to Caibarién.

"This is more money than I've ever seen in my whole life, Kiki." David said. "I'll be able to do a lot of good with this. *Gracias, mi hermano.*"

"Just be careful. Remember what you told me, David. 'The U.S. has the long arm of the law, but the Beard has many eyes.'"

"*Suerte, mi hermano.*"

We were away from the docks; I waved goodbye to the boys.

"Soon come back mon," Dreamer said.

Imitating an island accent as well as I could I said, 'Me soon come back, brotha." Dreamer laughed and waved us off.

Jorge maneuvered the big Hatteras down the channel and out of the cut by the old Paradise Hotel. It was a beautiful, calm, sunny day and in a few hours we would be back on Florida's gorgeous southeast coast. Our heading was Fort Lauderdale. We would work our way south along the coast, then I would call Charlie Alvarez and give him the surprise of his life.

It was a smooth ride across the Gulf Stream, and soon the sight of buildings began to appear on the horizon. It was late in the afternoon and civilization and the hustle and bustle of Miami seemed like an old friend calling me. I welcomed it—at least for the time being. Darkness set in on us on our trip down the Gold Coast. The sun sat behind the buildings, and the silhouetted skyline was engulfed in pastel colors. Another day in paradise.

I made a phone call.

"Hello?"

"Charlie, it's me, Kiki."

"Hi son, how are you doing?"

"Oh, it's son now. Last time I talked to you I was full of crazy ideas and I needed to settle down because I wasn't going to be around long if I didn't."

"Okay, Kiki, I told your old man I'd watch out for you, but I didn't tell him I'd put up with your shit. What's up?"

"Get your little museum nerds and your archaeologist friends and get on that nice Fountain boat of yours and go to Fowey Rocks. Head directly south one mile, and there will be a dinghy anchored there. I have some glow lights on the anchor line. There's a present there for you. Don't go alone, Charlie, you're going to need verification from the pros on this one."

"What are you talking about, Kiki?"

"Charlie, you might not like the way I lead my life, but I'm not a bullshitter. Remember what I said, museum curator, archaeologist—you're going to need them. Fowey Rocks in two to three hours, Charlie."

The good thing about Charlie Alvarez was that he was no nonsense. These priceless pieces of art and gold were going to get where they needed to be to have the best chance of being dated and identified. Charlie knew the right people.

It was quiet, not many boats were out, just the occasional boat trolling to see what would tighten their lines. We loaded the dive bags full of treasure onto the dinghy, then anchored it off of Fowey Light at the southern end of Key Biscayne. Charlie showed up a little while later. I watched with binoculars from the cover of the *Hawk Marine.*

With spotlight in hand, a crewmember boarded the dinghy and then handed up the dive bags to a man on Charlie's 42-foot Fountain. There were a few men with Charlie on his boat, but picking him out was easy, all five foot four, 250 pounds of him.

He stepped to the bow of the boat, put his hands on his hips and scanned the darkened waters of Biscayne Bay. The satellite phone rang; I had left it on, on purpose.

"Hello?"

"Hello, Kiki. If you're out there somewhere watching, your little joke wasn't funny. I'm lucky I have Miami Dade police with me; that kilo of coke wasn't funny," he said.

I couldn't control my laughter. "I just wanted you to know that the Beard is into everything. I know we can't do shit about it, but now you know," I told him.

"The Beard, where in the fuck..."

I hung up on him before I got a lecture. We waited around for a while until Charlie left, leaving the dinghy anchored off the lighthouse, then Jorge started up the *Hawk Marine* and headed to Islamorada, to my waiting *Quest.* I'd be on the *Quest* in a couple of hours, in my own bed. I could hear my pillow calling me, and it sounded great. It was going to feel good to take a shower and relax around my own surroundings.

The *Hawk Marine* pulled up to the dock where the *Quest* was tied.

"I'll call you in a couple of days, Kiki. We're going to have a little get-together with our families and I want to have you and Nadine there," DK said.

"That sounds great, *amigo*; I'll wait for your call."

I jumped over to the *Quest*, reached back and helped Nadine on board.

"*Gracias amigos*, see you soon," I said.

Jorge let out the big twin diesels in reverse and the *Hawk Marine* backed away from the docks, then spun around and was off to Miami. The *salsa* music began to play and I could see Jony begin dancing on the deck of the *Hawk Marine* as it slowly pulled away.

I walked into the *Quest* and the sights that had become home to me. Nadine followed. We had nothing with us except the clothes on our backs and one of Jony's dive bags with four million in it. I opened up the hatches and galley windows and welcomed the warm tropical wind. Nadine flopped down on the old beanbag chair in the corner of the galley and I lay down on my favorite couch.

"It's nice to be home, *niña*," I said.

That night we fell into each other's arms without the thoughts of upcoming or ongoing events. No fear, no anxiety, no falling asleep from the weight of fatigue. Her touch and embrace made me feel safe and secure. I'd never felt this way in a woman's arms before.

We spent the next few days cleaning up the *Quest* and doing little repairs. The long hot summer days of August made us lazy, and we slowly got back into the rhythm of the Keys. We went to Miami a couple of times for dinner and to see some friends, including DK and the boys. The sounds, sights, and smells of Miami were wonderful. But the throng of human flesh everywhere took the excitement out of it and made me feel caged.

Nadine and I decided to get the *Quest* ready to cruise the Caribbean for a few months, and she could show me the pleasures and relaxation of sailing like she promised. We were going to sail down through the Caribbean to Isla Margarita, Venezuela and spend the winter warm and cozy.

Nadine and I were sitting on the deck at the back of the *Quest* by the wheel when I heard a familiar voice. It was Banco.

"Can I come aboard?" he asked.

"You're always welcome, Banco, come aboard."

I helped the fat man on board. He had regained his weight, and was back to the old smiling, sharp-looking Banco.

"It looks like you're going on a trip, Kiki," he said.

"Yeah, we're going to slow cruise the islands and spend the winter down in Isla Margarita."

"That sounds great. I wish I was built like you, but look at me, I can't stay away form the game," he said. "I heard you were back in town and I just wanted to tell you that I appreciate what you did. I know not everyone would have come back for me and for that I thank you, Kiki."

I didn't say a word. I just nodded my head. Banco walked off the *Quest* and onto the dock. He turned to walk away, and then stopped.

"Oh, I almost forgot," he said. He pulled something out of his pocket and tossed it up to me on the deck of the *Quest*. I sat there in the chair and looked at Banco for a second, then reached down, picked it up and looked.

It was a Polaroid snapshot of Banco holding a recent edition of the Miami Herald in one hand with that huge Banco smile, and in the other hand he was holding the Golden Madonna.

I couldn't believe what I was seeing. Banco was halfway down the dock when he turned and with a huge smile waved to me and said, "I hope we can work together again some day, Kiki. I admire you, I really do."

And he turned and walked away with a little snicker on his lips. There was no sense in talking to him; the Madonna was probably on its way to some private collection in Eastern Europe by now. I leaned back in my chair, looked at the picture one more time and tossed it to Nadine. She looked at it in astonishment, and then looked at me. We both began to laugh.

"I guess the Madonna will remain a mystery, *niña.*"

www.ingramcontent.com/pod-product-compliance
Lightning Source LLC
Chambersburg PA
CBHW030807260626
47169CB00001B/230